D0790464

Praise for the second novel in Delilah S. Dawson's
scrumptious Blud series

WICKED AS SHE WANTS

Winner of the RT Book Reviews Seal of Excellence

"No sophomore series slump here. . . . Delightfully edgy
with hidden charms. . . . Dawson is on the fast track to the
top of the genre!"

—*RT Book Reviews* (Top Pick!)

"Fantastic writing through and through. . . . You'll find
any excuse not to put the book down."

—*Paranormal Haven*

"Dawson has created one of the most original and refreshing worlds in a time when I thought it had all been done
before. . . . If you are not reading the Blud series, you are
missing out!"

—*Under the Covers Book Blog*

"Amazingly creative and original."

—*Bitten by Paranormal Romance*

"This book has it all . . . vampires, romance, murder,
revenge, steampunk, and a special secret. . . . Amazing."

—*Dark Faerie Tales*

"A most interesting world filled with fantastical creatures. . . . Dawson is a gifted storyteller."

—*Fiction Vixen*

"Ahna and Casper are full of passion, which makes for a red-hot romance that adds to the brilliant storytelling. . . . A supernatural adventure that's hard to put down."

—*Romancing the Dark Side*

WICKED AS THEY COME

"As good as it gets!"

—*New York Times* bestselling author Nancy Holder

"A wonderfully fresh new voice splashes onto the scene. . . . In Criminy Stain, Dawson has created a delightful rogue with a dangerously sexy edge. Join the adventure; you won't be sorry you did!"

—*RT Book Reviews*

"Mesmerizing . . . holds the reader spellbound from its opening line until its last. . . . This reviewer recommends you make a trip to the fascinating Sang immediately."

—*Bitten by Books*

"I can't recommend this book enough. It's like every genre I love so perfectly blended together. If you want to fall in love with two great characters plus an entire new world, this is your book."

—*Badass Book Reviews*

"A wonderful start to a new series that had me dying to find out more. It is a dark macabre tale that Tim Burton would only wish to dream of. . . . Many a midnight hour was burnt with me not wanting to put it down."

—*Book Chick City*

"A complex and interesting book. . . . If you are looking for something new, different, and fresh I would encourage you to try this book."

—*Fiction Vixen*

"Dawson has a wonderful voice that hooks you with humorous sharp dialogue, smooth pacing, and descriptive details. An enchanting mixture of steampunk, fantasy, and paranormal romance."

—*Smexy Books*

"I was completely engrossed from beginning to end and could not walk away from this book for a moment. It is utterly enchanting."

—*A Bookworm's Haven*

"The novel flips from the familiar to the fantastical effortlessly. . . . It could have followed down the rabbit hole of previous vampire or Steampunk tales, but it takes the high road, with humor and insights into life."

—*Heroes and Heartbreakers*

DELILAH S. DAWSON

WICKED
AFTER
MIDNIGHT

POCKET BOOKS

New York   London   Toronto   Sydney   New Delhi

The sale of this book without its cover is unauthorized. If you purchased this book without a cover, you should be aware that it was reported to the publisher as "unsold and destroyed." Neither the author nor the publisher has received payment for the sale of this "stripped book."

Pocket Books
A Division of Simon & Schuster, Inc.
1230 Avenue of the Americas
New York, NY 10020

This book is a work of fiction. Names, characters, places, and incidents either are products of the author's imagination or are used fictitiously. Any resemblance to actual events or locales or persons, living or dead, is entirely coincidental.

Copyright © 2014 by D. S. Dawson

All rights reserved, including the right to reproduce this book or portions thereof in any form whatsoever. For information address Pocket Books Subsidiary Rights Department,
1230 Avenue of the Americas, New York, NY 10020

First Pocket Books paperback edition February 2014

POCKET and colophon are registered trademarks of
Simon & Schuster, Inc.

For information about special discounts for bulk purchases,
please contact Simon & Schuster Special Sales at 1-866-506-1949
or business@simonandschuster.com.

The Simon & Schuster Speakers Bureau can bring authors to your
live event. For more information or to book an event contact the
Simon & Schuster Speakers Bureau at 1-866-248-3049
or visit our website at www.simonspeakers.com.

Cover illustration and design by Tony Mauro

Manufactured in the United States of America

10   9   8   7   6   5   4   3   2   1

ISBN 978-1-4516-5791-3
ISBN 978-1-4516-5793-7 (ebook)

For my flower twin, for the Red Door,
for Team Capybara, for the Bludbunny Brigade,
for the YELLING ON TWITTER IN ALL CAPS.
For the readers and writers and trollers of darkness.
YOU GUYS ARE THE WIND BENEATH
MY WINGS AND WHATEVS.
Thanks for making the world less lonely.

Acknowledgments

Oh, I owe a lot of cupcakes this time around. Big thanks, hugs, and baked goods to so many.

With so many people to thank, I know I'll forget someone important. But rest assured that the love and gratitude are there. As this is the last book (that I know of!) in the Blud series, the thanks list got a little out of hand. NO REGRETS.

First of all, many thanks to everyone who helped with the *Wicked as She Wants* launch party, especially Seth and Leah at the Red Door Playhouse in Roswell, Georgia. To my amazing friends in the Red Door Writers Group, who put up with my not-so-subtle manipulation of writing prompts into scenes for this very book. To the Fabulous Foxes of FoxTale Book Shoppe in Woodstock, GA, for joining us at the book launch party and selling a ton of books—and for making sure that there's a way to order signed and personalized copies of all things Blud. To Ericka Axelsson for coming up with the book launch party's signature drink, the Tsarina's Kiss—it's Prosecco and lingonberry syrup from Ikea, in case you want to try it, and it looks just like blood mixed with champagne but tastes a lot better. To Andrea for taking pics at the party and Elizabeth for helping with setup and Jim for bringing the unicorn head and Meghan for playing the role of the Goblin King. To Cakes by Darcy for another delicious masterpiece—red velvet with almond buttercream, of course. Thanks to everyone who joined us to party!

To my amazing husband, Craig, who has been my favorite person since the year 2000. To my magical children, Cleo and Rex, who make every day brighter and weirder. To my parents and grandparents, who always support me. I'll dedicate a book to y'all, some day—but not a vampire romance.

For music and the playlists that keep me editing, thanks to Chris Casatelli, Thomas Strickland, Ken Lowery, Karina Cooper, Becky Zemansky, and Adam Christopher. You can hear the playlist for this book at Spotify under DelilahSDawson.

To the generous beta readers who helped steer me in the right direction for "The Three Lives of Lydia," "Love Song of the Lizard Boy," and "The Damsel and the Daggerman," thanks to Stephanie at Fangs, Wands, and Fairy Dust; Brent Taylor, Austin Lewis, Stephanie Constantin, Ericka Axelsson, Debbie Pascoe, Beth Ho, Allie Charlesworth, Lindze Merritt, Charis Collins, Kathy Epling, Kevin Hearne, and Andrew Schaffer.

For using mad graphic skillz to whip up emergency swag faster than a speeding bullet, Jon Plsek.

To my beloved agent, Kate McKean, who always steers me true and without whom this entire series wouldn't exist. Because when we were on The Call, she asked me what I was working on next, and when I said something along the lines of "a *Buffy*-inspired steampunk adventure with kind-of vampires and clockwork monkeys and then there's a Kraken and lots of kissing," she just went with it.

To my awesome editor at Pocket Books, Abby Zidle, who turns my coal into diamonds and marshmallows and treats me to duck confit and takes me to butterfly gardens, even though I almost got us thrown out. And to Parisa

Zolfaghari, who not only took care of me through almost this entire series but also took me to STREB Extreme Action in New York so I could finally knock "flying trapeze" off my bucket list. (For real. There's a video on my blog.) To Wendy and Nancy and all the copyeditors who keep me from looking like an idiot. And to Stephanie, Marla, and everyone else at Pocket Books, too. I'm so glad my first books were with y'all!

To the awesome Tony Mauro for the best cover yet. It's perfect! And to James Perales for the gorgeous covers of all my novellas.

To the Bludbunny Brigade: Maranda Melton, Sara Muller, Rachel Flesher, Beth Ho, Leslee Nevill, Nancy Marsh, Savanna Puterbaugh, Sherry Gladden, Melanie Marsh, Laura Helseth, Christine Forshner, Jennifer Goble, Meghan Ball, James Breen, Austin Sirkin, Wendy Dagley, Nita Gill, Jillian Venters, Lise Donnelly, Sharonda, Kevin Craley, Sasha Conley, Beth Blanchard, Deb Rasmussen, Karen Burns, Brandi Engeman, Jessica Collins, Stephanie Constantin, Carol Malcolm, Jess Richardson, Lisa Millraney, Melissa Gilbert, Penelope Crampton, Janice Pia, Lexie Cenni, Heather Jackson, Gemma Harding, Sullivan McPig, Carien Ubink, Arienne Wallace, Carrie Mirim, Kat Fish, Ellen Sandberg, Lori A. Arcelay, Esperanza Gutierrez, Gloria Barna, Dani Albrecht, Linda Larsson, Anna Nicole Ureta, Kaitlin Sivley, Jessica Stewart, Tonia Rodriguez, Francesca Bensi, Amber Bray, Melissa Gilbert, and PJ McCracken. And unofficial members Mark and Theresa Curtis.

To everyone who came to the *Wicked as She Wants* pre-launch party at Madame X in New York City, including Adam Wilson, Janet Reid, Jeffrey Somers, Danielle Duffield, and Cara Moore. And speaking of my epic New

York trip, thanks to *Sleep No More* for being one of the coolest experiences of my life.

To the cons and conferences who invited me to partake of their awesome, including Coastal Magic, Anachrocon, JordanCon, the Dahlonega Literary Festival, Phoenix Comicon, Authors After Dark, Dragon Con, and Crossroads Writers Conference. And to the booksellers who made my books available there, especially Mysterious Galaxy and Barnes & Noble. Special thanks to Murder by the Book in Houston for putting together such a lovely signing for the *Carniepunk* anthology. To Cindy Rittenhouse and Rivers Academy for my first chance to speak to high school students about writing. To Brian White for inviting me to be part of Fireside Fiction and Pip Ballentine and Tee Morris for allowing me to play in their sandbox for *Tales from the Archives: The Official Ministry of Peculiar Occurrences*.

To my fellow writers, who keep me afloat and commiserate and sometimes let me blather on their blogs and who name whores and strip clubs after me in their books: Kevin Hearne, James R. Tuck, Janice Hardy, Kevin Maurer, Chuck Wendig, Deanna Raybourn, Cherie Priest, John Scalzi, Jim C. Hines, Mary Robinette Kowal, Alethea Kontis, Leanna Renee Hieber, Sam Sykes, Ben LeRoy, Mark Henry, Nicole Peeler, Annabel Joseph, John Hartness, Lucienne Diver, Thomas Willeford. And, you know, everybody on Twitter.

To Brooke Stante of Villainess Soaps for capturing the characters of the Blud books so perfectly in scent and soap. Visit www.villainess.net/wicked to fall in love with her creations!

To the book bloggers and reviewers and everyone who's ever rated my books on Amazon or Goodreads, *merci mille fois*!

Thank you all, so much for joining me on this journey.

♥, d.

1

Here is a painful truth: the circus is a magical place only so long as you're allowed to leave when the show is over. My first year in the caravan was a dream. The next three years were purgatorial, and the last two were a nightmare, the kind where you endlessly grind your teeth to dust. And that's why the ringmaster now loomed over me, lips drawn back over his fangs in a hiss so long and soft that it had become a silent sigh that smelled of blood and wine. He was beautiful, murderous, and maddening, and I was completely in his power. And that really, really pissed me off.

I glared at the man who had killed me and saved me all in one fell swoop. In another life, he might have been attractive. Sexy, even. But here, now, he was simply annoying.

"You're not my dad, Criminy."

"I'm the closest thing you've got, love. And more important, I'm your employer."

I rolled my eyes. "Then I quit."

Criminy threw his head back and laughed. My eyes shot to Tish, but she was wearing a Mona Lisa smile.

"This isn't our world, Demi," she said gently. "This isn't

Earth. You can't just walk out the door and find an apartment and a job online. As much as I believe in being an independent woman, Sang simply isn't set up that way. As a female and a Bludman, you have almost no rights here. And, for the record, if Crim's your dad, I'm way too young to be your mom."

I smirked at that. She was only a few years older than me, even if I still looked like the college coed I'd been before one drink too many put me in the coma that transported me to Sang. When I arrived in this freaky parallel world naked and confused, the only thing that had saved me from death by a warren of murderous bludbunnies was Criminy Stain with his ability to turn humans into nearly invincible blood drinkers, Bludmen like himself. Tish was from Earth, too, and we'd had some heart-to-hearts over the last couple of years, reminiscing about movie stars and music and a world where women who weren't swaggering airship captains could actually walk around alone safely. But just like a real mom, she would never take my side over Criminy's.

"Besides," Tish added, "have you been to the cities? They're awful." She held up a creased newspaper from Criminy's desk. "I've seen Manchester, London, Brighton. You couldn't pay me to live behind those high, cramped walls. And it's much worse for Bludmen, to be quite honest."

Her voice went bitter as her eyes went far away, and I couldn't help noticing the crow's feet that hadn't been there last year. Tish had told me about the witch's curse and the enchanted locket that made her age far faster than was fair, the price for her life in Sang. My best friend, Cherie, and I had bets regarding how long she would hold off being bludded so she could stay with Criminy without regrets and wrinkles. Tish had told me her grandmother was in the final stages of her third round of breast cancer and that once the tough old bird had passed on, Tish would most likely join us in the life of a predator. More years, more resilience, more beauty, and all you lost as a Bludman was a taste for food and any real rights once you were inside the city. It was a far cry from the sparkly rich vampire stories I'd salivated over back home.

For example, I was twenty-six but looked seventeen, and I was currently so hungry that I could smell Tish's blood on the air, as yummy as baking cookies used to be. I swallowed and looked away.

When Criminy spoke again, his voice was gentle and kind. "The point, my darling girls, is that this is the best life I can offer you in Sangland. What precisely do you lack?"

I fluffed my bangs and stared down at my black-scaled hands. So gross, even with the nails painted hot pink. "Parties. Independence. Adventure," I muttered, not meeting his eyes.

"I think she means boys," Tish whispered.

Criminy snorted and looked offended. "There are boys in the caravan. Plenty of them."

"Charlie Dregs is not 'boys.'"

"You should have snapped up Casper when you had the chance. Or one of the daimon lads."

I spun away as if in anger, hoping I'd done it fast enough to hide my blush. I had, in fact, snatched up one of the daimon boys. Luc had been the most mysterious guy I'd met since waking up in Sang, but he was part of the reason I now wanted to leave the caravan. Underneath his suave, bad-boy exterior, he was as sweet and gushy as the filling in a jelly doughnut. The way he was following me around, mooning over me, begging me to be his *petite amie*—so not sexy. Even the hot Franchian accent didn't help.

Tish was wrong about one thing: I didn't need a boy. I needed a man.

"Cherie and I have been talking." I paused, chewing my lip carefully with too-sharp teeth. "We'd like to try London."

"Over my dead body!"

I'd heard Criminy could be terrifying, but I'd never believed it, not until that moment. He seemed to rise over me and spread out a vulture's dark wings, his sharp features going sharper and his hair crackling with lightning that wasn't there. I shrank down, all my bravado fled.

Almost.

"You don't want to go to London," Tish started, and Criminy hissed, cutting her off.

"She's not going to London. I'll never allow it."

Before he was done talking, I rose from the chair, feeling the sparks in my own dark hair. "You can't stop me! You don't own me. I'm not just another freak in your sideshow."

He chuckled darkly and leaned back, crossing his arms and going cold. "I can stop you, actually. I made your papers, and I hold them. Without papers, you don't exist. You can't get into any cities."

"I can forge new papers."

"With what money?"

"I'll . . . I'll . . ." I swallowed hard, the anger draining out through my toes and leaving me cold and empty inside.

He was right, the smug asshat. Without those papers and the years of back pay stored in the safe hidden in his wagon, I wasn't going anywhere. And Cherie was no better off. For all the freedom he claimed we had, we were trapped in his caravan like canaries with clipped wings—albeit fanged canaries in a very pretty cage.

I caught the sob, sniffling it back down. "I don't want to grow old here, Crim. Nothing ever changes. I never change. Let me fly free."

"Demi, love . . ."

I looked up at him, straight into those cloudy gray eyes. When I first saw a mirror after he bludded me, I had been horrified at the dancing shadows in my own sky-blue eyes. They snapped like the fire of a Bunsen burner. But when I cried, the tears were tinged with red. And I didn't want to cry right now. I'd been good for so long, but the rebellion had been simmering underneath. I hated, just hated, being told what to do, what to be. Maybe I couldn't get what I wanted by shouting, but I would get it. Or else.

"You have to kick the baby bird out of the nest sometime," Tish said, and I smiled my thanks.

"Around here, baby birds that fall without flying get eaten in seconds. The bludbunnies wait underneath the nests all spring, drooling." Crim waved a hand at me when I tried to interject. "You're no baby bird, Demi. But Letitia is right. A lone female in the city will generally become a victim. London is out of the question. But I do have contacts in other cities. What about Ruin?"

I plundered my memory, trying to match the one-off names of Sang to my own world. "Is that in Franchia?"

"Not too far from Paris but safe enough. There's a university there. They allow women, although you might be the only Bludman. The daimons aren't so picky, if you aren't."

I didn't breathe for a moment. *Not too far from Paris.* Images from the capital of France in my former life crashed with what I knew of the Paris of Sang like badly shuffled cards. The Eiffel Tower, the Louvre, and Notre Dame were the same in existence, if not in name, and much of the history I'd studied in high school and the art I'd studied in college were mirrored in Franchia. I was especially intrigued at the thought of finally seeing the famous paintings that straddled both of our worlds, live and without pesky guards and cameras. Paris called to me in both universes. But the colorful daimons who peopled the closest country across the sea changed the flavor entirely, and I had heard that there, the Green Fairy was more than just a potent drink. London felt safe and exciting, a short jaunt from which Criminy could easily rescue me. Franchia, however, was a different story.

And I liked that even better.

"Why Ruin?" I asked.

"Not too far from Sangland. Civilized, mostly safe. The university has everything a young lass could want—literature, languages, painting. Handsome young scholars. Baggy, unflattering robes."

"I thought Bludmen weren't allowed to go to university."

His smile quirked up. "Only in Sangland, *ma petite.* Can't have you getting any ideas in that pretty head of yours and trying to eat the Magistrate." His gaze traveled up and down me, sharp eyebrows cutting down. "I'll cover matriculation and a stipend. For you and Cherie. I know it's not the glamorous escape you've been hoping for, but will it suffice?"

"I—"

I didn't want to go back to college. Even though I'd been stuck in Sang for years, some small part of me kept expecting that one day, I would collapse, as Tish sometimes did, and wake up in my own world and go back to school as if nothing had ever happened. If I committed to college here, it was not only giving up that pleasant dream but also dooming myself to the same reality that had once brought me nothing but misery and a fatal drinking problem. Even in Franchia, college would be an acquiescence to doom, not a bright future. But if Ruin was near Paris, that meant it was near the famous cabarets. And I could always find a place in the cabarets. I gave a small smile, knowing Criminy would be watching closely.

"Yes. Thank you."

He nodded abruptly and turned back to his desk, rummaging in the drawers and pulling out papers and stamps. Tish rose and cocked her chin at the door.

"Crim—" I started, but Tish shook her head and pulled me gently out onto the stairs of their wagon, shutting the door behind us.

It was afternoon, in that pleasant lull between lunch and show time, and the caravan was limned in sunlight and surrounded by the usual gently rolling hills of the Sang version of an English countryside. I couldn't help frowning. I was sick to death of the usual gently rolling hills.

"Is he mad at me?"

Tish patted me on the arm, and we sat on the bottom step, her wide skirts tumbling over into the lap of my more spare contortionist's costume.

"He doesn't want to lose you, Demi. You struck him pretty hard, I think, when you said he wasn't your father."

"But he's not."

"But he thinks of himself as your guardian. He saved you, and he's gone to a lot of trouble keeping you safe all these years. This may not be an exciting life to you, but that's because you're already living it. To your average Sang girl in a city, trapped behind thick walls, you're the luckiest girl on the planet."

"Doesn't feel like it." I kind of hated myself for grumbling like the ungrateful teen I resembled. I was twenty-six. I should have been past the theatrics. But that was part of the problem. How was I supposed to grow up when everything always stayed the same?

Tish's hand landed on my shoulder, and I struggled not to bite it. "Look, Demi. I know you don't like to talk about it. But before you came here, what did you want out of life?"

"Ngggggggh." I shrugged away from her hand and put my head between my knees. "I wanted to get away from my parents, go to parties, get drunk, and figure out what I wanted out of life."

"Did you ever figure it out?"

I glared at her and exhaled through my nose. "I was doing shots of Jaeger, and then I woke up here, naked and covered in rabbits and my own blood, with Criminy's wrist in my mouth. Since then, I've been wrapping my body around my best friend while strangers whisper about what freakish monsters we are. I don't know what I want, but I know this sure as hell ain't it."

"Then Franchia is bound to be better, right?"

"I guess."

Tish stood and turned to face me. She said she had been a nurse back home, and I could see the steel rod up her butt from telling people what to do all day. But I could also see that she wore her heart in her eyes. "Easy things aren't worth much, and you never have adventures if you stay in one place. So take Criminy's letter and go to Ruin with Cherie. If it sucks, come back here. What have you got to lose?"

I couldn't help smirking. "Nothing, I guess. When you put it that way, I sound like a scaredy cat."

"So don't be scared."

"Easy for you to say, considering you won't get bludded."

Tish gasped, and I immediately felt like crap.

"I didn't mean that, I'm just . . ."

Hands on her hips and hat blocking the sun, Tish glared down at me. "If you want to grow up, quit acting like a baby. I didn't want to be here any more than you do, at first. I fought it every damn step of the way. The only reason I won't get bludded is that I'm afraid it'll mean I can't get back home to be there when my grandmother dies. If you're unhappy here, do something about it. You're just lucky Criminy loves you enough to let you go. And you'd better be smart and grateful enough to stay alive, for his sake. The caravan may seem safe and boring, but Sang is scary as hell out there."

I grinned. "But I'm a predator."

"And in London, a suffering minority. Franchia could be good for you. New things to learn, new things to see, living among the daimons. But you're going to have to be careful about those Franchian men. They're not all love-sick softies like Luc."

"You knew about that?"

I saw a Bludman's humor in her smile. "I'm a fortune-teller, Demi. I know everything. Do you remember what I told you the first time I touched your hand?"

It was my turn to grin. "You said, 'I see feathers, fairies, mortal danger, a handsome stranger, and a trip to hell.'"

"I didn't see those things here in the caravan, honey. You need to go out there and make 'em happen."

"Even the mortal danger?"

Her fingers went to the wrinkles at the corners of her eyes. She stared past me as if she could see through the glossy maroon wall of the wagon she shared with Criminy. "A little mortal danger never killed anybody," she murmured. "At least, not a Bludman."

"I guess I have to go, then. Maybe I can find that handsome stranger you mentioned."

She looked down, the spell broken and her eyes crinkled up with humor. "Then go tell Cherie and get packing. I'll set up the bon voyage party."

"Thanks, Mom," I said, and we both chuckled.

"I'd hug you, honey, but you look hungry."

"I *am* hungry." I sighed. "For so many things."

I stood and dusted off my breeches and bustle. Only in the caravan could I get away with a style like that, one that would have been outrageous in the cities of Sangland. But the breeches felt like skinny jeans, and I would miss them once I was costumed in fifty pounds of ruffles to blend with the humans for the trip. With a smile and a wave, I headed toward my wagon.

The only problem was that I had lied to Criminy. Cherie had no idea we were going away. And she wasn't going to like it one bit.

2

"No! I won't do it! You're insane!"

In six years of sharing a wagon and often two square feet of space on a very small chair, I had never seen Cherie so furious. I'd seen her homesick, shy, kind, and often prissy. But until that very moment, I had doubted her ability to feel passion of any sort. It brought out her Freesian accent a little more, too.

"But it's so boring here, Cherie. Nothing ever changes. And you've always wanted to see Franchia."

She paced the train car, skirts snapping. "Not at university! Not sitting still, having numbers drilled into my head. I like the caravan."

"Then we'll skip out of Ruin and go to Paris. Be the stars of a cabaret."

"The caravan is respectable, but the cabaret? I am not some tawdry showgirl!"

I shrugged. "You're a girl who performs in a show. Same difference."

She stopped in front of me, shaking a manicured talon in my face. "No. No. No. This is different. The caravan, it's an art. With Master Criminy, we are safe, cared for. Legitimate. But once you're in the cabarets . . . you don't understand. The men, they expect things from the girls there. It is not all dancing and then back into your wagons like good little ducks."

I sighed and flopped down on the bottom bunk of the bed we shared. "It wouldn't be like that. We're Bludmen. Predators. The men will probably be scared of us. But whatever. I'm going."

"All this time, and still I do not understand this 'whatever.' You, who fight against being told what to do all the time—do you not understand that all men are not as good as Master Crim? In Paris, we would be playthings, feathers to be batted about on the wind. It is debauched, dangerous. Bludmen are not so loved. You cannot go out alone."

She returned to her pacing, her blond curls flouncing in her wake. For a bloodthirsty killer, she looked like a china doll from back home, like Claudia from *Interview with a Vampire*. Except that she really was as sweet as she looked and swore she'd never drunk from a live human in her entire twenty-five years. Cherie was content in the caravan, happy with what seemed to her an easy life compared with the tiny wagon she'd grown up in, somewhere in a freezing forest. With carnivalleros coming and going over the years, she was sure the perfect man would arrive at the perfect time to sweep her off her slippered feet. Maybe because she'd been born a Bludman, she had a better sense of how very long three hundred years of life could be, how very much time she could give that mysterious man to arrive. Having been born human, I possessed a sense of urgency about life that she couldn't quite fathom.

I stood and stopped her with firm hands on her slender shoulders. "Cherie, I need something new. I can't stay here. I can't do this anymore. I have to leave, with you or without you. But I'd prefer with."

A battle of wills ensued, a test of friendship spoken only with the eyes.

I felt her deflate and knew then that I had won.

"Fine. But only Ruin. Not Paris. Just promise me that if it's wretched, we can come back here. Where it's safe."

"Of course. We can always come back."

She drew me into a hug, and I inhaled a cloud of her hair, scented with her favorite shampoo, a soft mix of Freesian pine and vanilla that she splurged on with her carefully saved coppers. Most of her earnings were shipped back to her family in Freesia a few times a year, whenever we were near London and Criminy gathered up the caravan's post.

"You're going to love it." I patted her back and pulled away to look into her eyes, which were as cloudy gray as Criminy's but balmy and pleasant. Criminy felt like a storm, but Cherie was like a quiet rainy day spent reading by an open window, as different as two Bludmen could be. "We're going to have an adventure!"

"Hmmph." She shook a finger in my face. "The things I do for you."

I just smiled. It was going to be fantastic. She would see.

Everyone in the caravan had some piece of advice for our trip to Franchia.

"Speak softly and carry a big knife!" Torno the strong-man roared. "These city men, they will take advantage of a sweet girl like you. You must be careful, *ma donna*. And you must take a man with you. For protection."

I snorted and shook my head. "No way. That's the whole point."

"If you were my daughter . . ." Torno's face went even redder than usual under his tight hat.

I patted the stretched leather over his bulging bicep. "If I were your daughter, you would have a lot of explaining to do."

He choked and turned puce, opting to dive into his trailer rather than continue to blush in my presence. Eblick laughed from where he lay on a log beside Torno's weights, his forked tongue flapping against pebbled green skin.

"You ever been to Franchia?" I asked him. For once, he didn't flinch or cower from me.

"Only home and the caravan, mistress. But I chose the caravan."

"Don't you ever wish for adventure?"

He sat up and looked over the hills, his strange eyes following the twin lines the caravan train had cut through the moor grasses. We'd been near Dover last week, and he'd been especially quiet in sight of the sea cliffs. He'd gone out one day for a swim and returned with skin an odd combination of red and black that had earned him more coppers than usual in the freak tent. No one in the caravan knew where he had come from or where he had gone, but the sea made him noticeably melancholy.

"Caravan's all the adventure I need. But I understand better than most why you need to leave."

I couldn't touch him—no one ever did. But I bowed my head slightly before walking on. "Thanks, Eblick."

I passed Veruca the Abyssinian sword swallower next, and she leaned on her scimitar and eyed me thoughtfully. She was possibly the only person in the caravan more stand-offish than Eblick, and I had no idea where she was from, either. Refusing to follow either Bludman or Pinky fashion, she sweet-talked the costumer into making tight leather outfits for her that showcased her muscles and revealed her dark brown skin. She always smelled like almond oil and spice to me, and one of Criminy's first warnings had been never to drink from an Abyssinian. Their blood would make a Bludman go mad and then die; the way he described it, it was a lot like instant rabies combined with LSD.

"You remind me of a jaguar," she finally said.

I stopped and grinned. "Lithe and dangerous as a jungle cat?"

"They fall asleep in the trees, thinking they are safe. A savvy hunter need only yank them down by the tail for a fancy new jacket. So I say to you, Demi: don't let anyone yank your tail."

With a curt nod, I was dismissed. I didn't really want to keep walking, though. I could already see Charlie Dregs sitting, distant and forlorn, by his puppets. Mr. Punch sagged over an arm as Charlie retied the hideous little man's strings. When Charlie's eyes caught me, I stopped, very much against my will. He always looked so sad and hopeful to me, like one of the Beatles crossed with a basset hound. I'd heard stories that he'd loved a girl once and lost her, a Stranger like me. Something drew me toward him against my will.

"So it's true, then, Demi. You're leaving?"

I mustered up a smile. "Yep."

"Need an escort?"

"I'm a big girl."

"Even big girls can find bad ends, lass. Promise me you'll take care."

"I promise."

I put my hand on his shoulder, and his mournful eyes

focused on my wrist before squeezing shut as if in pain. He patted my hand with his red glove. "I hope you find what you're looking for, Demi. I really do."

That's what finally drove home the sadness: realizing that it might be the last time I would see Charlie Dregs. I'd never really looked at him as a man—more like a fixture, a dedicated dog, a cousin, maybe. I'd never seen him as a man, but now, for a moment, I could see the boy he had once been.

"What was her name, Charlie?"

He looked down, rubbed a heart tattooed on his wrist. "Lydia."

He was gone in a flash, his shirt a spot of white against the moors. I didn't want to be like him, a pitied cog in the grand machinery of the caravan, joyless and ageless and never smiling, following Emerlie the tightrope walker around like an unwanted guard dog that never received even the stingiest pat on the head. Seeing that moment of grief in him hardened my heart further. I would get to Paris, somehow.

Looking around at the rest of the carnivalleros who had become family, I gave up and sought refuge in my own car. I didn't have much to pack in the trunk I shared with Cherie, but the wagon looked pathetically empty without our crap strewn all over it. It reminded me of the way my childhood bedroom had looked after I packed for college. Empty, like a cicada's husk. Unnaturally tidy. My mom had cried then—a lot. I hadn't. But I did now.

At lunchtime, I redid the tear-smudged kohl around my eyes and walked to the dining car. Even without a Bludman's keen hearing and nose, I would have known that a party waited within. It wasn't often someone left the caravan—and if they did, they disappeared after dark or were dragged off, shackled in the custody of the Coppers. With a deep breath, I smoothed my bangs and opened the door.

The entire caravan was there, shouting, "Surprise!"

I put on my most professional smile and pretended that I wasn't going to miss them. The jerks.

I was awake and ready before dawn the next morning, prodding Cherie with a foot until she tumbled from the top bunk and landed in a Bludman's crouch. She hissed at me like an angry cat, and I just poked her in the nose with my toe. With a sigh of resignation, she stood and yawned.

"Is it too late to back out? I like sleeping late. You can do that in the caravan but not at university. And clearly not on the day that I'm forced to dress up like a terrified human and leave my home."

"You're just grouchy because you're excited," I said.

She rubbed her eyes and fluffed her hair, giving me a stare that would have knocked down a bludstag. "You're giving me your vial at breakfast, foul thing."

I just nodded. I was too anxious to eat, anyway.

Together we dragged our trunk down the steps to the front of our car and left it there while we went to the costumer's wagon for our disguises. Antonin was polite and distant as ever, offering us each a selection of slightly out-of-date but decent enough Pinky outfits. No one knew where the tailor obtained his cache of dresses and costumes, but I was glad enough to slip on the billowing taffeta dress over the slim-fit trousers made for me by the previous costumer. When many of your best tricks involve handstands or being upside down and you live in a world without underwear, it's smart to plan ahead.

My dress was bright teal, and Cherie's was a salmon

pink that would have seemed frivolous on anyone else. But it just made her look like a fresh-faced country girl, especially when I helped her lace up the cuffs and button the neck tightly. When she laced me into mine, I wanted to claw the cloth away from my throat.

"Jesus Christ. Being eaten by bludrats has to be better than suffocating to death," I growled.

Antonin pulled my hands away and loosened the collar by one button. "Suffocating is better than draining, which is what the Pinkies will do if they discover you. So get used to it, and fast. The humans of the cities get crazy when they're scared. Remember what happened to the last costumer?"

I nodded. I'd watched the Coppers drag her away, kicking and clawing and tied to the back of a galloping bludmare. She hadn't returned.

Antonin brought us gloves and hats and handkerchiefs and sent us along to the dining car. Which I dreaded, because there's nothing more awkward than walking into a room full of people who had all drunkenly told you goodbye the day before. I couldn't tell if Crim and Tish were there, as they usually dined in their private booth with the curtains drawn, and there were too many smells to pick them out. Crim had avoided me since our fight the day before, but I wanted to leave on good terms. I really did love the uppity bastard, probably more than my real dad.

Luc fidgeted in his usual corner booth with his brother, and I steered Cherie in the opposite direction, toward the cauldron that held the blood vials. I'd managed to avoid Luc all last night, and I didn't want to deal with his love-sick-puppy routine this morning, not with my stomach in upheaval and my heart telling my head not to have second thoughts. After grabbing a vial at random, I sat in an empty booth so that I wouldn't have to make small talk or choose whom to sit with for the last time.

I rolled my vial across the table to Cherie, who struggled to pop the cork with her talons covered in kid gloves.

"Eat fast, *ma chérie*. I can't wait to *allez-hop* out of here."

She just stuck her tongue out at me, then sucked it right back in with a blush.

I looked up to find Luc's mother, Mademoiselle Caprice, standing over us, her black hair tightly braided and her red-skinned hands on her hips, black nails tapping. She normally wore flamenco-style dresses that accentuated her dance moves and flowed like an extension of her skin. But today she had on a traveling gown just as stylishly constricting as mine. She raised an eyebrow at me and waited expectantly.

Cherie's eyes met mine. Neither of us knew the haughty daimon well. She was probably glad to get rid of me so her son would stop staring and writing horrible poetry to slip under my door.

"Don't worry. We'll go soon," I said, and she nodded and left the dining car without a word to her sons.

Cherie gulped down both vials quickly and then looked as if she might lose them to nerves. The moment she was done, we both stood and hurried to the door. Being on the road would be better than dealing with this awkwardness a moment longer.

A small party waited outside our wagon. Tish kept dashing tears away, while Criminy did his best to maintain his usual smirk.

"Mr. Murdoch put this together for you, honey." Tish handed me a train case that was unusually warm, and inside I found a dozen vials of blood nestled in little holes. It felt like an incubator.

"This, too." I was surprised to see the reclusive Mr. Murdoch himself. He'd ventured outside his car more frequently since Imogen had come along, but I couldn't recall if he had ever spoken directly to me before, not in all my years of traveling with the carnival. Imogen and I got along fine, though, and I'd spent some rainy afternoons reading beside her fire while a butterfly flapped lazily on my shoulder; there was a swallowtail in her butterfly circus that seemed to favor me.

The reclusive artificer stepped back to reveal our trunk raised up on a small conveyance, almost like a wagon, with a steering wheel and a clockwork winding box on the back.

"Wind the key, and as long as you're on the road or flat ground, at least one of you can ride. Sell it in Dover for traveling money." His gloved hand lingered on the key as if he were adopting out a puppy of which he had grown fond.

"Thank you so much," I said, and Imogen stepped forward.

"It was my idea, you know. But Henry's design."

"Good Lord, woman. What isn't?" He sounded gruff, but he pulled her close and kissed her hair with a fondness that made my lonely heart ache.

Jacinda Harville stepped up next, handing me a knife in a leather sheath. "One of Marco's. Stay lively so I can read about you in the Franchian papers, yes?"

I'd liked the journalist ever since she'd drawn a flattering picture of me for her book on the caravan, and although her beloved knife thrower was a man of few words, he winked and nodded. Funny to think I'd crushed on him once. It felt as if it was a million years ago that I'd watched him across the fire, dreaming of passion and adventure that I still hadn't found.

"Maybe we'll see you there soon," Jacinda added. "Lots of juicy stories in Franchia."

"Lass is getting restless for adventure," Marco said, and I would've sworn he goosed her.

All the smiling faces were making me feel wobbly inside. Criminy and Tish, Mr. Murdoch and Imogen, Jacinda and her daggerman. They all had what I longed for: someone to love and a place to belong. I fought back tears and was about to launch into a big speech when Mademoiselle Caprice appeared, a valise in her hand.

"*Allons-y*," she said with great fanfare.

"Let's go where?" I asked.

Caprice looked at me as if I was a complete idiot. Criminy tried not to laugh and failed.

"To Ruin, of course." She pinned Criminy with a harsh glare. "Luc said she was intelligent, and you concurred. Am I missing something?"

Despite the fact that I was well aware that Criminy was the most vicious predator for hundreds of miles, I still bared my teeth at him and growled. "A chaperone? You're sending us with a chaperone?"

Tish almost stepped forward, but Criminy caught her, probably recognizing that she was an excellent target for an angry Bludman's fangs.

"Demi. Poppet. Darling. Surely you don't think I'm sending two young, innocent girls to Franchia by themselves? You've never been there. You don't know how to negotiate air travel. You don't speak the language. And even if I was willing to take the chance, no one will do business with young human girls unchaperoned in the Pinky world."

"We're not young. We're in our twenties. And we're dangerous."

He smiled, rubbing my shoulders with both hands as if calming a dog. I snapped at him, my fangs closing on air. "You are dangerous, yes. And Mademoiselle Caprice will keep you under leash until you're in a safe place. Franchia is a different country. Daimons have different rules. She'll fill you in and make sure no one takes advantage of you."

"No one can——"

He put a finger against my lips. "You lost this round, pet. Count your blessings, and write me an angry letter from Ruin, yes?"

I spluttered, and Tish stepped in to hug me again. Then, suddenly, Mademoiselle Caprice and Cherie were walking toward Mr. Murdoch's wheeled trunk conveyance. The twin tracks cut by our wagon caravan dwarfed it on either side as they stretched across the moors, back toward the port city of Dover. I was just about to ask who would ride first when Mademoiselle Caprice leaped up with a daimon's grace and settled her skirts over our trunk. Cherie and I exchanged glances; walking was so unglamorous.

"Have fun, honey," Tish said.

"Good luck, *ma petite*," Crim added, slipping something into my hand. A bludbunny foot on a chain. I stuffed it into my pocket and tried not to cry and mess up my kohl again. Criminy strapped the train case of blood and Caprice's valise on a ledge behind the clockwork box and wound the key on the back. Before I was really ready, I was walking across the moors, stumbling over tussocks of grass as I followed my own rumbling trunk.

It was the strangest good-bye of my life, but I was on my way to Ruin.

3

I intended to punish my companions with my silence, but Mademoiselle Caprice spoke enough for all three of us. As elegant and aloof as she'd been in the caravan, the daimon changed utterly once we were over the first hill. She was an endless font of dry stories, anecdotes about life in Toulouse, and tips for not getting drained by big-city gendarmes, the Franchian version of police. In Sangland, the Coppers had evolved to keep the Bludmen down, but in Franchia, the gendarmes worked to promote peace among the daimons, the humans, and the few rare Bludmen within the city walls. But they still carried seawater guns, just in case.

"Such fortunate girls you are, to have a champion like Monsieur Stain. The university is beautiful—lovely buildings and soaring windows and the very best professors. You can study art or music or dancing."

"Or business or bone setting or law," I added, bristling for the twentieth time since she'd opened her mouth. No matter that I'd been in Sang for more than half a decade, I still had trouble swallowing the misogyny with a polite smile. And considering that my livelihood no longer demanded that I play nice with customers, I didn't have to take it anymore.

She laughed brightly. "Oh la la. Luc did say you were a bold little thing."

"What's the city like?" Cherie asked.

The trunk conveyance stopped just then, and Caprice hopped gracefully down to rewind it with arms corded with muscles. When it was ready again, Cherie made a move to take her turn. But Caprice beat her to it, hopping back up to ride sidesaddle as we took off again.

"Ruin is like all Franchian cities: built with order and loveliness in mind. White stone, stained glass, statuary. We daimons require that things be beautiful, you know. Not like those wretched Pinkies behind their walls, living lives of fear. Although I do hear the Bludmen's cities of Muscovy and Constantinoble are equally beautiful. How fortunate that your people and mine need not grub in the dirt for sustenance."

"Do you not eat anything, then?" Cherie asked, before blushing and looking down. "If the question is not too personal."

Caprice flapped an elegant hand at her. "Eating is a messy business, is it not? As plants derive nutrition from the sun, so do we daimons draw energy from emotions. There are different classes of daimon, but you can't tell by looking what a daimon requires for health. I feed on passion. Some depend on comfort, happiness, awe. The dark daimons hunger for sadness, hopelessness, rage, pain. They cannot help craving such things, but it does tend to turn them to malevolent pursuits. Unfortunate, really, but they are the exception. Most daimons feast on forms of happiness and lust, of which there is always plenty. And we do drink, as you do, to relax and cavort. Our drinks are mostly made of fermented flowers and magic. But we don't need it. It's more like liquor is to the Pinkies."

"How very fascinating," Cherie murmured, and I realized I'd never asked Luc what he fed on. Considering his lackluster skills in the bedroom and the way he followed me around mooning, it had to be comfort. Before she'd hooked up with Marco, Jacinda once told me about an affair she'd had with a daimon in Paris, and it had given me high hopes for the dancing mistress's son. But Luc had been a complete disappointment.

I had to find one of these daimon men who fed on passion.

"So the cabarets are as much for the girls as for the audience, then?" I asked.

Caprice leaned back to gaze at the airships bobbing over Dover as they played hide-and-seek with the low-hanging clouds.

"You would think that. But they are often required to do more than they originally bargained for. The wealthiest and most powerful men of Franchia are humans, for what daimon cares for all that work and responsibility? We have ways of keeping the laws in line with our ways, but the cabaret audiences are mostly Pinky gents. And that sort of man, so accustomed to taking what he wants, will not pay to be teased again and again unless he eventually gets his reward, *non*?"

"That sounds wretched." Cherie crossed her arms and shivered. "At least Criminy keeps us safe."

"Ah, yes. Monsieur Stain is a truly unique creature. You would not find such care in Mortmartre, no matter how delightful the show looks from the outside."

"How do you know?" I asked.

Her skin had always appeared red, but now it shivered over briefly into an angrier, glowing burgundy shot through with stripes like a tiger's. Luc had explained to me once that every daimon was born a certain color and wore it when resting or not concentrating, but they could change colors and patterns like chameleons to varying degrees, both on purpose and when particularly affected by emotions. Luc himself had changed to a bizarre fuchsia every time he'd kissed me, which startled the crap out of me the first time.

Caprice closed her eyes, concentrating until the furious stripes melted back into velvety red. "I know because my father sold me to a cabaret when I was only sixteen to pay for his gambling debts. It happens often, when a daimon hungers for anticipation and chance but isn't rewarded with luck. Let us say only that I was fed well but heartsick, and I will stay with Monsieur Stain as long as he will have me." Her face was pointed toward the airships, but her mind was clearly in the past and troubled. She lay back on the trunk and closed her eyes, trusting the conveyance to carry her down the straight lines toward the port.

"See, Demi? I told you Paris was horrid."

I flapped a hand at Cherie, just as Caprice had. "You forget: we're not daimons. It would be different for a Bludman."

"Everything is," Cherie grumbled.

I slung an arm around her waist and walked in step with her. Speeding up the pace, we hurried ahead of Caprice, who was emitting soft snores. "You're looking at it the wrong way, honey. We're out of the caravan. We have a little money. We can do anything we want to. The world is our oyster."

Her gray eyes went wide and shocked as she stopped and pulled away from me.

"Demi, no. No! I don't know what an oyster is, and I don't want to. You're the one who's looking at it the wrong way. We're being given the chance of a lifetime. Do you have any idea how rare it is for girls like us to go to university? I didn't want to be part of this plan, but now I've never felt so grateful. Don't botch it up just because you always want more."

"Of course I always want more. A hungry animal lives longer."

Her gloved hands went reflexively to her stomach. "I almost starved to death as a child in Freesia. I don't want to be hungry ever again."

Just ahead, at Dover, all the possibilities in the world waited, tethered to the docks by long ropes. Mademoiselle Caprice would soon haggle our passage to Callais, probably on one of the large, fast passenger airships, where we'd huddle on the open deck and try to keep hold of our hats. Then we would spend our first night in Franchia at an inn before taking a carriage to Ruin. I dreaded spending more than six hours trapped in a tiny, airless, jouncing box with humans, even if Criminy had given us a vial of salve to rub on our collars to lessen the smell of their blood. The bottled goo stank of Vicks VapoRub mixed with perfume, and for me, at least, hunger would be less painful. I was better at controlling the blood hunger than Cherie, who'd been raised far away from humans and, unlike me, had never been one of them.

The trunk's clockwork key had worn down, and it slowly rolled to a halt behind us. Caprice sat up like a zombie coming awake, rubbing her eyes with red fingers. She hopped down from the trunk with a dancer's flair and stretched, cracking her back and settling her voluminous skirts.

"We will all walk from here, my dears. Demi, pull the trunk along manually. We cannot have the people of Callais eyeing our goods until they've paid, *non?*"

I was glad to pull the handle and lag behind Caprice and Cherie. As I watched their skirts sway and listened to the sort of polite conversation that bored me to blud tears, the airships played peekaboo with my hopes. We were so close to freedom. And I didn't want to go to Ruin. No matter what Caprice said, my heart hungered for the cabarets of Paris.

Cherie never liked my ideas at first. But eventually, she always admitted that I was right.

She'd thank me later.

The airship ride was exhilarating, even if we weren't allowed to stand up for fear that our skirts would fill with air and carry us over the railing and into the fatally salty sea below. Cherie buried her face in my shoulder, and I wrapped my arm around her and inhaled the brisk, briny air. I'd loved the ocean before becoming a Bludman. Now it could kill me. Half my senses wanted to suck in the sea spray, and the other half wanted to hold my breath until we were safely on the other side of the Channel.

No one seemed to have noticed that we weren't human, which was helpful. I'd seen a couple of Bludmen being abused in the streets of Dover, and it took everything I had not to bare my fangs and come to their rescue. Thanks to Criminy's ability to forge papers and Antonin's costuming prowess, we were safe from being flogged by some shaky-legged old Pinky man with a monocle. But it was hard for a Bludman to pretend to be anything less than an apex predator, and I was glad to get off the streets and into the privacy of the boardinghouse Caprice had selected for us. Not too fancy, not run-down, and just a block away from the depot, where carriages would line up in the morning to take us to Ruin. The daimon certainly served her purpose as a chaperone, as I still had trouble converting coppers and silvers into francs in my head and had no idea how to tell an inn from an apartment until she explained what the daimon symbols painted on the signs meant. I paid special attention to her lessons.

Upstairs at the inn, I fell onto one of the three narrow beds and kicked off my boots, grateful to be horizontal. Cherie went straight for the train case of blood and downed two vials, handing me a third. I sipped it carefully without sitting up.

"I'm going down for supper, *mes filles.*" Mademoiselle Caprice smoothed her glossy hair and straightened her dress. "Drink your blood, and get some sleep. We shall leave at dawn."

"Yes, *mademoiselle*," Cherie said.

"Good luck finding some sexy victims," I added.

Caprice shot me a glare. "You should take care to curb your attitude before you reach university, my dear. The professors have been known to strike deserving miscreants with a cane. Bludmen are not exempt from manners."

As soon as she was gone, I sat up and held out my hand to Cherie, so she could see what nestled in my palm.

"Demi. You didn't." She poked the pile of coins with a finger.

I grinned. "Criminy taught me well."

"We can't use it. Even if I agreed, even if I wanted to

go to Paris, all the carriages in Callais leave from the same place. She would find us in a heartbeat."

Tucking the coins back into my pocket, I sighed deeply. "I guess you're right. No point in trying to give her the slip. Oh, well. Good night, Cherie,"

She looked me up and down. "You're not going to change into your nightclothes?"

"Of course not. Good Pinky girls don't change in inns. Who knows if they have bludrats?"

"Excellent point. You're finally starting to be sensible."

She lay down on the bed beside mine, fully clothed, and blinked sleepily at me.

"It's strange, going to bed this way. I'm so used to being in the top bunk with you below me. And now you're staring at me. And we're in Franchia."

I rolled over, showing her my back. "Creepy staring problem solved. Don't worry, honey. Everything will be better in the morning."

But I hadn't shown her what was in my other pocket. And I wasn't going to sleep yet, either.

"**Cherie, wake up. We have** to hurry." I rolled her shoulder gently and glanced over her at Mademoiselle Caprice, who let out a roaring snore.

"Why? Are we late for the carriage?"

"We will be." I slipped a vial into her hand and guided it, uncorked, to her lips.

She chugged it agreeably and blinked at me. "Where's Mademoiselle Caprice?"

I stifled a giggle. "Sleeping off too many daimon drinks, I suppose."

But Cherie knew me too well. Her eyes went to slits. "What did you do, Demi?"

"Well, Cherie, I might have brought a bag of Criminy's famous sleeping powder. And I might have used it on her after she went to sleep. And I might have grabbed our papers and carriage tickets from her reticule. And she might be sleeping for another day, at least, because I might have used more powder than was necessary." I held up our forged papers in one hand and a sack of coins in the other and waggled my eyebrows.

Cherie groaned and stood, looking down at our insensate chaperone with her usual concern. "Oh, dear Aztarte. You are a horrible person and a bad influence, and Criminy is going to kill us, and we're just going to sit right here and wait until she wakes up and pretend like nothing ever happened, because I really don't want Criminy to kill us."

"Criminy has to find us before he can kill us, and he's not going to find us." I smiled and patted her shoulder. "At least, not until we're the most celebrated act in the cabarets of Mortmartre."

"No. No no no no no. I'm going to Ruin. I'm going to university. I am not, under any circumstances, going to Paris. And I'm definitely not going to the cabarets. Did you even listen to Caprice yesterday? It's dangerous. Even for us."

"And it's the only way to be a star."

"I. Don't. Want. To. Be. A. Star." She punctuated each word with a little slap on top of my head.

"I don't want anything else *but* to be a star. Besides, you're going to live to be three hundred. You've got plenty of time to make youthful errors. You can always use your mad cash from the cabaret to go to university later, after you sow your wild oats."

Cherie sat down and put her head in her hands.

"What are oats, and why should I sew them? I hate sewing. Honestly, Demi, I feel like a mother with an out-of-control child. You won't listen to anyone. Not me, not Mademoiselle Caprice, not even Criminy and Letitia. Why can't you just be happy with what you have?"

I stared into her cloudy gray eyes, begging her to understand, as pink-tinged tears spilled down my cheeks unbidden and unwanted. "Because I'm not happy, Cherie. I'm hungry. Why are you so ready to be complacent? Why don't you want more?"

She scooted over to me, folded our black-scaled fingers together. "I don't know how to get through to you. You're my best friend, and you'll never be happy until you've destroyed us both."

I shook my head. "It's not destruction. It's reinvention. Trust me. It's going to be the biggest adventure of our lives. We just have to reach out and take it."

She sighed deeply and reached to pull the coverlet over Mademoiselle Caprice's shoulder. "You'll never give up, will you?" she asked quietly. "No matter what?"

"Not until I get what I want."

"So my only choices are to join you on this mad caper to Paris or stay here alone and explain to Mademoiselle Caprice why I let you go?"

"Pretty much."

She took two more vials from the train case and twined her arm around mine. We uncorked the vials and sipped them at the same time, a Bludman's pinkie promise. Her eyes were sad and rueful, maybe the tiniest bit amused.

"Then I guess, yet again, I'll give in to you."

"It's going to be amazing, Cherie. I promise."

She tossed her empty vial at my chest. "If you're wrong, I'm going to kill you myself."

"Fair enough. But I'm going to be right."

We slipped out the door with nothing but the train case of blood vials, our papers, and a pocket full of dreams.

And by dreams, I mean money I nicked off our sleeping chaperone.

Little did I know how quickly we would lose them all.

4

I was giddy as I watched the muffin-shaped haystacks roll past like a live Monet painting, the sky shimmering pink behind them. Beside me, Cherie vibrated like a frightened chihuahua.

"Criminy's going to kill us."

"You've already said that a thousand times. It's too late to worry about it."

"It's never too late to worry."

I rolled my eyes at her and leaned my head against the worn cushion of the jouncing carriage, which was moving across the fields of Franchia at a fast clip, spiriting us from Callais to Paris. My best friend was starting to sound way too much like my conscience. I was fairly certain she would nag me to death before we even reached our destination, much less before Criminy found out.

"He's got to find us before he can kill us. And Paris is a big city, *mon petit chouchou*." I elbowed her in the ribs.

"And what is that supposed to mean, Demi?" She elbowed me right back.

"It means I called you a cabbage. It's a French—I mean, Franchian—term of endearment. And did you know you have seriously pointy elbows?"

Her voice went so quiet that surely the Pinkies in the carriage wouldn't hear. "I just don't think it's right, running out on Mademoiselle Caprice and taking all her francs. Criminy's going to kill her, too, for being a bad chaperone. What was so horrible about going to the University of Ruin, anyway?"

We hit a pothole, and my head knocked against the wood, loosening a dark brown curl to dangle in my eyes. I sat up straighter and shrugged. "I left her enough money to get back to the caravan. And Ruin wasn't horrible; I just wanted an adventure. I don't want to be a boring contortionist in the boring caravan anymore, and I don't want to go back to college, either."

"*Back* to college?"

I wedged my head onto her shoulder, my mouth to her ear behind a curled glove. The other passengers didn't know we were Bludmen or that I was a Stranger from Earth. We would be in serious trouble if they found out we were bloodsuckers—not the nice, normal, Pinky girls we appeared to be. "I guess I never told you. I was at university when I . . . when I ended up in Sangland. When Criminy found me and saved me. I was a student, in my world. I hated it."

"Why did you never say? And why did you hate it so?"

I scowled behind my hand, but her confusion was genuine.

It was easy to forget that Cherie had grown up poor and freezing in the forests of Freesia after her family fell out of favor with the Tsarina. To her, the caravan was a life of warmth and security. And I had taken that from her when I decided to leave. Breathing in the scent of her hair, I felt a rush of love for the first person who'd reached out to me when I arrived in Criminy's caravan, naked and confused and newly blood-hungry. She'd hugged me and taken me in like a lost kitten, teaching me how to drink blood from vials without staining my clothes and showing me how to line my eyes with kohl like the other girls. When I looked at her, I saw only my dear friend, the closest thing I'd ever had to a sister. Golden curls, eyes too innocent for a Bludwoman, pink cheeks, and an upturned nose. She looked like an American Girl doll, not a well-disguised wolf.

But to her, the University of Ruin represented untold wealth and opportunity. Most likely, no one in her entire family had ever been to university, much less a woman. I would have to keep reminding myself, before we landed in Paris, that women in Sang didn't have the sort of freedom I had known back home in Greenville, South Carolina. I hadn't spoken much of my life before Sang, it was true. But I owed her a better explanation for why I'd forced her to join me on a risky adventure.

"I never told you because I wanted a clean start, wanted to forget how I ended up here. Earth is different. Safer. I guess I thought that once I left home and got to a new city for college, everything would be different. That I would make friends and get a boyfriend and do well in my classes without really trying and that a degree in art history would actually get me a job. I thought life would be as pretty as it looked in the brochures, in the advertisements. I thought that just getting away from my parents would suddenly make everything better."

"It didn't?"

"Nope. Kind of the opposite. It just made me more depressed and alone."

The Pinky gentleman across the carriage watched our

whispered closeness with an unhealthy fascination, a creepy gleam growing behind his spectacles. My instinct was to flash my fangs at him and hiss, but that would get us thrown off the carriage, if not killed. Instead, I pulled my head away from Cherie and locked eyes with the older man. After a few moments of my intense glaring, he cleared his throat juicily and looked away. The prim nursemaid beside him sniffed in disdain and sidled closer to her charge, a girl of about seventeen. The girl gave us an innocent, hopeful smile, which I was sure Cherie would return behind closed lips. We might have looked her age, but we were probably ten years older. There were benefits to being bludded, after all.

"Well, I think it's important that we—"

I never found out what was important. Two sharp thuds outside set the bludmares screaming as the scent of fire reached my sensitive nose. Cherie's head whipped around, her eyes wide and alert. The coach shuddered with sudden violence, throwing us against each other and the walls. Flames caught at the curtains, black smoke rolling into the stuffy, airless space. The gentleman who'd ogled us earlier threw open the door and froze before tumbling out onto the ground, a flaming arrow lodged in his jabot.

I leaped out, tugging Cherie behind me, trying to make sense of the chaos, while the young girl behind us clutched at her nurse with one hand and the carriage seat with the other and screamed bloody murder. I forgot myself and turned to hiss at her, which only made her more annoyingly hysterical.

A loud screech in the road caught my attention. It was a metal conveyance, shaking and belching smoke as it skidded to a halt. Masked figures with bird beaks and round goggles appeared in the haze, and I started to run in the opposite direction. Cherie was motionless beside me, stiff with fear.

"Run, you idiot!" I hissed.

"I—I can't."

The figures hovered closer, dark arms up as if to calm us, as if creepy, masked monsters could ever calm anyone. I grabbed her hand and pulled, but she was rooted to the ground and stronger than she looked. Gritting my teeth, I slapped Cherie's white face. "You're a goddamn predator, Cherie. Act like it. Run."

"I can't. I'm . . . I'm scared of fire, Demi. You don't understand. I never told you—"

With a growl, I scooped her up over my shoulder and dodged around the thrashing, burning, screaming bodies of the once-white bludmares to charge into the waist-high grass of the moors. Crossbow arrows *thwack*ed over my head, carrying nets instead of killing points. I tripped and fell face-first into the grass. Cherie slipped out of my grasp and landed with a groan just ahead of me. I couldn't see her, but the plants up ahead swayed with her passing, her frantic breathing and grunts as clear as the sounds of prey being hunted.

I stayed low to the ground and followed her, but the smoke was everywhere now, blocking my view and filling my lungs with the greasy funk of magic. I didn't dare call to Cherie, but I had lost her in the maze of foggy grass. Waving the smoke away, I clawed through the chaos and into a thick pricker bush that would have torn apart anyone not wearing so many layers of city clothes.

"Come on. Come on come on come on," I chanted, listening for Cherie, waiting for her to join me.

I'd given up on sight, but my eyes were screwed, too. With the screaming of the girl in the coach and the blud-mares dying on the ground, the conveyance's rattling, the roaring of fire, and the thrashing of the grass as the cloaked figures hunted us through the smoke, I couldn't hear anything. I didn't dare peek up or call out for Cherie. I would have to hope that her inner strength had over-come her fear, that she was waiting somewhere, crouched, as I was, hiding under the heavy gray sky. I was one of the few people who understood Cherie's quiet tenacity and power, and I prayed it wouldn't fail her now.

The screaming stopped all at once, leaving only the rumbling of the conveyance, the crackling of the fire, and the eerie whispering of the wind in the grass. I took a deep breath, trying to scent Cherie, but I smelled only smoke and charred meat. When the conveyance's racket quieted, I rubbed my ears. It took me an extra moment to realize the sound was fading as the vehicle moved rapidly away. I stood in a crouch and found a trail of black exhaust lin-gering over the road as the mixture of smoke and magic lifted. The machine was far off now, low-slung, dark, and mean, like a blackened raven's skull. And faster than any-thing I'd seen since coming to Sang.

"Cherie?"

The only sound that reached me was the creaking of the burning coach as the timbers collapsed. I was about to rush over and hunt for Cherie amid the flaming pyre when I heard the loud, nasal sound of a horn. Were they coming back?

I dropped to the ground behind the bush, the adrena-line finally running out of my veins and leaving me cold and wobbly. A bludbunny darted past me with a bleeding human finger in its mouth. The next one stopped by my boot to hiss, nearly dropping an ear. I shook my head to dislodge the woozy funk of magic and smoke, and one of the rabbits hissed at me.

"I'm not that desperate," I muttered. When I started to sit up, I only fell back, dizzy.

My head was pounding—at least, I thought it was. Then the pounding turned into the slamming of hoof-beats against packed dirt. I froze. I needed to find Cherie and get back on the road without interference. The only thing I needed less than further trouble was a cadre of helpful Pinkies and Franchian gendarmes asking too many questions I couldn't answer.

"Damn. Just missed them!" an older man's gruff, gravelly voice shouted.

"Nicely done, Vale." That voice was younger, smug and nasty.

"Yes, of course. Blame the guy who had to take a piss." A third voice, sarcastic and dry. All three voices were heavily tinged with the boozy kiss of a French accent, which told me they were likely humans, as only daimons actually spoke Franchian in Sang.

The horses skidded to a stop somewhere to my left. I pried a hole in the bush but could only see more grass and a column of white smoke. That had to be the coach. I could smell it, wood and flesh melding into the now repellent scent of barbecued pork. Horses whinnied and pawed the earth somewhere nearby, far more beasts than were necessary for the three voices I'd heard. I struggled to hold very, very still. Bludman or not, with a crowd of any males, the likelihood of being raped was just as high here as at a frat party back home.

"You three, after the slavers. Another man in each direction, hunting for survivors. Don't return until you hear the horn. Lorn and Vale, with me." The old man sighed, and I could imagine him. Paunchy, starting to stoop, a barbarian in decline, wiping his balding head under the Franchian sun. "I'm getting too old for this *merde*."

Even with my eyes closed and my body hidden, I could sense a strange tension in the following silence.

"I'm going to look over there," said the dry voice.

"There's nothing over there, Vale."

"Exactly."

Soft footsteps spelled anger in the dirt. He was moving toward me, and if he got too close, the patchy bushes and grasses wouldn't conceal my overly bright teal dress. *Dammit.* Why couldn't I have just stayed unconscious for this part or dressed in the boring green of the moors? And where was Cherie?

"Only the coachman and a gentleman, Father. No women." The smug voice was far away and muffled, and I could easily imagine a piratical man with the arm of his floofy blouse over his mouth and nose to keep out the scent of burning flesh.

Nearer me, the man they'd called Vale struck the bushes. Breathing in, I scented a strange mélange of good and bad and spices. He reminded me a little of Veruca the Abyssinian, and I assumed he was a half-breed of some sort.

"No bodies over here. Just a bush." The shout was sarcastic and falsely bright, and I struggled not to grin. My teeth clacked together seconds later as his stick poked my thigh through several layers of skirt. "What ze hell?"

His hands parted the twigs, and in a moment of panic,

I sat straight up and grabbed him by the collar, yanking him through the bush and dangerously close without taking time to look at his face. To his credit, he didn't topple over or shout.

Into a caramel-tan ear with three gold rings in the lobe, I whispered, "I am not in the mood to be found. Or raped."

With a soft laugh, he whispered, "Excellent. I'm not in the mood to rape."

When he didn't shout or otherwise broadcast my existence, I let go of his shirt, noting that he smelled like a chai latte mixed with hearth smoke and starlight, with an undercurrent of something . . . wrong. But oddly tempting. He pulled away gently, no sudden moves, and studied me. I scooted back and wrapped my arms around my trembling knees, realizing how close my lips had been to a seriously hot guy. Peridot-colored eyes lined in black and set in molten tan skin regarded me with a cat's mixed disdain and curiosity. He had a two-day beard that framed full lips and matched his recently shorn hair, which wasn't normally my preference but worked in his favor. He was dressed in all black like the Dread Pirate Roberts, sitting back on his haunches with a loose-limbed confidence that made my limbs a little looser, too. His eyes blended in with the moors perfectly, an endless shifting amber green, like a glass of chilled wine that made me feel thirsty all over for something other than blood.

"Anything behind that bush, Vale?"

I jerked and flailed at his father's shouted words, and Vale's lips curled up, revealing white teeth.

His eyes raked from my mussed hat down to the tall leather boots peeking out from beneath foamy black layers of petticoats, as if he was pondering which end of a Chinese buffet to start at. I'd felt like a stone-cold predator since waking in Sang under Criminy's bloody wrist, but now my middle went hot and soft.

"Just ze prettiest girl I have ever seen."

My mouth dropped open.

"Lazy, lying bugger!"

Something *plink*ed against Vale's back, and he laughed and held up a river-smooth stone for me to see.

"Get to work, you worthless ass!"

Vale shrugged, unaffected. Barely loudly enough to be heard, he said, "Sometimes I tell ze truth. It keeps them guessing." Another stone *thwack*ed him in the head, and he rubbed it with a black-gloved hand. "Stay here. I will return." Before I could respond, he had disappeared, leaving shivering grass and skin in his wake.

I flopped onto my back, just in case one of the other men should doubt his lie this time. Eyes open, staring at the lavender-gray clouds, I listened for more footsteps. Partly because I wanted to avoid notice and partly because I wanted Vale to come back and look at me as if I was a candy apple waiting to be licked all over. But most of all, I wanted them all to leave so I could find Cherie.

I didn't smell her anywhere near, couldn't smell anything over the smoke and now the highwaymen and their predatory mounts. But from the men's shouts, at least I knew they hadn't found her body. Cherie was small and agile and clever, and I could only hope she was hiding in another copse or backed into an empty bludbadger den, waiting for the pesky band of brigands to finish their plundering and go the hell home. Maybe Cherie was a predator, but she was also a beautiful young woman, and all we knew of Franchia was ancient history from the daimon dancing mistress and tips on navigating city life. Who knew what dangers actually lurked here in the wilds?

The hooves of a single horse pounded close, the bludmare's scream protesting her rider's harsh treatment.

"You were right, boss. Usual slavers riding hell-bent for Paris in that damnable fast conveyance. Farther along than we thought. But the others might still catch them before they reach the underground."

"Great humping Hades!" I could hear echoes of the old man's greatness in the bellow of his baritone. Bludmare squeals and the squeaks of butts in saddles meant I would soon be alone again. "Lorn, you're with me. Vale, you continue investigating your precious bushes. Dig through ze rubble. Bring in at least a silver's worth of plunder, or don't bother to come home, you spineless coward." He spit in the dirt, and despite my ambivalence, I flinched. That was some cold shit.

I barely heard Vale's muttered, "Have fun in ze catacombs, arsehole."

The horn sounded, and the horses took off amid the men's whoops and hollers. I sat up before Vale could pry his way through the bushes, smoothing my bangs and licking my lips and hoping I looked less like a terrified girl and more like a sophisticated, exotic, and possibly dangerous lady on a mission gone awry.

"We keep meeting like zis." He grinned and held out a hand, and I took it, well aware that the two gloves between us lessened the heat no more than grabbing a hot cast-iron skillet with a paper towel. I stood, but he didn't let me loose. "I'm Vale Hildebrand, first son of Curse Hildebrand." He paused as if waiting for a response. "Lord of ze infamous Brigands of Ruin. Nothing? Really?" Dark eyebrows swept up, and he rubbed the stubble on his chin. "Damn. You're very hard to impress."

In just a few moments, his hot Franchian accent had become my new normal. I could have listened to him talk all day—if I hadn't been so hellbent on finding Cherie.

"I'm not from around here. Name's Demi Ward." Then, before he could derail me, "Have you seen another girl about my age and size but blond?"

"Unfortunately, you're the only one today. Perhaps I should start setting snares."

He released my hand, and I stood tall but not quite tall enough to look him in the eye.

"My best friend is gone. We were on the coach together—it was just us and another girl and her chaperone and a gentleman. Headed to Paris."

He put a hand on the small crossbow on his belt but refused to look away. "Who wore the pumpkin-colored dress?"

"The chaperone. An old nursemaid."

Vale exhaled and jerked his head toward the smoking coach. "There is a blood-stained scrap of orange fabric caught on an arrow. Two men are dead and burned. I see no sign of your friend or the other girl." His hand landed on the puffed shoulder of my gown, and I took a deep breath to meet it. "I'm sorry. We try to catch the slavers before they swoop in, but they're fast."

"Slavers?"

"We call them slavers, although we don't honestly know what happens to their victims once they abscond to the catacombs under Paris. They mostly take young girls, although they'll sometimes take an older woman or a young man. We believe they take girls off the streets, too. And from the cabarets. We try to track them, but . . ." He shook his head. "They simply disappear. Like smoke."

I couldn't breathe, and my back felt more boneless than usual. "Do you never find them? The girls?"

"Not once they're underground." His eyes went skittery, and I knew he was lying.

"What about my friend?"

He squeezed my shoulder and gave me the warm but useless smile someone might give a child at a funeral. "I know I'm a complete failure, but the rest of our band are sharp as hell and twice as fast, I promise you. There is still time."

I nodded once and walked to his giant black-and-white-spotted bludmare where she stomped around a picket driven deep into the earth. She tossed her muzzle at me, and I shoved the metal cap away, sending bloody froth flying.

Vale blanched. "Please, Demi. You will want to—"

"Hang on to your waist really tightly? Yeah, I know. Let's go."

He allowed himself a smirk. "Look, *bébé*. I beg you. Just wait until the rest of the band returns. We'll take you to our camp, and the women can feed you and help you wash up. We're brigands, but we are honorable, and we can get you home safely in a wagon with far less bouncing and biting." He winked. "Not that I would mind you bumping against me."

"You're wasting time, Vale."

"And you waste your breath. Nice girls don't ride into Paris bareback on a brigand's hellbitch."

With a snort, I stepped out of the mare's reach, took a

deep breath, and bent over backward into a C. From the backbend, I walked my hands between my feet, curling under until my forearms were on the ground beneath my skirt. Putting my boots on my own shoulders, I felt the frothy layers of the dress fall down around me, giving him a fine look at the slim-fitting trousers I favored for just such an occasion.

"I'm not that nice. And I'm not just a girl." I grinned, showing fangs.

To his credit, he didn't freak out. Just put his head to the side like a crow watching a jewel glint in the sun. For the first time, his tone went serious, quiet. "Now, that I did not expect. Tell me, Demi. What is it that you want?"

"Right now?" I did a front walkover and turned to face him with a swirl of skirts. "I want you to take me to Paris and help me find my best friend."

"Say we find her. Say we don't. What's your endgame, *bébé*?"

I windmilled my arms, loosening up. I was a little sore after the crash, not to mention the previous hours I'd spent crammed between Cherie's shoulder and the wooden wall of the carriage. Just to see what he would do, and to stretch out further, I slowly lifted one leg until it was right beside my ear, perfectly pointed straight up.

"I want to find Cherie and then go to Mortmartre and be the stars of the cabaret, of course."

"There are no Bludmen in the cabarets—"

"Not yet. There will be. Once I find Cherie, there will be two. We're an act." I dropped my leg—and my smile. "But I have to find her first. So are we going now or what?"

He shook his head, earrings winking. "But where will you stay, *bébé*? Where will you sleep? How will you feed?

If you drink from a human, they'll drain you. Unless you have money, which I don't believe you do, you are destitute. Even with my connections there, I cannot keep you."

My narrowed eyes shot to him, my shoulders rising and my mouth drawing down as I prepared to give an earful about what exactly he could keep.

He cut me off before I could start, a hand slicing the air. "Forgive me. The language barrier is perhaps as unkind as your tongue. I don't mean to keep you like a pet. I mean that nothing is free, more so in Paris perhaps than elsewhere." But his eyes said something different about keeping me.

"Then take me to a cabaret, and let me earn my blood. It'll be a good base of operations."

He exhaled, his head on the side. "You understand that women here are sometimes sold into cabarets as chattel. That it's a life no sane girl with options would choose."

I swallowed hard against a lump in my throat approximately the size of Cherie's white fist. "Then I'm not sane, and I don't have options. I'm choosing it."

He crossed his arms over his chest and looked off into the hazy distance, where a single dark spear pierced the clouds. The Tower, they called it—some daimon scientist's clever way to attract and channel lightning into electricity for the City of Light. Funny, how it looked exactly like the Eiffel Tower from my world but actually served a purpose here. Paris wasn't tall and humpbacked like Sanglish cities but sprawled, orderly, and leisurely, in neat squares. The daimons weren't known for leading lives of fear, nor were the humans who had taken up residence alongside them. There was a wall around the city, of course, but they'd given the artists free rein to make it beautiful, from what I'd heard. Daimons made things much nicer than Pinkies, as I was learning since touching down in Franchia.

I'd always wanted to see Paris on Earth. And now it was the key to finding Cherie in Sang.

Vale followed my gaze and nodded, rubbing his buzzed head. "It will be a hard ride. If you fall off, I will laugh at you. Odalisque is a bitch of a mare, and there's no room for you on the saddle." He met my eyes, steady and unblinking. "And odds are we will not find your friend."

"I'm not scared. And I *will* find her."

"Perhaps you are deaf. Do you understand that girls are kidnapped from the city, too? The brightest stars of the cabaret are often among the victims. It may be your dream, but *ma chère*, it could become your nightmare. The safest thing for you to do is let me return you to your people, or at least to mine. Getting taken yourself will not bring your friend back."

I rolled my eyes. "But it sounds like getting taken *is* the fastest way to find her. Can we go now? At least try to catch her?" I paused, let a little of the brave front down to show him the blud tears gathering. "We have to try. She's all I have."

He held out his hands as if grasping for sense and finding nothing but air, a gesture I recognized from both Criminy and Cherie when dealing with me. "It's suicide, *bébé*. Life in the cabarets isn't easy, even if they will hire you on. And if you survive the ride to Paris, sneaking in will be messy." He looked me up and down, and I gave him my Bludman's stare, promising all sorts of yummy violence. "But if you really are that determined, I will take you."

"If you don't take me now, I'll start walking." I realized what I'd said a heartbeat after he did and almost dived back into the bush to die of embarrassment in peace.

His grin was luscious. "How can a gentleman turn down a threat like that?"

With practiced movements, he snatched out the mare's tether and slid the picket spike through a slot in her metal muzzle cap to make reins. He threw them over Odalisque's head as she danced, then put a foot into the wide stirrup to leap into the saddle. Still grinning, he held down an arm for me. I took it, surprised at his strength as he swung me up behind him, his wide crystal-green eyes showing in turn his own surprise at my agility. The mare screamed and crow-hopped, trying to shake me loose, and he jerked the reins and kicked her. Odalisque reared and bucked before collecting herself for a pounding gallop.

I fastened my arms around Vale's lean waist and settled my cheek against his back, inhaling deeply and willing the beast to run faster toward Cherie. Back in the caravan, I had ached for a goal, an adventure, for something to care about. My wish had definitely been answered but not in the way I had hoped. The adventure wasn't important anymore, not until I got my best friend back.

"Aren't you afraid I'm going to rip you to shreds?" I asked, trying to cover the fact that I'd all but nuzzled the hard muscles of his back through the worn black shirt.

"I'm half Abyssinian. My blood would drive you mad and kill you," he shouted into the wind. "But please, *bébé*, keep trying."

I snuggled against his back as the bludmare thundered toward Paris, my cheek nestled up to his ribs, hoping he couldn't feel my tears soaking into his shirt. I might have shown him my brave face before, but inside, I was falling apart. Cherie had trusted me, and I had brought her nothing but disaster. I let out a racking sob, and Vale tensed in the cage of my arms, muscles taut as the horse leaped and skidded across the road. Finally, he exhaled in a sigh I felt more than heard, and his hand reached down to squeeze mine where it held on to him for dear life.

He didn't let go.

5

We didn't talk much, which I appreciated. Staying on the horse's wildly undulating rump was a struggle, even with my performance-honed muscles. The cacophony of hoofbeats made conversation almost impossible, and every time I opened my mouth, I got a face full of shirt scented with woodsmoke and herbs, which wasn't so bad but definitely distracted me from my strategizing.

"Not much longer." His words thrummed against my chest before the wind snatched them away from my ears. "Are you perhaps scared of dark, dangerous places full of bones?"

"Not if Cherie is waiting on the other side."

Thunder vibrated the clouds, and the mare tossed her head and screamed a dare at the sky. It was darker over Paris, and a bolt of blue-white lightning arced from the gray thunderheads to the Tower and briefly lit the stark black skeleton of iron beams like a neon sign. A fat raindrop plunked on my cheek, and I burrowed further against Vale's back, glad for my hat's wide brim and annoyed with all the layers of my Pinky costume, which would soon be soaked and weighing me down when I wished to be fast and unencumbered.

The road turned from hard-packed dirt to a slick slurry that slid beneath the mare's hooves. When Vale turned her off the road and into the waist-high grass, I was glad to be on more solid ground. The wall was finally in view, but we were galloping swiftly away from the grand iron gates. Vale angled the mare toward a dark, boggy area surrounded by cattails. An enormous pipe jutted from the earth like a fallen Tower of Pisa, broken and overgrown with moss and filth. I smelled it then—deep, old death soaking up through the ground. Even closer, jagged tombstones poked up from the sludge like black pegs of rotten teeth. No one but the richest families in Sang buried bodies anymore, thanks to the lack of land within the cities and the possibility of a funeral party being eaten by a troop of bludsquirrels. Cremation and pretty urns were the fashion. Not surprisingly, the graveyard was long abandoned, untended, and falling back into the earth.

So this was the door to the famous catacombs, the portal into the decaying underbelly of Franchia's greatest city. The stories were true.

"Are you sure this is the path you wish to follow?" Vale asked, slowing the horse to a trot.

My teeth clacked as I jounced behind him, wrapping my aching thighs more tightly around the mare's barrel belly and against the backs of his legs. I dashed away old tears and ran fingers under my eyes, hoping to clean up the kohl I'd smeared all over his back.

"Looks like fun. I've been needing a vacation." In my mind, it sounded jaunty and brave, but it came out with a hitch that I couldn't hold in. Poor Cherie. She had to be terrified, if she was in there. She hated being dirty.

The bludmare picked her way through bunches of

cattails, sometimes plunging into a boggy bit as we aimed for the yawning mouth of the pipe.

"Oddly enough, it's not so bad once you're inside. The rain and sewage collect and pool out here over the graves, but underground it's channeled through rock. The threat of horror keeps most people out, though. Not to mention the blud creatures. Just remember not to touch any of the bones. They're cursed."

"You actually believe that?"

He chuckled. "Let us consider. Touch moldy bones and see if I'm cursed forever, or keep my hands to myself? Not a difficult decision."

We reached the pipe, where a trickle of grayish water splattered to the boggy ground. The mare sneezed against her metal muzzle, adding bloody foam to the sludge. Vale edged the horse closer to an old log, and without being told, I leaped off her back and landed heavily on what felt like permanently bowed legs. Vale dropped beside me, steadying me with a firm hand as the log wobbled. He slapped the mare's rump, and she took off with a splash, her hoofbeats merging with the near-constant thunder overhead.

"Won't she run away?"

He smirked and stared after her high-flung tail. "We plant a carcass nearby to draw the bludmares and leave a young lad to catch and picket them. Hungry predators aren't so smart when it comes to half a bloody pig on the moor."

It was my turn to smirk with a flash of fang. "Funny, I'm pretty good at resisting bloody pigs."

"One point to the *mademoiselle*." Vale tipped an imaginary hat; I pictured a fedora and couldn't stop myself from giggling.

· Surefooted as a fussy cat, he leaped onto the lip of the

pipe and straddled the slushy water. I followed him into the darkness, my skin prickling as I left the weak light of a cloudy day for the sucking shadows of the cylinder. Just before the pipe's curve shifted to aged stone, the light gave out. Vale pulled a heavy pendant from the neck of his shirt and twisted its base, and a gentle green glow filled the space, showing a long tunnel of orderly bricks and stones. Perfectly set in patterned niches were artful groupings of smooth white bones and polished skulls. Sluggish, lumpy water flowed down a channel set in the middle, just wide enough to straddle. Each side had just enough space for a slender person to walk without turning sideways. Vale's shoulders were almost too broad and occasionally bumped the wall as he led me down a ladder and deeper into the catacombs. I threw out my senses, hoping for any sign of Cherie.

"My father's band is ahead of us somewhere. The slavers never return by the same route, and there are endless tunnels and ladders and stairs and secret niches set into the maze of underground crypts. The good news is that I haven't seen blood or signs of combat yet, but the bad news is that if they reach their destination in the city and get topside before the brigands find them, we will have no idea where your friend was taken."

"Then what?" My boots rasped on the stone, and the smell shifted from death and decay to something slightly more tolerable, a mineral smell tinged with iron.

"Then whatever the lady wishes. I can return you to Callais, take you back to our camp, or deliver you to your new life in Paris."

"Dropped on the front step of a cabaret like a baby in a basket," I muttered.

He turned to give me a horrified look. "I do believe they call that murder in the city. The bludrats of Paris are monsters. And so are some of the men who frequent the cabarets."

The American teenager in me peered down into the water with a frown. "Speaking of which, anything nasty live in the catacombs?"

Vale chuckled and kept walking by the light of his pendant. A flash to the side caught my eye, and I watched him twirl a wicked-looking blade. "That depends on your definition of nasty."

"Dude, don't try to scare and impress me. I seriously want to know."

We passed an open tunnel, and I heard faraway shouting and felt a damp breeze. When I paused, he gently grabbed my wrist to pull me along. "Paris looks ordinary topside, all orderly rows and squares. But down here, in the old city, things are twisted and strange. There is no complete map, no limit to how wide or low the tunnels can go. Men have gotten lost and never come back. Or they've come back changed. Some say that even deeper than the tunnels, there are caverns filled with glowing crystals and albino bats. Sometimes bludrats find their way down here and go blind and bald. Sometimes feral dogs find a cavern and live like wild, half-mad creatures." He trailed off, his footsteps the only sound. But I smelled a lie.

"There's something you're not telling me, Vale."

He exhaled, shaking his head sadly. "Sometimes we find daimons down here. Ruined. Walking corpses. Mostly women."

"And you don't know what happened to them?"

"Not a clue. The best we can figure is that they got lost and went mad with it. No emotions to feed on, no clean water, no light. After a few weeks of wandering around down here with nothing but the sewage and pitch-black darkness, it makes sense." He stopped and spun, blocking my path. The green light lit him from below, a fiendish ghoul, all sharp edges and shadows. "I see that you wish to ask, so I will tell you. We kill them. Quickly and as kindly as possible. If you bring them topside, they scream and panic. Father brought one back to camp once, and she killed a child."

"I'm sorry."

"Life is dark, and then you die, *bébé*. Just let it be a reminder that you never want to get lost down here. And if you do, go very quiet and follow the sound of water."

Up ahead, a burble of voices. Vale stilled, and I nearly ran into his back before he relaxed.

"It's my father. And he's angry."

I held my breath but caught no sound of Cherie, no soft rasp of skirts against stone. What little hope I had tumbled away in the darkness. "Bad news, then."

"Today does not appear to be your lucky day, no."

I fingered the rabbit's foot still hidden in my pocket. "And how's your day?"

He drew a deep breath and gave the call of a hunting owl, which was swiftly answered from the bowels of the tunnel. Leaning his shoulders against the wall, he regarded me, smirk back in place. "Could be worse. No silvers, but I already made my hunting quota for the week, catching you behind that bush. Such a big, tame bludbunny would win prizes at any festival."

"I bet you say that to all the girls."

He sighed, almost sadly, before turning to greet the group of men materializing from the shadows, lit by the glowing green of their own pendants. Their leader exactly matched my mental image for Vale's father, leader of the brigands. A pro-wrestler type going to seed, with a paunch that stretched his vest, gray hair marching backward off the top of his head, and a scarred leather eye patch.

"Lose the trail? Lorn's fault, I'm sure." Vale's voice was dry and silky, every word a dare.

The old man shot a disgusted look at his older son. "Your responsible brother is still tracking the bloody bastards. They're faster than ever. Didn't see a single one. Found this, though."

I peeked around Vale and almost oozed into the water when I saw Cherie's hairbob.

"That's hers. My friend Cherie's."

The old man squinted at me with his one good eye. "Who the hell is that?"

Vale winked at me over his shoulder. "The girl I found behind the bush."

"I thought you were lying as usual."

"Then you owe me an apology, old man."

The head brigand turned red, which was quite an accomplishment in the green light. "I don't owe you a goddamn thing, son. You want something, you take it. If you can."

Vale stilled in front of me, going stiff all over like a stalking cat. He snatched the hairbob and handed it to me. As I fingered the ribbons that I had helped tie under Cherie's hair just that morning, Vale hopped across the water to the ledge on the other side of the tunnel.

"Care to join me, *bébé*?" He held out his hand.

His father glared at me, his single eye going narrow. "*Mademoiselle*, we'd be glad to escort you to safety. Despite Vale's bad manners, the Hildebrand tribe is known for stout hearts and valor." His eye roved over me, as if calculating the worth of my figure and costume. When he smiled, it was cold, like a shark.

I smiled sweetly, showing fangs. "Stout hearts? But I thought you were thieves."

Vale swallowed a laugh, and I took his hand and leaped lightly to the other side, where he caught me with a palm splayed across my back.

"Vale, it's your duty—"

"To escort this *mademoiselle* to her destination in the city. Don't worry, Father. I'll be home eventually."

"Already told you, don't come home unless you plan on living up to your birthright."

Someone snickered behind the old man, and Vale released me and walked stiffly along the ledge, away from his father and deeper down the tunnel toward Paris.

"Thanks, but no thanks," I said with a wave as I followed him.

The ledge wasn't as well kept on this side. It crumbled in places and felt almost spongy in others. Whenever there was a rough spot, Vale slowed and held out a hand to help me across. I could feel conflict and unease roiling in him, and I wasn't exactly calm myself. I wanted to break free, to run, to howl, to show my fangs to whatever creature had dared to take my friend Cherie. The ghostly plague doctors in the smoke now seemed like nothing more than nightmare visions I'd conjured myself. All we had was the hairbob clutched in my gloves. The anger and helplessness were maddening, but we had no choice but to creep along carefully, feeling our way down the narrow ledge, half-blind in eye and heart.

Which was probably why I decided to badger my savior.

"So . . . your dad."

"He is a terror, no?"

"Is he trying to start a fight or something?"

Vale chuckled. "Something like that."

"You want to talk about it?"

"You want to be tossed into the sewage?"

"Shutting up now."

The next few moments were tense and silent, and when we came to a jumble of femurs, I hopped back over to the other side of the water.

"What are you doing?" he asked.

"The silence is so thick over there I couldn't breathe. Figured the air might be a little more clear on this side of the crap river."

He failed to hold in a chuckle and leaped to my side. "*Touché, bébé.* Here's the thing. The Brigands of Ruin are patriarchal, which means leadership is expected to pass from father to son. Follow?"

"Got it."

"My Abyssinian mother was part of the camp only long enough to bewitch my father and leave me behind, which means I have less status and don't fit the pattern. I have always been rather a disappointment, while my brother, Lorn, is a boot-licking bludweasel with champion bloodlines." I cleared my throat, and he smirked. "Pardon the comparison. In any case, my father is past his prime, and I am expected to challenge him for leadership, but everyone knows I would be horrible at it. The obvious choice would be for my brother to challenge me, but he knows it would kill my father if something bad were to happen to either of us. So we're all bound by ridiculous traditions, and no one can do what he wishes." He reached back to help me over a little avalanche of broken stone. "But he is still a nasty little bludweasel."

"So run away."

Vale snorted. "Everyone half hopes I will. But that's the thing. As much as I don't wish to be responsible for dozens of families and a hundred mares, I love my father and don't care to disappoint him. So I abide, getting on everyone's nerves and mucking things up, hoping the slavers will just shoot me with a flaming arrow so the whole damned thing will be over."

I turned and put a hand on his shoulder, stopping him in mid-step. "There's no shame in being unsuited to your expected role."

He cocked his head, considering.

"At least, that's what my guidance counselor told me once when I disappointed my parents in high school. Wouldn't it be better to just make the choice and leave and have it be over with?"

Vale looked down, face lit by the green glow. "Not if I have to see my father's heart break when I tell him." He motioned forward with his chin, and I obliged him by continuing along the ledge. After a few footsteps, he went on, voice low and sad. "When I was ten, I asked him if I could go stay with my mother, learn more about her people and their ways, and he turned me over his knee and whipped my arse until I bled. Not only because no Brigand of Ruin had ever asked to leave the tribe before but also because it showed the people I would one day lead that I didn't feel proper responsibility for their safekeeping. That I would leave my duties and go to stay with foreigners, giving up my place as a man. It was the worst thing I could have done to him. Emasculated by a weak son, disappointed in his firstborn, and then the poor man had to make me cry to save face." He snorted softly, sounding much like his mare. "I don't think either of us can withstand a repeat of that night. No amount of freedom is worth that price. Not that he could whip me now. I'm much faster than he."

I tried to imagine a tiny version of Vale going through the regular preteen rebellion. I couldn't help smiling, just a little.

"How were things, after that?" I asked him.

"Ah, yes. The fallout. You see, after that, I had to prove myself, do something to save even more face on behalf of myself and my family. It was simply understood. So when my father and his men galloped away on their next raid, I took up my bolo and an old man's neglected gear and slipped away to capture my first bludmare. I returned that evening missing a chunk of my arm and riding Odalisque's mother, Olympe, leading a wobbly little filly behind me. Men of my tribe are supposed to go through careful training and ritual before they bring home their first horse, and I skipped all that and just took what I wanted, times two." He laughed and rubbed the back of his head, the rasp of skin on stubble the only sound in the tunnel and one I already recognized even though I couldn't see it. "Best mares in the camp, and I'd pulled it off four years before tradition allowed."

"And then?"

"And then he beat me again for breaking the law. And complimented my horsemanship. And told me he'd done the same thing at my age and my grand rebellion had just convinced the camp that I was the one who must lead them one day."

"Is there no other choice? No other role you could fulfill?"

He held up his fingers, counting them down. "Target? Eunuch? Laughingstock? Stew meat? Bludmare bait? Sadly, nothing appeals."

"But what do you want to do? With your life?"

He exhaled raggedly, leaped over the water, and ricocheted off the far bank and back to my side, landing in front of me without missing a beat. As if I didn't even exist, he started moving again, this time with more purpose and anger. I scurried behind him, boots slipping on bits of rock and bone.

"Vale, what?"

"If I knew what I wanted to do, if there was some secret calling in my soul, then I could walk away from Ruin and my father's tears with a light heart. If there was meaning, if there was passion, if there was anything I was good at besides thievery and sarcasm, he would understand. As it is, I have no plans. No future. No wish. I am merely a rebellious bastard and a well-trained brigand who no longer cares to brig."

"I used to be that way, too."

The words were tiny, swallowed up by the huge weight of an entire city overhead, but I know he heard them, because he stopped moving.

"And what happened then, Demi? What did you do?"

"I got depressed and almost died." I paused, not sure how much to tell, how many secrets the darkness and his desperation could coax out of me. "And then I woke up hungry."

"And then?"

I giggled at a line from a movie he'd never seen because there are no movies in Sang, and for just a moment, I felt infinitely far away from anything resembling home or comfort, the weight of an entire country pressing down on me with the feather touch of a girl's hairbob clutched in one hand. He turned to stare at me, Chardonnay-green eyes glowing, and something in my chest shifted.

"And then I ran away," I said finally.

He reached for me, his fingers stretched out toward my face, and I closed my eyes and parted my lips slightly, needing to feel something, anything, other than crushing defeat. Instead, I heard a blood-curdling scream, and Vale's arm flung me into the stone wall before drawing away suddenly.

I opened my eyes, heart beating an insane cadence, and found only darkness.

6

I reached for him, but he was gone. "Vale? What the hell!"

He was breathing heavily—that meant he was alive, at least, his boots scuffling on stone. There was another creature with us, something that smelled as stale and deep as the catacombs. And underneath that mildewy reek, there was pumping blood.

No. Wait.

Blud.

"Is it a bludrat? Can I help? God, it's so dark. I can't see anything. I frigging hate the dark!"

He growled and shuffled, and I wasn't sure whether to run or fight or scream for his dad to come back. I was just about to start feeling around with my toe for something useful to kick when I heard the solid thump of stone hitting flesh.

"Mangy. Little. Bastard!" Each word was punctuated by a thump, the last one accented with a gushy splat that peppered the air with the reek of hot blud.

"Vale?"

He grunted with effort, and something dropped into the water. After a few moments of fiddling and cursing, his green light flickered back on, showing black splatters up his arms, a few on his cheeks. "Remember what I said about bludrats getting underground and going bad?" He pointed down, and the twitching thing I saw smashed at his feet looked more like a shaved capybara than a rat, its pale skin sprinkled with wiry pink hairs and its sunken eyes white and unseeing.

"Are you okay? Did it bite you?"

With a laugh that echoed through the tunnel, he kicked the scrawny carcass into the water, where it bobbed and floated sluggishly with the flow, webbed feet up. "It tried. And failed. Let this be a lesson to you: don't try to kiss anybody in the catacombs."

I was blushing before he'd turned around and started walking. I'm pretty sure he knew.

Time went as thick and slow as the water beside us as we trudged through the underground tunnels. We chatted of silly things to keep our minds off reality and flirted as much as a giant graveyard allowed. But we never got close enough to attempt another foolish, desperate kiss. Then, all at once, the air congealed, and I knew the tunnel was about to end.

Although slogging through sewers and catacombs wasn't my ideal day, much less date, it had been all too easy to concentrate on the immediate, on the shiver that thrummed through me when I took Vale's hand to step over rubble and long-gray bones. I was in the worst trouble of my life, beyond terrified for my best friend, but every time he touched me, my betraying skin jumped, my heart raced. Being on the move at his side was far preferable to holding still. I sensed the stone wall before Vale stopped but let myself run into him anyway. Whatever happened next, his warmth was a comfort, and this might be my last chance to indulge.

"Shh, *bébé*. The door to the cabaret is just overhead."

It was darker here, and the scent of cold stone was overlaid with a fine patina of spilled liquor and echoes of cheap perfume and something else. Something rotten. A shimmering rectangle of gold light limned a trapdoor in the ceiling, and as I looked up, pounding feet sent dust to scatter over my cheeks.

"What's it called?" My own voice startled me in the darkness, almost overbright with worry I could no longer hide.

"Paradis," Vale said. "It means——"

I gripped the bludbunny foot in my pocket. "Paradise. I know. But probably not a paradise for me."

"Madame Sylvie's not so bad. She doesn't hit her girls, at least. She won't allow opium or absinthe or bludwine among the performers. And the daimon girls are . . ."

I could hear his smile, the ass. "Accommodating?" The word dripped icicles..

He cleared his throat. "They're lovely girls. Just watch out for Limone. That name's no coincidence. Sour as hell, that girl."

Looking up at the trapdoor, I pinched my cheeks and rubbed my lips with the back of my glove, hoping to bring some pink to the surface so I wouldn't look like the grime-speckled, scared-to-death monster I was.

Vale put a hot hand on my shoulder. "Are you sure this is what you want?"

I drew myself up tall, as if pushing back my shoulders could send the filth dripping off my back like a discarded cape. "If my only choices are giving up on my best friend and going back to the caravan or becoming a star in the cabaret while I hunt for.her, I choose cabaret. All the way."

"You're crazy, *bébé*. And I don't like it."

"You don't have to like it." I smiled, then frowned. My mouth didn't know what to do with the odd mixture of excitement, terror, and expectation. "You don't think they'll mind me?"

He snorted and rubbed dust off my cheek with a wide thumb, sending unexpected shivers down my skin. "A pretty girl in a cabaret? No, I don't believe they will mind at all."

That wasn't what I meant, and he knew it. "Where I come from, they consider me dangerous."

Vale held up his pendant, and the green glow bloomed between us. Honestly, he looked as nervous as I felt. "They'll take you in because you're beautiful. They'll keep you because you're talented. And because you have fangs, they won't try to take what you don't wish to give." His eyes met mine and went soft under long lashes.

I swallowed, digesting his words. "And what about you, Vale?"

Looking up at the trapdoor as I just had, he gave a lopsided grin that made his teeth a ghastly, electric green that reminded me of ghosts and raves and phosphorescent waves in the ocean, of too many things roiling under the surface. "I told you, *bébé*. I don't want what isn't given."

The green still meant he couldn't see me blush. I hoped. "Not . . . that. Up there. Are you coming with me?"

Reaching up, he flicked a lock and threw back the door, blinding me with lights as hot and welcome as the morning sun after an endless nightmare. "You heard my father. I have no money. I can't go home, either. So I'll follow you to Paris and Paradise." He winked. "You're going to need my help finding your friend, *bébé*. It's a big city."

Bits of feather and glitter fell down from the shaft of light, and someone called, "Oh la la! Careful, *chérie!*"

My heart leaped, hearing my friend's name. Vale's hand on my shoulder reminded me almost instantly that *chérie* was one of the most common words that might be uttered in a cabaret. Darling. Dearest. People might be calling me that soon, if things went according to plan. A shadow appeared, and I put up a hand to shield my eyes. The face that peered down through the explosion of light was shamrock green, dusted with diamonds and graced with eyelashes as long as plumes.

"*Quoi?*"

"*Bonjour*, darling!" Vale called, with lusty cheer that made my hackles rise.

"Vale? But why are you coming in the back door? You know that is not allowed here."

His face burned bright red, and the daimon laughed gaily and held out a hand clad in an emerald-green elbow-length glove. He recovered quickly, at least. "I've brought a surprise for Madame Sylvie. Let us up, will you, Mel?"

The face disappeared, and Vale nudged me toward the ladder with a gentle push that involved the warmth of his hand searing my back. Twitching my long bustle behind me, I took a deep breath and climbed upward into the light. Before, I would have been vexed that he was watching my butt. Now I was careful to move gracefully, making the skirts sway with my hips. Why I wanted to impress the vagabond, I wasn't exactly sure. Maybe it was the way the daimon's eyes had twinkled at him with secrets fondly remembered and excitement over future possibilities. Or maybe it was the memory of every single touch we'd shared and the fact that he had been about to kiss me before a mutant mole-rat tried to kill him. Maybe it was because he was the only friend I had here, and I'd already told him half my secrets, and if my ass would keep him close, I would take whatever advantage it gave me.

When my head rose through the trapdoor, it took a few moments for the scene to coalesce into any sort of sense. We were backstage, the red velvet curtains casting everything in a blushing glow. Stage lights shone in every direction, blinding me no matter which way I turned. Girls ran back and forth, dozens of daimons in a rainbow of colors, speckled all over with satin and sequins, which made me feel a little at home, at least. The face I'd just seen, Mel's, waited just a few feet away, attached to a petite but stunning body with proportions molded by years of tight corseting. I briefly wondered where the girl kept her innards and if daimons even had innards, seeing as how they fed off of human emotions. Did you need a liver to digest joy? Before I could speak, Vale popped up behind me and swung the trapdoor closed, where it merged seamlessly with the boards.

Oddly, I felt more trapped upstairs in the soaring theater than I had in the dark, dank, crumbling catacombs. Up here, everything felt very final. For so long, I had dreamed of the cabarets of Paris. But now that I was here, I felt like a very small, bloodthirsty fish in a very big pond filled with colorful frogs. I had always hoped to tread the boards for the first time with Cherie by my side, and missing her was like losing a limb, an ache that wouldn't go away.

"Not here for ze show tonight, eh?" Mel stared pointedly at Vale's empty hands and smirked. Her accent was heavy, her green lips plump and welcoming. I put a hand on Vale's forearm on the pretense of steadying myself.

"And not making a delivery. So what is ze occasion, *monsieur le brigand?*"

"A delivery of a sort. I've brought you a new girl. Where's Sylvie?"

"Oh, la. Two moments until show time. Stand still long enough, and she'll find you. But I wouldn't recommend that. Shoo. Go to the hallway and wait. Or watch from the back, if you wish. Just don't let Auguste see you." She winked, eyelashes brushing her green cheek like a bird's blessing. "You know how he is about strangers backstage."

"*Merci*, Mel. You look gorgeous."

Mel fluttered a hand at him and focused on me, cocking her head. "What's your name, *chérie?*"

I hoped she didn't see me flinch. "Demi Ward." I gave her a big, charismatic smile.

She leaned closer, breathing in with an open mouth like cats back home would do when smelling something rank. Her eyes flew wide, and I saw that her pupils had points like stars. "Do you know what she is?"

Vale grinned. "Oh, I know."

"But there has never been——"

"Such a pretty girl with such an unusual talent. Trust me, Mel. Even daimons can't do what Demi can. Not even Limone."

A sick, acid yellow washed over Mel's skin for just a second before it returned to a glistening emerald green. "Don't even say that. Zis new girl doesn't need help finding enemies here."

The crowd beyond went quiet, and a woman's dusky voice rang out as if seeking every hidden corner of the theater with silken fingers.

"My fine Parisian *messieurs*, have you been good?"

A cheer shook the rafters, making the curtains wobble beside us.

"I must go. Good luck." Mel grasped my wrist for just a second before running off to find her place in the flock of brightly clad daimons waiting closer to the curtains. Vale drew me back into the shadows toward a dark hall, but I balked. I didn't want to miss the final moments of calm before the show began. It was my favorite part of the spectacle, but I was far more accustomed to being part of it, to taking that deep breath that would hold until the curtain rose. This was where I belonged, not out there, among the rabble. The cheers quieted suddenly, as if someone had sucked the air from the room. The voice went on.

"Have you been very, very good?" A meaningful pause and a low, sexy chuckle. "Or have you been . . . wicked?"

The yelling and whistling intensified. My skin prickled all over, considering how very large the theater must be to hold so many voices. Even parked right outside London, the caravan had never drawn such crowds. I ached to be in front of them, to feel their excitement and hear them calling my name. I swallowed hard, felt every hair on my body rise. Even here, beyond the curtain, I could smell the hot blood pulsing through the building, the sweat rising off their skin, the goatlike stink of overexcited men and their lust. The immediacy of the stage struck through my homesickness and heartsickness, lighting me up from the inside with the otherworldly transcendence of lightning striking the Tower.

"Then let me be the first to welcome you . . . to Paradis!"

If I thought the cheers had been loud for the first two invitations, the third round was deafening. The orchestra began with a frenzy, and I shivered all over as the dancers went completely still on their marks.

So this was Paradis. Heaven. Although I had neglected to mention it to Cherie, I had been an art history major once, and I had spent an entire semester delving into the Impressionists and the Paris they'd envisioned in paint and dreams. In my world, Montmartre had featured, among the Moulin Rouge and the other cabarets, two clubs with very different names that did basically the same thing. Whether you were in Paradis or Enfer in the nineteenth and twentieth centuries, you were still in for the bawdiest, most daring, most exciting shows in the world.

As I watched the daimon girls rustle, I noted that they all looked bright, healthy, excited, and colorful, nothing like the dark daimons I'd occasionally encountered while in Criminy's coterie. They reminded me of Mademoiselle Caprice and her sons, and I felt a brief twinge over breaking Luc's heart which quickly dissolved into the girls' bright chatter. The cabarets were meant for stealing hearts, not pondering regrets. And possibly for breaking hearts, too, since many daimons would gorge on heartbreak. If Paradis was filled with good daimons, who were the denizens of Enfer?

A firm hand wrapped around my wrist and tugged me back into reality and down a pitch-black hallway just as I felt the air change and the curtain rise.

"We can watch from out here. Being caught backstage is not the best way to make an impression with Madame Sylvie."

Vale could have let go then, but he didn't, and I liked that, liked the feeling of being dragged along on an adventure. Even with a Bludman's eyes, it was hard to see back here, and I had to wonder just how intimate he was with Paradis that he could navigate the twists and turns of the corridor without running into anything. When he finally slid a door open and pulled me through behind him, I was nearly overwhelmed by a riot of color and heat overlaid by the delicious scent of bodies crushed together. We were in the back of the theater, behind the crowd. Hundreds of men and a very few women sat at round tables packed tightly on a well-polished dance floor, while dozens more watched avidly from plush velvet boxes and booths around the periphery. It was a sea of black and white and flesh tones and a few blooms of color, with every single human or daimon in some version of a classic black tuxedo, even the women. Onstage, dozens of daimons danced in a line, their skins and dresses arranged according to the rainbow's spectrum. Oddly, they weren't doing the cancan, or even raising their legs overhead to reveal the colorful petticoats under their skirts. Still, their performance was masterly. Even I could feel the palpable excitement and joy rising from the crowd. For the daimons, it had to be like the breakfast buffet at the Ritz.

And of course, it was slightly painful to me, as I'd taken no blood since before the slavers' attack. I rubbed my nose, curling a finger to block my nostrils. I hadn't been hammered with so much humanity in an enclosed space since being bludded in Sang. It was lucky I had such excellent self-control, as if my body still remembered human food and was barely willing to settle for blood. I'd never experienced that rabid hunger that Pinkies expected from my kind, but if I wanted to stay focused and at Paradis, I was going to have to remain well fed. All the barely contained blood made it hard to concentrate.

"Impressive, is it not?" Vale elbowed me in the side, forcing me to suck in another breath of warm, enclosed person-stink.

"I'd be more impressed if I didn't want to eat the audience."

He grimaced and glanced at the bar, where a male daimon with purple skin, slicked-back hair, and a mustache shook and poured drinks faster than seemed possible. "Oh la la. I forgot about your troublesome appetite They don't often serve Bludmen here, but I'll ask at the bar. Can you wait?"

I rolled my eyes and held up my hands, curling them into faux claws inside their gloves. "No. I'm totally going to kill everybody. Roar. Rawr."

His teeth flashed when he laughed. "Try not to, for both our sakes. I'll be right back."

I watched him leave, unable to escape the fact that his worn but well-fitted breeches were a thousand times more impressive than all the expensive tuxes in the room. If there was one thing that was true in Sang and on Earth, it was that money could buy a lot of things, but a tight butt and sexy swagger weren't among them.

In order to tamp down my hunger, I focused on the daimons onstage. The music changed, and dancers hurried off in a flurry of petticoats. The crowd hushed as a large silver ring descended from the ceiling, twirling slowly on a rope. It was empty, and for a moment, I thought perhaps they'd already botched the show. But no. A spotlight clicked on, and golden dust danced in the harsh glare like glittery pollen. A lithe body slid down the rope with snakelike grace, the beautiful daimon girl writhing and posing around the hoop with boneless precision. In the interest of professional disdain, I studied her form, her movements. She was flawless, really, with long limbs of shining gold carefully hung with a minimal costume of cloth as flowing and languid as liquid. The tinkling music playing behind her made me think of fairies and sunlight and dainty things easily broken. But the girl's face told me she wasn't the fragile sort. She was concentrating, every line focused and harsh. Her painted mouth may have fooled the crowd, but my Bludman's eyes could see the tiny lines of annoyance that assured me that she didn't find the joy in her act that her movements suggested to the ignorant and mesmerized crowd.

I smelled Vale before I saw him, already attuned to his strange half-Abyssinian odor. The vial he presented was cool in my hand, refrigerated instead of warmed. I sucked in air through my teeth.

"It's cold, I know. Sorry about that, *ma petite*. Can you choke it down?"

I popped the cork, held my nose, and tossed back the slightly clumpy blood, thankful that in Sang, for some strange reason, there were no germs, no blood-borne pathogens, no way for me to get sick from old blood. Even if it was like slurping a liquefied scab.

The taste was rancid in my mouth, and when Vale pressed a glass of red wine into my other hand, I rinsed and swallowed before thinking. The blood was so bad that the wine wasn't disgusting.

"Thanks for that." He took the wineglass from my hand and finished it off himself, which caught me by surprise. I wasn't accustomed to daimons and humans wanting much to do with Bludmen or anything our foul, murderous, bloody mouths had touched. Being half-Abyssinian must have made a big difference to his worldview.

After slipping the wineglass onto a passing daimon waiter's tray, Vale gestured with his chin to the golden girl dangling from the hoop. "That's Limone. She is bad news."

"Bad news how? Does she feed on pain?"

He chuckled. "Thankfully, no. But she is the cruelest daimon here. I would avoid her if I were you."

I cocked my head, watching Limone swing and spin and flip through her ring. "It's a shame that someone so beautiful should be so nasty."

Limone struck a final pose as the ring smoothly rose into the ceiling like a full moon, taking her with it. The crowd whispered excitedly as a trio of daimons dressed as parrots ran out onto the stage. I stifled a chuckle, considering how insulted the tightrope girl in Criminy's caravan would be if she knew that the Parisian daimons were pulling her shtick and making a total joke of it. Emerlie had favored the brightest costumes in the show back home. Although I'd never really liked the nosy busybody, she'd been a hell of a performer, riding her unicycle on a slender rope in leather tutus of lurid green and pink while the humans below trembled in fear for her.

My heart wrenched momentarily. Would I ever see Criminy and the caravan again? And what about Cherie? She should have been there at my side, her arm linked through mine as we witnessed the cabaret for the first time. We were a duo. Partners. Best friends. And there was no way for me to find her unless I could persuade the cabaret's mistress to hire me and let me stay here while I searched for clues. If only I had let the slavers steal me, too. Now all I wanted was to be one of the girls who disappeared, because it would get me one step closer to Cherie.

But first, I had to secure a place right here, at Paradis.

"So how do I nail this job interview?"

Vale turned, looking me up and down with a critical eye that seemed more for his personal enjoyment than any professional critique. "Beauty won't be the issue. Neither will temperament or skill. What you must do is make Madame Sylvie feel that she can't do without you. That if she doesn't hire you, you will run along to the next cabaret and bring in such a crowd that she'll stand in her office and weep." He put a finger under my chin and tilted my head up, and I jerked my face away and snapped at his fingers in faux annoyance. He grinned. "That. That, right there. Dance the line between dangerous and desirous, and she won't be able to turn you away."

"And don't kill anyone."

"Well, obviously, *ma petite*. Professionals rarely eat their customers."

Vale snatched another glass of wine from the tray of a passing daimon man dressed as a waiter. With a shouted "*Merci!*" he flipped a franc onto the platter as he led me away. I walked backward, watching the coin twirl for a moment, and my hand clamped down on Vale's wrist and drew him to a halt.

"Wait, I thought you said you didn't have any silvers."

Vale grinned, light eyes dancing above the wine like footlights. "I *don't* have any silvers. I do, however, have a limited supply of francs."

"But you said . . ."

"I said if you delved too deeply into my business, I would gladly toss you into the sewer." He looked around the room, posh and sensuous down to the carvings in the scarred bar. "Although I suppose up here, I'd have to settle for dumping some third-tier gin on your pretty head. Rest assured I don't have enough for a third glass. Yet. Come, now. Madame Sylvie should be in her office, counting her own silvers. Let's catch her while she's still optimistic, yes?"

He reached for my hand, and if he felt the same strange chemistry I did at the touch, he didn't show it. In moments, I understood that it was a utilitarian gesture, that it was the only way to stay connected as the crowd pressed dangerously close. We wove in and out among tuxedo-clad, overexcited gentlemen, and I pinched my nose closed against their extreme edibility. When I felt a hand caress my bustle, I had to bite back a snarl. Getting into a fight and throwing hot, tempting blood into the mix of posh black and white was no way to get a job.

Vale twitched a damask curtain aside and pulled me into the plush darkness of a hidden hallway. For just a moment, it was like being in the bowels of a great, velvety beast, and then another curtain moved aside to show a simple brick wall that looked like the backdrop for a mass murder by confetti cannon. Glitter, ribbons, and feathers littered the dusty boards, and a slender young daimon boy with bright blue skin hurried by, his arms laden with the biggest hoop skirts I'd ever seen.

We halted before an unmarked door.

"Any last words of encouragement?" I asked.

Vale squeezed my hand and let go. "Don't fail."

7

Vale knocked on the door, three quick raps. An annoyed sigh echoed within, followed by the sound of a heavy bag filled with metal clanking on wood.

"*Entrez!*"

He squeezed my shoulder briefly and opened the door, holding out an arm to usher me inside. A large, heavy desk dominated the elegant office, framed by thick velvet curtains and a window of opaque black glass. The aging daimon sitting at the desk reminded me of a ballerina in slow decline. Her erect posture, swanlike neck, slender carriage, and studied grace marked her instantly as a past performer, and I relaxed just a bit. Someone who knew what it was like to be onstage would be far easier to deal with than someone whose only skills lay in managing artists as if they were as foolish as wayward kittens.

Still, the well-powdered and stern lines around her mouth spoke of discipline and snobbery and a woman who didn't take rebellion lightly. To almost anyone else, she might have appeared human, with her dark hair and milk-and-roses complexion. But I could smell her, and she was daimon through and through.

Vale tilted his head. "*Bonsoir*, Madame Sylvie."

She tilted her head in almost mocking return. Even though she was seated, she still seemed to regard us from on high over the top of her half-moon glasses.

"*Bonsoir*, Monsieur Hildebrand. What have you brought me?"

Her voice was cultured, careful, and sultry. Madame Sylvie must have been an unstoppable force of nature when she was younger. Even now, she was in total command of the room. I couldn't help imagining what would happen if she and Criminy were to meet. Would the cabaret explode?

"Madame, this is Demi Ward, recently of Sangland. She wishes to secure a place in your cabaret."

"We don't take Bludmen, fool. You know that. Why are you wasting my time?"

Dipping a hand into the bag sitting on her desk, she rattled the coins within and raised an eyebrow at us. Vale looked at me expectantly and mouthed, "Your turn."

I took a deep breath to center myself. In one smooth leap, I landed on top of Madame Sylvie's desk, balancing on my toes and fluidly transitioning into a backbend. Walking my hands under my skirts as I had for Vale, I lifted each leg into the air with practiced sureness until I held a perfect handstand. Balancing on just one hand, legs spread and skirts aflutter, I plucked Madame Sylvie's quill from its stand, dipped it into her ink, and wrote, "Contortionist extraordinaire, at your service."

"How fascinating." She snatched the quill from my hand and stuck it back in place. "But this is a daimon cabaret. Try Darkside instead."

"I'm the most tame Bludman you'll ever meet. I dare you to test it."

"She did walk through your crowd without so much as a drop of drool, Sylvie."

The daimon's fingers drummed on the polished wood, the pointed tips of her red-lacquered nails making staccato clicks that grated on my nerves. "Show me something else."

I kicked over and stood, my toes in the small space recently taken by my hands. With a dancer's flair, I twisted and curled a finger at Vale. As if we'd done this a thousand times, he stepped forward as I beckoned and stopped when I held out a flat palm.

"Hold still," I said.

I lifted my leg straight up until it was beside my ear. Then, with perfect grace, I fell forward until my ankle landed on Vale's shoulder. To his credit, he made no sound and barely shifted, easily absorbing the impact as I used him as the stand for my split, one toe on Madame Sylvie's desk and one ankle on the brigand's shoulder. I straightened my torso and held my arms up like a ballerina. My splits had always been perfect, and even Cherie had trouble keeping her legs so straight, taut, and unshaking.

"Really, this time, don't move."

Finding my center, I exhaled and slowly rolled to the side until I held the split upside down, my head and arms dangling between Vale and the desk and my ankle cradling his neck. Before he could freak out, I grasped his leg, just above the knee, and used it to gracefully kick down from the split. Standing before the grand desk, I wrapped a leg around my own neck and curtsied.

Madame Sylvie's face didn't change. "Can you fit into a hatbox?" she snapped.

"Easily."

"Are you a front bender or a back bender?"

"Both."

"Are you frightened of heights?"

"Only if there's a tank of seawater below."

"Marinelli bend?"

"So long as the mouth grip has extra padding for my fangs."

"Spanish web?"

I sighed and rolled my eyes. "Yes. *Oui, oui, oui.* Anything your daimons can do, I can do better."

"Golliwog act?"

"I'm the perfect rag doll."

"Have you worked with a partner?"

My throat closed, and I struggled to swallow. "I have."

"But your partner is not with you?"

I shook my head no, blud tears burning hot in the corners of my eyes.

Vale rushed to fill the silence I couldn't touch. "Her partner was stolen by slavers outside of Ruin. They reached the catacombs before we could catch them."

Madame Sylvie's eyes sharpened, boring into me. "Will this loss affect your performance? I can't have heartbreak on my stage. It shows."

"I'm a professional above all else." I glanced at Vale, my eyes pleading, and he shrugged as if to say, *You're on your own now.* "This is my dream, Madame Sylvie. I've been traveling Sangland in a caravan for six years, and I've always wanted to be a star. I'm a hard worker, no bad habits, no vices, no biting, and I'm willing to do anything."

One sharp eyebrow went up. "Anything?"

It was as if the air was sucked out of the room, as if all of

Paris waited to hear what I would say. The word fell heavy as an anchor. "Anything," I answered.

Vale looked pained, which in turn pained me. I would have to talk to him later. He had to understand that I would have said anything to get my foot in the door, to stand on Madame Sylvie's fine stage and feel a thousand eyes on me, a thousand hands clapping, my name on everyone's lips, their whispers and cheers carrying me to the top, all to find Cherie and share the spotlight as I'd promised.

But that one word—*anything*. It didn't mean what he thought it meant. I wouldn't be a courtesan. I wouldn't sink into the dirty side of Mortmartre, become just another lost girl with smeared lipstick and dead eyes. I had read enough about Sang and seen enough movies on Earth to know that my current position was dangerous. But I was a Bludman, and I was determined, and no matter what I told Madame Sylvie, I would be able to withstand the darkness, the temptation. I would keep my pride. For myself and for Cherie.

The daimon nodded once, and a transformative smile spread across her thickly powdered face. "Zat is the answer I like to hear," she said, the tiniest bit of a Franchian accent leaking out. "It will be a trial period, at first. The daimon girls will not like it, and I'm not sure how the humans in the audience will feel. If you are anything other than a rousing success, I will kick you out on your *derrière*, you understand?"

I couldn't hold back my gummy smile. "You won't be disappointed, *madame*."

I turned to leave, and she snorted behind me. "We are not done. One more thing."

I had to breathe in through my nose to hold in the Bludman's beast-rage. To give me what I wanted and then take it away? It was unbearable. I held out one hand as if testing for rain.

"There is a final test. Just because you two children say something is so does not make it so. We will see what you are capable of, *ma chère*."

I couldn't contain my annoyance any longer. "I am beyond capable. Find a single daimon in Paris who can match me, pose for pose, and I'll walk out now."

Her smile was irritatingly pleasant. I wanted to slice it off with my talons. "No, dear. Your contortion is clearly exquisite. I had never considered that a Bludman's resiliency and flexibility could be harnessed for such beautiful and effective work." She paused for a moment, allowing me to soak up the compliment before the kicker. "But I must ensure that you will not eat the guests." She plucked a brass bell from a row on her desk and rang it delicately between thumb and forefinger.

I looked to Vale, who only gave a Gallic shrug. Anger shook me for a moment before I realized that he was possibly doing me a great favor. He seemed to annoy Sylvie as much as he annoyed his father, and perhaps his silence wasn't so much cowardice or bewilderment as it was the gift of not getting us thrown out of the cabaret on our butts for saying something disrespectful.

Within seconds, there was a soft knock on the door.

"*Entrez*," Madame Sylvie called, and the little blue daimon boy poked his head in.

"*Oui, madame?*"

"Bring me Monsieur Philippe. Tell him I have a surprise."

The boy nodded once, ink-black hair shaking, and was gone. Madame Sylvie ignored us, straightening and sorting various papers on her desk and momentarily hefting her bag of coins as if reassuring herself that we hadn't stolen a single sou. When my eyes met Vale's wine-gold ones, he mouthed *I don't know what she wants* with exaggerated care that made me giggle.

When the knock came next on the door, Madame Sylvie stood gracefully and struck a pose that highlighted her height and grace.

"*Entrez, s'il vous plaît, monsieur,*" she purred.

I composed my posture and brushed down my rumpled skirts, hoping the sewer spatters of the journey weren't apparent. Vale was the picture of rakish vagabondry and merely stood, hands on hips and eyes narrowed, as if daring the person coming through the door to say a single thing about his wrinkled, tear-stained shirt.

The man opened the door, and already I could smell him. Overweight humans were a rarity in Sang, thanks to diminishing food supplies and an environment pushed to the brink of disaster by chemical fug and fear. But this Monsieur Philippe could have fed a dozen Bludmen happily, which meant he had to be very, very rich and therefore a very, very good customer. My eyes shot sideways to Madame Sylvie, whose professional smile didn't waver. It had to be quite the gamble for her—either I passed her little test and was accepted into the company, or I went insane with bloodlust and ripped open the florid neck of the biggest man I'd seen since passing out on the floor of my dorm room on Earth.

"Madame Sylvie, what a pleasure to see you again." His accent was classically French, to my ears, his eyes beetle-bright over an impeccably cut suit. But no tailor's tricks could make this man handsome. The scent that rose from his flesh when he looked at me was lust, pure and hot. I struggled not to shudder.

"Monsieur Philippe, you are known for unparalleled taste and an eye for quality. This young girl would like to join our company. I was hoping you might be so kind as to share your opinion."

He quivered with pleasure, his eyes narrowing further to regard me sharply. Stepping close, lighter on his feet than I expected, he held out a bare hand. Unsure what he wanted, I put out my own tentatively. He didn't take it.

A snort and an eye roll. "Gloves. Must be Sanglish. What's your name, dear?"

The Demi who had died on the floor on Earth would have been meek, deferential, desperate, pleading with the man who now held my future and possibly Cherie's life in his hands. But the Demi on Sang was a Bludman, a predator, and a performer. She was reckless and knew her job. I gave Monsieur Philippe my most sultry smile and used my teeth to loosen the fingers of my glove. A slight intake of breath told me he'd noticed the fangs. Locking my eyes with his, I sensually rolled the glove off my hand. The other one, too. After they both lay on the ground, I smirked at his still-outstretched hand and leaned close, up on tiptoes and hands light on his wide shoulders, to kiss him on both cheeks in the Franchian style.

"Je m'appelle Demi Ward. Monsieur."

I could smell his prey response, the deep-down knowledge that sent him conflicting signals to hold still and run away. And judging by the look in his eyes, he hadn't had as much familiarity with Bludmen as most Sanglish Pinkies. From what Luc had told me, the racial breakdown of Paris was about fifty-fifty daimons and humans, with less than one percent of the population made up of Bludmen. After all, why would humans go to the trouble to give up their own blood when trading in emotions was far more painless and often involved being purposefully amused or pleasured? I had been just as exotic to Luc as he had been to me. At first.

"And what is it you do, Demi?"

On Earth and in Sangland, they'd pronounced my name with an emphasis on *Dem*, but in Franchia, it took on an entirely new flavor that I wished to practice alone and taste on my own tongue.

De-MEE. Yes, I could get used to that.

I smiled at Monsieur Philippe and stepped as close as his stomach would allow. To his credit, he didn't back away, although the way his nostrils flared like a frightened horse told me he wanted to. I leaned forward, just enough to almost press my chest into his body, raising my right leg behind me until I could reach overhead and catch my own foot. My skirt cascaded down around me, and I heard Vale grunt behind me; he now had a prime view. But all my attention, of course, was for Monsieur Philippe. Leaning forward and gently pressing my torso against him, I brought my foot up until it was inches away from his face, showing just the tiniest sliver of skin between my leggings and the top of my boot.

"I'm a contortionist, *monsieur*. The best Paris has ever seen."

I placed one splayed hand against his chest and let my lips nearly brush his before pushing away, arcing gracefully and falling into a split on the ground. Monsieur

Philippe cleared his throat and fussed with his coat. From my vantage point on the floor, I could see the effect I was having. And I struggled not to get smug.

"I can see that. But *ma chère*, a Bludman in a cabaret? It's unheard of!"

"Then hear of it," I said.

I stood with a twirl and took a deep breath. I didn't want to do what I was going to do, but I didn't see that I had a choice. With Mademoiselle Caprice's lessons in my head and steel in my spine, I stepped close to him and lifted his hands, placing them in their proper places at my waist and in my other hand. Palm to palm, he was warm and clammy, with just the faintest tremor of unease, and his blood burned high in his cheeks, spicing the air with nervousness and desire. The blood hunger tugged at me but wasn't problematic. I'd seen other Bludmen lose it—especially Catarrh and Quincy, the two-headed twins at the caravan, who'd run hotter than most and needed to keep both mouths satisfied. Even Criminy got peckish if he went too long without feeding. But for me, it had always been like this, the same sort of polite hunger you would get waiting for a meal while staring at food behind a glass display. Sure, you wanted it. But you weren't about to break the glass and steal it.

I began to hum a well-known waltz, and after a beat, he moved with me, surprisingly light on his feet. Madame Sylvie took up the song with a strange quaver in her voice, which freed me to talk.

"You see, *monsieur*. I am a very unusual woman. I was raised in a caravan, performing for humans every night. I've never drunk from a live subject. I don't even know how to break the skin. My hunger is as inconsequential as my talent is enormous." I leaned close, my lips brushing his ear. "I am as tame as tame can be."

He twirled me out and stared at me, just flat-out stared, as if he couldn't quite figure out what sort of curiosity I might be but wanted to put me in a locked glass case in his bedroom. I swept a deep curtsy, knowing it would show off the tight fabric over my bosom to best advantage.

"How much, *madame*?"

Madame Sylvie chuckled, low and husky. "I don't believe the girl wishes to offer such services, *monsieur*."

All three of them looked to me. I hid my panic behind an enigmatic smile, as Criminy had taught me long ago.

"Is that true, Mademoiselle Ward?"

I winked. "For now. But please, *monsieur*, keep asking."

He shivered all over and closed his eyes as if he couldn't take another moment of looking at me without carrying me away to a bed, and that's when I knew I'd won.

"She will be in tomorrow's show?"

Madame Sylvie regarded me, taking in, I'm sure, my ragged hems and tangled hair. "Her debut will be Saturday night, I think. That gives us three days to get her in shape." She walked close, lifting a lank curl that had fallen from my updo. "Interesting coloring, though. Blue eyes and hair the color of thick coffee."

Monsieur Philippe nodded hungrily. "Exotic, just so." He gasped and chuckled to himself. "That's it. La Demitasse. The cup. Delicate and small and curved, perfect for holding both darkness and sweetness, yes?"

Much to my surprise, Madame Sylvie's skin shivered over pink as she laughed and clapped her hands like a little girl. "But *monsieur*, that is brilliant! We'll have to have posters made up *tout de suite*. I wonder if Monsieur Lenoir would . . .

but no. He won't even look at her until we've made her a star. I'll send for Steinlen. If you believe she is safe?"

Monsieur Philippe licked his lips like a toad. "Perhaps . . . one last test?"

I struggled not to bare my teeth and hiss at the expectant silence that followed. My eyes flashed to Vale, his jaw so hard that I winced as if struck somewhere soft. The interview was getting out of hand, testing the bounds of that one word: *anything*. One step after another. And now it all came down to something I very much didn't want to do. Something that meant nothing to me and yet also meant everything.

I turned my quavering lips into a quirked smile and went up on tiptoes to kiss Monsieur Philippe on the rosy, blood-hot cheek.

"I'm very young, *monsieur*. Please forgive my shyness."

A tremor ran through him, and he pulled a silk handkerchief out of his pocket to wipe away the sweat that beaded his brow.

"Understandable, my dear. How young?"

"Only eighteen, *monsieur*," Madame Sylvie said.

"Eighteen. And a tame Bludman." He shook his head, a quiver in his chin. "*Mon dieu.*"

Madame Sylvie rang her bell again, and the blue daimon boy appeared through the door, which had been ajar. "Blaise, dear, please take Mademoiselle Demi up to Mireille's old room. You know what to do."

"*Oui, madame.*" The boy jerked his chin at me, his eyes flashing a warning. I glanced back at Vale, and he nodded and followed me. A dash of blue told me the boy had collected my gloves.

"Monsieur Hildebrand, gentlemen are not allowed

upstairs. You know that. I hope you'll accept the hospitality of the bar while I conclude some business with Monsieur Philippe."

Vale quaked with fury, and I wrapped my arm around his and dragged him toward the door with me. He balked, but I was stronger than I looked, and I managed to pull him out before he said something we would all regret.

"*Merci, madame. À bientôot, monsieur,*" I cooed. As soon as the door shut, a whispered argument began within, and I leaned my back against the brick wall of the hallway.

"If Madame catches you listening in, she'll beat you with a riding crop," the daimon boy whispered. He shoved my gloves into my hands, and I slipped them over my fingers before Vale noticed. Not that he was looking at my hands.

"If she ever kisses that pervert again, *I'll* beat her with a riding crop." Vale was suddenly there, in front of me, blocking out Blaise and the lights and everything but his avid, searing eyes. "Run along, boy. Wait at the bottom of the stairs."

"But Monsieur Vale——"

"Have you ever seen me angry, Blaise?"

"No, *monsieur*, but——"

"People who anger Hildebrands don't live to complain. Now, run."

The boy threw me an exasperated, frightened look and scuttled away. Vale's fingers tightened around my upper arms, and he half-dragged me down the hall toward a bricked-in niche.

"Vale, you can't get me in trouble on my first day——"

He cut me off with a hand under my chin and soft lips pressing, insistent and desperate, against mine.

8

It was the last thing I expected but the first thing my body wanted. With damnable quickness, my arms wrapped around his neck and pulled him closer. An electric current shot through me, making me quiver with heat that pooled low in my belly. When his mouth opened, just slightly, I moaned for more and ran my tongue between his lips, frantic to gain entry.

This, this was what had been missing. This this this.

With Luc, with the boys on Earth. This mad, insane passion. The way his fingers tightened at my waist, the way my hips sought his, the way my heel dragged up the back of his calf as if pointing out the right road on a map. He felt it, too—I could tell by the frantic curling of his tongue, the hardness in his arms as I slid my hands down to his wrists, struggling not to dig in my nails. Everything inside me went liquid and hot, like molten chocolate. He tasted like masala, like chai, like spices both hot and sweet that were too fiery to savor undiluted.

I dipped deeper, chasing his tongue, frantic to remove the taste of Monsieur Philippe from my lips. I was so hot, so hungry, so avid, that I completely forgot I had fangs.

Until he pushed away roughly, almost tripping over the leg I'd wrapped around his thigh.

"Come back here," I growled. He shook his head no, his eyes burning golden in the low lights of the hallway.

"Can't. You nicked me."

He stuck a finger to his lips and pulled it away barely painted with blood. My breath caught on instinct, but then I smelled it. Half-tainted. Wrong.

How easily I had forgotten that Abyssinian blood would drive me mad—and not in a good way. Although there were no germs and therefore no diseases in Sang—which, honestly, I still couldn't quite believe—it would appear that insanity here could be chemically induced in a way that sounded a lot like rabies. Bludmen who drank any Abyssinian blood at all were said to foam at the mouth and bleed from the eyes, nose, and ears, all while running around, blind and screaming and clawing at whatever their talons encountered. It was an ugly way to go that often resulted in the death or dismemberment of anyone else nearby. This made the Abyssinians undaunted warriors, much respected and somewhat feared all over Sang, especially considering that many of them painted their weapons with their own blood.

Vale had said he was half Abyssinian, but I didn't know if that meant his blood would make me only half-mad, or if it would take longer to kill me, or if it would just make me sick for a while. And I definitely didn't want to find out after I'd just been offered a job and was one step closer to finding Cherie. I would have to be more careful, more controlled, the next time he kissed me.

Because yes, I realized, I wanted there to be a next time. I'd never wanted there to be a next time before.

"Why are you smiling, *bébé*?" He was leaning against the wall directly across the hall from me, mimicking my posture with one leg kicked up against the bricks. He looked as dazed as I felt, his eyes unfocused and wide. I hadn't realized I was grinning until he asked, and that only made me grin wider.

"I was thinking about something funny."

"You think going half-mad is funny? Or you think me kissing you is funny?"

"Neither." I tried to control the grin and failed. "Definitely neither."

"*Mademoiselle*? The ladies will be back soon. Please hurry."

Blaise's voice carried, faint and nervous, from the top of the stairs at the end of the hall. I didn't want to get him in trouble, but I wasn't ready to be without Vale. He was strange and dangerous, but he was the most familiar thing I had in Paris and also my main link to finding Cherie. And more immediately, I wanted him to kiss me again. After my first taste of passion, I felt open for more, like a book with the spine cracked, waiting for more ink. Just staring at him from five feet away made my heart speed up. Damn, but chemistry is a demanding bitch.

"I guess I need to go."

He nodded sadly. "If you don't, Blaise will get beaten. Madame Sylvie is kinder than most, but she doesn't care to be crossed. And neither does her choreographer. Be careful—they're two halves of the same serpent."

"When will I see you again?" The words rushed out of me so fast I felt like Liesl in *The Sound of Music* and mentally cursed myself for acting like a sixteen-year-old idiot instead of the stylish cabaret girl I was bound and determined to become. The way his searing gaze roamed over my mouth made me feel slightly better.

"I will go around to the other cabarets. Spread the word about a kidnapped girl who's worth a great deal of ransom. Small and blond, yes?"

I nodded. "Curly hair, gray eyes. Last seen in a salmon-pink dress and bludbunny skull fascinator."

He stroked my hair gently, his smile going sad.

"Oh." I touched the polished skull myself; I'd forgotten I'd pinned it on after nearly losing it in the catacombs. "Never mind that last part." Then, more softly, "It was her favorite."

"I'll do my best, Demi. Keep your ears open, eh? The daimons are good at keeping secrets among themselves, but perhaps you will hear something useful. I'll be back sometime tomorrow. I have a delivery to make."

"Another cabaret girl?" I said, trying to put on a brave face.

"Oh, I only deliver those once a week. This would be wine. Cabarets always need wine."

"But where do you get it?"

He shook a finger in my face, *tsk*ed, and grinned, his teeth looking, for a moment, as sharp as mine. Something in my heart thrummed like guitar strings, seeing that wicked look in his eyes. When I'd crushed on the knife thrower in the caravan, I'd been told he was too danger-ous for me. Maybe Vale was just dangerous enough.

"I'm not a daimon, but I know how to keep secrets, too, *ma petite. À demain.*"

With a swift kiss that bypassed my glove to send ten-drils of fire up my hand and arm and straight to a blush in my cheeks, he spun and walked down the hall with a delicious amount of brigandine swagger.

"*Mademoiselle!* Hurry!"

I glanced toward Blaise's voice in consternation, not wanting to miss a moment of Vale's retreating form. When thunderous applause shook the boards under my feet, I picked up my skirts and hurried up the narrow stairs toward the daimon-shaped shadow on the top steps.

"Forgive me, *mademoiselle*. I thought you would wish to be in your room before the ladies arrived for intermission."

His blue tail danced in the orange gaslights as I followed him past narrow wood doors, each bearing a sliding name plaque. Some of the names I recognized from my art history studies, but others were clearly stage names. Melissande had to be Mel, whose sign had an added "et Beatrice." I also saw Victoire, Calliope, Charmagne, Edwige. And then there were the earth-famous names like La Douce, Chi Chi, and La Goulue. And, of course, Limone. The door Blaise opened for me had an empty placard, and I had a brief vision of "La Demitasse" written there in curling letters. Monsieur Philippe had given me the name, and I would do my best to get it onto everyone's lips.

"Dang. Is this it?"

My dreams of opulence fluttered sadly to the floor with the dust bunnies. The room was a quarter of the size of the wagon I'd shared with Cherie and contained nothing but a narrow wooden bedstead with a sagging mattress, two ratty old chairs, a bedside table, and some hand-carved hooks for hanging clothes I didn't own. The walls were a sorry, washed-out blue with a cracked mirror hanging dispassionately in a corner, and the sea-green floors were bare and dusty, in some places so gappy that I could see top hats moving below like shifting herds of cattle. My thighs clamped together instantly, just in case one of them should happen to look up. The lone window opened onto a dark alley.

"It could be worse, *mademoiselle*. You could be sharing a room with Limone or La Goulue." Blaise shivered, his skin going over with dark blue spots like a pox.

"Are they that bad?"

I had always loved Toulouse Lautrec's painting of La Goulue, the saucy can-can dancer who had ruled the Moulin Rouge, high-kicking the hats off her ensorcelled fans. Maybe she wouldn't make the best roommate, but I still couldn't wait to meet her in the flesh. Being here in the Paris of Sang was almost like traveling back in time on Earth and witnessing firsthand the larger-than-life historical celebrities from my art history books.

"La Goulue is all too real for my taste, *mademoiselle*." The boy shook his head. "They do not call her the Glutton for nothing."

"What does she feed on, then?"

"There is nothing she will not devour, *mademoiselle*." He paused at the door, although I hadn't seen him move across the room. "If you have everything you need?"

I spun around, which took almost all the space in the tiny chamber. Empty. So empty. "I don't have anything. Do I get a nightgown or a blanket or . . . anything?"

The small boy shrugged his narrow shoulders. "You must earn it first, *mademoiselle*."

He made to dart out the door, and I snatched him by the collar. "Wait."

He half trembled, half sneered, waiting as if I might strike him. Instead, I sank down to my knees and gave him the closed-mouth smile that made me look sweet instead of dangerous.

"Please call me Demi. *Mademoiselle* is way too long."

"*Oui*, Demi. But you know, La Demitasse has just as many syllables." And before I could ask him how he had managed to listen in on that conversation, much less how he knew what a syllable was, the impish blue daimon was gone.

There was nothing more to see in my room, of course. I would have to earn a blanket soon or freeze to death at night, if Franchia was anything like Sangland. As the hallway was still quiet, I went out to see if any other famous cabaret dancers called Paradis home. The fanciest door placard by far belonged to La Goulue, and I was certain I recognized the names Jeanne La Folle and La Cascadeuse. All the other names were Franchian, the same names my French teacher had assigned to us in high school.

As I traced La Goulue's name with a finger, the long bout of applause far below ended, and footsteps sounded on the stairs like a herd of giddy wildebeest. For girls who were light on their feet onstage, the dancers of Paradis were noisy as hell when they were off the clock. As they appeared over the top stair, I felt very much like Simba in *The Lion King*, about to be run over by a gallumphing herd but without a tree to cling to.

"*Attendez*. Who are you?"

The woman at the head of the colorful flock stopped halfway down the hall, and I whipped my hand behind my back as if the letters I'd been tracing on her sign had burned me. I knew her instantly, of course. La Goulue as a daimon was very similar to La Goulue from the paintings: thin, sharp, bendy, and with a head of golden hair. As I struggled to find words, her skin shivered over from sunny yellow to the same angrily striped red that I'd seen earlier on Mademoiselle Caprice.

"*Bonjour*. I'm Demi Ward, but they call me La Demi-tasse." I sketched the curtsy Criminy had taught me in the caravan, a courtly gesture that showcased my litheness and made my skirt fan out behind me. After a moment of silence, the entire coterie of daimons broke out in laughter.

"I wouldn't be too proud of being a cup, if I were you."

I recognized Limone's neon green skin and matching acidic tone.

"If you are not a daimon, why are you here?" asked another girl, this one bright orange.

"She's new, aren't you, doll?" Mel rushed forward, her skin the cheerful green of four-leaf clovers. She put a bare arm over my shoulders and drew me close in a sisterly side hug. "Vale brought her up from the catacombs tonight. And if you're up here, I suppose you got the job?" I nodded, and she pulled me into a real hug. "Good for you, darling. And this is your room? Ah, *bon*! But it's empty, isn't it?"

La Goulue shrugged as if she'd seen a million girls come and go. She walked past us and into her room, slamming the door. Everyone else pushed toward my open door and peered inside.

"You have nothing? But that is so sad, *chérie*. Where is your trunk?"

"Were you robbed?"

"Paris was so nice before all the humans showed up, *non*?"

As if on cue, they gave a collective sigh.

"Except for you, Demi, darling," said a purple daimon as she patted my arm.

I was boggled, yet again, by the fact that daimons, so

sensitive to every emotional change in a person's heart and mind, could fail to see or smell the difference between a human and a Bludman, a predator and the prey, until they got very close, as Mel had, or saw the telltale fangs. But I wanted to start out here as myself and avoid the sort of lies that might make the daimons hate or resent me later. I wouldn't tell them I was a Stranger, but I would let them know exactly what I was.

"Oh, I'm not human," I said. I grinned, showing off my fangs, and the daimon girls drew back with a gasp.

"A Bludman?"

"It can't be."

"She'll eat all the customers!"

"Will she eat us?"

"I don't think so. We don't taste so good, on the inside."

Mel let out a piercing whistle, and the other daimons stopped sidling backward and chattering and instead stared at me as if I was a bludbear walking on two legs in galoshes.

"Silly things. Do you think Madame Sylvie would let her into the cabaret if she was dangerous?" She turned to me and put a hand on my shoulder as if to help me prove my point. "Demi, darling. Have you ever killed anyone?"

"Never. I've never even drunk from a live body. And Bludmen don't care for daimon blood."

The girls began whispering again, and Blaise stepped out of their throng.

"It's true. Madame Sylvie tested her against Monsieur Philippe. She kissed him on the cheek."

The purple daimon let out a glittering laugh. "If you can get close to that buffet of flesh without drawing blood, you can withstand anything."

"I almost killed him just last week, and I can't even eat him," added a pink daimon.

They all laughed and crept forward, and I closed my lips over my fangs to smile.

Limone pushed her way past the girls and stood to face me. Her cheekbones were hard-cut, her face pointed and austere. Hers was a cruel beauty, and in a way, I envied her. Even after being bludded, I still felt too soft, too curved, too pink-cheeked. No one would mess with Limone.

"Just because a dog licks your hand does not mean it won't turn on you."

I showed my fangs, my posture as straight and aggressive as hers. "I don't plan on licking you or turning on you," I said. "I'd rather be friends."

Her nostrils flared, her eyes narrowing to glittery green slits like cracked glass. "I don't have friends. And I don't keep dogs. And if you ever try to lick me, I'll cut off your tongue." Her long fingers waggled in the air, their wicked points even more dangerous-looking than my actual talons. "You don't belong here, Demi. Go back to Darkside where you belong."

My human instincts told me to cower. My Bludman instincts told me to murder. I fought them both and took a step toward her with a steely smile. "Oh, I belong here."

She snorted and shoved past me, knocking into my shoulder in a way that made me bite back a hiss. "Not for long."

After her door slammed behind her, Mel pulled me close again by my shoulder. "Here, Demi. I think I have a spare blanket. And Leola, didn't you keep one of Mireille's night shifts?"

With nods and murmurs, the other daimon girls disappeared into their rooms, returning swiftly with small gifts that I didn't know how to repay, considering I had nothing but what was on my back. The talents that would earn my keep in Paris were no good to them.

Tears filled my eyes, and I clutched the worn old nightgown to my chest as Mel fluttered her hands at two girls carrying pillows and blankets. A blue daimon with a cheerful smile made the bed carefully, tucking the ripped quilt as if it were made of finest silk and fluffing the old pillow.

"I can't thank y'all enough," I stammered. "Your kindness is too much. I can't repay—"

Mel held my face in her hands and closed her eyes, breathing in deeply. "You already are, *chérie*. We can taste your thanks on the air. Your heart is sweet, like flowers in the spring."

I noticed that the other girls had set my bed to rights and were also smiling dreamily, their mouths open as they breathed.

"It will be good to have you around. Like a midnight snack, yes?" Mel said.

The violet daimon nodded eagerly. "Lads below bring only lust and the smallest bit of amazement. But you're still fresh, you see." Her short, curly hair reminded me of Emerlie, and I gave her a wobbly smile.

"I'm Lexie," she said with a curtsey. "Even if the door says Alexandra."

"And this is Beatrice, though we call her Bea." The blue girl who had made my bed nodded and gave a little wave with long, elegant fingers. Mel slung an arm around Bea's waist, and Bea put her head against Mel's shoulder. "She can't talk, but you'll pick up some signs pretty quickly."

Remembering a few simple bits of sign language I'd learned in elementary school, I signed *Thank you*, hoping that the gestures carried the same meaning. Bea's face lit up, a shiver of sky blue rippling over her skin. Her fingers flew excitedly with a flurry of signs, but I didn't recognize anything else, except something that looked like *crabapple*, which wasn't helpful.

"I'm sorry. That's all I can remember. But I'd like to learn more." Bea waved a hand, and I didn't need to wait for Mel to translate *Don't worry about it. Thanks is enough.*

A gong rang below, and most of the daimons scurried out my door. As they disappeared, I felt the warmth go with them.

"You're leaving?"

Mel turned around, her grin quirking up like it had when she talked to Vale. "It's only intermission. We still have the second half of the show. And after . . ."

Lexie snorted, and Leola sighed heavily and blew a puff of air into her bangs.

"What happens after?"

Mel rolled her eyes and shook her head. "Nothing you need to worry about tonight. Get some sleep. Tomorrow we'll teach you the ropes."

"Oh, I'm from a caravan. Shouldn't be a problem."

All three of them burst into laughter.

"Oh, la," Mel said. "You have no idea what you've gotten yourself into."

9

Falling asleep was all but impossible, thanks to the whoops and catcalls and clapping and stomping and music, always music, beneath the floor. That was one thing I'd taken for granted about caravan life: for the most part, it was quiet and allowed for privacy. After the last round of applause and demands for an encore died away in the theater below, I enjoyed a brief period of soft murmurings and shufflings as the house cleared out. And then silence. I waited for the girls to thunder upstairs again, but they didn't. Only a few tired footsteps and gently closing doors broke the calm. I was on the verge of sleep then, but I did note that there should have been more of them, and I wondered where the others were. It bothered me but not enough to keep me awake.

It had been a long, long day, as if an entire week had passed since I'd stepped out the door of the inn in Callais, giggling and whispering with Cherie, Mademoiselle Caprice's silvers heavy in my pocket. Now all I had there were a few francs and a bludbunny foot that had proven far from lucky. Funny how I had skipped the city of Ruin only to find true ruin. My outfit was destroyed, most of my money long gone. The only thing I had in excess were hairbobs, mine and Cherie's.

When I woke up the next morning to the sound of a woman's harsh, nasal cawing, I was clutching the bedraggled feathers of Cherie's fascinator in my hand as if it had been my friend's fingers. My dreams had been only of smoke.

"*Vite*! *Vite*! *Vite*! Wake up, my little hens. It is time."

My door flew open, and I sat up blearily. The daimon staring at me from the hallway was a stranger, but that didn't stop her from rushing across the room and dumping me out of the bed onto the dusty floor. She hadn't very far to go, after all.

"Oh, so zis is the little tame Bludman I hear so much about, eh? Ze Demitasse? Looks like ze cup is half empty this morning. *Vite*, now! Hurry! The sun is up, and so will you be!"

I was too sleepy still to bother hissing and simply stared at her as if she had three eyes, mainly because she did. Of course, the third one was painted on her forehead in what would have been an Egyptian style on Earth. She wore a cobra headdress and golden robes and sandals. Her skin was the molten gold of sand in the sunset, and she was long-limbed and unnaturally skinny. She leaned down to slap me across the cheek but gently. I bit my lip to hold in a growl.

"Now," she said firmly. "Or you're out on the streets."

I could only nod.

She flapped out the door like a crane that had crashed through a costume shop, and I stood, still a little sore from my time on horseback. Funny, how I could contort my body into all sorts of unnatural positions but could barely walk after a few hours of riding behind Vale. I closed the door and dressed quickly without benefit of the ewer of water that seemed the bare minimum for bathing in Sang. Yesterday's clothes were now dirt-infused rags that needed to be boiled in lye, but I couldn't very well go out in the cobweb-thin nightgown I'd been given. With no mirror, I could only pat my hair and hope there was a dressing room somewhere below so that I wouldn't seem an utter mess to my new coworkers.

There was no lock on the door, but I checked that it was closed firmly before slipping a small pouch from my pocket and stuffing it into a hole in the mattress. I hadn't told Vale about the few coins that remained from Mademoiselle Caprice's stash, not to mention my stolen supply of Criminy's sleeping powder. As of right now, they were the most valuable things I owned.

Outside in the hall, I ran into Bea and gave her what I hoped was the sign for *Good morning* and not *I spit on you and chop off your arm*. It must have been close, because she gave me a radiant smile and repeated the gesture. The one she tried next was familiar.

"Eat?" I shrugged. "I don't eat."

She shook her head no and did another sign.

"Mouth rain?" I guessed. "Drool?"

With a silent laugh, she made fangs of her fingers and tapped them against her neck.

"Oh! Do I need blood?"

An enthusiastic nod.

"It would help."

She inclined her head, and I followed her down the stairs. In the hallway, my eyes went straight for the niche where Vale had kissed me—and I had kissed him back.

Part of me hoped to see him there, maybe leaning against the brick wall nonchalantly and smirking, waiting for me. But he wasn't there, of course. If all was going according to plan, he was out in the city, trying to find information on a pretty blond Bludman who had recently appeared under mysterious circumstances.

I almost missed it when Bea ducked down a different niche that was actually a hallway. Just a little ways in, she opened a hobbit-sized door and scrunched over before disappearing inside. With little choice, I followed her into the dark. Small tendrils of light occasionally filtered in from up high, but below my knees it was so dark that I couldn't tell if the sandy debris under my feet was dirt, stone, or more crushed bone. When Bea finally knocked softly on a wooden door, I stopped behind her and held my breath, hoping for fresh air. At least I wasn't trapped in here with a yummy human.

The door opened a few inches.

"Eh?"

The face that appeared in the gap surprised the hell out of me, as I'd written a paper on the symbolism of, well, pretty much her. It was the girl from Édouard Manet's *A Bar at the Folies-Bergère*, except that her eyes weren't dead. They were narrowed and annoyed under hay-colored bangs that had lost any luster they originally possessed.

Bea mimed the same thing she'd originally tried with me, the one that looked like *mouth rain*.

"No blood magic, Beatrice," the girl said severely. "You know how Madame Sylvie feels about . . . oh."

Bea had moved aside to reveal me, doubled over in the tunnel. "Hi," I said with a little wave.

The girl sucked air in through her teeth. "Must be the

new Bludman." She put a reddened hand to her plump white neck, rendered pale by the deep blue velvet of her gown. "Are you as tame as they say?"

I grinned. "Want to step into the tunnel to find out or just give me some blood to be sure?"

Bea shook with a silent laugh, and the girl shrugged as if cleverness was an itchy flea in an especially tender place. The door closed, leaving Bea and me in the dark, her breathing strangely silent.

When the door opened again, the girl shoved a chilled vial into my hand. "It's cold and old. But if you slip me a few coppers, I can maybe find some fresh."

"I don't have coppers now, but I will soon."

She raised one plucked eyebrow. "I don't have fresh blood now, but I will . . . then."

The door closed, and Bea's hand patted my forearm swiftly in apology.

"It's okay. Everybody gives the new girl trouble, right?"

I caught a flash of her nod as she moved around me and back down the hall the way we had come. Considering that I couldn't sip without throwing back my head, I curled my hands around the vial to warm it while I followed Bea out. I did notice a little gust of air about halfway through, and when I looked up, I saw a flash of lavender clouds lit by the weak sun. I hadn't seen a window since entering Paradis, so it was the first time I'd seen the sky since stepping into the catacombs with Vale. The scent of ozone and impending storm filtered down like dust, and a lone raindrop sizzled on my cheek. Up ahead, Bea tapped the walls, and I hurried on.

I stepped out and straightened, leaning backward to crack my spine. As I lifted the vial to pop the top, Bea grabbed my arm and dragged me away, and I chugged it just as we entered the wings of the stage.

Paradis looked different in the morning. With no crowds, only half the lights, and a chill in the air, it called to mind a cavernous old church built on the bones of sacrifices and still echoing with noise that had fled. The girls were gathered in small groups or standing alone, practicing dance steps and bits of arias and acrobatics. A few daimon men moved among them, their foppish clothes and bored gazes indicating they had no interest in the rainbow of sleepy cabaret girls running through their acts in various states of undress.

"Did you get any sleep, *chérie*?"

Mel was the same emerald green she'd been when I'd met her last night, a color almost exactly the opposite of Mademoiselle Caprice and her sons in Criminy's caravan, at least according to the color wheel. She was dressed in what amounted to a ballet costume on Earth—a leotard, tights, toe shoes, and a ragged tutu the color of dust. Four more daimons in similar costumes waited in a half-circle, whispering behind their hands and staring at me.

"A little," I said. "After things got quiet."

She laughed. "Oh, la. That's probably the last time you'll have the opportunity to sleep at all while Paradis is open. You'll be so exhausted tonight you'll barely be able to fall into your own bed."

"Oh, goody."

"I'm sorry, Mademoiselle Demi, but is honest work a problem for you?" The daimon who had so rudely awoken me appeared, toes tapping beneath her golden gown.

"No, *madame*."

"Mademoiselle Charline. Your choreographer."

I snorted to myself. Of course. Of course there would be a Sang version of Charles Zidler, the famous mastermind behind the Moulin Rouge.

In response, I was slapped across the face for the second time that morning, and this time, I most certainly did hiss. She didn't even flinch. "If you wish to work at ze most famous cabaret in the entire world, you will learn respect, hard work, and my goddamn name, you vicious little scab."

I swallowed down my desperate need to rip her to shreds but only for Cherie's sake. "Yes, Mademoiselle Charline."

Her mouth pursed. "Better. Now. Show me every single trick of which you are capable."

"Here? Now?"

All the other daimons had stopped their own practice to stare at me, and I felt the full force of a hundred eyes of all different colors and shapes, some with unnerving horizontal pupils like a goat's.

It was Mademoiselle Charline's turn to snort, but hers was an elegant French snort.

"Fifty daimon dancing girls will be just as cruel as a thousand rich Parisian gentlemen. There's no better trial of your mettle."

I nodded. I could do this.

"I need three chairs, a mouth stand, a glass box, and a large ball."

Mademoiselle Charline jerked her chin at the daimon girls standing behind Mel, and they scurried into the wings like terrified mice. Charline's foot tapped as we waited, and I went through the abbreviated series of stretches Cherie had taught me years ago, the bare minimum that would limber up my body enough to perform the full range of motion required by someone in my profession. It was rote now, as natural as taking a shower or making a bed.

After years of careful practice, my elbows and shoulders could hyperextend easily, and my spine could curve in unnatural ways that I tried not to contemplate too deeply. I'd taken gymnastics as a child on Earth, but being a Bludman made my entire skeleton feel like a Slinky. I forgot, most of the time, that I wasn't human anymore, but it was never more apparent than when I was contorted like a snake, my fangs digging into the stand while I balanced my feet on my head and salivated over the audience.

The daimon ballerinas reappeared, carrying much-mended practice pieces, not the more showy equipment that would be used during actual performances. I checked each item carefully to ensure that if I embarrassed myself, it would at least be on my own and not because of a weak chair leg or cracked mouth stand. Satisfied, I replicated the setup I had used at Criminy's Clockwork Caravan and stood gracefully, arms up and show persona in place.

"Music?" I asked.

Charline nodded. "What do you wish?"

Did I detect the barest note of curiosity in Charline's voice? I had to hope so. And I had to choose carefully . . . and quickly.

I glanced at the collected company, wishing everyone was in costume so I would know which niches might still be available to exploit and therefore which music to request. One group of girls wore Egyptian-style costumes that matched Madame Charline, and there were several butterflies, tons of ballerinas, and a collection of rococo-style ballgowns, but that didn't help.

"What's the most popular song for the can-can?" I finally asked.

Mademoiselle Charline raised one thin eyebrow. "What, pray tell, is the can-can?"

I barely restrained myself from bursting out into a Bludman's characteristic, devil-may-care laughter. If the can-can hadn't yet been invented in the Mortmartre of Sang's Paris, then I suddenly knew exactly how I would make my name as a performer.

Was it cheating? Maybe.

Did I care? Hell, no.

Especially considering that popularity would, I hoped, bring me to Cherie. If Casper Sterling could become the world's most talented musician just because Sang didn't have a Beethoven, then Demi Ward would become La Demitasse by teaching the daimons how to kick their legs in the air. But I wouldn't show that off today, where Charline might claim it for herself. No, I would wait until I was onstage and unstoppable, facing thousands of soon-to-be adoring fans. I'd wanted stardom before, but now that it was my key to being taken by the slavers and finding my best friend, I wanted it even more.

"Well, Mademoiselle Ward?"

"Do you have 'The Infernal Galop'?"

She rolled her eyes. "Of course. We did the operetta last season." When she snapped her fingers, Blaise ran from the wings with a disc and placed it reverently on the flower-shaped gramophone half-hidden by the curtains.

After a few moments of fuzz, the song began, tinkling along, and I went into my act with the quiet professionalism of a well-oiled and many-jointed robot. I hadn't performed to the song before, but I knew it well enough from a lifetime of Earth cartoons and movies that I could anticipate the changes in pace and work them into my routine.

Although I had used a few flashy moves to persuade first Vale and then Madame Sylvie to take me on, I understood that this wasn't a job interview; it was a dictionary of Demi, a catalog of my abilities that would determine my place in the show. Mademoiselle Charline alternated between scribbling in a notebook and staring at me with narrow, dark eyes, her small lips pursed like a dog's ass.

I was flawless, of course. After doing the same routine for years on top of my wagon, I knew the moves by heart. The only thing missing from my act was a partner. Without Cherie, I had to skip the trickier parts or rely on the stacked chairs or mouth stand or ball to make it interesting.

"That move is traditionally done with a partner. Would you like to borrow someone?"

As my teeth gripped the stand, I glanced at Mademoiselle Charline in annoyance. Elegantly stepping out of the move with a flourish, I murmured, "I am a solo act, mademoiselle."

"But you had a partner."

"Yes. Had. And I don't care for another."

"I see."

More scribbling, and I bent over backward into the next move.

When I was done, the crowd clapped politely. There had even been some whispering during the trickier parts that Criminy had devised for Cherie and me, moves that couldn't be accomplished by a human or daimon. But Mademoiselle Charline had never cracked a smile or stopped her frantic note-taking; she and Madame Sylvie had to be a true force of nature when they were both in the same room and focused on the same thing. Now she closed the red leather book and stared at me so hard that I felt as if someone had set a lit match under my nose. Even her third, painted eye seemed in on the scrutiny.

"This song—why did you choose it?"

A light laugh hid my crafty smile. "The operetta is traditionally performed by daimons, and that song is about a party in hell, correct?"

"Of course. Everyone knows this."

"Then debut the Bludman as the queen of hell. Let there be a party of dancers around me as I writhe. Fake fire, imps, whatever. Make it a spectacle."

"Hmm." More scribbling. "You did not answer the question."

So I told her the truth. "Because it's wild and unstoppable and dark and mad."

"Interesting. You're dismissed to costuming. Tonight you will be backstage, helping with makeup and dress. Learn as much as possible. You'll debut Saturday. Our biggest night. I'll have notes to you after tonight's show, including choreography."

"Okay."

"No. You will say, '*Merci*, Mademoiselle Charline.'" The sizzle of her gaze lit my cheeks.

"Thank you, Mademoiselle Charline."

"Now go. *Vite*. We have things to do besides stare at your pasty flesh."

She turned and began yelling at Mel and her friends, and I felt a tug on my bustle. Blaise.

"Hurry, Demi. Before she notices you a second time."

I followed the daimon boy across the stage and into

a new hallway, one I hadn't seen before. He waved and abandoned me in front of an open door, and I tentatively knocked on the jamb, just loudly enough to be heard over the sound of the sewing machine within.

"*Entrez.*"

The daimon hunched over the black machine was the oldest-looking creature I'd seen in Sang thus far. She was going gray all over, the stripes of her wrinkles dusted with what must have once been the same blue skin shared by Bea and Blaise. The bright orange wig on her head and the paint on her lips showed that she was still trying, and her obvious disdain for the aging process made me smile.

"Hmm. The Bludman. Don't typically care for your kind. But Bea says you're a good egg, so I suppose I won't sew poison into your skirt." Unlike the other daimons, she didn't have a wholly Franchian accent, and I suspected she had spent time in Sangland.

"Uh . . . thank you?"

She finally looked up, giving me the same all-over scrutiny that was starting to feel invasive and annoying. I had been with Criminy's caravan so long that I had forgotten what it was like to be the new kid. Fortunately, my natural Bludman's pride superseded my human insecurity, and I stared her down as I had everyone else, as I would continue to do until eyes met me with curiosity and interest instead of doubt and suspicion.

"You're filthy."

"I'm well aware. My coach was attacked by slavers, and then I spent most of yesterday on horseback or in the catacombs."

She wheezed laughter. "Smoke, horse, and shit. We need to burn those rags. Take 'em off. Toss 'em in the fire."

I searched the room for a changing screen and found nothing but the open door and racks and racks of the same sort of costumery that filled Master Antonin's wagon in the caravan.

"Is there a changing room?"

Another wheeze. "You're in it, kid."

Close to the fire, I stripped off my boots and stepped out of the leggings that had once been artfully ripped and ruffled but now resembled mummy wrappings. I'd left my corset off that morning, knowing I would need to either perform or practice, both of which were almost impossible with tight steel bones running up my ribs. I briefly had bruises after showing off yesterday in my Pinky costume. Feeling cold and tender, I untied my bustle.

"Is this salvageable, at least?"

She squinted. "Two years out of season. Won't do. Burn it."

Luckily, I remembered to remove my lucky bludbunny foot before tossing the mud-rimed skirt into the fire, where it smoked with the dark hint of bone rot and mud. Now I was in nothing but my short chemise, my jacket, and the abbreviated bloomers I'd introduced around the caravan. It had been disturbing enough to learn that in Sang, I would hunger for and drink only blood. It had been even worse to discover that no one had yet invented a decent set of women's undergarments, and most women just let the breeze blow by. After several exhaustive sketches and very ticklish measurements, Master Antonin had finally caved and constructed bloomers that were tight and stretchy but perfect for performing. The lace-ruffled edge was his own design and itched me horribly.

"Are you wearing a diaper, girl?" Finally, I had the old daimon's attention.

"I call them bloomers. Women's undergarments."

She stood and hobbled over to me on feet so curled I wondered if daimons had ever practiced foot binding. Gnarled gray fingers poked me with impersonal curiosity, tugging at the fabric and pinching the tea-stained ruffles. "Don't know why I never thought of that," she finally said.

"Does that mean I don't have to burn them?"

"Leave 'em there, in the bin. I'll have 'em laundered and tear 'em apart to make a pattern. I take it you'll want more?"

"If it's not too much trouble. I'm not accustomed to . . ." The Earth girl inside me almost said "free-ballin' it," but the Bludman of Sang interceded. "Feeling a breeze down there."

Another wheeze. "You'd better get accustomed to a breeze, *chérie*. This is Paradis. The day may start off still and fair, but it's bound to end in a hurricane. Fancy bloomies won't change that."

"Bloomers."

"Yes, yes. Take 'em off, and get over here. You're wasting my time, and I don't have much left."

With a last glance at the open door, I stripped off my jacket and chemise and, last, the bloomers, leaving them in a heap on the floor. When the old daimon snapped her fingers and pointed to her side, I walked to the appointed spot and stood, naked and not quite shivering, as Bludmen didn't do that. But it still felt completely freaky, being stripped down to the soft parts. Everyone in the caravan, especially in Sangland, was so careful to keep skin carefully covered, in part because of people like me. But I'd developed a habit of using my clothes as armor, perhaps, and that was to end now.

"Is this for my act?" I asked, and she wheezed away.

"You don't get your own costume until Mademoiselle Charline orders it. This is to keep your measurements on hand and get you decent enough to run around backstage. You want to be fancy, you have to earn it."

She bade me step up on a box before a mirror and took my measurements with sharp efficiency. I did my best to hold still and not hiss when she hit a particularly tender area. She didn't write any numbers down until the end, when she entered them in a large ledger, licking the point of a pencil in between. I glanced over her shoulder, noting line upon line of names and measurements in neat columns. Several of them had been crossed out with one definitive stroke of her pencil.

Noticing my interest, she snapped the ledger shut and went to sort through a long rack of clothes, clearly the everyday stuff. The colors were washed-out and simple, probably made from old sheets or refashioned from the last generation of attire. I longed to run my hands over the hanging racks of brightly glittering costumes. Clouds of tulle and shimmering sequins and the spark of glitter called to me, and I couldn't wait for the day when I would go backstage to dress and wait for that breathless moment before the curtain rose.

"Petticoats: black. Skirt: dark blue. Chemise: eh, used to be white." She shoved a stack of fabric into my arms and shooed me away while she turned back to the rack. I dutifully slipped on the chemise and stepped into the petticoats, tying the frayed cord tightly. The skirt had to go over my head to fall over them both and had buttons up the back. The first few times I'd gotten dressed in Sang, back when Mrs. Cleavers had ruled the caravan's costume wagon with an iron, pointy fist, I'd mucked it all up, trying to step into the skirt or putting my corset on before my boots. Now it was as simple as putting on underwear, jeans, and a T-shirt. I had long ago given up hope of ever ending up in a world where you could walk outside in only one layer of clothing or show sleek, tanned legs in shorts.

At least I got to enjoy the sensation of life without the typical corset. Most girls in mainland Sangland put on a corset at age twelve and only took it off for half an hour at a time for the bare minimum of bathing. By the time they were my age, they were permanently molded into hourglass form, most of them, and couldn't laugh deeply for want of lung space. My life, although strange, was an improvement on that front.

Speaking of which . . . "Is there a shower?"

The costumer didn't turn around. "There's rain."

"Then how can I get clean?"

"I told you: there's rain." She wheezed herself into a coughing fit. "But if you don't like shaking your rump in the alleys, it's ewer and cloth, same as anywhere." I sniffed my armpit and grimaced. "What, you don't have a ewer in your room?"

"No, ma'am."

"*Tsk*. Girls around here. Sticky, sticky fingers. And not just the ones that were born with 'em. I'll have that fixed."

That earned a genuine smile from me. "Thank you."

She handed me a capelike jacket and went to rummage in a drawer. "Never been as fine a life as it looks like from the audience. Out there, they only see the lights, the glamour, the feathers. Never see the freezing attics in winter, the bruises on your waist, the girls who'll stab you in the back just to swallow your pain and fear. Never think about how the brightest stars wink out the fastest. All the magic happens onstage, and real life starts when the curtain goes down. Back here, behind the curtain, the world stands still."

"Are you saying I should find other employment?"

She smirked. "You're a lifer, honey. We can smell our own. I'm just saying to watch your back. Wherever you came from, it's a smaller, sweeter place than this. Don't let Mortmartre kill what's best in you."

I was so intent on her words that I accidentally misbuttoned the jacket, and she smacked my fussing hands away to fix it herself.

"And watch out for Limone. That girl's as sour as they come. Men like that, for some reason." She handed me a pair of worn linen slippers, which were a little loose without . . .

"Stockings?"

She wagged her head. "No point. Not in here. Not until show time. No men and no customers allowed past the door until dusk, and then only in black tie and after paying. Girls here have already seen everything you've got and then some."

Although the air felt good on my legs after so long in dirty leggings, I wished for the millionth time that they made disposable five-blade razors in Sang. I'd never appreciated drugstores until I woke up in a place where toiletries were sold by traveling tinkers or mixed up from a magician's grimoire.

When the old daimon handed me a brush, I pulled down the rest of my hair, making a neat stack of pins on her table. As I gently brushed the dried sweat out of my dark waves, she shoved me back and pressed my shoulders until I landed with a thump in her chair. Soon the brush was in her claw, and she was ripping through my hair until it snapped with static. Once it was all done, she began braiding it so tightly the corners of my eyes pinched. I had grown up calling it a French braid. But here it was a Franchian braid, and if I remembered correctly from the papers, it had fallen out of favor with anyone of taste and class.

I sighed, and she patted my shoulder.

"You'll be onstage soon enough, dear. Impatience is a bitch of a mistress."

"I could perform now."

"Ah, but you won't."

Her hand stayed on my shoulder as if she understood that my every instinct screamed for me to leap up and run away. I wasn't sure which bothered me more, that I wasn't allowed to get onstage and begin my ascendency to stardom or that Cherie felt farther away than ever while I sat here, hopeless, doing nothing. I looked up at the bare lightbulb shining directly onto the sewing machine and realized that I wanted—no, needed—to see the sky. Criminy had always told me that cities were awful for Bludmen, and I began to understand what he meant. We were wild things, predators who didn't take well to obedience. We belonged out in the wild, no matter how nicely we dressed up to pass, harmless, among our prey. I'd felt more myself bareback on Vale's mare than I did sitting here, still, tightly braided, and obedient.

"Go on, then. They'll be expecting you backstage." I perked up, and she added, "To sweep up feathers, probably, or act as a pretty net for the high fliers. Don't get excited yet."

"At least my feet will be on the stage."

"That's the spirit, kid."

I stood and stared at the open door. It stared right back.

"Thanks for your help and advice . . ."

"They just call me Blue."

"Thanks, Blue."

"Be careful out there, kid. You will never be the most dangerous predator in Paradis."

I nodded, one hand on the doorjamb. I really didn't want to go out there. I was far more terrified of being backstage than I was of feeling the spotlight and a thousand eyes. I already knew how to perform. I didn't know how to fit in with my new coworkers, especially without Cherie at my side. In the past six years, I'd come to rely on her, for her knowledge, friendship, and understanding. Now I was alone. And I couldn't get through the door.

Until I heard a certain familiar voice on the other side.

"*Bonjour, bébé.*"

10

Vale's voice pulled me through the door, grinning in anticipation.

The grin died when I saw that he hadn't been talking to me.

"*Bonjour*, Monsieur Hildebrand," trilled a daimon girl in a tutu. She put her hands on his shoulders and went up on pointe to kiss him on both cheeks, a gesture he returned. In the process, her skin shivered over to a warm caramel that matched his, which contrasted oddly with her maroon hair. Vale hadn't noticed me yet, but if the heat I felt in my cheeks was any indication, I was turning as red as a daimon myself.

"You haven't been around lately." The daimon girl pretended to pout, pooching out her lips and sucking in her cheeks.

"I'm a busy man."

"Mm. I know how you like to get . . . busy."

As she stepped closer to him, he saw me over her shoulder and took a step away from her reaching hands. She stumbled on her toe shoes and caught herself against the wall with a muttered, "What's wrong with you?"

His eyes didn't leave mine as he stepped around her.

"Told you. Busy. Later, Jess."

She did her best to storm away, but it's awfully difficult to stomp successfully in toe shoes and a tutu.

"*Bonjour*, Monsieur Hildebrand," I said, mimicking her exaggerated Franchian accent as soon as she was out of hearing range.

"What can I say? The girls love me."

"I can guess why."

"You would guess wrong."

I raised one eyebrow.

"Fine. Half wrong."

"What else do you give ze *mademoiselles* besides ze kisses?"

"Let's not talk about me. Let's talk about you. How is your first day at the cabaret?"

I sighed. "I thought I would be a star tonight. Instead, I'm an errand girl. Or something. They dressed me like a servant and told me to go backstage. Not cool."

He snatched my hand and twirled me around. "Looks fine to me, *bébé*. We all have to wear costumes in Mortmartre."

And it was true. He'd traded in his all-black outfit for clothes that would blend in with the crowds I'd seen at the caravan recently. Criminy had never let me into the cities, and the papers we got were often out of date or missing the pertinent bits on fashion, so the only comparison I had for menswear came from noticing the customers while balancing upside down on top of my wagon. Tight, striped trousers, waistcoat and shirt, cravat, pointed boots. And yet he gave Parisian normalcy a dangerous edge.

"Aw. You're trying to look respectable."

"Trying?" He clutched his chest and staggered backward. "*Bébé*, you wound me. I am very respectable."

"Today."

He grinned. "Today, yes."

"Have you heard anything about Cherie? Or the slavers?"

He shook his head. "Such things take time. I can't just appear in the streets with a poster, shouting. In Paris, especially in the dangerous parts, the more they know you want something, the higher they set the price. And if they know you cannot afford it, the more locks they put on the door that hides it. So I'm making my usual rounds, taking my usual orders, dropping hints nonchalantly over a glass of bad wine. I've only hit three cabarets."

"Only three?"

"The three biggest ones, *bébé*." He put a hand on my shoulder, and little thrills sang through me. I'd grown so accustomed to the touch of gloves that there was a new intimacy to the warmth of a man's hand felt through my jacket. "I will go out again this evening. I told you we would not find your friend overnight."

"So no one's seen anything? At all?"

He let go of my shoulder and leaned back against the wall, crossing his arms and smoldering at me. "What am I going to say? 'Oh, *bonjour*. Been buying any illegal slaves? Because I would like to take one back. Without paying. And I won't tell anyone about the butchering slavers who kidnapped her. Brigand's honor.'" One finger crossed an X over his heart and then went to his lips to mime silence, and I giggled despite my instant depression.

"I guess not. But there has to be something I can do."

His eyes skittered away, uneasy. "Besides rise to stardom and get kidnapped yourself?" He shook his head bitterly. "I still do not like this idea. Are you sure you have nothing of value to sell?"

I crossed my arms and leaned back, shrugging my shoulders against the brick wall. I wouldn't give him my only coins. I wasn't even sure I could trust him. "Nothing."

"You have no money. I don't have much. If we had more, I could grease some palms, open some doors. And you could drink fresh blood and sleep on a pillow. *Oui?*"

"Somewhat tentative *oui*."

"But if you have nothing to sell, we are at an impasse." He reached out to tug a curl that had fallen from my updo. "I would offer to sell your hair to the apothecary, but I think you will need it to become a star." Leaning closer, he whispered, "Also, I like the way it curls."

I shook my head and slipped the curl behind my ear, grateful that he'd given me an out . . . and a compliment. I would sell my hair for Cherie, if that was what it took. But I agreed with him; short hair didn't suit me, and it definitely wasn't the fashion in Paris. The way Vale was looking at me, though, as if weighing me—there was something he wasn't telling me.

"What?" I asked.

Shrugging it off with a falsely bright laugh, he patted my shoulder. I immediately felt I'd failed Cherie with my fear.

"Don't worry about it, *bébé*. You won't start earning until you're onstage, so you'll just have to put on a brave face until then. Oh." Vale reached into his vest pocket. "It's not much. But I thought this might make it easier." As he curled my fingers around something hard wrapped in a handkerchief, voices came down the hall, and he whispered, "Keep it hidden."

I felt around my new costume for a place to hide the

mysterious package, and he stepped away to a less personal distance as a group of daimons appeared.

"Allo, new girl! Mademoiselle Charline is looking for you." I didn't recognize any of the arms, but I nodded and thanked the pink-skinned daimon.

"Why, Vale Hildebrand," she cooed, catching sight of him. "Brought us anything good today?"

The girls circled him, and his grin slid from me to them. I snorted and turned, doing my best not to storm off to the stage, considering how quickly his attention had shifted.

"Wait, *bébé!*"

I just held up a glove, wondering what was the Franchian equivalent of *talk to the hand 'cause the face don't wanna hear it.* He didn't call to me again, and even though I slowed down a little to give him the chance to catch up, no hand landed on my shoulder. It made me feel rejected, even though it was childish and ridiculous. I had grown used to Criminy's brand of brigandry, in which he held the utmost loyalty to his people and especially to his wife but gave the world the face of an outlaw. Even though we'd barely shared a few hours of each other's company and one kiss almost gone deadly, I had no real reason to feel that Vale owed me anything, much less loyalty. His relationships with the daimons appeared long-standing, warm, and real. Who was I, one desperate Bludwoman, to suddenly show up and turn the world on its head?

That's what I told myself, but it still rankled. I might have been the predator, but I wanted to be chased, damn it all.

"Idiot, come here."

Mademoiselle Charline tapped a long, elegant foot

beside a rope ladder. I walked to her, chin high. I wasn't going to start by apologizing—not to her, not to anybody.

"You're hard to kill, which means you're a natural for the catwalk. Climb up and replace the cold bulbs, *oui*?" Blaise scurried out from the wings with a wooden box of milky glass. I was unsure how they could possibly expect even a Bludman to climb a ladder carrying a box, but he showed me how to hitch it onto my back with two wide leather straps.

"Yes, Mademoiselle Charline."

Thus began a long list of mundane tasks, the sort of manual labor that had been done by subservient humans in Criminy's caravan, mostly Vil. Maybe I was spoiled, but it seemed counterproductive to waste my potential with mops and feather dusters and gallivanting high above the ground if it wasn't related to an act. I watched the daimons below, first as they stretched and worked in small groups, then, after noon, when they ran a rehearsal for the night's show in full costume. Charline ran a tight ship, much tighter than Criminy, who had mostly allowed his carnivalleros to control their own acts. More than one daimon girl was rewarded with a whack from a small leather whip after missing a cue or not smiling brightly enough. Watching Charline's face, I couldn't tell which sort of daimon she was, the sort that thrived on success or on pain. She seemed to enjoy a perfectly executed act as much as she enjoyed snapping her whip.

I was again walking the catwalk, this time knocking down rogue bird nests and dusting cobwebs, when I bent too far and felt the package Vale had given me dig into my side. Pulling it out and unwrapping the handkerchief, I found the glowing green pendant he'd worn in the catacombs. I'd told him I hated the dark, and he'd given me his light, given me comfort. And I'd snubbed him for smiling at his friends.

"Idiot," I muttered to myself, twisting the mechanism that made it light up.

And that's when I heard the metal rails creak.

"Poor little Cendrillon. No one will let her go to the ball."

I didn't have to turn around to know who addressed me. "*Bonjour*, Limone."

"Not such a *bon jour* for you, is it? Didn't think you'd actually have to do work, I bet. Thought you'd just waltz in and be a star?"

I shrugged, careful not to show weakness as her footsteps made the catwalk sway between us. Her aerial hoop waited just beyond me. It must have been time for her rehearsal.

"Bad news, bloodsucker. Here in Paradis, you have to work for what you want."

She stopped behind me, and I swept an especially large cobweb from a corner and turned to face her, letting the gray tendrils trail over her face and making her cough and swipe at it. Her acid-yellow skin flushed an ugly dappled mustard.

"I'm working. I'm not complaining. What's your problem?"

Purposefully taking up as much of the catwalk as possible, I returned to dusting. Making enemies hadn't been part of the plan, but I absolutely refused to grin and give way. Being nearly immortal had given me an attitude I'd never had as a human. If Limone was so very determined to hate me, I'd rather give her a good reason than suck up to her. If I wanted to be a diva, I had to act like a diva.

I waited for her to say something else, to shove past me, to turn and stomp down the catwalk and demand that I be ejected from Paradis.

When I began to think that perhaps I had won, that's when I felt firm hands clutch my shoulders and push, hard. Before I understood what was happening, she had tipped me over the metal rail, and I fell from the catwalk, trailing feathers and cobwebs.

11

It was a long way down, so long that I had time to realize that I was falling and wheel my arms and legs, trying to land any way but head-first. I was nearly invulnerable, but "nearly" left a lot of wiggle room. I managed to get flat, like a starfish, and that's how I landed: on my back, splayed out, still holding the damn duster in one hand. Vale's green pendant had shattered on the boards beside me.

Daimons screamed and scurried about as if I might explode. But I just lay there, contemplating the bizarre pain of falling a hundred feet and landing on solid wood planks that had shivered beneath me, probably sending dust into the catacombs just below, where I'd once stood with Vale. Everything onstage moved in slow motion, the rainbow-hued circle of faces now gathering above me making the cheerful noise of dolphins laughing underwater.

I just shook my head weakly. My teeth were clenched so hard I could feel my fangs digging into my gums. Something blue waved and wiggled to get my attention, and I squinted. It was Bea. She made the universal sign for *Okay?* And I barely managed to connect my thumb and forefinger. She smiled, and I allowed my eyes to close. Dozens of fingers helped lift me, and I went limp and boneless as they carried me away. Looking up, I saw an acid-green face far, far away, high in the sky, glaring at me with eyes like lasers. I bared my teeth in a smile.

Limone wanted me dead. I had not obliged. And that made me happy.

The daimons deposited me in my bed, which now had a much thicker blanket. I was curious if it was from Vale, but everyone was fussing too much to listen to me. Finally, Mel cleared them all out until it was only her and Bea, tucking me in.

"Come on, y'all. I'm fine."

Mel tsked. "Oh, la. That was a big fall, *chère*. We need a chirurgeon to check your bones. You might have broken something." The green shards of the pendant matched her skin as she gently placed the remains of Vale's gift on the table beside my bed. "Sorry about your heartstone."

"Heartstone?"

"Vale used to have one. They're very special to his people. Maybe he can find a replacement."

Tossing off the blanket, I rolled to my feet and stretched, cracking my spine in four places as if that would help heal the part that ached inside when I looked at the broken necklace. Vale had told me to be careful with it, and it had been special, and I had let it get destroyed. Growling, I did a backbend, satisfied at the pops in my hips. The green girl in the tutu and the blue girl in the shepherdess costume both stared at me as if I was the strange one.

"Why aren't you dead? Why are you standing? What happened?" Mel asked, her arms held out to catch me should I suddenly topple over.

"I was on the catwalk. Limone started an argument and pushed me off."

Mel sucked air in through her teeth and tapped her toe shoe. "Oh, la. I saw her skulking off while everyone gathered around you. If Mademoiselle Charline finds out, they will take Limone to the gendarmes, and they are . . . not kind to us."

Bea tapped Mel on the arm and signed something in a flurry.

"Are you going to tell?" Mel asked.

"Who, me?" I thought for a moment, understanding that I was being given some sort of test. "No, of course not. I'm not hurt. Besides, if she ran away, my problem is over, right?"

Bea held up a finger, then fled the room. Moments later, she returned and signed to Mel.

"She's gone. Her room is a mess. Looks like you've rid us of some trouble."

I chuckled. "I didn't really do much. Just fell. But who will . . ." A milky, old-fashioned lightbulb flashed over my head, and I grinned. "Wait. I have an idea. Will you help me?"

Their eyes met, shifty and suspicious but curious. Bea shrugged a *How?*

"First of all, go put Limone's room back in order, and don't tell anyone she's gone. Second, can you find a makeup kit? With paint?"

I twisted back and forth, getting limber. I had work to do.

*   *   *

I spent the rest of the afternoon holed up in Limone's room, planted in front of her full-length mirror. Her door actually had a lock, a good one, and no matter how many people knocked, I ignored it. The ewer held rose-scented water, and the first thing I did was take what my grandmother always called a whore bath, exhaling in relief as the dirt I'd carried with me from Sangland dribbled down onto a plush rug. Limone's closet held almost everything I needed, but I struggled with the final piece of the puzzle. Without needle, thread, or scissors, I couldn't make what certainly felt like the most important part of my wardrobe.

Therefore, it seemed like more than providence when I heard Blue's voice on the other side of the door.

"Limone, dear, I have a special delivery for you." Her wheezing told me she was in on the joke, and I cracked the door open just wide enough to let her slip in. Her eyes twinkled as she held out a pile of cloth. "That's what you needed, yes?"

I held out the bloomers and smiled. "Exactly. But how did you know?"

"You have your secrets, and I have mine. Now, let me help you not muck it up."

The basket she set on the floor held all the little details that only a costumer remembered, and I was soon ready to put my plan into motion.

"Break a leg, dear," Blue said as she hobbled back out the door. "I'll be watching." She winked and was gone, and I checked the clock under glass on Limone's dresser. Her room was three times the size of mine and much more beautifully appointed. And if tonight went as planned, it would be mine completely tomorrow.

A soft scratch on the door startled me. "It's time," Mel whispered. I gave her a few minutes to get into place, as being seen with me could get her thrown out of the cabaret—at least, until my plan reached victory.

I took one last look in the mirror, and damn if I wasn't impressed. Each of the cabaret's daimons had a personality or theme, and her costumes and colors reflected it. Bea was a dainty shepherdess, Charline was an Egyptian queen, Mel was a butterfly. And now I was marked in every way as exactly what I was: a blood drinker. The deep-red jacket, short but billowing black skirts, red lipstick, kohl-lined eyes, and red-lacquered claws would stand out even among the bright daimons.

With a deep breath, I opened the door and hurried down the hallway, down the stairs, and past the niche in the brick where Vale had kissed me. Without really meaning to, I trailed the points of my claws along the bricks, a little hitch in my breath and a tingle in my belly. Would he be in the audience, watching? God, I hoped so.

I pulled the veil from my small top hat down over my face. The double layer of black lace hid my features, but still I hurried before anyone bothered to ask who I was and what I was doing. The first act was in progress, the audience warming up with swirling dancers and the pounding of feet on boards—the very boards that had shuddered underneath me when I fell. The cabaret hadn't paused for even a moment; rehearsal had gone on, and neither Madame Sylvie nor Mademoiselle Charline had been up to check on me, that I knew of. If it hadn't suited my purposes so well, I would have been insulted. Criminy would have been there for an hour, holding my hand and stroking my hair back with a concerned look on his sharp eyebrows and threatening to kill me if I told anyone of his soft heart in regard to a scruffy little orphan like myself.

But we weren't in Sangland anymore.

Finally backstage, I wrapped my hands around the rope ladder and climbed quickly and without looking down, lest someone see my face. The first act ended, and I hurried faster as the daimon girls ran behind the curtain. Halfway up, I checked to see that Mel and Bea were in their places. Mel gave me a smile, and Bea giggled silently into her hand, each where she was supposed to be, waiting to play her part in the plan that would either make me or break me.

The catwalk swayed as I hurried past the place where Limone had pushed me. What a gift the bitch had given me. Stepping out over thin air, I caught her hoop and settled myself on it in the same position she had taken the first night I'd come to Paradis. I'd never used a hoop before, but my body knew exactly what to do. It felt sturdy, cold, and sure beneath my bare hands. The second I found my mark, the anxiety melted into the same beautiful calm I felt every time the spotlights came on. Performing had become part of me, the place where I knew myself and my body and my part in the world. And tonight I would steal the goddamn show.

The audience went quiet, and the curtains parted with the whisper of velvet on wood. The hoop trembled, and I began to descend. As the spotlight hit me and the hoop stopped in midair, I let go with one hand and swung back into a dramatic arch that Limone herself couldn't have achieved. Lifting one leg in a perfect point, I let my skirts fall down to reveal black fishnet stockings and a high-heeled red boot. The crowd went mad.

Instead of Limone's signature music, Mel had managed to coax the orchestra into producing "The Infernal Galop," and I went through a series of contortions on the hoop, writhing around it as Limone had but with more finesse, more flexibility, and more daring. She had slithered around the metal circle, but I contorted around it, bending and arching. At just the right moment, I swung down, a move I'd never practiced but which I knew I could stick.

I hung from my hands now, my heavy skirts pulling toward the stage. The hoop began to descend, right on cue, and I willed Bea's hands to speed up, to ensure that I hit the ground exactly when I wanted to. On a whim, I scissored my legs out and around and got the hoop spinning, letting my skirts flail out in a move that got an appreciative howl from the crowd. Thank heavens for Blue's bloomers.

After landing daintily in the center of the stage, I got into place, hands on my hips. And then the music hit precisely the right moment, and I threw back my veil, tossed off my hat, and became the first girl in the Paris of Sang to dance the can-can.

The first time my leg rose over my head straight up, the crowd gasped and whispered. Then again and again, and they roared. They fucking roared! I kicked high, kicked in circles, and even did that little leg-shake thing that made my skirts fall all the way back to show the lacy bloomers. At that sight, the men nearest the stage took to their feet and surged forward, clamoring. I moved toward them with a suggestive smile and began kicking the top hats off their heads to laughs of disbelief and the hot growls of universal lust. Francs and roses rained at my feet and clattered under my boot heels.

I glanced offstage and found Mel and Bea watching me anxiously, their arms entwined. Jerking my head, I held out my hands to them, and Mel laughed and rushed onstage, linking arms with me and matching her kicks to mine as well as a regular body allowed. Bea was beside her in seconds. More and more of the audience left their seats to rush the stage, and Mel thrummed with joy. For a daimon, this sort of response had to be like an ice cream buffet for a little kid. She waved offstage, and other daimons joined us, linking arms into a long line as they learned quickly how to do my bastard version of the cancan. I briefly wondered what they wore under their skirts and whether they were truly giving the audience a show, but it had been their choice to join me, so I wasn't going to worry about it.

The song was drawing to a close when the first of the men clambered onto the stage. The curtain fell early to cut him off as the orchestra fumbled to a halt. Mayhem followed, with men in tuxedos trying to crawl under the weighted velvet curtain and Charline darting back and forth with her whip and cane, trying to smack them away. The mustachioed male daimon I'd seen behind the bar that first night grabbed the push broom and tried to hold the men off of us, his barbed tail wagging dangerously over his shoulder. The daimon girls had glassy eyes and couldn't stop laughing, and I was filled with the power of the stage, with the knowledge that I'd started a complete and utter sensation. It was getting dangerous behind the curtain, but it felt good, and no one made a move to leave.

Strong fingers dug into my wrist. Even when Madame Sylvie dragged me offstage and shoved me hard against the brick wall, I couldn't stop smiling.

"What is this farce?" she growled, her face hot, bright red under flaking flesh-colored paint.

"It's not a farce. It's a dance. I call it the can-can."

"How dare you! I take you in off the street, and you drive away one of my stars and take over the show? Unforgivable."

I swallowed my grin, tried to look contrite. I failed. As I licked my lips and tried to plan my next words carefully, Blaise tugged on Madame Sylvie's jacket.

"*Madame!*"

"Away, boy. This is business."

"But *madame*. This note is from the duke."

The paper he held out was pristine and creamy and thick, the seal that held it still wet and glistening with a rampant gryphon. A hungry look passed over Madame Sylvie's face, and she let go with one hand, still pinning me to the wall with the other. After ripping the note open with her teeth, she read it one-handed and sucked in her breath. Ever so gently, she untangled her fingers from the front of my jacket and placed me back on the ground as if I were made of porcelain.

"There are more, *madame*." Blaise held out a fan of paper in his other hand, and Madame Sylvie took them with a giddy chuckle.

"Would you like to be the mistress of a duke, my Demitasse?" She raised one eyebrow at me as if gracefully conceding defeat and moving on to the next stage of negotiations.

"I'd like to meet him first."

She stepped back, tucked the duke's note into her cleavage, and brushed down the front of my jacket where she'd wrinkled it with her fist. "The can-can, eh? You've named a dance 'the scandal.'"

"We are also sold out for tomorrow night, *madame*." Blaise melted into the shadows.

Madame Sylvie crowed and looked at me as if I was edible—but in a regular way and not the harmless daimon way. "And what a scandal it is! Already sold out for tomorrow, and it's not even intermission. I would call you an instant success if it didn't cause me pain to do so." She took a deep breath and put her hands on her hips. "Outfoxed by a Bludman. What have I come to?"

"A grand success, tons of publicity, and oodles of money?" I ventured.

She patted me on the head. "Just so. Now, off to your room and lock the door before they find you. You've driven them to a frenzy, you know."

I straightened my jacket and put up my chin. "I'm taking Limone's room."

Her mouth quirked up, and she looked me up and down. "Fair enough. Just stay away from La Goulue, or she'll stab you in the throat."

"I've already died once on your stage. I'm not scared of round two."

"Be scared of tomorrow, my dear. There will be even more men in the audience. And this time, they'll be waiting to eat you alive."

"Not if I eat them first."

My eyes dared her to retort. She raised her chin a notch. On a whim, I caught the corner of the duke's note and whipped it out of her corset, tucking it into my own cleavage instead. Her gaze continued to measure me, and I raised my eyebrows.

As I turned to hide my smile and take the stairs, she called, "Speaking of which, I'll send out for some blood, shall I? Can't have you getting too hungry."

I raised a hand in thanks and muttered to myself, "You have no idea just how hungry I am."

My elation and smug self-satisfaction lasted until I opened the door to Limone's room and found a man standing by my open window, his face obscured by billowing white curtains.

"Shut the door and close your eyes," he said.

12

"Honestly, Vale. Breaking in?"

He shrugged and grinned, his hands behind his back. "The window was open, *bébé.*" His finger sketched a circle in the air. "Now, at least turn around and shut the door."

I leaned back against the wood, my breath catching as the door clicked shut. Last night's room had been a closet with a cot, but Limone's room was like a lady's sitting room, with pretty damask wallpaper and rugs and a fire in the grate. The bed was sumptuous, iron with posts and draped in swaths of gauze and vines made of paper. I'd spent the afternoon trapped in here, waiting for my moment, but I hadn't given the actual surroundings much thought. Now, with nothing between me and Vale but warm, smoky air scented with cinnamon and flowers and a jacket I'd already unbuttoned, it felt like a room made for seduction.

I nodded and closed my eyes, just to see if he would kiss me again.

"Good girl."

A cork popped, and liquid glugged against glass. He stepped close enough for me to feel the warmth radiating from his skin and wrapped my fingers around the belly of a goblet. Gently, slowly, he brought it to my nose.

"Smell that, *bébé*?"

Breathing in deep, I smelled a million things. Blood, lots of it. Red wine, deep and perfectly aged and carrying hints of berries and vanilla and summer fruit I hadn't tasted since passing out in Earth on my dorm room floor. He hadn't let go of my hand, and his other hand now wrapped around it and brought the rim of the glass to my lips as he stepped even closer.

The scent of the wine was overwhelmed by the scent of him, just as powerful, just as dangerous.

"Careful, now. Just a taste."

The goblet tipped up, and I opened my mouth, taking the small sip that he allowed me.

"Keep your eyes closed. What do you taste?"

I rolled the wine around my mouth, letting it wash over my tongue. "Blood. Wine. It's greater than the sum of its parts."

"There's something else. Try again."

I swallowed the wine, felt it caress my throat all the way down to my belly, where it settled, hot and mellow. I'd had bloodwine a few times since coming to Sang but not much. Criminy didn't want any risk of his carnivalleros descending into drink or other illicit substances that tended to make one lazy or feral. But Vale was right—the wine he pressed insistently against my lips was different. I drank deeper this time, wrapping a hand around his wrist to hold it there. The flavor eluded me, and I opened my eyes. Vale was smirking, delighted. My fingers tightened around his arm as suspicion rose in my gullet.

"Is it your blood, Vale?"

"No. Of course not. I don't want to make you go mad, *bébé*." He winked. "At least, not that way."

My fingers didn't relax, and his bones ground together in my grasp, but to his credit, he didn't flinch.

"What, then? Something dangerous? Magic?"

A peculiar distrust rippled through me. I dropped his wrist and threw the glass into the fire, where it shattered and sent sparkly red flames roaring up the chimney. I bared my teeth, my heart speeding up as I tried to puzzle out what he had given me, what he had done.

I had grown too comfortable with Criminy's honor among thieves and had given this avowed brigand more trust than was wise. He could have poisoned me all too easily simply because I had a schoolgirl crush on him and felt as if I was filled with helium every time he stepped near. Funny, to think I had survived college frat parties without getting roofied, only to fall for the first drink set to my lips in Sang. I didn't want to believe he was a villain, but that smirk he'd given me . . .

He took a step back, hands down, eyes wary. "*Bébé*, you're taking it all wrong. It was unicorn blud, nothing more. There's a certain cabaret where the Maestro and his Freesian Tsarina stay sometimes, and they keep the cellar stocked with special vintages of bloodwine. I nipped one and thought I'd surprise you. I assumed you would recognize the taste of unicorn. I'm told your people prize it."

I licked my lips. True, I hadn't tasted such magic before, and I was angry now but not insane. "Is it supposed to taste . . . fizzy? Warm?"

"Airy, yes. Effervescent, they say. That bottle of wine is one of the most expensive ones in the city, but they were unloading a crate as I came through the catacombs." He carefully moved the bottle away from the edge of the desk, pushing it closer to a brilliant bouquet of mad sunflowers in a matching golden pot marked with a card that read "Limone." "I thought it might make a nice gift to celebrate your debut," although I was saving it for Saturday.

I moved to inspect the bottle, struggling to read the Sanguine type. Criminy and Cherie both had tried to teach me the rudiments of the Bludmen's mostly secret tongue, but it didn't follow the usual rules of language, and I'd given up. The bottle was thick, green glass, the label hand-painted with tiny letters and edged with gold. A fierce unicorn stood rampant on it, and I didn't need to read the writing to know I'd just thrown a hissy fit over something completely stupid. The taste still tickled my throat, utterly delectable. I had to change the subject or start crying over what an idiot I was for doubting him. Rattled by annoyance, I snatched the card from the flowers and tossed it into the fire.

"Did you see it?" I blurted out.

"See what?"

I kept my back turned so he couldn't see my reaction. "The show."

"I'm so sorry, *bébé*. I missed it. Didn't think you'd be onstage for several days and made Blaise promise to let me know as soon as you were on the schedule. You surprised the hell out of everyone today. Twice." He stepped close behind me, his hands landing gently on my shoulders as if testing the tension in me after the glass-throwing incident. His voice went soft. "Were you hurt?"

I shook my head no. "Told you I was mostly indestructible." My eyes strayed to a poster on the wall that showed Limone dancing, and I spun around suddenly. "Wait. How did you know I was in Limone's room if you just showed up? Were you coming to see her?"

He choked on a laugh. "Oh la la, so jealous. Do you think I'd be bringing a daimon a bottle of stolen blood-wine? And do you think I'd actually want to spend time with a nasty tart like that, even if she could stand me?"

His firelit eyes found mine, and my heart wrenched at the light golden-green that recalled the moors of Sang-land. I pushed the homesickness down to focus on the thrill I experienced every time he settled on me.

"Blaise said Limone was gone and you'd spent the afternoon in here, and there's a convenient window, and I had some news, so I took a chance. I do believe that's the quickest I've seen a girl move from backstage to stardom. I have never heard of a crowd going mad like that."

I looked down, the scrap of creamy paper in my corset catching my eye. "Well, I did receive a proposal from a duke. I guess that's a good start, right?"

Vale's nostrils flared, and with that same uncanny talent Criminy had, he suddenly seemed a foot taller and wider, capable of pummeling a tiny duke into the floorboards with a fist. "Which duke?"

"You mean there are more than one?"

Half giggling and half worried, I pulled out the paper and unfolded it. I hadn't actually read it after taking it from Madame Sylvie and was more than a little curious about how a duke might offer to buy a woman's body and time.

> *Chère Madame,*
>   *The new girl is a delight, and I will be the first to taste her charms.*

*The usual details apply. Please have her de-
livered after tomorrow's show.*

F.

The handwriting was overly curly but hasty, and I
could see the lust written into every loop. Although
I hadn't considered the offer for even a moment, anger
flared at the assumption.

"Doesn't look like he's offering you a choice, bébé."

"I always have a choice."

"Will you go to him?"

"I'm not some piece of meat . . ." A fierce grin replaced
my rage. "Wait. I understand you're a bit of a brigand," I
said. "Do you work on spec?"

His grin matched mine. "I'll need a down payment,
you understand." He pointed to his cheek.

I lightly slapped it. "The whole point of this plan is that
I'm not that kind of girl."

"And I appreciate that, especially as pertains to dukes.
So I'll extend a line of credit, but you'll owe me interest."

"Oh, I think you'll like this plan. Now, hand me that
bottle of bloodwine, and get ready to take notes. Here's
what I need."

It was all business after that. I told Vale what I needed,
and he agreed to get it. But when I tried to tip up the bloodwine to test the airiness of unicorn blud again, he snatched
the bottle from my hand and shoved the cork in harder.

"The rest of this vintage will make it easier to find Cherie. And buy your supplies. I only offered you a taste, *bébé*.
Not the entire bottle."

"But I wasted it!"

"That's your fault, isn't it? Perhaps next time you will trust me."

I stuck my tongue out at him, and he returned the gesture. Throwing me a kiss, he slipped out the window with the bottle in his bag and a last, hot gaze that swept up and down my body and ended in a look of desire and regret. The room felt suddenly empty and quiet, so much so that I had to wonder if he'd even been there. Leaning out the open window, I found a narrow ledge and darkness, hazy with streetlamps. Vale had disappeared. Only the glitter of shattered glass around the fireplace and the lingering warmth of wine on my lips told me that I hadn't imagined him in my room.

Alone now, I felt the little pangs and annoyances of a long fall and a thrilling debut. Slight aches, including the balls of my feet, much abused by my first public can-can. We would need better shoes if we were to perform it every night. My back still stung, thanks to my tumble from the catwalk, but it hadn't affected my performance. When I undressed and sucked in a big breath, I had to wonder if perhaps I'd bruised a few ribs. In the excitement and adrenaline, I'd completely ignored the needs of my body. And I was deliriously hungry for blood, of which I had none. At that moment, I would have gladly licked the bloodwine from the floorboards, had any spilled there during my little rage.

I undressed and slipped on a night shift I found in Limone's armoire, a far nicer one than the ragged, worn thing I'd borrowed the night before. Would Limone come back for it? And did I care? Probably not, and no. Just as I had once walked the caravan, telling myself that it was home and I should forget Earth, now I paced Limone's room, telling myself that it was mine and I should forget the caravan.

I couldn't put down the duke's note, couldn't stop reading the cold words that turned me from a thinking, feeling woman into a commodity. Even after six years in Sang, I still hadn't internalized the general sentiment that women were things to be used and, when they'd outlived their use, discarded. Women had practically no rights here, unless they had a father or a husband to stand behind them—or a big-ass sword to swing at whoever threatened them. The caravan was better than most places, thanks to Criminy's liberal worldview, but here in Paris, I was on my own. And I was practically chattel.

I had no idea what Madame Sylvie had planned for me, whether she had any control over my destiny and my body—or whether she thought she did. This duke could likely own the lot of us if I made him too angry. The shit would probably hit the fan in the morning, but what did I care? My answer to the duke was already in motion, out of my hands, and if Sylvie didn't like it, I would find another cabaret and teach them the groundbreaking, scandalous dance I'd just invented.

I undressed, turned down the lamp, and slid between the rich coverlets. The bed was luxurious compared to what I was used to, the feather mattress cupping me like angel wings under blankets as soft as melted butter. I stretched and writhed and stared longingly at the window. I'd noticed since becoming a Bludman that lust and hunger were painfully intertwined. When I hadn't had enough blood, my thoughts grew dark with needs I'd never known on Earth. And when I couldn't stop thinking about a guy, I couldn't stop thinking about his blood and staring at the little vein in his neck. The last guy I'd dated had been poor Luc. He'd been hot, but his daimon blood hadn't appealed, and neither, I'd soon realized, did his personality. I'd wanted Marco Taresque and had spent more than a few nights in my wagon car thinking about what it would feel like to drink the knife thrower's blood while he traced my body with the points of his daggers. But Marco had been too old for me and then rightfully claimed by Jacinda, and my hungers had cooled.

The caravan meant two vials a day, one show a night, very little lust. A simple life.

Now I was again at the mercy of a hunger that didn't quite fit. I wanted Vale, but I didn't trust him, and I couldn't drink from him. Still, something in me kept watching the curtain billow from the open window anyway, hoping to see his pointed boot slip over the sill, bottle in hand and eyes on fire with mischief. Was it foolish to think his kisses could sustain me?

Something had been bothering me all along, some restless sense that I had forgotten something important. I went over every look, every word in my conversation with Vale. I could never sleep when something evaded me like that and had sprung from my bed after midnight more than once to Google an actor's name or pull up a thesaurus online back on Earth. I couldn't stand being eluded.

And that's when I remembered it. Vale had said that he had news. I'd glossed right over it in my excitement over the show, and he'd never returned to the subject. News about what? He had to mean Cherie, but he hadn't said her name. I leaped out of bed and went to the window as if he might be lurking outside, waiting for me.

Of course, he wasn't. That was just stupid.

As I slunk back into bed, the thrill that had lit up the night vanished. I'd been so self-obsessed that I'd forgotten the entire reason I was here. I had let Cherie down again. There wouldn't be a third time. Despite what I'd told him, Vale could have all the pecks on his cheek he wanted, if only he would bring my best friend back.

The next morning, an unmarked package arrived at the duke's doorstep. Underneath the beautiful wrapping that I could only describe as Tiffany blue despite the fact that there was no Tiffany's in Sang, the duke found a box. Inside that box, packed carefully in bunched tissue paper, was a cow's tongue.

> *I am not a piece of meat for your amusement.*
> *Hope this charm is to your "taste."*
> *La Demitasse*

By lunchtime, a new card had arrived, tripling his price.

When Madame Sylvie delivered it herself, demanding to know what I had done to inspire him so, I laughed and threw the creamy paper into the fire.

"I told him he couldn't buy me. At any price."

She tapped her foot, shook her head. "Someone will find your price, *ma petite*. That, or they will take you and tell you what you are worth after the fact."

I grinned, showing her my fangs. "Let them try."

13

Everything had changed overnight. After Madame Sylvie left, fed up with my feral and cocky attitude, Blaise appeared with a teacup of warm, fresh blood and a nicely folded napkin. An apothecary's glass jar sat beside it on the tray, filled with notes. Apparently, this was the preferred way to win a cabaret girl's attention, and I went through them one by one, sorting them into little piles on the silky bedspread.

They promised me love, adoration, bedroom skills, trinkets, private rooms in costly hotels, and willing necks that longed to see if it was true that a Bludwoman could incite a climax just by feeding the right way. I was half disgusted and half fascinated, and as the unfamiliar names and their offerings swirled together, I called Blaise in and requested a notebook and a pen. I made a spreadsheet of names, their offers/requests, the quality of the paper and handwriting, and their perceived creepiness. Each of these men was suddenly on my list of suspects, a self-selected group of supposed gentlemen who thought of women as things to possess and who might have a reason to abduct a young, beautiful Bludwoman and keep her somewhere in secret for their own selfish purposes.

No one bothered me as I worked. No one knocked on my door or called my name or demanded my attention or help. Cabaret stars, apparently, were allowed to sleep in. I luxuriated, reading the newspapers and gossip magazines Limone had kept in a slippery heap by her bedside. Paris was a place of beauty, intrigue, sensation, and melodrama, worlds away from Criminy's quiet caravan, where Emerlie's whispers were the only true source of scandal. Fashion in London was clearly years behind Paris, which was odd, as they were less than a day away in a fast airship. With dresses and the disappearance of bustles on my mind, I turned a page in my new notebook and sketched costume ideas for Blue and practiced signing "La Demitasse" with an ink pen, just in case cabaret stars were required to autograph things.

One time in the caravan, I had asked Jacinda if her writing could make me a star and had been disappointed when she tried to let me down gently. Now I *was* a star, and I had no idea what that meant, except that dozens of men wanted to do raunchy things to me, and if I did well enough, I might find myself stolen by kidnappers in scary masks—and that was my goal. And yet all I could think about was a half-Abyssinian brigand's eyes, his hands on my waist, and the prickle of brick against my back as he kissed me. A dozen different hungers held me, things I shouldn't have wanted yammering over the one thing I needed most: my friend safely back by my side.

A light knock on the door startled me, and I huffed a "Yes?"

"La Demitasse?"

It was Charline, wearing a painted smile that was at least half false. While she must have loved the monetary benefit I would bring to the cabaret under her tutelage, she had to hate that I had tricked my way to the top instead of earning respect the old-fashioned way. I couldn't keep the snark out of my own smile. At least Sylvie had accepted her defeat gracefully. The bagload of silvers cleaned up off the stage last night probably helped.

"*Entrez*, Charline." No more *Mademoiselle*.

"Did you sleep well, *chérie*?"

"Very."

"I'd like to discuss tonight's show."

My grin widened. "I'd love that."

She cleared her throat and pulled out her red notebook, and I noticed that it matched mine exactly. So they'd given me one of her private stash; no wonder she was annoyed. "What we must decide is whether to replicate last night's act or try something entirely different. Of course, it will not be such a . . ."

"Surprise?"

Charline pinched the bridge of her nose. "Indeed. It won't be a surprise. But it doesn't inconvenience the rest of the girls, and we already have the equipment and music. I'm sure you'll want to work with Blue on costuming, and I did have some ideas."

She held out her notebook, and I held out mine. The two drawings had nothing in common whatsoever, and laughter burbled in my chest as she fought the urge to screech at me in her typical manner.

"Look, Charline. I refuse to wear a hat shaped like a coffee cup, even if it works with the name."

"But this costume you propose is . . ."

"Utterly indecent?"

"Unprecedented."

"This is Paris. We set the fashion. So let's set it. Besides, very little skin is revealed. They'll see more when the other girls dance than they see when I contort."

Angry mauve spread over Charline's gold skin like ink on tissue. "Must you be utterly contrary at every juncture, *mademoiselle*?"

I shrugged and settled back against my pillow. "Why not? Someone needs to. You don't become a star by doing the same thing everyone else is doing. *N'est-ce pas*?"

"Perhaps. But you don't keep the established clientele by suddenly changing everything they've come to expect."

"So keep everything the same."

She smiled in triumph.

"Except for my act."

The smile died.

"My act should be last, and it should start the same way, on the hoop. Or maybe a trapeze. Lower me to eye level, I'll do my thing, then bring all the girls out to dance the can-can together with locked arms. Easy."

"And for the costumes?"

A brief image of one of my favorite childhood movies flashed through my head, and I grinned. "Dress them as forks, napkins, salt cellars, sugar bowls, teacups. Like a giant table, putting on a show just for the diners. Inviting the audience to be our guests."

One eyebrow went up as she considered it. "I regret to say that it's not entirely horrible. Perhaps instead of a hoop, you could emerge on a giant chandelier?"

I nodded eagerly, imagining it. Me, sliding down the rope to a majestic chandelier of gold and jewels, slithering around it as it slowly descended to the floor. Paris had surely never seen its like, and that was exactly what I was hoping for in my act.

"It will take a week to prepare this grand finale. Until then, can we count on an exact replication of last night's sensation?"

"Yes."

"Good."

"But I have a rider."

She cocked her head. "Do you require . . . a horse? Perhaps a saddle?"

I laughed. I guess she'd never heard of M&M's, either. "It's a list of demands. I want posters of me. And a better costume for the interim."

She snorted a very Franchian snort and rolled her eyes. "Both requests are already in process. We are not idiots, *mademoiselle*. If the people want you, we shall give you to them, and gladly."

"Excellent."

I nodded and sipped my blood, picking up a magazine. Recognizing that she'd been released, Charline spun on her slipper and left, muttering under her breath in Franchian. Her last line bothered me still. I had felt powerful all morning, knowing that I had proven myself, made a good bet, and cast myself one step closer to the stardom I'd always craved.

But her carelessly tossed words reminded me who was really in charge of my future: the people. More specifically, a slavering crowd of rich, lustful men who weren't accustomed to being told no. Were they really so different from the slavers who had stolen Cherie? The duke's response had been amusing, but the fact remained that he hadn't written "I appreciate your rejection and respect your empowerment," he had simply upped his price.

I was still for sale; the bids would just have to get a lot higher.

The show went off without a hitch that night, and the crowd's mad yammering and stomping filled me with elation and terror. The purple daimon dude, Auguste, ushered me out of view before they could storm the stage and tear me apart, his hand wrapped around the top of my arm, gentle but firm. He was like a bouncer, Mel had informed me, working many of the cabaret tasks that couldn't or wouldn't be performed by the girls. But Auguste didn't escort me to my room upstairs. Instead, he dragged me down the opposite side of the wings, through a maze of hallways, and outside into the starlit night.

The air was chill and as clear as the air in a Sang city could get, and I opened my eyes as wide as possible, until I blinked away tears. I hadn't been out of doors since I stepped into the catacombs with Vale, and Paris was ridiculously, impossibly beautiful. The City of Light merged the pictures in my world mixed with the topsy-turvy paintings of absinthe-riddled artists to shimmer with brighter-than-life colors and energy and movement. The effect was beyond distracting.

Overhead, the clouds swirled and curled around the stars in a dreamy dance. The moon was a perfect crescent, the warm yellow of fine cheese, its glow painting indigo mountains and throwing sharp black trees into shadow. The sky mesmerized me so completely that I nearly tripped on my own feet as Auguste pulled me toward a towering elephant of copper and glittering enamel, its giant legs each the size of a lighthouse and the rivets that held it together as big as my fist.

"You've got to be kidding me," I muttered.

As he opened a hatch in its front left leg and yanked me inside, I felt the first sting of panic. Where was he taking me? Then I heard the first calls of the crowd on our tail. It was pitch black and cold inside, and Auguste let go of me long enough to turn the wheel behind us, locking the door.

"Steps, miss," he said softly, and I reached out a toe until I felt the first one.

Up and up we went in a tight spiral. I kept one hand on the smooth copper wall, running fingers over solder and rivets and cringing as gentlemen's fists banged on the metal. Outside, Madame Sylvie's voice carried, but I couldn't catch any words. Had they sold me, or had I been given away? Was this ridiculous elephant my new room? Something about it—maybe the echo of my steps or the cold scent of metal on the air—felt like a prison even a Bludman couldn't escape. My heart sped up. Could this be where they kept Cherie?

A glow ahead made my feet move faster, and I soon stood in the most opulent room I'd seen yet in Paris. It was the elephant's belly, the glowing copper hung with velvet and silks like a maharaja's palace, with expensive furniture pressed close to the curved walls. The floor, at least, was flat, the wood boards new and polished and covered with sumptuous rugs. A painted screen broke the space up into two distinct rooms, and I would have bet everything I owned that a bed was on the other side of it. But there was no one else there; it was empty. And not a single sniff of Bludman rode the air. No Cherie.

Not that kind of prison, then. Unfortunately.

"You'll stay here tonight. Outfit's on the other side of the screen. Best get ready."

"Get ready for what, Auguste?"

His smirk was pitying and a little leering. "What do you think, *mademoiselle*? Being a star ain't free."

With a faux-courtly bow of his head, he ducked back into the elephant's leg, leaving me alone. Unnerved but still amped from my performance, I went to the gramophone on a small table and pressed the button without checking to see what music waited on the disc. Having grown accustomed to Casper's masterly playing in the caravan, I was generally disappointed by popular music, but I needed something soothing. The song that started after a mechanical buzz was slow and sleazy. I was flipping through the other records when I heard footsteps on the copper stairs. I gasped and ran behind the screen.

Oh, what a bed. Round and covered in a mound of pillows, it was clear that only fools would sleep on such a sexy piece of furnishing before they'd completely exhausted each other. All around the bed, the copper walls were painted with bright blue skies, pink-tinged clouds, and daimon children dressed as cherubs with mechanical wings and crossbows. Hanging from a hook on the wall was a delicate wire hanger, and hanging from that by two pathetic silken strings was the slinkiest, most nonexistent dress I'd seen since waking up in Sang, half-dead and craving blood.

A foot landed on the wooden boards with a creak.

"La Demitasse?" a cultured but unfamiliar voice called gently.

The breath caught in my throat. Who was it? Surely

not the duke. Or was it? And not Monsieur Philippe, thank heavens. But that left an awful lot of rich, horny men in tuxedos who might have bought their way into my life.

"Just a moment, *monsieur*," I called, keeping my voice low and light.

"I'll pour the wine, *chérie*, while I wait."

The offhand use of my best friend's name was all it took to propel me into motion. Every man I got close to here was one more suspect on my list, one more possibility. With my sharp sense of smell, I would know immediately if he'd been near her. And that meant that I had to slither into the dress on the hanger and make nice with whatever silver-tongued predator had landed on the doorstep.

My hands were numb as I untied the skirt and undid all the layers of my costume. I almost missed the impenetrable armor of a corset, but in this case, every breath was welcome. The gramophone music buzzed and wheedled, echoing off the metal and filling the room with the promise of sensuality. After checking that the gentleman's back was turned, his hands busy with cutting the wax and uncorking and pouring the wine, I stripped off my costume and kicked it under the bed.

The male form I'd seen had been utterly unremarkable in every way. Darkish hair, slimmish figure, the same black tux required of every visitor to Paradis. His hat sat on the table beside him, and a long coat was draped possessively over a chaise. Before he could turn around, I tugged the dress down over my head, the soft cotton and filmy lace whispering over my bare skin. I kept on the new bloomers Blue had made for me, this pair in black lace with foamy layers of ruffles. A full-length mirror by the bed showed a slight rumple at the waist, as the negligee wasn't designed to conceal anything, but I wasn't about to go into this unexpected meeting without underwear on.

I was a fool for being at all surprised. I had been warned in different ways that being a star came with certain requirements, including spending time with the customers, who paid heavily for the privilege. But I had never agreed, in writing or in words, to barter my body or sexual favors of any sort. No matter what the gent in the other room might have been thinking, no matter what he thought he had paid for, no matter how Sylvie defined "anything," I didn't owe him shit, and I wouldn't forget that. I'd tease the hell out of him, but I wasn't going to be a whore. Not now, not ever.

The cork popped. Liquid gently gurgled.

"The wine is ready, *mademoiselle*. Won't you join me?"

I shivered at the confident, low timbre of his voice. This was a man accustomed to getting what he wanted, what he'd paid for. Like the duke—and maybe he really was the duke—he thought I was for sale. Time to inform him differently.

"Alas, *monsieur*. I cannot partake."

A soft laugh. "I beg you to reconsider. It's a special vintage from the Tsarina's personal cellar. Tell me, Demitasse. Have you ever tasted unicorn blud?"

I struggled not to giggle. I bet I knew what was on the label and whose pockets had been lined through its procurement. At least I'd get to taste it this time without suspicion.

But wait. Just because Vale hadn't drugged me didn't mean this so-called gentleman shared the brigand's scruples. I had a lot of questions for the girls of Paradis regarding taking drinks from patrons and what could be slipped into those drinks that a girl might find reason to regret later. For now, I was stuck. But considering that he hadn't watched American television, perhaps he didn't know all the same tricks that I did.

Checking myself in the mirror, I used a finger to wipe off stray lip paint and compose my smile. The dress hung daintily from my shoulders and billowed around me, short and voluminous, and I slipped my feet into a pair of kitten-heeled slippers lined up below the coat hanger. The look wasn't unflattering, but I hadn't seen such a fashion in Sang, much less Paris. I felt a little like a child in a nightgown, which was creepy in an entirely different way. Taking a deep breath, I curled fingers around the painted screen and cooed, "Perhaps I will reconsider, then."

His head snapped around, and I was disappointed. He was older, distinguished, not unattractive, but nowhere near my age and tastes in men. Not that it mattered. I had enough problems with handsome men who kept turning up and setting my heart thumping. Seeing me, he grinned with tobacco-stained teeth and ran a hand through his slicked-back hair, which was graying at the temples. His eyes would have been kindly if they hadn't been filled with dark, avid lust.

"Saint Ermenegilda, preserve me. You've forgotten your stays, *ma chérie*."

I blushed, suddenly understanding why the short gown was so voluminous. Of course. It was meant to go under a corset and balloon out prettily, highlighting my small waist. Except for bludded carnival contortionists, no woman in Sang went out without a corset. It was the equivalent of walking out of the house topless. But the hunger in his eyes ratcheted up a notch as his gaze crawled over me. I took a half-step behind the screen to cover my embarrassment.

"Leave it off. Please. I have never seen anything so ravishing."

I'd broken another rule. And it was already paying off. As I'd learned long ago in a different world, when men started thinking below the belt, they stopped thinking above the neck.

I smiled and struggled not to cross my arms over my cleavage. Letting my hips sway, I walked to the table, where a familiar bottle of wine sat, open. One wineglass sat beside it, the deep red liquid seeming to slosh gently on its own, glitter swirling like silt. I didn't know enough about that drink or this world, and I wasn't about to sip from the glass he must have brought himself, as it hadn't been here before I'd disappeared behind the screen.

I wanted to drink it. I just didn't want to end up unconscious and assaulted for my curiosity.

"Mmm, unicorn," I murmured. As I reached for the goblet, I tripped on the kitten-heeled slippers and knocked the slender glass to the ground, where it shattered against the painted wood. A deep red stain spread across the floor, seeping into a white fur rug, and I gasped melodramatically. I felt like a Barbie doll, or at least, as if I had to act like one.

The gentleman cleared his throat in annoyance, probably tallying the cost of the lost wine. "And to think you looked so graceful onstage, *mademoiselle*. I haven't brought a second glass."

He had gone stiff and was looking at his hat. I didn't

intend to woo him, but I needed him to stay close, to lure him into conversation and discover if he knew anything about Cherie. And I needed him to leave the copper elephant with tales that would bring all the other men knocking on its knee.

"Have you a piece of paper, *monsieur*?"

Surprised and leery, he pulled a billfold from his coat and handed me a single thick sheet that matched the first note I'd received, with only a small letter-press F crest in the corner.

So this was indeed the duke.

I swallowed hard and made a mental note to screech at Charline. It wouldn't have hurt anything to tell me what was expected, how powerful this man was, what he would do to a woman who rebuffed him, for clearly he was unaccustomed to rebellion. With a smile and a bob of the head, I folded the paper into an origami cup and tucked in the edges.

"*Et voilà!*" I held out the cup, eyebrows raised under my thick bangs.

The duke chuckled, a very French sound. Or Franchian. In any case, it was utterly confident and appreciative, and it carried the tone of dark, easy promise. Lifting the half-full bottle, he poured the shimmering bloodwine into my makeshift cup. Whether or not he had drugged the first glass, I had no choice now but to drink and hope for the best. Surely a man like this—a powerful, handsome, wealthy man—wouldn't wish to bed an unconscious form. The seduction and fire had to play a part in it. Dozens of girls would have lain with him for free. He'd probably paid enough for my time to run Criminy's entire caravan for a year. My heart raced, terrified of giving him what he wanted and even more terrified of denying him.

I caught his eyes as I tipped back the cup, the wine running from the sharp paper corner and into my mouth. It was delicious. No, more than that. It was like champagne made of love and lust and magic, effervescent and smooth and sweet. A fire licked up my insides, and my smile turned real as I caught the last drop from the burgundy-stained paper.

"You have excellent taste, *monsieur*," I purred.

His smile returned, and he sat down on the couch of shimmering copper velvet that matched the elephant, one arm along the carved wood back. When he patted the seat beside him, I had no choice but to leave the paper cup leaning against the bottle and saunter to him, hips swaying. I wanted more wine, but more than that, I needed my wits about me.

"Please join me, *mademoiselle*." Instead of sitting where he'd indicated, I sat at the other end of the sofa, my legs tucked under the ruffles of the flared dress. The couch was short enough to allow his fingers to play with the curls hanging down from under my hat. "I found your little gift this morning terribly clever. It's not often I meet a cabaret girl with any fire."

"But I'm a Bludman, *monsieur*. I'm filled with fire."

"Oh, I know. I know everything about you. Even about that little caravan in Sangland, although I have trouble envisioning you performing for the country rubes, surrounded by freaks."

I turned my snarl into a toothy grin. "I'm flattered by your interest."

"I make it a point to scout the land before making an investment."

My eyebrows rose. "So I am merely a piece of property, then? How peculiar. I had always imagined myself a person."

He leaned close, drawing a finger along my jaw. I shivered as if a shark had brushed against my leg. It's rare a woman challenges me, Mademoiselle Ward. I find it rather intriguing. But dukes must be careful where they spend their time and with whom. I always do my research."

"Considering you're here, I can only assume you found me harmless."

His fingertip lifted my lip a little further, just over a fang. I struggled to maintain composure, my lip trembling in his grasp. "I consider you anything but harmless. Fortunately, I have ways of rendering a woman, shall we say . . . less dangerous?"

He leaned in for a kiss, my chin in his hand. I whipped my face away and stood, putting the arm of the couch between us. The look he gave me then—he was like a reptile, a lizard, head cocked and eyes hard and fathomless.

"Demi, surely you understand that I've made an arrangement with Madame Sylvie? A great deal of money exchanged hands. Normally, I don't mention such crass topics, but you appear to need a reminder of your precarious position." His hand patted the couch again, harder this time. "Sit."

"Ah, but sir, you haven't made an arrangement with me. No money has found my hand. And so, you see, I haven't agreed to anything." His face was going over red, so I looked down, batted my eyelashes at him. "I don't normally mention such crass topics, but I may be the last virgin in Mortmartre. I'm only eighteen, and I wasn't prepared for . . . this."

It was a lie, of course. They were all lies.

But he believed me.

And he didn't care. His breath caught.

"Eighteen," he said, slowly and carefully, "is more than old enough."

"Not for me, *monsieur*."

He licked his lips. "Surely we can agree on a compromise?" Leaning back and twitching his coat aside, he revealed his bulging "compromise," and a rush of rage overtook me.

"You want my mouth on you, *monsieur*?"

"Very much, *mademoiselle*."

I grinned, and the sight of my fangs made him gasp. "As you wish."

And I dove for his throat.

14

I didn't kill him, although I wanted to. But I did make a terrible mess. I'd never fed from a human before, and my teeth slid across his skin like a car over black ice. When his arm latched around my waist, I bit harder, finally opening the skin and releasing a dribble of blood. My tongue found his neck with the impersonal kiss of licking a stamp.

Although Criminy had strictly forbidden feeding from customers and Cherie had never drunk from a live victim, the two-headed boys of the caravan had plenty of experience and loved to brag. Catarrh and Quincy had shrugged their extra-wide shoulders, saying that where they'd come from in Freesia, two minutes of drinking could conclude a full day's work for lucky humans with a healthy constitution.

While Quincy filed his teeth, Catarrh detailed how very easy it was to make the bloodletting enjoyable for them if we wished. Bludmen did have a sort of residual magic. That was how they got away with snitching blood in the darker corners of the freak tent. Their willing victims never complained and sometimes enjoyed the experience so much they left a copper behind. The high-necked gowns and winding cravats meant to protect the humans from us sometimes protected indiscreet Bludmen from the repercussions of a pilfered meal.

Knowing that feeding from the duke could, much like my stage antics, be another triumph or end with me being chased out of the city with fire and pitchforks, I tried to make it as good for him as I could without sacrificing my honor. Judging by the way he tried to drag me onto his lap and over the bulge in his expensive trousers, it worked. He was putty in my hands, whimpering and blissfully writhing under my lips. When he moaned and shuddered suddenly against me, hands digging hard at my waist, I knew we were done.

I pulled away with a long, seductive stroke of my tongue. He lay back, drained and panting.

"That was the most sensual experience of my life, my Demitasse."

I stood, wiping my mouth with the back of my hand. "Happy to oblige, *monsieur*."

I slipped on his frock coat, opened the copper door, and walked down the stairs of the elephant's leg on the balls of my bare feet. The night was dark and cold and still when I emerged, stepping out of the elephant's foot to run across the courtyard and into the cabaret. The halls were empty, the theater silent. With a sniff of disgust, I plundered the coat's pockets, all empty, and dropped the expensive pile of fabric on the boards, disappointed to find not a single whiff of Cherie on its lapels. Feeling humiliated and cheap, I ran up the stairs, not stopping until I was in Limone's old room, now marked with a sign reading "La Demitasse" in curling silver letters, just like I'd dreamed of seeing on my first night here.

Thankful my window was closed and locked from

the inside, I curled up in my bed and quietly shook. The duke's blood made me feel strong, beautiful, invincible. It was almost enough to quiet the tiny, shouting voice saying that I would be thrown in jail in the morning. But it had been my only choice.

My hand slid to the place under the mattress where I'd hidden my coins and the pouch of Criminy's sleeping powder. Although I trusted Mel and Bea, there were dozens of daimon girls I still didn't know who had access to my room every moment that I was gone. My treasures were still there, and it suddenly occurred to me that not only did I have a powerful and mutually beneficial gift for the men who bought my time—because I knew without a doubt that the duke wouldn't be the last—but I also had a way to render them unconscious while I hunted for clues. A tiny sprinkle of the harmless sleeping powder would give me plenty of time to search each body that found its way into the copper elephant for any hint of Cherie or the slavers. Tomorrow night, after the show, I would begin my investigation.

I could only hope that my second gambit would turn out as well as the first.

My sleep was long and delicious, right up till the dreams turned from the mad clapping of packed crowds to the thunder of hooves and a black conveyance, the air shimmering from spotlights to smoke rent by the flailing legs of screaming horses. But in the nightmare, Cherie was torn crying from my arms by a man in a bird mask, our talons breaking as we were ripped apart. I woke gasping and muttered, "Holy shit."

As if on cue, my door opened to admit Blaise with a dainty teacup filled with deliciously warm, high-quality blood. On the tray sat the same apothecary jar filled with notes, even more than before. I sat up, rubbing my eyes at the sunlight filtering through my open window. It felt like a dream within a dream within a dream.

"What's going on? Am I in trouble, Blaise?"

He giggled into his hand. "I don't think that's what they're calling it, *mademoiselle*. Read the paper." I unfolded the Parisian newspaper on the tray, the fear in my heart giving way to curiosity. I had fallen asleep half dreading Madame Sylvie's harsh screech or the stomp of gendarmes with billy clubs and guns filled with seawater. After all, feeding from humans was strictly forbidden and punishable by death in Franchia, as it was in Sangland. Blaise, fresh blood, and a newspaper had to be good news.

The first page was all politics, the second all society. Boring. A full-color page caught my attention. It was a slick insert titled "Diversions," and the main illustration featured a slightly familiar, if overly beautiful, slender girl with dark hair and bangs kicking one red boot high over her head. "La Demitasse: The Angel of Paradis," the headline said.

I read the story hungrily, knowing that at least half of it would be lies. As Criminy had always said, journalists were worse than novelists, because novelists at least try to tell some truth. *Mortmartre has ever been the pleasure district of distinguished gentlemen and high-spirited daimons, but a new addition has the crowd clamoring for more. A Bludman? In Paris? And performing? Do not faint, ladies, for she has been proven as safe as a muzzled and broken bludmare by Monsieur Philippe himself. Our esteemed Duc de Fournier agrees, saying only, "La Demitasse is a singular creature of unparalleled grace and beauty, and I look forward to giving her more of my attention."*

Tickets through the next week were sold out before noon at Paradis, and interested parties may inquire from Madame Sylvie regarding personal boxes and champagne. A grand finale is planned to stun and surprise all viewers beginning Saturday next.

Your heart will be this Bludman's next victim!

I sipped my blood and laughed.

So they would indeed be coming after me . . . with roses and bottles of bloodwine. I'd triumphed again, this time by simply doing what came naturally. If the duke continued to spread his story, then my parlor trick would become feeding daintily from my suitors while waiting to search their bodies or be kidnapped.

I could do that.

That afternoon, I had a costume fitting and was politely requested to indulge Charline with a rehearsal. I acquiesced gracefully, knowing deep inside that while I had to keep up the untouchable-diva front to the gentlemen who wanted my favors, I didn't want to be a bitch to my coworkers and employers. Criminy had included rehearsal in every day's plan, so it felt good and refreshing to go through the motions and accept a page of overly polite notes from Charline, who actually had excellent ideas on improving my work on the hoop. Thanks to last night's drink from the duke, I was sated and strong and smiling when I sauntered back to my room, enlivened by solid work and feeling like a queen.

I sensed the man waiting within before I opened the

door this time. Vale sat by the fire, feeding my apothecary jar of notes and love letters into the flames.

"What the hell, Vale?" My new skirts tangled around my legs as I jogged to him and snatched the half-filled jar of notes from the rug by his side.

His look was dark, threatening, and I drew back a little even though he posed me no danger. "They wish to make you into a whore. At the very least, a kept thing. It makes me sick."

My blud boiled, and I bared my teeth. "You don't get to decide what I am. No one can do that but me."

His mouth dropped open as he stood. "*Bébé*, you can't want . . . that is . . . I wouldn't have thought you'd be angry at me for wanting to keep you from being sold as a prostitute."

I gave a dark chuckle. "I appreciate the thought. I'm just not willing to tolerate the assumption. And I'm keeping notes on all the letters they send, sniffing them for a trace of Cherie."

Vale dusted off his pants and resettled his shirt while he hunted for his words. In the end, he settled for placing the half-full jar in my waiting hands and shooting me his wicked grin. "We started off on the wrong foot. I'm sorry for burning your clues. You were beautiful last night, *bébé*. And not in a way that intrudes upon your personal freedom. Beautiful like . . . a wild mare or a sunset. Something completely independent."

"Thanks? I guess."

"Do not give me that attitude, *chère*. You say you're the one making the rules. I just wanted to check in on you, make sure you are being treated well." He looked down, rubbed the back of his head. "Considering I'm the one who brought you here, I feel more than a little responsible for your happiness."

I faltered. It was nice that he cared, but I would have preferred that he was there because he liked me and wanted to be around me. I'd had enough caretakers and had just told him to buzz off in that area. Or, better yet, I wanted . . . "Do you have any news? On Cherie?"

His smile was rueful, his eyes angry and perplexed. "It's tricky, *bébé*. The word on the cabaret circuit is that more and more daimon girls are disappearing. No one calls it 'taken.' There's no mention of slavers or kidnapping. But they all seem to descend into drink and worse before just . . . vanishing. Most assume they wandered into the streets alone while under the influence of absinthe and met dark ends. The bludrats will strip any corpse they find, regardless of species. And the gendarmes refuse to investigate."

A thousand possibilities went through my mind. I imagined street gangs, giant bludrats, open manholes into the catacombs, and the slavers themselves in their dark cowls and plague masks. But then I imagined the damage one angry Bludman could do and the fact that it took an awful lot of bloodwine to render us stupid. And of course, the fact that Cherie had been directly taken, had never gotten so far as to take a single drink in Mortmartre. She was more than some silly drunk girl, stumbling into a dark alley with the wrong man.

I shook my head. "Sounds like something different entirely. Can I draw a poster for you to show them, perhaps?"

He shrugged, a sad thing. "If it will make you feel better. But . . . have you not noticed that having a Bludman in a cabaret is big news? Whoever has your friend is keeping her secret. Especially after your debut, I imagine that any other cabaret hiding a Bludman with any contortion skills whatsoever would instantly set up shop to take advantage of your popularity. And believe me, *bébé*, if I hear anything of the sort, I will be in the front row to steal her back for you."

That finally softened me up, and I let the smile spread over my lips. Putting a gloved hand on his shoulder, I looked into his eyes, soothed by their golden glow, so like a cat's. "Thank you, Vale. She's everything to me."

"Everything?"

The possessive hardness in his eyes made me angry again. "Of course. She's my best friend, my partner, the closest thing I have to family. Just because I go through the motions here and get sent to that blasted elephant with dukes doesn't mean I'm not thinking about her constantly."

"The pachyderm?" Anger twisted his fine features. "You've been to the pachyderm?"

"Last night. With the duke. And you can't say a damned thing about it."

We were nose-to-nose now, each filled with fury and breathing hard. His nostrils flared, and the anger writhed off his skin, sharp as cinnamon.

"Oh, I have something to say, *bébé*."

I opened my mouth to tell him exactly how much he could say, but he grabbed my shoulders and kissed me, hard. His tongue forced its way past my lips and raked me possessively, and I let out a little moan and curled my fingers into the front of his shirt, unable to resist his pull. His mouth claimed me, his hands moving to my waist and pressing me close.

When he changed angles, he murmured, "Watch the teeth, *bébé*. Can't have you going mad."

"I'm already mad. Shut up and kiss me."

"I like you when you're angry."

"Shut. Up."

I gave him no choice, kissing him hard but without fangs, mouth wide and eyes closed. As cold as the duke's practiced attempts at wooing had made me feel, Vale filled me with passion, half furious and half hungry. I took a step backward, pulling him with me, still kissing him. Step by step, we stumbled toward the towering, soft bed, his thighs brushing against mine as our tongues danced and licked. With my back to the bed, and one more nudge from his thighs, my butt hit the mattress. His controlled fall took me to my back and brought him over me on his elbows, the kiss never breaking.

"Mm. You're good," I murmured.

"You're better."

I took his lip, gently but as a warning, in my teeth. "What are you implying?"

He drew back, raised an eyebrow. I let go of his lip. "That you're a good kisser. Every word out of my mouth isn't a fight, *bébé*."

I grabbed his chin in my hand, licked his lips. "Then stop talking and kiss me."

"Normally, I'd argue, but you've made it clear that you are a woman who does what she wants."

With a growl, I hooked a leg over his and rolled him over onto his back so that I straddled his hips, my skirts cascading around us in a puddle of black ruffles. "Damn right I am."

I leaned down to kiss him again, and he didn't resist

at all. His hands found my hips, and I settled in to take whatever I wanted, slow and deep, my fingers tracing the buzzed stubble of his hair. When the knock came, I hissed at the door and hoped that whoever had interrupted that kiss was human and edible.

"*Mademoiselle?*"

I sighed and quickly arranged my skirts so that Vale was barely visible. His bemused smile told me that he looked forward to seeing how I handled the sticky situation. "Yes, Blaise?"

The door creaked open, and the young daimon cleared his throat. "Madame Sylvie asked me to tell you that you'll be in the pachyderm again tonight with another very important guest. The great Lenoir wishes to paint you."

Vale shifted beneath me as if he might rise up and argue, but I planted a hand against his chest and let my talons prick, just the tiniest bit, through my gloves.

"Thank you, Blaise."

But the boy didn't budge. I spun to raise my eyebrows at him in inquiry.

"The duke was much impressed to learn that you were unspoiled, *mademoiselle*. It's said that you'll make your fortune in one night, should you choose to do so. The gentlemen have already begun to bid."

The door shut softly, and Vale erupted, tossing me over. "You're a virgin?" he hissed.

I blushed hot. "No. But I would've told the duke anything to keep him away. That's just what slipped out."

He licked his lips, rubbed his jaw. "Probably just made them hungrier for you. That will be a tough lie to hide one day, *bébé*."

"Then we'll have to find Cherie soon, won't we? Before anyone has to find out."

"I'll do my best. I *am* doing my best." He fell back on the bed as if suddenly realizing that I still straddled him and he wished to enjoy the view. Elbows out and feet crossed on the ground, he grinned. "Lying to the duke. Such spirit, *bébé*."

"He also thinks I'm eighteen." Feeling his interest coalesce beneath me and knowing we couldn't take it further just now, I slipped off his body and stood beside the bed, rearranging my costume in the mirror. "And tonight I meet Lenoir."

Vale bolted up again, swinging his legs over the side of the bed. "Demi, no——"

I spun on him, staring daggers. "No?"

"No. . . torious. He's notorious, *bébé*. A Lothario. Paints all the stars of the cabaret."

"And that's bad?" Hands on hips, I waited for him to choose his words. "That's not what I want?"

"*Bébé*, do you know what happened to Jane Avril? Nini?"

"I've seen their paintings . . ." By Toulouse Lautrec, in my world. But still.

He stood to pace the room. "But where are they now? Not running their own cabarets. Not touring Sangland. They rose to the top, Lenoir painted them and everyone assumes slept with them, and then . . . nothing."

"Good! That's what I want! That's how I'm going to find Cherie."

"And you're not frightened? Of disappearing?"

I shook my head. "No. Because I'm expecting it. If the same people who took Cherie are taking the cabaret girls, and if the girls Lenoir paints disappear, then it seems like the fastest way to get where I'm going is to get painted by Lenoir and disappear."

"You're insane, *bébé*. Suicidal."

"I'm a Bludman, Vale. And he's just a painter."

"A painter with a reputation."

I laughed brightly. "Then I don't need to worry, do I? Because I'm not going to sleep with him, and if he tries anything, I'll drain him. He'll paint my portrait, and I'll get even more famous. And considering he's painted some of the girls who've disappeared, maybe I'll smell Cherie."

Vale shook his head. "You're buying trouble, *bébé*."

I tossed my hair. "Wrong. Trouble is buying me."

Another knock at my door startled us both.

"Your costume, La Demitasse," Blue called. She snickered. "But I can wait a moment if you're busy."

Vale kissed me, hard and quick, and I stopped breathing. "Just promise me one thing, *bébé*."

"Maybe."

He cupped my face, ran a thumb across my lips. "Don't trust him. Don't trust anyone."

And then he was gone, leaving me hungry for more than his words. I waited until he'd slipped out the window before opening the door for Blue.

"Windy day." She held out an armful of silvery fabric. "But the wind is wise, don't you think?"

"Full of hot air," was my only answer.

He meant well, but I hadn't left Criminy's nest just to be bossed around by another man.

I would meet Lenoir and decide for myself.

Tonight.

15

The show was flawless, of course. I'd long ago ceased to doubt myself or my abilities, thanks to the natural grace and confidence of a predator. As Auguste ushered me back to the elephant, I smoothed my hair and patted the sweat on my forehead. I could still feel the heat of the stage lights and the hot press of hundreds of drunk, lust-filled bodies. The men in the audience were so rabid for me that Charline had rearranged the finale so that all the other girls formed a tight, interlocking line of high kicks that no one dared to breach. That's right—in Sang, the first true can-can line was invented just to shield me from my admirers.

At the elephant's leg, Auguste paused and fussed with me for a moment, setting my hat at an angle and pinching my cheeks, although I didn't know how he could see me in the darkness.

"You don't want to displease him, miss," he said, his voice low and rich like coffee. When he opened the door and bowed, I went in alone, my nerves on fire and shining out my eyes.

From what I understood from the papers I'd read in Sangland and the few discussions I'd had in Franchia, Lenoir was an amalgamation of several Impressionist painters from my world. At the very least, his body of work included things I remembered as the work of Édouard Manet, Claude Monet, Toulouse Lautrec, and Pierre-Auguste Renoir. But the man himself was said to be a mystery and a wealthy man. He was the only artist in Sang who couldn't be bought, who chose his own commissions and pursuits. And now he had chosen me.

My heart was beating so loudly that I imagined it echoing against the copper as I took the winding stairs upward. Was Lenoir already here, waiting for me, or would it be like last night, when I had a few moments to compose myself? There was no way to know, although Auguste's brief primping made me suspect that I was already being judged by the timbre of my footsteps. I was more nervous than I should have been, probably because while I had confidence in my skills as a contortionist and dancer, I had never felt glamorous or seductive. Lenoir painted only the most beautiful girls, the stars, and I felt a little like a fraud. But I quickly smothered that little voice of doubt in my heart and put on my best smile as I entered the chamber.

He was there on the couch, watching me with the sharp eyes of a hawk.

No. That's not true. Hawks have kind of stupid, round, golden eyes. Lenoir's eyes were too smart, too dark, already narrowed as if measuring me for a frame. His Van Dyke and hair were ink-black, with one streak of distinguished white. But it didn't lessen the man; quite the opposite. There was a confident, smooth stillness about him that drew me in like a vacuum. A sexy vacuum. I breathed in deep and barely held myself from hunching over into attack mode.

Lenoir smelled of Bludman, which meant I'd finally found my link to Cherie.

He tipped his head, just the tiniest gesture, and his mouth quirked up in a sly grin. I gasped when I saw his fangs, and with that gulp of air came the full power of his scent. Not Cherie, then; I had smelled his own blud.

"And now you know my secret."

His voice was butter and bourbon, sipped in a lightless room. The accent was mostly Sanglish but rich and royal. He stood, his shadow-gray suit as crisp as if he'd just had it starched for the first time. He was all angles and corners as he bent at the waist and reached for my hand. My bare fingers were dark against his white kidskin glove, and I shivered when his mustache and lips brushed the back of my hand.

I bobbed my head and looked up through my eyelashes. "We're all filled with secrets, *monsieur*. But you have surprised me, which is one point in your favor."

He grinned in a way that reminded me very much of Criminy Stain, except that a bit of playful good humor lurked always behind Crim's wickedness. I suspected Lenoir held all of the danger and none of the amusement that made my mentor so very lovable. And yet I couldn't help mimicking the smile. We were both dangerous things, weren't we?

"So you're saying you owe me, then, *mademoiselle*? Fine. I accept the debt. I wish to paint you."

"I'm flattered, *monsieur*."

"Don't be. You knew I'd come for you. They all do."

"All of whom?"

"Coyness doesn't become you, Demi. The girls I paint know I will come for them because that's exactly what they want. After I paint you, you'll be immortal, your name on every man's tongue. You're a rising star, but I will turn you into the sun."

"Sounds hot."

His grin widened, went darker, if that was possible. "Oh, little one. You have no idea." He returned to the couch, taking up a sketchbook and leaning back. "Stand there, one hand on the table. Don't look at me. Look at . . . oh, say, that painting."

Bemused, I did as I was told. He shook his head in annoyance and walked to me quickly, his gloved hands businesslike and cold as they posed my arms and changed the angle of my torso. I'd felt like an object ever since arriving in Paris, but under his posing, I felt less like a morsel or a doll and more like a vase of flowers that just wouldn't cooperate. When he'd finally contorted me into the correct pose, he returned to the couch and began sketching, the pencil's rasp harsh in the silence.

"I thought Bludmen weren't allowed in Mortmartre," I murmured through mostly closed lips.

"And yet here we are, you and I. The thing is, once you're in, it's awfully hard to get you back out. And if you were here all along and have never taken off your gloves and can't be seen to smile very often under your mustache, no one ever looks closely enough to tell. It's the beauty of daimons; since we're no danger to them, they don't really notice the difference."

"And none of your . . . subjects has ever noticed?"

He stopped sketching to glare at me from under heavy brows. "You say subjects, but you mean lovers."

"I am a student of history, *monsieur*, and I understand that an artist's muse often finds his bed as well as his brush."

He chuckled as he made angry slashes with his lead. "A muse is a muse, and a portrait subject is a thing. One is more trouble than the other. Your head should be tilted, Demi."

I dutifully tilted it. Maybe he was gay? He certainly didn't look upon me with lust, at least not the open, crass sort I'd grown accustomed to when performing. But there was something deeply sensual in his close scrutiny, in the calculations going on behind his eyes. Whatever he wanted, it wasn't some giggling daimon dancer. And whatever path he chose, I suspected, would be thorough and purposeful and would allow no turning back.

When I shivered, he only murmured, "Hold still."

It might have been ten seconds or ten minutes or ten hours later before the mad scritching stopped and he looked at me as if I was a person again.

"You may sit."

I stretched and twisted, cracking my spine in four places. Odd parts of me were asleep, and my eyes were dry as if I'd held them open too long at the beach.

"Tiring, isn't it? Holding one attitude too long."

I shrugged elegantly. "I'm a performer. I perform."

Lenoir nodded thoughtfully. "So you do." I was about to sit and lure him deeper into conversation, hoping to discover more about his past and how he'd hidden so long in plain sight and if he knew any other Bludmen in Paris, but he stood abruptly and tucked his sketchbook under one arm.

"I'll expect you tomorrow morning. Before nine, while the light is still good. Take extra blood, as I'll want pink in your cheeks and lips. I'll have a costume ready. I utterly defy you to be shy." He slipped a card into my hand and turned for the door with a whirl of his gray coat. A breath of lavender and anise trailed him, and I took two steps toward his retreat.

"You wouldn't care to stay, *monsieur*? I could order up a teacup, perhaps a cigar?" Considering that he'd most likely paid through the nose for the privilege of my time, I didn't want him to leave disappointed.

He didn't turn back to me, merely shook his head as he put on his top hat. "*Bonsoir, mademoiselle*. I need you rested. Do not disappoint me."

And with a tip of his hat, he was gone, footsteps echoing against the copper as he hurried down the stairs.

He was one of the strangest men I'd ever met.

And despite Vale's dire warnings, I was riveted.

Last night, I'd been anxious to flee the giant elephant and hide in my room. But tonight the door was locked from the outside, and no amount of banging on the metal brought any sort of help. With my patron gone under his own odd auspices and no use for the sleeping powder in my pocket, I settled into the plush circular bed in a huff to flip through racy postcards, pornographic playing cards, and books about sensual bootblacks and burly firefighters who caught and ravished swooning women. I'd found an elegant hatbox brimming with such gems sitting on a tuffet, and it felt more than a little surreal, reclining in a metal pachyderm and staring at photos that were currently the height of vulgar pornography but showed less than a geriatric lap swimmer's bathing suit from my own world. If these guys saw my triangle bikini, they'd probably have an apoplexy.

So that was one more thing I could "invent" in Sang.

I was grinning to myself and planning a cabaret-style version of *Beach Blanket Bingo* when the door opened far below and footsteps tapped up the circular stairs. I'd never moved as fast as I did then, tossing the photos and cards and books back into the hatbox and shoving it under the bed before the owner of the footsteps appeared. Even if it was just Auguste or one of the daimon girls, I didn't want to be seen looking at porn.

"La Demitasse?"

I groaned silently. It wasn't a familiar voice, but it carried the same apologetic ownership as the duke's had. Charline must have double-booked me, the greedy bitch.

But wait.

I didn't have to put out or even fend him off. Just play nice for a few minutes and feed, then use the sleeping powder. They'd sent up room service that paid for itself.

I grinned. "On the bed, *monsieur*," I cooed.

A red-faced elderly man appeared around the screen, cane in hand. I patted the bed.

"*Mon dieu*, but you are even prettier up close, *ma chérie*. Can you believe I've never met a Bludman before? I've long waited to make your acquaintance."

I stood and draped an arm around his neck. "And I yours," I whispered into his ear.

It was too easy. Far too easy. One caress, and he had what he needed, while I earned a full belly. I sprinkled a few grains of sleeping powder over his head, and soon he was snoring softly on the bed, fully dressed and cheeks enflamed with imagined passion. With a grimace of distaste, I gave him a thorough pat-down but found nothing useful. A wallet, several nice handkerchiefs, a horribly creepy-looking condom that looked as if it had been used before stuffed in a small book of Saint Ermenegilda's better quotes. There wasn't a whiff of Bludman about him or the stench of magic and catacombs.

Before descending the stairs, I slipped a calling card from his wallet and used his handkerchief to dab the blood away from the little rip in his neck. I would add his name to the "Innocent" column of my spreadsheet. He said he'd never met a Bludman before, and oddly enough, I believed him. In six years among Crim, Tish, and the people of the caravan, I'd learned to read faces, and as far as I could tell, he hadn't lied.

I slipped off my boots so I could take the metal stairs silently. Pebbles bit into my stockinged feet as I fled across the uneven cobbles to the back door of Paradis. With one ear against the door, I made certain that it was quiet inside. The only thing I wanted less than to further entertain the old man was to encounter the other girls doing the walk of shame and have to answer questions about why I was so quick at my work. The hallway seemed empty, and I turned the doorknob as slowly as I could, knowing after last night that it had an unfortunate tendency to squeak.

"You work fast, *bébé*."

I bit back a scream and spun, hands curled into claws. Vale's amused and skeptical calm made me even more likely to rake out his eyeballs.

"So—what, Vale? You're following me now?"

"Don't flatter yourself. Stargazing in the courtyard of

the—" He chuckled and rubbed the back of his head. "Yes, I'm following you. But only because I have something that I thought you'd want to see, as soon as you were done . . . entertaining the great artist."

Rage shot up my spine, making me clench my teeth with a click that rang in the night. "First of all, entertainment is my job. Second, *entertaining* is not code for sex. Third, I just assumed you'd kissed half the daimons here, and I've never thrown that in your face. So how dare you judge me?"

He stepped closer, reaching for my hands. I jerked them back, feeling all too inhuman.

"Simmer down, *bébé*. I didn't come here to start a fight."

"Then keep your meaningful, judgmental pauses to yourself." He tried to take my hand, and I smacked his wrist. "Keep your paws to yourself, too. I've had enough of being grabbed at."

Hands in the air, he stepped backward, and I shook myself like a dog shedding water, feeling tightly wound and unpredictable in my anger. It was true, what I'd told him. Except when I was in my own bed, I spent a lot of time being touched against my will. Whether Charline was placing my hands on the hoop or Blue was dressing me or Mel and Bea were fixing my hair and makeup, I was sick to death of being touched like an object.

"Fair enough, *bébé*. I don't want to make you unhappy. But look."

The thing between his fingers was so small that I couldn't see it without stepping close. Duh—he'd been trying to hand it to me.

It was a tooth. A fang, actually.

I took it with shaking fingers, holding it up to the meager orange glow of the gaslight.

"I know there is no way to know if it belongs to your Cherie, and I know it's unsettling, but . . ."

"But if you're using a Bludman as a slave or a concubine, she'd be less dangerous without her fangs."

"That's what I was thinking."

The fang matched mine, bright white and smooth, with a long, two-pronged root. I had a sudden curiosity regarding whether little Bludmen lost their fangs and hid them under their pillows for a creepy, blud-spattered Tooth Fairy.

"Where did you find it?"

I held it out to him reluctantly, but he shook his head and crossed his arms. It felt good in my hand, curled within my fingers. Macabre as it might be, he was right; this was actually a good sign. After all, it could have been a fanged skull.

"Well, you see . . ."

"Stop acting cagey, brigand."

"Being a brigand involves a certain amount of smuggling and trading, and from time to time, unusual objects come into my possession. Dragon claws, unicorn hairs, mysterious valises covered with stamps—"

"The Freesian Tsarina's bloodwine?"

"That, too. Francs and silvers aren't the only form of payment, after all, and I know the sort of folk who need certain things and the sort of folk who pay with certain things, and I connect them."

"All very legal, I'm sure. Totally aboveboard."

He chuckled into his fist. "Believe whatever you wish, *bébé*. But it just so happens that tonight's bounty included a handful of glittery little trinkets, and that was among them. I asked for some background—which is all part of the game—and the gentleman in question got very nervous and would only say again and again that it was very fresh and he'd won it at cards. Which means, if it's hers, that she is in Paris."

My hand stole to my own fangs, which felt foreign even after six years in Sang. I still remembered the strange, searing pain as the old canines had fallen out, the tips of the new fangs pushing through right behind them with a dull ache in my jaw. I'd been terrified. But back then, everything had been terrifying. Now I was mostly angry. When I found who had done this to my best friend, who had torn off part of her body just to make her weaker and more helpless, I would sink my claws into the bastard. And I would bleed him dry in some very choice, very painful spots, withholding the magic that gave the feeding any sort of pleasantness. I would teach him what a Bludman truly was.

But that made me think again of Lenoir's secret.

"Wait. Aren't there any Bludmen in Paris at all?"

"There are a couple in Paris but not Mortmartre. As it's the pleasure district and gentlemen can't spend money or unlace their breeches if they're scared, the gendarmes guard the wall very carefully. Only humans, daimons, and a few harmless freaks like myself are allowed in." He rubbed his head again, a nervous habit that I found endearing in spite of myself, like a little kid rubbing his nose. "Technically, I'm not allowed in, thanks to some rather choice warrants, but I stay far away from the walls and the billy clubs."

"Then why haven't they come for me?"

His eyes went tender-soft with pity. "Oh, *bébé*. You're so very naïve. They did come for you. That night after your fall, after your first show, where you took over Limone's act and sent the crowd mad. Limone must've tipped off the local gendarmes."

I felt cold all over, synapses firing uselessly. "Why didn't I know? Why didn't they take me away?"

"Because Charline met them at the door and paid them a very large sum to let you stay." His gaze was kindly, fond, almost parental. "And they wouldn't have taken you away. They would have killed you."

"I'm hard to kill."

This time, when he reached to stroke my cheek, I let him. Cold as I was in the early spring night and filled as I was with rage and fear, his touch seared me.

"Good," was all he said.

I stood up on my tiptoes to kiss his cheek, the fang wrapped in my fist where it lay on his shoulder. "Thank you."

"*De rien, bébé.* Pay me back later."

His playful grin was back, and my wobbling smile joined it as I pulled away and turned to go. I slipped through the door and up to my room, never meeting a single soul. My cheeks were red, my eyes bright with unshed tears. I wasn't sure what to do with the fang, so I tied it up in a piece of lace and tucked it into the armoire drawer next to the remains of Vale's pendant and Cherie's lost fascinator.

I'd put my life and my friend back together piece by piece, if I had to. At least now I knew she was nearby.

As I fought wakefulness, knowing that Lenoir wanted me early and fresh, I couldn't help wondering exactly how much Charline had paid for my life. And exactly how much interest she would charge me. For as I was learning, everything in Paris came with a price.

And an expiration date.

I had to find Cherie before she lost more than a fang.

16

I awoke in a panic. Without alarm clocks or school or a nine-to-five job, it had been years since I'd worried about a wake-up call. Everyone slept past noon in the caravan. But my window was tinted lavender with early dawn, and I breathed a sigh of relief. Angering Lenoir would be dangerous in more ways than one. I still had time.

The hallway was empty, but the animal part of my Bludman nature could sense wakefulness somewhere beyond the closed doors. I was right—as I passed, one opened to reveal Mel and Bea. Their eyes were bright, their lips turned down. They'd been waiting for me, then.

"Oh, la, *chérie*. You're going to Lenoir, aren't you?" Mel asked, arranging a curl over my shoulder with a kind but sad smile.

Bea's fingers flew excitedly, her eyes wide.

"She says to be careful," Mel supplied.

"Be careful? Why?"

We both stared at Bea, who blanched ice-white and fidgeted, her eyes darting back and forth. She signed slowly, as if trying to find the words, and Mel translated.

"'I can't say why, but he scares me. Always has. The streets aren't safe. Just be careful.'"

The poor girl was so flustered that I reached out to hug her. Over her shoulder, I saw a small pallet in the corner of the room and Blaise's blue face relaxed in sleep. Something clicked into place in my mind, but I only said, "Don't worry, y'all. I know what I'm doing."

Mel patted my arm. "Tell us all about it later, eh? We could use some good gossip."

Bea signed *Good-bye* and something that looked like *Good luck*. I took the stairs to the brick hallway, careful not to let my new dress catch on the loose nails. As I had expected, Auguste waited by the door in street clothes. He looked different, dressed in waistcoat, tailcoat, and trousers, complete with a slit for his tail. His face was kind but guarded as usual.

"I'm to deliver you to Monsieur Lenoir's studio, miss. Oh, and there's this."

He held out a brown paper bag, as if someone had packed my lunch. Inside was a vial of blood, and I turned my back to him politely as I drank it. No point in taking to the streets with any lingering hunger, although the old man's blood last night had fortified me well enough. At least it wouldn't be a problem, trapped in Lenoir's studio all morning, as he wasn't the human everyone assumed him to be.

I had expected to walk, but a posh conveyance waited outside, chugging in a puff of smoke that matched the violet clouds and lingering drizzle of early morning. I hadn't seen many private vehicles in Sangland, as everyone came to the caravan in heavily built, carefully guarded bus-tanks. This vehicle was shaped like a fussy miniature boat, with carved ribbons, flowers, and fleurs-de-lis, and the prow was a carousel-type horse, as if they just couldn't give up the idea that horses had to pull carriages. Auguste helped me up the step, and I settled onto the cushy mauve bench within.

Perfume was heavy in the air, and handprints marred the porthole-shaped windows. I guessed how the passengers generally kept busy. Auguste climbed into the front compartment and pressed buttons with patient familiarity, and I watched the streets with interest as the conveyance rattled away. The pastel-painted buildings lining the gray-cobbled avenues were tall and angular and squashed together, with long windows and ironwork balconies and doors painted in bright colors. It was too early for promenading, and most of the figures I saw were dashing about in a businesslike manner, with iron-gray umbrellas bobbing overhead. It looked a little like my mental image of Paris, down to the bludrats that scattered in the gutters, which were a lighter burgundy than the ones in Sangland and somehow managed to look a little more chic and slightly less bloodthirsty.

I couldn't keep track of the turns we made or the landmarks we passed, although the scent wafting from a lavender-painted bakery made me simultaneously nauseated and heartsick for my human life. We finally screeched to a stop outside a building like any other, the walls a smoky bluish-gray with elegant copper statues of dancers flanking the doors. Auguste left the conveyance chugging and held a black parasol over my head as he helped me down to the street and walked me up the steep stairs to the front door.

"*Bonne chance*," he murmured. He was gone before I could ask him how I was expected to get back to Paradis.

I took a deep breath and drew back my shoulders as

I lifted the door knocker. It was shaped like a lion with gigantic fangs, and my three knocks rang up and down the alley and sent a flock of pigeons squawking into the grayish-purple clouds. Footsteps echoed within, and soon the door opened to reveal Lenoir himself in an impeccably clean artist's smock. He didn't smile, but then again, I didn't expect him to.

"You're barely on time."

"And you're barely personable. I expected better, *monsieur*."

That earned a snort but still no smile. "Come in, then, and enjoy my hospitality."

"Said the spider to the fly," I murmured under my breath. But if he heard, he made no comment.

I stepped into his foyer, which was ten degrees colder and a deep shade of ombre. Lenoir was already taking the stairs, which were thickly padded by a carpet patterned in thorns and roses. I hurried after him, hoping not to displease him further. Something about him felt dangerous in a very welcome way, and I wanted to learn more of his secrets. Two Siamese cats the color of marshmallows with singed corners darted past us, silently preceding us up the staircase. I longed to touch them, as the only cat I'd seen in six years had been the tailor's cat in the caravan.

Lenoir passed the second level, and I only had a moment to glance down the orange-lit hallway at two closed doors and an elegant table holding a huge bouquet of flowers. My nose crinkled at the vegetal decay of funeral lilies, but I suspected that to a human or daimon, the odor would have been pleasant. Still Lenoir didn't speak, and still I followed him, past two more floors likewise beautifully closed off, up to the very top floor, where the cats posed daintily on a chaise. The plush carpet ended in a frayed strip, and then dusty wood floors the color of new honey spread out, their smooth stripes broken only by the occasional stain of spilled paint.

A grand window let in a strip of sun as narrow and targeted as a laser, with the promise of a gold-rimed sunbath once morning was officially in full force. Directly in front of it was a rug so deep and luscious-looking that I wanted to rub my cheek against it. A velvet chair with curling arms sat at an angle, a cushy pillow and a whisper-soft blanket thrown over it. Lenoir turned to me with a dress draped over both arms as if the body inside had simply dissolved.

"Put this on, and take your hair down. There's a screen." He jerked his chin at the corner and dumped the dress into my arms. It was a heavy thing and had the old, rubbed look of a royal gown from the previous century. The deep chocolate-plum would perfectly complement my hair, eyes, and skin, and Lenoir knew it.

The screen was a paltry thing, paper and ripped in places. A pair of forgotten stockings were draped over it like shed snakeskins. I checked that Lenoir was readying his palette before turning my back to the slightly chill room and quickly slipping from the many layers of cabaret attire to the rich, hand-stitched dress. It was off-the-shoulder and sleeveless, hanging like a bell from my hips. When I took down my hairpins and shook the black curls over my shoulders, I couldn't help smiling. It felt a little like I was going to vampire prom. And yet something about the costume made me feel vulnerable and small, like a child playing dress-up. Like one shove at my shoulders would draw it down and leave me completely bare in seconds.

"Hurry, Mademoiselle. We need the light."

I walked to the chair and sat down.

"Too prim. You're a sensual woman, Demi. Sit in the chair like a lazing queen."

His dark eyes engulfed me, one fist under his chin. I slumped back and slid down, hooking a leg over the chair arm and letting my head fall to the side. His mouth barely twitched.

"Better."

He had an easel ready, a large canvas waiting. But he didn't start painting. Merely scrutinized me as if something still weren't quite right.

"You're too tense. The painting will appear unnatural. But I know what will help."

I shifted the cushion to where my leg met the chair arm and watched Lenoir open a cabinet filled with bottles of all shapes and sizes. He selected a wine bottle and a shorter squat thing of heavy green glass. I narrowed my eyes as he pulled a leaf-shaped flat spoon from a drawer.

"*Monsieur*, forgive me, but I don't care for absinthe."

I didn't actually know if I cared for it; I just knew that I didn't want any. I'd heard enough stories in Sangland, read enough penny-dreadfuls, and studied enough art history on Earth to know that Sang's combination of wormwood and laudanum would render me a useless, addicted zombie.

"My dear, this isn't the rot-gut they sell on the street. This is an herbal preparation by the esteemed Dr. Ordinaire. I take just the tiniest drop in my own blood-wine."

He added a dash of green liquid to a wineglass, placed the flat spoon over the rim, set a sugar cube on it, set the sugar on fire, and poured a full glass of red bloodwine over the blue-flaming sugar cube, causing most of it to melt away. After stirring the deep purple mixture, he poured half the liquid into another wineglass and brought it to me. I took it as if grasping a viper. I was suspicious, angry, and scared, but the dare in his eyes kept me from flinging the unwanted drink across the studio. Angering Lenoir could be the end of my stardom; one word from him, one breath that he'd rejected me, and the seats of Paradis would be empty, the paper full of lies surrounding my name. I would never be snatched up and delivered to Cherie, to save her from whatever hell held her. This man—this strange, dark, secretive man—held the keys to Mortmartre.

It also didn't escape me that girls disappeared all the time in Paris with no repercussions, no justice. I was better equipped to survive than most, but no one knew my weaknesses as well as a fellow Bludman. The bravado I'd shown Vale was no longer justified.

Lenoir clinked his glass against mine and sipped, his mouth curving up in a lazy, sensual smile that served as a dare. We both knew he was proving that it wasn't poison. We both knew I now had no choice but to taste it.

"To the Red Fairy," he said.

I held the glass to my nose and sniffed. It was a cacophony of smells good and bad: the sharpness of anise, the maple-syrupy sweetness of fennel, the bite of wormwood, the sour velvet of wine, and, most attractive, the warm, salty goodness of fresh blood. I wanted to taste it. And I hated myself for that.

Lenoir took another sip and raised his eyebrows. "You didn't strike me as the sort of woman easily frightened by rumors and a few bits of plant. Would I be drinking it myself if it were deleterious? Would I stand where I stand, hold the power I hold, if this drink was dangerous?" He sipped again, his Adam's apple bobbing. "Drink, Demi."

I touched my lips to the glass, let the plummy liquid wash against my mouth. The Red Fairy, he'd called it. Taste exploded over my tongue, and without another thought, I sipped it. What was the point of being nearly indestructible if you didn't enjoy the hell out of yourself every now and then?

After my second sip, he nodded slowly, his dark eyes smoldering like storm clouds at night. "That's better, *chérie*. Lean back. And hold still."

Taking his half-empty glass with him, he found his place behind the easel. After a brief pause, his brush began to move furiously, faster than seemed possible. The oily tang of paint filled the air. Moments later, the sun lit on my hair, warming me all over with the feel of crayons melting on a radiator. I took another sip and relaxed, my eyes caught on the glittering motes of dust dancing in the sunbeam. They looked like fairies, and if I squeezed my eyes shut and watched through my eyelashes, I could almost see their wings.

"Your head, *chérie*." He waved at the air, and I realized my cheek had fallen over completely.

I righted myself and felt the room spin sweetly, but something he'd said had caught my attention.

"Cherie," I murmured.

"Yes?"

Cherie sounded the same as *chérie*. I giggled. That wasn't the way to go about it.

"You paint lots of girls, don't you, *monsieur*?"

He peeked around the easel, brush moving furiously. "You know I do. Have you been to the Louvre yet?"

"No. But I've seen reproductions. When I was in Sangland."

"I'm sure one of your paramours will take you there soon. A reproduction misses the life, the subtlety, of the original."

"Have you ever painted a Bludman before?"

"Of course. A private client. Ahnastasia Feodor, the Tsarina herself. She's in Paris often so her mate can perform, you know. Such ostentation." He sighed and sipped his bloodwine. Or absinthe. Bloodsinthe? I giggled again.

"So most of your victims are daimons?"

He raised an eyebrow at me. "Of course. As this is the pleasure district of Mortmartre, most of my subjects are daimons. There's occasionally a human girl in the mix, but honestly, who could expect a mere human to keep up with the performance a daimon can provide? When you feed on joy or lust, you're always going to have more to give to your work." His eyes twinkled for just a moment. "To be quite honest, it's been so long since I've painted a girl with flesh-colored flesh that I know I'll have to mix and remix the colors, trying to capture all the subtleties. Blue and red are so much more straightforward."

Glancing down at his empty wineglass, he seemed surprised to see that he'd drunk it all. When I looked down at my own glass, barely a few deep-red drops remained, and it hung from my talons just a few bare inches from the plush carpet. I had completely forgotten I was holding it.

Talking to Lenoir was hypnotic, like having tunnel vision. When I was around him, he was all there was, a vacuum.

Wait.

I looked up. The afternoon sun had moved all the way across me and now painted me with dark shades of red, like a rash.

"*Monsieur*, it's late! Past time to go. I must perform soon."

He looked confused for the briefest moment, before placing his brush reverently on his table. "Is it? Time does have that tendency to fly." I rushed to the door, and he stopped me with a hand on my arm. "Your dress, *chérie*," he said gently, his voice low and husky. I realized for the first time that he'd taken off his gloves to paint me, and his hands were dark like mine, their nails white and sharp. I'd never been touched by the bare hands of a male Bludman, if you didn't count Criminy, and I shivered all over like a spooked horse.

All I could do was nod and rush back to the screen. I didn't look back at him as I changed into my layers, more glad than ever for the Sang cover of a corset and the safety of petticoats. The cats attacked my skirts and the laces of my boots but darted away when I tried to pet them, slicing at me with their claws. When I was mostly dressed, I looked for a mirror in which to arrange my hair, as fashionable ladies never walked the streets with their hair loose.

"Allow me."

He appeared behind me, his fingers nimble as they twirled my hair into a low chignon and pinned it swiftly into place. I wanted to bolt; I wanted to stay; I wanted to turn and kiss him and see if he tasted of absinthe and blood. Lenoir sent confusing signals through me, but I understood that my predator's blud respected the inherent danger in the famous painter and wished to flop on the floor and show him my belly as the lesser creature.

"Where did you learn to dress a lady's hair?"

He leaned down, his lips against my ear. "You're no lady."

I jerked away and spun to face him, mouth open to shout about who got to tell me what I was.

"You're a Bludman, Demi. You might forget it among the daimons, but at least here, in this room, under my brush, you can be exactly what you are." I closed my mouth. He smirked. "And it's not difficult. One night backstage at a cabaret could teach an idiot how to pin a chignon."

"So you've worked backstage?"

He stood at the door, waiting. "I didn't say that. *Au revoir, mademoiselle.*"

I hurried past him and down the stairs, a blush hot in my cheeks. Throwing open the door, I found the conveyance outside and Auguste sitting on the steps wearing a forlorn expression.

"I'm sorry, Auguste——"

He looked up and saw Lenoir standing in the doorway, a dark and silent form. Shaking his head mournfully, the daimon only said, "My pleasure, miss. Let me help you up. We must hurry."

"I'll see you tomorrow morning, *mademoiselle.*"

Lenoir stood in his door like a god atop a mountain. His dark eyes didn't blink, just stared at me, capturing me, searing me with an odd sort of ownership that my body wasn't fighting as hard as it should have.

"Yes, *monsieur*," was all I could say.

That night, I went to the pachyderm feeling optimistic and hungry, which was a great change from my usual nervousness. Although I'd had the two vials to which I was accustomed, not to mention whatever blood was in Lenoir's wine, I felt sapped and more tired than usual. A hot, willing victim would be more than welcome. As I hurried to the mirror to touch up my face and hair, I pondered what vintage I would have tonight. Rich, of course. But young or old? Shy or confident? I could taste the men's personalities in their blood, and it was fascinating.

I was powdering my nose behind the screen when the door opened.

"Are you ready, La Demitasse?" a man's voice called.

I emerged from the bedroom, one hand to my bosom and a confused look on my face. "*Monsieur?*"

I didn't recognize the slender gentleman waiting in top hat and coat by the door. A velvet cape hung over his arm, and his red beard glinted in the gaslight.

"Didn't they tell you? We're going out. Have you ever seen the pleasure gardens?"

"But *monsieur*, I thought . . . that is, I usually make a gentleman's acquaintance here . . ."

He waved that away with the enthusiasm of a young boy utterly unaccustomed to hearing the word *no*. "The Tuileries. The fruit trees are in flower and lit up. It's like a fairyland. We'll ride donkeys. Come along."

I glanced around the pachyderm, with its rich appointments and nods to sensuality. Could it be possible that a client had paid for the privilege of taking me out on a date in the most fun and fashionable garden in the world? I had to admit he looked pleasant enough, young and bright-eyed and dapper. And what was he going to do, anyway? I was almost invincible, and I was very nearly bigger than him, and Jack the Ripper was at work in London, not Paris.

I smiled and reached out for the cloak he waggled enticingly.

"I'd be delighted, Monsieur . . .?"

He laughed and wrapped the cloak around me. "Does my name really matter?"

I gave him the most genuine smile I'd worn all week. "I guess not."

Taking his hand, I let him pull me down the stairs, laughing all the way.

17

When they called the Tuileries the "pleasure gardens," they meant it.

In this peculiar parallel universe, they were more like Central Park than a palace, and what happened under the acres of leafy boughs was far from governmental. My date didn't give me his last name or the important title I'm sure he held, based on the cut of his clothes and the servant daimon who followed us at a respectful distance with a large bag of coins and a small crossbow. But he did give me a spectacular night that reaffirmed my reason for leaving Criminy's caravan in the first place. And with a saucy wink, he told me to call him Louis.

We saw ballerinas and operettas and parades and a puppet show almost as good as that of Charlie Dregs. Louis enjoyed flagon after flagon of beer and surprised me by purchasing a snow cone and pouring a vial of blood from his pocket over the grainy white hill of ice made by a clockwork machine. Considering that I hadn't had a popsicle in six years, it was quite a treat. We had carousel rides and donkey races and dancing, and I laughed so hard that I fell down on my ass—and not the donkey.

Paris was beautiful at night, and had I been there at

the right time with the right person, I would have understood why they called it the City of Love. The trees were in bloom, as Louis had promised, and strung with millions of twinkling lights like stars caught in nets of silk. As we promenaded down the Boulevard Mortmartre, the golden lights glowing on either side cast the cobblestones in indigo shadows, as if we might keep walking on and on forever and never reach the horizon. The crowds were jewel-bright and filled with joy, the daimons mixing among the humans and sighing happily as they sold balloons and toys and nosegays. The Tower was likewise strung with lights and rose over the city like a doting parent, calmly keeping watch yet always waiting for lightning to strike.

Louis was excellent company, in part because he wanted nothing more from me than a lovely evening. I suspected he was glad to spend time with someone who had no expectations and treated him like an equal, as everything about him pointed to royalty. I also guessed, judging by the way his eyes roved to gentlemen's backsides, that his interests lay in other domains. But I hadn't laughed so hard in years, and I almost forgot all my problems and ambitions, for a time. It was relaxing, being with someone who had no expectations of me, either.

Right up till I saw the blond girl, I had one of the greatest nights of my life. Even though I hadn't had a drop of bloodwine, I still felt half-drunk and free and easy, and I was leaning on Louis's shoulder and giggling over a gendarme's misbuttoned pants when a flash of light blond caught my attention. The girl passed under a gas lamp at a fast clip, trailing a cloak, and I knew instantly that it was Cherie.

"Excuse me, *monsieur*." I untangled my arm from Louis's

and bolted off the walk and across the green, my boot heels sinking into the soil. "Cherie!"

She didn't turn, and I didn't stop running. All around me, female heads shot up—of course, because *chérie* was the most common name men in Franchia used to address women they were sweet on. I twisted through the crowd, my breath short in the spring night, hoping I could catch her before she disappeared. I didn't know why she would run from me, but I was damned well going to find out.

Her heels clicked onto the cobbles as she ducked down an alley. A human or a daimon would have stopped, but not me. Bludrats scattered with Franchian disdain as she stopped at a narrow door, knocking frantically. But I was faster than whoever was inside, and with talons dug into her shoulder, I spun her around. She lurched back, banging her head against the door.

"Cherie?"

She was already sobbing. "Please, *mademoiselle*. Please let me go."

It wasn't Cherie; I knew that the second I saw her face. But she was the closest thing I'd seen to my friend, and the disappointment hit harder than a fist in the gut. This girl was a human, and a sickly one at that. I could smell her, but she evoked more pity than hunger, as if there wasn't enough of a meal to bother breaking the skin.

I let go of her shoulders and took a step back. The door opened, revealing an indigo-skinned daimon, her cheeks drawn and her hair braided back tightly. Behind her, colorful ribbons hung from hooks along with sausages and strips of meat. The scent of magic was just as heavy on the air as the copper tang of bloody meat.

"Zis is not ze place for you," she said with a heavy

Franchian accent, ushering in the human girl. The door slammed in my face. I looked up, curious about what the building was, if perhaps it was a beggar's house or a soup kitchen or a hospital, some place that took in pitiful, fleshless wretches. There was no sign, no daimon code like at the inn. I walked around to the front and found only a butcher shop, with lank pink meat hanging in the window and a pig's face staring at me, the eyes flat and bulging. The Parisians seemed to favor fanciful door knockers; this one was a cow's behind, the clapper a long, curled tail. Perhaps the girl was a servant here, a pig girl or some such. In any case, she wasn't my business; Cherie was. And that meant I had to get back to Louis and feed my way into his good graces, if need be. His pockets were surely full of secrets.

I hurried back toward the laughter and music of the Tuileries, which reminded me more than a little of Criminy's caravan—the way the light drew you forward and each new act within seemed more magical and colorful than the last. Perhaps the daimons used some of the same spells as my clever godfather. In any case, I felt at home here, more than I had since leaving my wagon.

As I entered the crowd, hand after hand landed on my arm. Whether they knew who I was or were simply drawn to a pretty girl without a man by her side, I didn't know. But I shrugged them off, one after the other, telling them with a fake smile to come to Paradis and see me. It was exhausting, or maybe I was just coming down from the elation and adrenaline of thinking I'd finally found Cherie. By the time I found Louis, deep in his cups by the donkeys, all I wanted was to drag him back to the pachyderm and drain him half dry for the contact high.

"You're the first woman who's run from my charms," he said with a slur. But he was smiling.

"I wasn't running from your charms, *cher*. I thought I saw an old friend and wanted to introduce you." I sat in the chair by his side, draping an arm over his shoulders, and he melted against me. I'd long ago struck his name from my mental spreadsheet of suspects. There wasn't an evil bone in his body.

"Shall we head back to the pachyderm, then? You must be exhausted. I don't know how you girls do it, putting on such an energetic show and then entertaining the lads until dawn."

I nodded, finally understanding completely why the halls were always empty when I returned from the elephant. I guess I'd already known—had been told repeatedly but hadn't really internalized—that the girls sold their bodies to the clients of Paradis. I hadn't fully explored the entire cabaret, but there had to be other apartments somewhere, places far more sumptuous than the tiny, threadbare rooms where they slept. Mel and Bea and the rest . . . they were prostitutes.

It didn't sit right with me. But again, it wasn't my business. I'd seen in Sangland that women were in every way less free than they were on Earth, but I hated to think that the beautiful, talented, kind girls I knew here had turned to bartering their bodies for their livelihood.

Louis stood, wobbling, and held out a hand. Arms around each other's shoulders, I half dragged him back to Paradis. I had to help him up the winding stairs and onto the plushy couch, where he collapsed in a lanky, boneless heap, wrapped in his wool coat like a very wealthy and elegant burrito.

"I've heard you don't do . . . what the other girls do." He blinked at me through glowing ginger eyelashes.

"Well, *monsieur*—" I pursed my lips, but he waved his arms to stop me.

"No, I'm saying that's why I chose you. I have . . . other tastes. But I've never met a Bludman before, and it's very rare that I find something to pique my interest. Is it true you drink from your paramours?"

I cocked my head at him. What a peculiar man. "It's true."

"I'm told it feels rather pleasant. That some men find independent release in your arms."

"That is also true."

"Then will you drink from me? I'll probably make you drunk, at this rate. But I like new experiences."

And so, taking him in my arms, I gently tipped back his head and pierced the tender skin of his neck.

I couldn't help grinning. I had studied history along with art, and after an evening on his arm, I knew what I was doing.

I was feeding on the future king of Franchia.

It was a pleasure to root around the rich fabrics of his costume, looking for clues that I knew weren't there. All I found were bits of horrible poetry, licorice pastilles, a tight roll of silvers, and some mustache wax in an adorable tin. Louis looked so sweet, innocently sucking his thumb in untroubled sleep. But I left him there as I left all of them, hurrying through the courtyard and back to my room. I didn't stop at the door to Paradis to listen for footsteps; either they were elsewhere doing their work or asleep, exhausted, in their beds. And I didn't see Vale, either.

As I brushed out my hair and prepared for bed, all I could think about was how much easier life would have been if I'd never left the caravan. Safe under Criminy's wing, I'd resented the endless, marching army of dull nights and duller days. But now, on an adventure and facing challenges that definitely seemed insurmountable, I missed knowing exactly where I stood. My heart was buffeted on all sides by feelings I didn't want to have. One minute, I was dragged down by sorrow and loss and hopelessness over Cherie. Moments later, I was buoyed by determination and confidence regarding my career and talent. And then my skin and belly swirled with confusion and lust whenever Vale came near, as if my brain completely shut off. And just now, I was overcome by an odd, floaty, tipsy sensation that made me dream of dancing.

I didn't feel like myself. But I didn't know who I was anymore, either.

Besides the future king's wine-drenched blood, what had gotten into me?

The next morning, I arrived on Lenoir's doorstep a few moments too late, late enough that he gave me a cold, disapproving stare.

"Cavorting with princes is no excuse."

Instead of answering him, I stared him down. I didn't owe him anything, and if he thought I did, he'd spent too much time around weak-willed humans and emotionally dependent daimons. He snorted and jerked his chin toward the stairs. With grace and without hurrying, I walked the stairs to the attic studio and went directly to the screen to change. When I emerged, a glass of blood-wine with the strange, plum-sparkly hint of absinthe sat beside my chair, and Lenoir stood behind his easel. The cats appraised me coldly from their chaise, their green eyes the color of Limone's skin.

"*Monsieur*, I told you, I don't care for absinthe."

He chuckled, a dark and humorless sound that made my eyes stray to his lips. "Your empty glass from yesterday says differently. Whether or not you care for it, you enjoyed it. Now, sit. Drink. I have work to do, and I need your limbs to be pliant."

I took a step toward his easel, curious about what his furious brushstrokes had accomplished yesterday. A paint-stained cloth hung over the canvas, blocking my view entirely.

He shook his head and *tsk*ed at me. "No one sees my paintings until they are complete."

"Not even a peek?"

"Don't even try."

With a melodramatic sigh, I flopped into the chair and tried to find my pose. As I adjusted the pillow under my leg, I watched him through my bangs. He whipped off the cloth, his eyes shining with love and fervor as he looked at his work. Damn, but the man was sexy, and without really trying. Every heterosexual gentleman I'd met in Sang had fawned over me like an overanxious puppy, but Lenoir treated me as if *I* was the poorly trained dog. The suave elegance of his every movement, the sharp cut of his mustache and beard, the perfectly tousled and European way his hair was swept back, just the tiniest bit overlong—this must be how my mom had felt about Sean Connery. When I was around him, I felt his pull like gravity.

"Drink, Demi."

The glass was to my lips before I realized I'd picked it up. The liquid washed over my tongue like a symphony, welcome and nourishing and dizzying all at once. I drank half the goblet before setting it down and settling into my pose. As the liquor spread, I could feel my heartbeat slowing, my limbs lengthening, and my spine going soft and loose as I all but melted into the chair. Squinting my eyes, I looked again for the sunbeam fairies. They danced in time with Lenoir's brush, and time fell away into ribbons of gold.

I didn't show up for rehearsal—and why should I have? I'd never made a mistake, never taken a single misstep or botched my cue. What I was doing here, with the country's most influential painter and tastemaker, was far more important. I sat for Lenoir until evening, somehow ended up in the conveyance back to Paradis, albeit upside down, and went straight to Mel and Bea's room for makeup. Auguste avoided my eyes and didn't say a word. I had barely arrived in time for the show.

"What is he like?" Mel asked, as she attached extra-long eyelashes to my half-mast lids with tiny dabs of glue.

Bea signed something, and after several days in her company, I didn't need a translation.

"He scares you, Bea? Why?"

In response, she just shivered and shook her head, her skin quivering into a milky ice-blue, like the heart of a glacier. She didn't know. Or she wouldn't say.

"Hmm." I blinked my eyes, focusing on the flutter of false lashes made of bits of feather. "What's Lenoir like?

Austere. A little scary. Stern. But a genius, so you put up with it."

Mel held my chin firmly as she lined my lips. "How's the painting coming along?"

I shrugged. "I have no idea. He keeps it covered. Won't let me see it until it's done. He says he always does a grand unveiling at the Louvre, a big party. I'll see it then, when everyone else does."

Mel sighed with longing. "Painted by Lenoir. Every cabaret girl's dream. He started one of Limone, you know, but she made him so mad he never finished it. That's why she never really became a star, they say. Always on ze edge but never quite arrived."

I tucked that bit away for later: so it was possible to anger Lenoir to the point of no return. Every day, I felt as if I'd come close to trespassing on his last nerve. But I also left his studio feeling as if I'd been manipulated, treated like a thing instead of a person. And yet I wanted to go back and didn't want to lose his approval. I needed to know exactly where the boundary between spirited and destroyed might lie.

Mel ducked her head close to mine to whisper in my ear. "Does he give you absinthe?"

I felt cagey answering, and I felt even worse for lying. "I told him I don't care for it."

"They say he's an addict, that his genius is fueled by the Green Fairy."

"Such is the price of greatness, I suppose."

Bea shook her head and signed. "'Not worth it,'" Mel translated for me.

"Just be careful, yes?" Mel squeezed my arm briefly. "Paris is dangerous, outside of Paradis."

I squeezed her back. "Is it dangerous . . . *inside* Paradis?" My eyes flitted to the bed.

She looked at me, and I looked at her, and she dropped her head, blushing dark green. "Oh, la. Not like you think. It's different for daimons. You do what you must to feed, and so do we. There's no shame in it. There's no real danger. It's an exchange of spirit, of emotion, of hunger for satiety."

"Then why are you blushing?"

She looked up, caught my eyes in an angry glare. "Because you're making me feel like there is something to be ashamed of."

It was my turn to look down and blush. "You're right. I'm sorry. I don't know much about daimons. But I'm willing to learn."

Bea patted my hand and signed.

"'There is much to fear, much darkness,'" Mel translated slowly. "'Especially outside the cabaret.'"

"I'm being careful," I said, and the look they gave me was one of pity.

"You can never be careful enough," Mel said.

That night's gentleman caller arrived in the copper pachyderm with a bouquet of flowers that smelled like death. Unsurprisingly, he was another shy but domineering old man. I flirted with him for an appropriate amount of time, sat in his lap, wiggled a little, and drank enough blood for us both to feel satisfied. I left him there on the couch with a stain on his breeches, hoping he wouldn't have a heart attack and die. With the absinthe still echoing in my blood, I skipped downstairs and across the courtyard. But considering that I wasn't sleepy at all and it was relatively early, I decided that it was high time I explored more of my gilded cage.

There was a brick hallway, then the backstage of the theater, and then another brick hallway mirrored on the other side. Aside from Blue's costume room, Madame Sylvie's room, and the secret tunnel Bea had shown me, I didn't know what might lie behind any of the other doors along either passage. I felt a little giddy, a little wicked, as I slipped off my red boots and tiptoed down the wooden boards to discover the secrets of Paradis.

The first door I opened was filled floor-to-ceiling with dusty, broken things. Bits of stage, old doors, steamer trunks, sand bags, and coils of rough rope piled so high that I couldn't even step inside. Seeing that the dust lay undisturbed, I closed the door gently.

Boring.

The next room was locked, but I'd been under Criminy's tutelage for long enough to know how to pop a lock with a hairpin. I had the door open in moments and pressed the light switch, burning with curiosity. Barrels of spirits, wooden boxes filled with wine bottles, and racks and racks of glasses were pushed neatly against the walls, a few tables and chairs stacked in a corner. My eye was drawn to a wooden crate that held vibrant oranges, a rare sight in Sang. A narrow door in the far wall surely connected to the bar. If I'd been a normal girl with a taste for liquor, it would have been heaven. But considering that I only liked my wine mixed with the finest blood, I relocked the door and slipped back out into the hallway.

Backstage was a little creepy when dark, with ropes and curtains swaying in a nonexistent breeze and unidentified lumps throwing shadows on the ground. I hurried across to the other hallway and past Blue's door, running a hand along the niche where Vale had once kissed me. The bricks there were a slightly different shade from the rest, and I was curious about what had been there and why someone had sealed it off. So many mysteries abounded in Paris, even in places that seemed safe. The next door opened silently, and I stepped into a high-ceilinged practice room I'd never seen before, mainly because, again, I didn't really need practice.

The floor was polished and waxed and warm as sunshine, and one wall was all shiny mirrors and a barre. Costumes on racks took up another wall. But what really delighted me were the circus props that we'd never had at the caravan. A Spanish web rope, a trapeze, silks, and a practice hoop hung from the ceiling on adjustable pulleys, while a giant wooden ball and balance boards rested in a corner. Charmed and curious, I went to the wall and let the trapeze down to a height I could reach from the floor. I'd never done aerial work until the moment I'd stepped onto Limone's hoop, and I'd always wanted to try the trapeze. Flying would have been better, but this would do.

I double-checked my knot and pulled on the trap, making sure it was secure. Not so much because I was scared of falling, obviously, but more because I didn't want to make a big, embarrassing noise and get in trouble. I kicked my legs over the bar and hung upside down for a brief moment before shimmying upright to sit. Checking my form in the mirror, I pointed my toes and smiled at myself. As a little kid, I'd threatened again and again that if I didn't get my way, I would run away and join the circus. And now I had, twice.

A shadow filled the doorway, and I almost fell over backward.

"*Bonsoir*, songbird."

Vale leaned against the doorway, all too pleased with himself.

"You really like scaring the shit out of me, don't you?"

His grin widened. "Very much, *bébé*."

"And why are you skulking around Paradis late at night?"

"One might ask you the same question."

He walked to me slowly, his boots somehow silent on the boards. He wore the tight, striped trousers and paisley waistcoat that all the dandies under a certain age wore, but the addition of his gypsy shirt and brigand's honed physique only served to highlight his wildness rather than indicate the usual cultured aloofness. The Parisian gents also favored wild, long, foppish hair and purposefully messy ponytails, as if every one of them was trying out for the part of the Rosetti that hadn't yet been discovered in Sang. But Vale's shorn head and rough beard only made his golden-green eyes shine brighter. My fingers tightened on the ropes of the trapeze as he wrapped his hands around the bar on either side of my hips, just beyond the black ruffles of my skirt.

"Can't blame a girl for being curious."

"Oh, I never would blame anyone for that."

"The door was open."

"Of course it was."

With every volley, his hands drifted closer to my body, and my breathing sped up in response. With the height of the trapeze, his eyes were level with my cleavage. He took one step closer, and my knees pressed against his chest.

I couldn't even think of where my feet pressed, farther down.

He looked up at me, humor in his eyes. "But really, *bébé*. Why are you here?"

I swung my hips back and forth, taking the trap with me. "Maybe I felt the need to explore a little."

His hand found my ankle and traced up the back of my leg, running one finger seductively up and down my stockinged calf.

"Exploration, eh? That's an excellent preoccupation." His eyes met mine, and even though they were as light as a summer meadow, they held all the promise of a shadowy bedroom draped in velvet. "I like exploring. I could help you with that, you know."

His hand settled on my thigh, and I squeezed my legs tightly together at the rush of warmth he caused.

"But you're going to have to loosen up first, oui?"

18

I smirked and perked up in mock indignation. "I may work in a cabaret, but I'm not a loose woman, *monsieur*."

"But in your profession, surely you must remain limber. Lithe. Flexible."

"Flexibility is just one of my many talents."

"I'd like to see more of your talents, *bébé*. Maybe I could teach you a few things myself."

"You're so very altruistic."

"I don't know that word, but I'm guessing it's similar to sexy."

He reached for my face, and I leaned down to meet him, his lips pressing gently to mine, almost nibbling. Heat shot through my body, and it took effort to stay on the trapeze. But something was off. I pulled away and licked my lips.

"Wine. You taste of wine."

"I must test the vintage before I can sell the wine properly, *bébé*. Part of the job, being a brigand."

I looked closer. His eyes were slightly red, which was making them glow an otherworldly green.

"Are you drunk, Vale?"

He grinned, hands back on the trapeze on either side of my hips.

"*Peut-être.*"

With a whoop, he pulled the trapeze back and ran, pushing me high into the air and swinging with me, dangling from the bar. He couldn't go far, as the wall was near and I'd adjusted the ropes to keep it close to the ground, but I still felt the sensation of flying. I took advantage of the mirror to watch the fine lines of his back and the way the trousers hugged his butt. A red-striped handkerchief fluttered from his back pocket. When he hit the wall, he kicked off it and swung back, tucking up his knees so the trapeze could swing in the other direction.

I tried to hide my childlike glee at flying through the air on a trapeze with a seriously hot guy dangling just underneath me, his buzzed hair tickling my ankles through the stockings.

"Yep, you're drunk."

"Just a little. Just enough."

"Just enough for what? Wailing and waking up the entire cabaret?"

He let his feet down, dragging his boots to bring the trap to a stop. I held on tightly and recomposed my legs, crossing them demurely at the ankles. With more agility than a drunk man had any right to possess, he swung up and turned in the air, landing on his feet, facing me again.

"Just enough to come to you when I don't have any information, any tips, any trinkets, any advice. To come to you with nothing but myself."

"Vale, you don't have to—"

I tried to slide off the trapeze, but he pinned me there and stepped close, spreading my knees to stand pressed against me. His arms wrapped around my waist as he ran his nose up the buttons of my jacket and planted a kiss in the V of my cleavage. I couldn't breathe and suddenly felt as if I was upside down, as if everything had gone topsy-turvy.

"No, I don't have to. I want to. And if it took half a cask of the best wine in Paris, so be it. *Bébé*, I'm not just your errand boy. I want more."

Maybe it was the absinthe still bubbling in my blood, or maybe I was just sick of being an object of lust who never gave in to her own passions. Hell, maybe I felt the same way, not that I was about to admit it. But I bent my head and pressed my lips against the gold rings set in the curve of his ear.

"More what?" I let my breath play over his scalp. "Eh, *bébé*?"

He drew a deep breath and buried his face between my breasts. I gasped, caught entirely by surprise. The hot, wet touch of his tongue would have sent me flipping over backward had his strong arms not held me firmly down.

It was insane, the way he devoured me with lips and teeth, and all I could do was hold on for dear life, feeling as if I was floating a million miles over the ground.

"Ouch!"

His teeth had nipped too hard, and I drew back with a hiss.

"What the hell?"

Vale's lips didn't budge, and I realized exactly what he was doing. Bludmen tended to smell and taste of hot pennies and old meat to humans and, I suppose, half-human, half-Abyssinian brigands. But once someone had ingested a certain Bludman's blud, even one drop, that changed completely for them both. If what I knew of Crim and Tish applied, I would now smell delicious to him, and were he human, I wouldn't be rabid for his blood. He had always smelled strange to me before, but I suspected the hunger I felt for his body, mouth, and mind wouldn't lessen a bit.

He sighed and pulled me closer. "Oh, *dieu*. Now you're like butterscotch. *Mignon*, I could eat you alive."

Arm by arm, I slipped off my jacket, revealing the snowy chemise underneath. He ran his tongue along the edge of the deep neckline until he found my nipple, held high and trapped by the built-in cups of the lingerie. Other girls in my position wouldn't be able to breathe, thanks to their corsets. But with the barely-boned stays Blue had crafted to enhance my shape but allow me to contort, I could feel the press of his hands at my waist, and the way his fingers grasped tighter told me he found it just as hot as I did.

I let my head fall back and held on for dear life as he pulled my nipple into his mouth. The sensation was so deeply sensual that I wrapped my legs around him just to keep him there. With his arms holding me in place, he couldn't use his hands, but there was a primal hunger in the way he licked and sucked his way across my skin, eager to find the other nipple and bring my breast to float above the chemise, the nipple peaked and eager for his mouth.

"Let me down. I can't . . . I can't do anything."

I wanted to touch him, to run my hands over the rasp of his head and cheek, the smooth line of his throat. I wanted to trace fingers along his hipbones and cup his ass and trace the firm ridge pressing against my legs. But I couldn't let go of the ropes.

"No, *bébé*. I like you where you are. And I can make it

worth your while." He let go of my waist and wrapped his fingers hotly, briefly, around mine, around the ropes. "Remember to hold on, yes?"

"Vale . . ."

His hands were already on my thighs, pressing them gently apart and pushing the layers of ruffled skirts and petticoats back over my hips. I sucked in a breath, knowing what he was doing, half mortified and half aching and fully expectant. His fingers danced up the insides of my legs, drawing lines up the ribbon ties of my stockings. Flat palms spread over the brief, lacy bloomers.

"That's different," he murmured, curling a finger under the hem, up and down.

As if his touch had been a question, I spread my legs wide to give him better access. He murmured appreciatively and let his finger rove deeper, just under the lacy edge. I quivered and closed my eyes as his fingertip slipped all the way under, stroking me softly. When I moaned, he set his mouth to my breast and murmured, "So wet," with his lips wrapped hotly around my nipple.

His fingers curled possessively over my knees, holding them apart as he nibbled along my inner thigh, slipping his tongue under my bloomers. He could just barely reach the core of me, and he teased me like that, barely licking, barely tasting, until I whimpered and bucked against his hands.

"Dance for me, *bébé*," he murmured. One hand stroked down my thigh and gently moved the bloomers aside to give him full access. I felt the caress of a breeze before I felt his mouth, and it nearly undid me.

He alternated light, breathy, teasing caresses with more aggressive tastes, and it was all I could do to hold on and not scream. I was molten inside, a pool of lava and hunger and need, and I hadn't been touched this way ever, not even on Earth, with passion and confidence and pure, unselfish finesse. The combination of the taut trapeze and the possibility of getting caught and my pent-up need and his perfectly timed licks were too much, and I shuddered and flew apart, my fingers twitching around the ropes as he kept licking in perfect rhythm, sustaining *la petite mort* for longer than seemed possible.

"Come down, *bébé*. Let me catch you."

Barely thinking, barely capable of thought, I let go of the ropes and fell backward into his arms, still shuddering.

"You put on quite a show, Vale Hildebrand," I murmured.

"Hope you like encores, *bébé*. The night is still young. And I'm not done with you yet."

I was loose and boneless in his arms, and he turned toward the corner, where mats and curtains were puddled behind a barricade of boxes. A smile curled over his lips.

"That will do, yes?"

Before he could take a single step, motion caught my eye. A blue blur slipped into the room, making me gasp and lean against his chest. Vale spun around, muscles tense.

"Bea? What's wrong?"

The blue daimon zipped past us, blocking the corner where Vale had planned on ravishing me and where I'd planned on letting him. She couldn't speak, of course, but she shook her head at us and navigated around the boxes. When she motioned me over with anxious eyes, Vale set me gently on my feet, and I wobbled over to investigate. Bea pointed down, showing me where Blaise lay under a faded burgundy curtain, his blue cheeks tinted violet with sleep.

"Oh." I was mortified that he'd been there all along and extremely grateful that the lights and our banter and my moaning hadn't woken him. "I'm sorry, Bea. I didn't know."

She shook her head and smiled, then pointed at the door, then at Blaise, then put her finger to her lips.

"I won't tell." Bea raised her eyebrows at Vale. "*We* won't tell." She exhaled in relief and hugged me. "Wait. Are you in trouble? Is someone . . ." I wasn't quite sure how to ask the questions I wanted to ask. Was someone trying to hurt the boy? Or was she trying to protect him from knowledge of her nighttime business? How could a young boy grow up in a cabaret and not know what his mother and the other daimons did to earn their place?

Her eyes shot to the door, then back to Blaise. Her hands flew up briefly before clenching into fists. She shook her head sadly. She pointed at me, then Vale, then Blaise, then raised a hopeful finger to her lips.

"No worries, honey. We're leaving. We won't bother him again, now that we know he's here at night."

For just a second, her eyes went impish, her eyebrows shooting up. Her message was clear. She knew exactly what we'd been doing. I blushed, and she smiled sweetly and patted my arm. She gave the sign for *Thank you*, hugged me again, and slipped around the boxes to pick up the limp boy. Cradling him against her chest, she slipped back out the door as quickly as she'd come in.

Vale and I watched her go with matching frowns and crossed arms.

"I wonder why Bea is so scared," he finally said.

"I'm going to find out tomorrow."

He chuckled. "Good luck, *bébé*. Even for a mute, Bea is locked up tighter than a Kraken's arsehole."

I swatted his arm, then clutched it. "You won't tell, right?"

He patted me, just as Bea had. As if I was a child. "I'm a professional brigand, *bébé*. Keeping secrets is what I do best."

I raised my eyebrows at him and stared hard at his mouth. "Maybe second best," was all I said.

Falling asleep at Paradis was never easy. The high of performing, the dizzy fizz of the absinthe, my worries about Cherie, my mixed feelings about Vale and Lenoir, the secretive whispers and bare feet of the daimons returning from their assignations: no matter how long I stared at the patterned ceiling of my room, things never coalesced into a complete picture. It was like being too close to a Monet painting, and I couldn't step back to see what all the smeary dots meant.

Tonight, at least, my body was exhausted and sated and deliciously boneless. Part of me was utterly shocked at what had happened on the trapeze. Most of me felt a grand sense of relief. Being around sex and lust day after day was pretty boring when you weren't feeling it yourself, but this was different. Unlike the men in the audience, Vale liked me for more than my body. And yes, I knew I had a crush on him. Back in Criminy's caravan, I'd dreamed of a man—not a boy but a man who was dangerous but safe, funny but effective, strong but willing to support me instead of caging me. To think that I'd found all these qualities in an entirely hot man I didn't want to eat? Unbelievable. And after tonight, I had to hope he felt the same way. Surely a man didn't do that to a woman on a trapeze without caring about her?

The fact that he'd willingly ingested my blud also spoke volumes. Other than Maestro Casper Sterling's time in the caravan, when it'd been a bit of a joke how willing he was to trade blud for temporary freedom, I'd never known a non-Bludman besides Tish who was willing to risk the trade. Could Abyssinians even be pushed toward madness by blud? Veruca the sword swallower was the only other Abyssinian I'd known, and she'd mostly kept to herself.

For the millionth time since waking up in Sang, I wished for a laptop and a fast Internet connection. It was painful, not being able to access information immediately in a private manner. I wanted to know more about Paris, about Paradis, about Lenoir, and mostly about Vale. I chuckled at the ceiling, picturing what a wild brigand's Facebook page would look like. And then I thought about how in another world, there would be fewer places where my best friend could be hidden. Technology made things more transparent, but magic only obscured things further.

I dreamed of dancing in a grand ballroom, a huge, bell-shaped dress swirling around me. But I couldn't see the dark figure who held me in the cage of his arms.

After sleeping in and enjoying a good scrubbing at my ewer the next morning, I sauntered into the theater to find an enormous chandelier hovering a few feet off the ground.

"I kind of thought you guys were joking about this."

Charline tapped her pen against her notebook, which was her polite way of showing annoyance, now that I was a star. Just a few hours ago, as I'd drunk my blood and smiled at an innocent and still-sleepy Blaise, they'd delivered my finished poster to my room. It was like the gorgeous love child of Mucha and Lautrec, with "La Demitasse" emblazoned across the top on a banner and an overly stylized version of me doing the can-can with impossibly bent legs and, of course, the dreaded cup on my hat.

It was possibly the only thing more ridiculous than the giant chandelier, which had been cleverly fashioned to include plenty of places for me to sit, swing, dangle, and contort. And Charline had already handed me a sheet of paper covered in her tiny, perfect script, outlining exactly what I was expected to do. I folded it up and tucked it into my corset.

"Can I go now?"

Her face screwed up, and she went red all over. "Of course you cannot go! We have a new show to rehearse! The entire theater is sold out, including the boxes. This poster is being pasted on every wall in the city. They say princes from all over the world will be flying in on their private dirigibles. We're planning a masked ball. You must be perfect."

"I'm always perfect. And Lenoir is expecting me."

She rolled her eyes. "Lenoir can wait. Now, on the chandelier and into position."

I glared at her and lifted my lip to show a fang.

"If you please, Mademoiselle Demitasse," she added, although it pained her.

I stared longingly at the door, where Auguste waited, hat in hand. All too easily, I could imagine Lenoir waiting in his attic, mixing his paints, pouring our absinthe, watching the sunlight move across my empty chair while his cats stared disdainfully at the door. My own distress bothered me more than his anger. He couldn't ruin me now, even if he didn't finish the painting. But I wanted him to finish it, wanted to spend those swooning, magical, timeless hours under the spell of his brush and the dark scrutiny of his cloudy eyes. Whether it was the fellow feeling of the only other Bludman in the city or the pull of a knowing and charismatic older man, I felt the distance between us like a slender string pulling me from afar.

"*S'il vous plaît*, Demitasse." Charline waited, arm out invitingly, skin the warning red of a stop sign. "I'll call out your marks."

I sighed. "Of course. But only once through. And then I must go to Lenoir."

"Of course," she answered with a cold smile. "But first, you earn it."

When I finally reached Lenoir's doorstep, I knocked with trepidation, hoping the bruises on my arms and legs would fade before the master could paint them. Practice had taken longer than I'd hoped, and my anxiousness to finish had meant that I'd made foolish mistakes. New equipment always meant new sore spots, and Lenoir's low-necked gown would show dark blooms that most Sangish clothes covered up. I didn't want him to see me any less than perfect.

After a few moments of silence, I knocked again, but

still he didn't come. I stepped back and looked up, but the windows were all covered with gauzy curtains, blocking my view. One of the curtains quivered, and a Siamese cat's face appeared, glaring at me like the judgment of God. With a grunt of frustration, I dropped the knocker and pounded on the door with my bare fist.

No footsteps in the hall. No open door.

I wiped away a blud-tinged tear and let Auguste help me back into the conveyance, where I flopped in a heap of dejection and loss that seemed utterly useless and stupid even as I was crushed under it. It was like having vampire PMS.

That night, after the performance, I drank so hungrily from my suitor that I was afraid he might stop breathing. Clumsily plundering his sleeping body, I accidentally popped off one of the buttons on his pants and wasn't sure if I'd put all his effects back where I'd found them. I ended up just stuffing all his papers down the front of his vest and getting drunk on the subpar bloodwine he'd brought as I kept vigil by his unconscious body. I didn't leave until he murmured in his sleep and reached for me. Exhausted, bruised, and frustrated, I crawled around the screen to the bed in the elephant's belly and pulled the thick covers over my head. I fell asleep there to the tune of his snores, feeling utterly lost and a million miles from home and still hungry.

The next morning, I found a fang on my pillow. There was no note.

19

There was no hangover like a bloodwine hangover. Well, unless you included the way I had felt when I woke up in Sang after nearly dying of alcohol poisoning on Earth. Being simultaneously hungry and nauseated was even worse when the only thing you could ingest was blood. I dragged myself back to my own bed before dawn, puking sour blood in an urn on the way. When Blaise appeared with my teacup a few grueling hours later, I grabbed at the cup as if I might die without it. Blaise stared at me with pity and disgust as I licked at the dry red droplets that had fallen on the handle.

"Are you well, *mademoiselle*?"

I looked closer at Blaise. I'd taken him for granted, which I often did with children, as I felt myself too young to have them and too old to consider them people. Blaise was young but seemed like an old soul; he was probably seven or so. I'd seen him running errands or crouching quietly in every corner of Paradis but never in the elephant. He was a lighter shade of blue than Bea, almost like an ink wash instead of a solid hue. And I'd never seen him change color. His hair was black and unruly, his eyes yellow, with horizontal black pupils.

He was very strange but very beautiful, as most daimons were.

Before he noticed me staring, I cleared my throat and smiled at him, relatively sure the blood wouldn't come back up.

"I'm okay, Blaise. How are you?"

He shrugged with that careless grace of young boys, suggesting that it was ridiculous even to contemplate how one might or might not be, most likely because one was too young to have a raging headache, a roiling gut, and a guilty conscience from almost murdering a randy old dude the night before. I didn't really know how to talk to the kid, but I wanted and needed to know more about him.

Which gave me an idea.

"Blaise, is it hard to learn sign language?"

"I do not know, *mademoiselle*. What is it?"

"Talking with your hands. So I could understand Bea."

His shoulders rose up to his ears. "I do not know, *mademoiselle*. I have always known how to do it."

"Could you teach me a little every morning? Maybe just a couple of words?"

He glanced quickly at the door and fidgeted.

"How about one word?"

"Perhaps. Which word do you want?"

I thought a second, dragging my pinky around the dregs of the cup to capture every drop. Blaise danced from foot to foot, anxious to be gone and about his business again.

"What's the word for *scared*?"

He showed me, his hands hovering over his torso as if electricity and fear were shooting through his body. No problem remembering that one.

"Is that all, *mademoiselle*?"

I smiled and signed *Thank you*, and he nodded and ran off.

I needed a better teacher. Or better yet, a book. If Mel, Bea, and Blaise didn't know that I understood their personal language, I might pick up on something that was assumed to be private. There was something important and silent going on in Paradis, and I wanted to know what it was.

"So can you get it?" I tugged at my gloves, cheeks hot under Vale's cool glare.

"Depends. You got money, *bébé*?"

Vale was acting more distant and Franchian than usual, blocking my way to the conveyance outside and my much-anticipated date with Lenoir. Surely the peculiar painter would let me in today? If Vale would get out of the way and do as I asked in time for me to beat the golden morning sunlight to Lenoir's attic, I would at least have a chance.

I rolled my eyes and edged toward the door.

"Of course I don't have money. They haven't paid me yet."

"Then I can't get you a book, *bébé*. They're expensive. But we could barter."

His eyes slid sideways, and I had the distinct impression that he was punishing me for falling asleep in the elephant and missing his delivery last night. Stuck-up bastard probably thought I'd actually enjoyed the wrinkly old guy who'd paid for the privilege of feeling my teeth and nearly died for it. But that was my business. If Vale wanted to court me properly, or even say something kind,

I would soften. But if he wanted to be nasty, I could play that game, too.

"Fine. What do you want, brigand?"

A slow, dark smile spread across his face, showing straight white teeth. And in that moment, I knew exactly what he wanted. But he *tsk*ed and shook a finger at me.

"It's not me we're talking about. It's what I can sell to get what *you* want. And the most expensive thing you have is under your skin. Blud is worth more than gold."

I almost told him to fuck off, but then I thought about it. "More than gold? Seriously?"

"You are the only Bludman in Mortmartre. One of only a handful in Paris and a few dozen in Franchia. And as you've seen, the rich men of Paris will pay anything to taste something new, exotic, and rare."

I'd always hated needles. Even though I knew there were no germs in Sang, I'd seen the unkempt and rusty tools in every chirurgeon's black bag. There was simply something dirty about the process of selling a piece of myself, not to mention the thought of part of my body being used, enjoyed, outside of my knowledge. And I knew well enough, thanks to Criminy's warnings, what happened to humans who drank too much and became addicted. It was an ugly life and a slippery slope that was too steep to ever climb out of for all but the most wealthy and determined halfbluds.

So that basically made me the Sang equivalent of a meth cooker.

Was I willing to sell myself to save Cherie?

Hell, yes, I was.

If the rich old bastards accepted the consequences, that was their problem.

"How does it work?"

He shrugged and leaned back. "I know someone. Will you be working late again tonight, or . . .?"

I sighed and sidled closer to the door. "Or will I meet you outside the giant copper elephant and crawl through the catacombs to see your shady friend who'll remove my blud and pay me for it so you can buy me a book? Yeah, it's a date. Now, move it."

With a disgustingly handsome grin and a chuckle, he moved aside and opened the door for me. I couldn't help flouncing out and bouncing through the carriage door.

"See you tonight, *bébé*."

I waved a dismissive hand at him as I settled onto the seat.

"And wear something dark, would you? Try not to look like a courtesan."

If Auguste hadn't slammed the conveyance door, I would have leaped out to slap Vale for that. Instead, we were rumbling down the road before I could get to him.

I suddenly understood why he was acting so cold: I'd never told him I was only feeding on my midnight visitors. He thought I was prostituting myself. I'd set him straight tonight.

For now, I had Lenoir. And peace.

If the great artist had again refused to answer the door, I probably would have sat on the step and wailed like a hungry stray cat. As it was, it swung open on the second knock to reveal a glare that rivaled the one my dad gave me the first time I came home drunk after curfew in high school.

"You appear to have forgotten a day, my dear."

"It wasn't my fault—"

His lip twitched up in disgust. "It never is. You disappoint me, Demi."

I cocked a hip and stared at him. "I'm a muse, not a slave. You're too used to weak-willed daimons. Should I go?"

It killed me—killed me—to say it. I wanted so badly to be back upstairs in the sunlight that always seemed to shine there, even on days as dreary as this one. I wanted to watch the fairies and feel his eyes pry me open like a ripe peach. But the diva in me was already raising her red-painted lip to show fangs. Even the great Lenoir didn't get to speak to me as if I was a child.

With a long, unblinking, measuring stare, he drifted back to reveal the stairway. I brushed past him, still flouncing, and took the steps at a pace that belied my anxiousness. He followed sedately, silently. He didn't speak again until I was behind the screen, all but purring as the dress slithered over my skin.

"I waited, you know. All morning. There was an emptiness."

"I wasn't having fun, either," I snapped.

"You'll sit an extra hour today."

"You're not my father."

A gloved hand clutched my wrist, hard, leading me to the chair waiting in a sunbeam. Lenoir leaned close enough for me to smell the sharp stab of violets and anise and paint oil that clung to him. His lips brushed my ear, and the breath caught in my throat as if someone had pulled the strings of a corset too tight.

"I never meant to be," he whispered.

I sank into the chair, his other hand firm on my shoulder, pushing me into place. He arranged me gently but with purpose, as if I were a doll without feelings that he could easily choose to break. Did I imagine a caress as he pulled the pins from my hair and arranged the curls on my shoulders? I had to pull my lips back down over my fangs, stop trying to catch his scent. Like his absinthe, Lenoir was mysterious, heady, overpowering, and impossible to resist. The glass was in my hand moments later, and this time, I was sure I felt his fingers linger on mine, curling around the globe of sparkling liquid. One finger under my chin raised my face to his.

"Don't displease me, *chérie*."

I shook my head no, just a little.

"Good."

As he walked to the easel, I couldn't help admiring the austere but fashionable cut of his suit and the silent strength in his every movement. His eyes met mine as he slipped on his smock and whipped the cloth off his canvas. He seemed to embody what a Bludman should be, so very controlled and dangerous and beautiful. He must have caught me watching, for his mouth curled up in that rare, rare smile.

"Don't look at me, Demi. Drink. Look at the fairies."

The cup was to my lips before I willed it. For a moment, I fought the urge to taste it, knowing that I shouldn't give in so easily. But that silly instinct disappeared once my tongue darted out to test the swirling sweetness. I took a long drink of the absinthe-laced bloodwine and unfocused my eyes, gazing into a sunbeam that had no right to be there when I was sure I heard drizzle on the windowpanes. It was like looking at one of those Magic Eye posters, waiting for the foreground and the background to switch and the dancing motes of dust to form into mesmerizing patterns. The cats batted at them, purring, and I reached black fingers out to join them, laughing.

It seemed mere seconds before Lenoir was helping me up from the chair, my bones aching and my eyes bleary. My hand was empty. The goblet lay on the thick, plush carpet, one lone drop of glittering red swirling against the unbroken glass. The sunbeam was gone, and the night was starless and black outside. Panic shot through me, but my body felt utterly drained.

"I'm late. Charline's going to kill me."

Lenoir led me to the screen and politely turned away. "She can't touch you, *chérie*. You're my star now."

I dressed as quickly as I could and dived into the carriage, avoiding Auguste's quiet but measuring gaze. Lenoir was right about Charline; although she grumbled in Franchian and wouldn't stop sneering, she didn't yell at all. I barely made it up to my hoop before they began to lower it in the spotlight. For a brief second, I looked for the dancing fairies, but they were gone. Then the music started, and I was again an object, a plaything, a puppet.

I smiled and spread my legs in a split.

Charline caught my arm as I bowed offstage, and I jerked it right back out of her grasp with a hiss. She recomposed her face into something similar to politeness.

"Listen, *chérie*. Tonight, you hurry with your patron. You don't drink wine. You get sleep. Tomorrow is the debut of our grand finale, followed by a dance, a grand ball. You will be sold to the highest bidder. And you will dance with him, do whatever he wishes. Do you understand?"

I tried to count back the days, but I had no idea what day it was. "It's time for the finale? With the chandelier?"

She made an elegant huff of annoyance. "Yes, of course. We have been rehearsing like mad while you sleep until noon and swoon for Monsieur Lenoir. Blue will fit your costume and ballgown tomorrow morning." Charline leaned close, studying my eyes. "Less wine, more blood. We need you with us, Demitasse. Your grand finale can make our mark on the world. Or end us. We are all counting on you, you know. This is your chance to shine." She gestured to a poster of me, pasted crookedly on the wall over a thick, faded collage of past posters. La Goulue and Jane Avril peeked out, as did a slender acid-green leg that had to be Limone's. The message was clear: I might not be on top for long, and it was my duty to make it as spectacular and worthwhile as possible.

"But Lenoir is expecting me tomorrow morning."

Her nostrils flared, and she flashed red with anger. "Lenoir"—she paused dramatically—"can wait."

I couldn't turn red, but I could still be pretty scary. I drew myself up tall despite the silly costume, pulled my lips back over my fangs, and took on the predator's mantle that I spent so much time suppressing. Charline swallowed hard, turned a sickly shade of pink, and made herself smaller. Even if we both knew that I didn't want her blood, it was clear enough that I could spill it all over the dusty wooden boards if I so desired.

"Then I take the next day off. Whatever day it is. I haven't had a day off since I showed up here, and I'm damned well taking one. Got it?"

"Of course. Of course. Only fair," she muttered, hurrying away from me with tapping slippers.

I grinned to myself. I still had it.

Instead of going directly to the pachyderm after the show, I whipped my arm from Auguste's hold and ran upstairs to rifle through Limone's vanity for a pen and paper. I found an elegant stationery set marked with skulls and peonies, still wrapped in its ribbon and including a quill and acid-green ink. It wasn't exactly my style, but it would have to do.

> *Monsieur,*
>
> *I am regrettably detained tomorrow. I will attend you the day after, when my schedule is entirely open. Such is the life of a star.*
>
> *Yours,*
>
> *La Demitasse*

Double-checking the note once more for silly mistakes, I folded it and skipped downstairs to put it in Blaise's hand.

"Take this directly to Monsieur Lenoir, please."

He stared at the paper, then looked up at me quizzically. "*Désolé, mademoiselle,* but I'm not allowed to leave Paradis."

I'd seen him running so many errands in the cabaret that I'd assumed he performed such duties all over town.

"Why not?"

He shrugged. "Not sure, *mademoiselle.* But Bea says I mustn't, so I don't. Never been outside."

I fought the urge to crush Blaise in a hug. A young,

vibrant, lively boy, and he'd never been outside? Never ridden the elevator up the Tower? Never danced through the streets or played ball with the other daimon boys under a bright blue sky? It was possibly the most depressing thing I'd ever heard. But since it didn't seem to bother him too much, I didn't want to make it seem like a big deal.

"I'll ask Auguste, then. Thank you."

He ran off, and I found Auguste and sent him on his errand. As I passed the open door of Blue's workroom, I found the old daimon bustling around a huge dress on a mannequin.

"Is that for the ball?"

She sighed and poked her needle through a ruffle. "Of course, kid. Everything is. You ever been to a cabaret ball?"

"Nope. Never been to a ball at all." I was pretty sure Homecoming at Riverdale High didn't count.

She shook her head sadly and jabbed the needle through the fabric, pulling it taut again and again. "It ain't the sort from fairy tales. Normally, I'd tell the girls to relax and enjoy it. But I think I just need to remind you to step lively and not kill anybody that grabs you wrong." She gave me a significant look over her half-moon glasses. "Daimons and Bludmen got a lot in common, but you got to understand. We're not predators. We're prey. The girls here need what the men give them and don't mind the exchange most clients demand. Like eating a food that ain't your favorite— you can still live on it, can't you? Don't judge 'em for it. If you don't want something, just disappear. Understand?"

I wasn't sure that I did, but I ran a hand over the thick corset and long, frothy skirt. "This is for me, isn't it?"

She nodded, a pin sticking out from the corner of her mouth. "I shouldn't have to tell you this, but be careful out there. You stay in Paradis, you're mostly safe. You leave here, bad things could happen. Did they tell you Victoire disappeared?"

I shook my head. "No one tells me anything."

"They keep it quiet. But it's getting worse."

I glanced into the hallway, too worried to ask if girls ever disappeared from the pachyderm.

"You got somewhere to be, don't you, kid?"

I sighed and looked at the door. "More of the same."

"Girls come here, they want to be stars. You know what stars want?"

"What?"

"They want to be girls again. And they can't. Not ever. Now, go."

I hurried out the door and down the hall, feeling for the first time as if I was avoiding something besides grasping hands. Blue's words had made me feel small and helpless, and the pachyderm and a throat full of blood seemed a good enough place to hide my blazing cheeks from her pity. I darted through the drizzle, head down, and ducked into the elephant's leg, leaving my waterlogged boots to dry on a step. Upstairs I found the duke, the first man who'd written me and the first one who'd purchased my time. When I saw him standing there, wine bottle in hand, my heart sank. What if he wanted more than what I'd given him last time? What if he wanted what the daimon girls were glad to provide?

And if not him, what of the man with the deepest coin purse tomorrow?

"*Bonsoir, monsieur,*" I said coyly.

"La Demitasse, you're a vision." It was a lie. I was sodden and shaking. He poured a glass of wine and held it out enticingly. I could smell the unicorn blood and snow from across the room, and I wanted it. Badly. All of it. I bit my lip. I had to take control. And there was only one way.

I sashayed across the room, took the goblet from his hand, and sipped delicately, savoring the kiss of blood and magic on my tongue. But then I set it down and stepped close to whisper in his ear.

"It is delicious, *monsieur*. But there's something I want even more."

I could smell the change in blood flow as his face went red and he swallowed hard. I untied his cravat and pulled him toward the couch by his jacket lapels. He followed willingly, the powerful diplomat reduced to a hungry, overexcited little boy. He said nothing, his mouth hanging open like a randy goat's.

With a hand on his chest, I shoved him back onto the couch and straddled him.

"Come into my parlor, said the spider to the fly," I whispered.

And then my teeth found his neck. It was becoming my best way to shut someone up.

20

I fled barefoot from the elephant like Cinderella being chased by her glass slippers, a ticket from the Louvre wadded up in my fist, the only helpful thing I'd found in his pockets. The duke hadn't spoken again, had simply jerked and moaned when my blood magic helped him find his relief. It was grotesque but helpful, the way that happened with my clients. I giggled to myself, considering how this happened every night. I had become silent but deadly.

I had a foot on the stairs up to my room when Vale called my name, his voice soft and urgent as it echoed down the hall. We both knew there was no one else around to hear it. My heart lurched as it always did when he was near, but my brain was impatient. I really did need sleep, not to be up half the night thinking about the mysterious brigand. Still, I stopped. I couldn't *not* stop.

I turned back to wait for him. He didn't hurry. He never did.

"*Bébé*, it's all set. Run up to your room to lose the bustle and grab your boots, and we'll take some blud and get your book. And maybe some information, too." He held out a disreputable umbrella and grinned. "Enough room for us both under here, if you stay close."

I dug a bare toe into a knot in the wood floor. "I can't. Tomorrow's the finale and some sort of ball. I have to get sleep."

He shook his head. "Oh, *bébé*. I do not understand you. You'll go to the gardens, you'll meet men in that ridiculous pachyderm, you'll go to Lenoir. But I try to help you find your friend, and you brush me off like a pestering child. Have you forgotten the whole reason you're here?"

Anger flared, my cheeks going hot and my fangs bared. "I didn't forget. I can't stop thinking about Cherie. Everything I do is for the sole purpose of staying here, to buy more time, to find more clues." I held up the ticket. "See this? The duke was at the Louvre today, and there's some sort of code on here, but I can't even go there by myself to investigate because I have no freedom during museum hours. I'm constantly trapped. I don't like what I do. I need the blood to live, and I need the men for the blood, and I need the performing for the men. I'm caught here."

"You're not caught right now. Come with me. We'll be back in an hour."

I shook my head again but with warning this time. "I told you. I can't."

For a moment, he just breathed, watching me. "You'll do anything for anyone. Except me. And except Cherie."

"Oh, I'm the one who won't do what I'm supposed to? Aren't you supposed to be taking over the family business? Aren't you running away, too, hiding in Paris from your real responsibilities?"

"For you, *bébé*! For you!" The shout was sharp, and he strangled it quickly. He looked me up and down in my ridiculous costume and chuckled bitterly. "We both have issues with men who want things we don't wish to give, I suppose. Except I run away from mine, and you run right toward yours and start sucking on it."

I exhaled in a growl and poked him in the chest. "I like you, but you make it so damned hard, Vale! Everyone else here worships me, and you just push and push and push."

"I could not have said it better myself."

"I thought after last night—"

His grin curled up, his eyes dancing. "What about last night?"

"I thought we'd found something good."

"Oh, we did. I would like to find it again." He licked his lip, and my knees nearly melted.

"Then stop pissing me off and pushing me away, and start wooing me, you ass."

I spun around to flounce away, but he caught a fistful of my bustle and yanked me back. No man I'd met yet in Sang would have dared it, but he held me there with a chuckle.

"As you like, *bébé*. Leave with me now, and I'll woo you in the most romantic place in Paris."

Stifling a yawn and twitching my skirt out of his grasp, I turned. "More romantic than the catacombs?"

"Oh, you'll enjoy this place. It is dark, private, and filled with surprises. It was once a fortress, then a palace, now a national treasure. And at this time of night, you can touch . . . whatever you wish."

He pulled me close, and the breath caught in my throat. "You want to break into the Louvre?"

His hands tightened on my waist. "Break in? We won't break anything. It is considered trespassing only if they catch you. And no one ever catches me." He held up the duke's ticket, which I had slipped into my pocket moments ago. "These are directions to a painting's placement in the gallery. Let's go see what it is that so interests your duke, shall we?"

"He's not my duke."

"That's what I like to hear," he whispered in my ear.

I borrowed a cloak and some boots from Blue's empty room and felt the first fine thrill of being bad. We left through the same door I used for my assignations, and I stared up through the rain at the copper elephant with foreboding as we slipped around its giant legs, Vale's fingers entwined with mine. Lights shone from the portholes and hung from the ornate headdress and enameled howdah on the pachyderm's back, and I saw what looked like a gazebo on top. I'd never been up there, but then again, all my suitors really wanted were my teeth and my body, not the foolish pretense of romance. I ducked back under the umbrella.

Once we hit the street, Vale whistled for a conveyance—a cheaper one than I'd used before and so small that we were stuffed together, touching from shoulder to ankle. Vale gave the dull-faced driver an unfamiliar address instead of giving the museum's name, and the trap took off at killer speeds, leaving a puff of violet smoke hanging in the gaslight behind us. The machinery was so loud that we had trouble hearing each other, but there was a new intimacy to being so close and doing something so normal. He was wearing his striped pants and vest, and the umbrella sat sentry between our knees like a bony chaperone.

In lieu of talking, he walked his fingers up my arm

every time I paid attention to something else that wasn't him. Each time I swatted him away, we both knew it was only a matter of time before I would pretend to stare at something else.

Rain dotted the roof as the conveyance pulled to a stop, and Vale slipped a franc into the man's filthy fist and helped me down. My boots slipped on the cobbles, and I tried to orient myself. As usual with Vale, we were in a dark alley in a place where no lady would go during daylight.

As if reading my mind, Vale opened the umbrella over my head and pulled me deeper into the shadows with a murmured "Quiet, now, *bébé*. I would normally go underground, but I am attempting to woo you, which requires a giddy stroll through an evening rain, yes?"

I glanced at the soot-streaked bricks and piles of bones and rocks. "It's just like I always dreamed—slimy carcasses and all."

"I would kiss you to keep you silent, but around here, we might be eaten."

The words sent shivers to dance along my spine, but I took his hint and went quiet as he pulled me into a maze of ramshackle buildings and fallen walls. There had been a fire here; my nose told me that more than my eyes did. But they were rebuilding, and the scaffolds and piles of stone and wood left plenty of shadows to shield us from prying eyes. When Vale lifted the edge of a manhole cover, I realized why he'd encouraged me to leave my bustle at home and tried to put on a brave face as I followed him into the yawning hole.

Once we were both underground and standing on stone, he produced a metal object from his pocket. With a few flicks of a switch, a fire bloomed, and I was delighted to see my first cigarette lighter in six years. He hooked the umbrella over my arm and handed the lighter to me so that he could replace the manhole cover above, and I admired the flower and vine design chased in the brass. I almost asked him about his green pendant before remembering that he had given it to me, and I had broken it the same day during an attempted murder. *Oops.*

With a heavy *clunk*, the tunnel went pitch-black around my small flame. Vale landed beside me. He took the lighter gently, careful not to hurt me or let the fire go out, his fingers caressing mine.

"It's not far," he said, and I shrugged.

"I'm pretty tough."

He pointed to my borrowed boots. "I would not wish you to get blisters."

That small kindness reached past my cold heart, the warmth spreading as he held out a hand and guided me over a puddle. Rain *plink*ed overhead, and further down the tunnel, I could hear more water moving. As we walked, Vale held up the lighter to show me an ancient rock wall that subtly curved.

"We are just outside the base of the original fortress. A great daimon king built it to protect the city from humans who wished to overrun it. Legend says the daimons repelled the humans with magic and by catapulting bludrats into the human armies."

"That's smart. Ratapults."

Vale laughed, and it warmed the cold tunnel like a blast of sunshine. "Come, my clever *bébé*. You're about to see the inside of the gentleman's loo. Brace yourself."

We turned off into an empty chamber with a high ceiling. Vale handed me the lighter before whipping away a moldering old cloth to reveal a wooden ladder, which he leaned against the stone wall. He climbed carefully as I waited below, holding up the lighter to enjoy the rare chance to see him from a different angle. He was about twenty feet up when tiny rays of light struck his face in a sunburst pattern, shining through a drain. After putting his ear up to the ceiling, he slid a chunk of stone to the side with a grunt. A beam of light shot into the chamber, illuminating a beautiful mural of daimons in medieval armor, rippling flags held aloft by their tails.

"It's clear, *bébé*. If you'd care to join me?"

I clicked the lighter shut, tucked it into my pocket, and started climbing. On Earth, I couldn't imagine how terrifying this entire outing would be: navigating a treacherous city after midnight with a strange and dangerous man, followed by tromping through the sewers and climbing thirty feet into the air over stone and into a government building. But considering who I was and where I was, it was an exciting trip. And that's when it hit me: I was about to have unfettered access to the greatest art museum in the entire world of Sang.

I had to hold in the squeal as Vale gently took my arms and helped drag me onto the tiles above. I stood and dusted off my leggings . . . and looked directly into a urinal.

"You weren't kidding."

"It gets better, I promise you."

Taking my elbow, he led me out into a wide hall. I sucked in a deep breath, considering how many atoms of paint and oil and genius I might be taking into my body forever with each lungful of air. I wasn't sure exactly how much this Louvre had in common with the one on Earth, but it was close enough to make me drunk on art-nerd giddiness.

"Where do we start? Is there a map? Do you have Impressionists here yet?"

"Let me see your ticket again, and I will tell you."

Vale flicked on the lighter, and I handed him the crumpled paper. The building around us was utterly silent and beautiful in its moonlit austerity, and it took every ounce of self-control I possessed to stop myself from running down the long hall, doing cartwheels and whooping with joy.

"This way."

When Vale took off, I followed. There was scant light from the moon outside, and I wished to see more, but he didn't ask for his lighter again. Bumbling around in a high-profile building with fire probably wasn't the best way to remain unnoticed, after all. I didn't know much about the layout of this Louvre or the one in my original world, so I just tried to take in as much as the shadows allowed, soaking in the sculptures, paintings, and ancient wonders when I wasn't watching Vale's butt. He walked with determination, moving through the Louvre as if he owned the place, and I liked that. It didn't hurt that he was bringing me closer to what I hoped would be a clue about Cherie.

"The gallery should be through here . . ."

He turned left, and I followed so closely that when he drew up short, I ran into him. Normally, I think he would have rather enjoyed having my front plastered to his back, but this time, he was so tense and alert that he didn't even notice.

We stood in the doorway to a portrait gallery, surrounded by daimons frowning, laughing, dancing, and seated astride screaming bludmares. Almost one entire wall was a version of *La Grande Jatte* but with daimons mixed among the humans and a clockwork monkey playing with the puppies in front. I hurried over to read the card and see if Seurat existed in Sang and was surprised to learn that it was the first painting created solely by automaton in a style entirely new.

"*Bébé*, you need to see this."

Vale was a dark and stalwart shadow before a wall of dancing girls, many of them doppelgängers of paintings from my own world but with the twist that these girls were daimons instead of humans. The canvases were in all shapes and sizes, each in a heavy gilt frame. Vale flicked open the lighter, and a hand to my pocket told me that yet again, I'd been pickpocketed without my knowledge. He raised the flame, and I nearly barfed duke blood onto the dainty tiles of the Louvre.

The image of Limone didn't look like Lenoir's work, and the brass plaque on the frame was blank. In my world, this masterpiece by Toulouse Lautrec showed the Moulin Rouge, so this evil twin most likely showed the inside of the Moulin Bleu of Sang. In the bottom right corner, lit in lurid absinthe-green, was an image of Limone so true to life that I could feel hatred and disgust radiating from it in waves. I stepped closer, but Vale threw an arm out to hold me back.

"When was the last time someone saw Limone?" I asked.

"The day after she pushed you."

"She went to the Moulin Bleu, didn't she?"

He nodded. "There's dark magic at work here," he said, and I gulped and shivered but didn't move forward again.

I could feel Limone's cold presence in the room with me, and I spun suddenly, certain that I would feel her hard hands pushing me off into space. But the gallery was empty, peopled only with whispering shadows. I looked from portrait to portrait, trying to sense if perhaps it was only my history with Limone and the perfection of her likeness that was freaking me out. I saw faces I half recognized, a maroon girl stretching in a tutu and a pink-skinned girl laughing. But I couldn't remember their names or when I'd seen them last.

I pointed with a trembling finger. "I know those girls . . ."

"Jess and Edwige. They went missing from Paradis. Together." His voice was dark, torn between anger and sadness. "Neither painting shows the artist's name, but at least it was not Lenoir." His fists clenched at his sides.

"Why did you bring me here?" I asked.

Vale put an arm around my waist, and I shuddered as he pulled me close and led me from the room. "The words on that ticket were directions to this gallery. There was something here the duke wanted to see."

"Ugh. I don't know why. I feel like I need to go wash in boiling water or something. Like that painting is still staring at me." I shivered all over like a dog throwing water, trying to get back to normal. "Do you know who painted it?"

The hall outside felt ten degrees warmer and much less haunted, and Vale clicked off the lighter and pulled me into a desperate hug, his hand cupping the back of my head.

"I do not know, *bébé*. Many are by Lenoir but not that one. He takes on protégés and students sometimes. I will try to find out. Do you feel . . ."

He trailed off, and I wrapped my arms around him, too. If he felt half as shaken as I did, then I was glad to give him my warmth. I couldn't believe a painting had inspired such horror in my heart.

"That painting hates us," I whispered, and he nodded as he rubbed my back.

"I did promise you romance, but I didn't wish to frighten you into closeness." He pulled away and held my face for a brief, bright moment. "How easily one forgets the hunt when one is hunted."

"Wait." I wanted to look through the door again but couldn't bring myself to do so. "Did you see any paintings of Cherie? Of a Bludman or a human with long blond hair and gray eyes?"

"So far as I know, there are no humans in the cabarets, and if there were another Bludman, everyone would know. I saw no such painting."

I sighed heavily and slumped over. "Then this whole trip was a waste of time."

"Not so, *ma chère*." He slipped his hand into mine, walking backward and pulling me after him. "We tried. And trying is worth something. We also know that there is something strange about that painting. I will come back during the day, ask around. See who painted it, and the ones of Jess and Edwige, too. Some ideas take more time to bear fruit, but you must not lose hope."

My steps were shuffling and coy. I felt more than a little like a princess in a palace, surrounded by the dripping gilt and excess of the grand museum. The farther we got from the painting, the better I felt. "You're right. It's not like Cherie was going to be here and we were just going to walk in and find her. And it's not a wasted trip." I blushed and looked down, tracing the marble in the floor. "I mean, I've always wanted to see the Louvre."

He stopped walking backward and smirked as if he knew exactly what I wasn't brave enough to say. "Oh, you have always wished to see the Louvre? I think perhaps I can help with that."

Before I could protest, he'd swept me off my feet and tossed me over his shoulder, taking off down the grand hall at a run. I started to shriek but slapped a hand over my own mouth. Vale ran through the Louvre like a little boy chasing a soccer ball, pointing out unhelpful things such as "Here's a statue of a naked man with an unfortunate nose," or "I think those are the king's petticoats." I laughed so hard that my stomach hurt, and when he finally stopped and placed me on my feet, we were both out of breath and far enough away from the portrait gallery that the malevolent tension was gone.

"Did you see everything?" he asked.

Without thinking, probably because of the lack of blud in my brain, I blurted, "I mostly watched your butt."

That got his attention. He was instantly focused on me, his light eyes shining in the darkness. "Did you now, *bébé*?"

"Oh, well, I . . ." I looked down and fidgeted, very un-Bludman-like.

Light hands settled on my hips as he stepped into my personal space. "What is it you fear, Demi? You walk right up to the line and kick dirt over it and laugh, yet you won't step over. Do you think a man minds being admired?"

"Of course not. I just . . ."

"Are you ashamed of me, then? Do you not find my backside pleasing?"

"What? No! Vale, come on." My cheeks were red, my insides all twisted up. "Your butt is . . . awesome. I just . . . I didn't break into the Louvre with you to talk about . . . this."

"This?"

"Us."

"And yet here we are. All alone in the greatest museum in Franchia. Think of all the things we could be doing here, and yet we stand arguing in a hall. You could always kiss me to into silence."

For a brief moment, I let myself think of all the things we could be doing—against this very wall, on one of the velvet couches, upstairs in the Sun King's old bed. And yet . . . I couldn't.

"My life is really complicated right now, Vale."

"Yes, and that is why it's good to have someone on your side."

"You're already on my side."

"But I could be on your inside, too."

A fire burst into life in my belly and radiated outward. I knew what he meant, but it was the double entendre that really caught me. And maybe it would have been easy to give in. But I knew how relationships happened in Sang, and no matter what I had thought about romance from the confines of the caravan, I wasn't ready to give up my autonomy and start letting him call the shots. Especially when his first demand would be that I stop seeing Lenoir and drinking absinthe.

But I couldn't tell him that, so I chickened out and went for the cheap shot.

"Maybe once I've found Cherie. But until then . . ."

"Until then, you dance on your side of the line." He dug tight fists into his eyes. "And I dance along with you. From the other side."

"I have responsibilities."

"You keep saying that. As if I don't know. *Mon dieu, bébé*, do you hear yourself?" He rubbed his head as he paced back and forth, more agitated than I'd yet seen him. "I have halted my life to help you. I have not been back to my tribe since I found you. I haven't seen my horse. Do you think I am a boy playing a game?"

"I do, actually. You're using me to avoid your real responsibilities."

"You are the only thing I've ever cared about besides horses! You are my responsibility! So do not toy with me, because I am not a toy."

His passion shook me, and I was torn between running away and clawing off his clothes to screw him senseless on the floor of the Louvre. But I did neither. "I'm not used to you being serious, Vale."

"Perhaps I hide my true intentions behind jests because in truth, *bébé*, the way I feel about you terrifies me. But you don't wish to hear that." He pulled out a pocket watch and checked the time. "But for now, let me return you to your giant, lonely bed, as I know you have . . . business tomorrow."

I snorted. "Oh, so you get to sleep with all the girls at Paradis, but if I don't fall at your feet and do whatever you say, you get to call me a whore? That's fair."

Vale's jaw dropped, and I'd never seen him look so caught out. "*Bébé*, no. That's not what I—"

I put up a hand. "That's exactly what you meant. You

imply it almost every day. And I've never slept with any of them, never even kissed them. So let me do my job, and I'll let you do yours. Which way is the bathroom with the ladder?"

Giving me a long, charged, measuring look, he pointed down the hall. "I might hide behind humor, but you, ma *chère*, hide behind cruelty."

I started walking with my back as straight as a curtain rod, and he followed. We didn't talk all the way through the Louvre, which had lost its midnight luster for me. Down through the hole in the floor, we were silent. Tromping through the sewers, we didn't say a word.

And I hated it. God, how I hated it. But he hadn't apologized. And he needed to.

Conveyances were scarce, but at least the one we finally landed had more room in it, which meant we weren't forced to touch. The air was too thick with resentment for words, anyway. Still, he insisted on seeing me to the back door of Paradis.

"Thanks for a shitty date in a sewer," I said.

"And thank you for ruining a lovely experience in a romantic museum."

We stared at each other, breathing audibly through our noses.

"Weren't we supposed to go see some shady friend of yours and bleed me out?" I spat.

He shook his head, smiling the saddest little smile. "It was only pretense, *bébé*. Just an excuse to enjoy your company. I was going to take you out for a stroll. There is no way I would put your blud into another man's hands. Not now."

"Well, why didn't you fucking say so? You romantic

idiot!" I stormed upstairs, hating the way my hat was bobbing stupidly and even more the way I felt like a spoiled, silly child.

"Good night, *bébé*," I heard just before I slammed my door.

There was something on my pillow, and I picked it up with hands still hot with anger.

"*Merde*."

It was a small book. "The Elements of Signing with Style" was printed in gold on the cover, along with a hand making the *Okay* sign.

I ran downstairs to screw his brains out and confess my feelings, in that order.

The hall was empty.

21

It was good to wake refreshed and without a headache, even if I was sleepy and still conflicted over my time with Vale and our troubling good-bye. I was alert enough to slip the book back under my blankets before Blaise entered with my teacup of blood. When he presented a second vial nestled in his tiny blue hands, I shrugged and drank that one, too. Wholesome warmth bloomed in my belly, but when I licked my lips, I longed to taste bloodwine tinged with Lenoir's special cocktail of absinthe. Tomorrow seemed very far away.

The morning was a flurry of makeup, hot hair tongs, fitting dresses and skirts, and the occasional sting of a pin when Blue wasn't satisfied with the fit. Fully dressed in my Demitasse costume, I called for a break, taking a quick cup of perfectly warmed blood handed over by the surly bartender. The afternoon belonged to two run-throughs of the chandelier act in my new outfit while dangling high over the stage. Charline and Sylvie knew me well enough now to avoid the fury they would have caused by requesting that I start my practice just a few feet from the floor. I never slipped, never faltered. The confidence and grace of a predator were well suited to performing onstage, and all the high-quality blood had done its work. Even Charline was pleased, and when the curtain went up on a packed house, I was ready.

Every performer dreams of the flawless opening night, and that night I had mine. No one missed a cue. The daimon orchestra's music was perfection. The girls had never smiled so brightly or kicked so high. The collective gasp as I descended on a giant golden chandelier covered with dripping faux diamonds—well, I drank up their adoration and wonder with the hunger of a daimon. They loved it. They loved us.

They loved me.

And I loved performing for them. This was what I'd dreamed of every night in Criminy's caravan. A packed house, a sea of tuxedos and faces suffused with red. The hot kiss of spotlights, the breathless exultation of a standing ovation. I was a star, and no one could take it away from me.

The only thing that was missing was Cherie, and as they lowered the chandelier to the stage for our final bow, I felt a stabbing ache deep in my heart. I'd had enough time to become famous, but all I had of my friend were a ragged hairbob, two pulled fangs that might not even be hers, and a jar full of meaningless notes that didn't give me a single clue as to where she might be. As I bowed and was buffeted by the patting hands of my daimon friends, I swore to myself that after tonight and the insanity of the ball, I would redouble my efforts to find my partner. Stardom was empty without her.

Normally, I hurried to the elephant once the curtain was down, but tonight I let the avalanche of laughing daimon girls carry me back to Blue's room, where most of them changed every night. Mel and Bea helped me squeeze out of the costume and into the waiting black-and-white ballgown, and Blue double-checked the seams and retied the ribbons before I was allowed to leave. The dress was a wonder; the white organza fit perfectly and spread from the tight corset waist to a wide bell skirt that was so out-of-date as to reinvent fashion in one night. Determined black lines swirled over it like iron scrollwork on a gate, as if one need only grasp my waist and pull to open me wide. Kohl-rimmed eyes with black feather eyelashes and a slash of bright red in a Cupid's bow at my lips marked me as a Bludman. My bloomers had become all the rage, I noticed; all the girls were wearing them, albeit in more colorful and ridiculous versions than my plain black ones.

As Blue pinned up my hair, I watched Mel and Bea get dressed at another mirror. They helped each other tenderly, with little touches and smiles. Mel whispered to Bea, and Bea answered in gestures, some of which were becoming familiar after a few hours with the book. They made a lot of sense, actually, the gestures describing the words cleverly. I saw Bea sign the words for *scared* and *nightmare* and *hungry*, and Mel pulled her into a hug and rubbed her back before kissing her gently on the lips. When Blaise ran by, they pulled him into their embrace, and my heart wrenched at how nice it must be to have a relationship of such easy affection and trust.

"Good luck tonight." Blue's grumble broke my musings as she slipped a half-mask over my face. "You're going to need it."

I thanked her and headed to join the gaggle of girls waiting by the door.

"You go first," Mel said, dragging me forward a little. "It's you they want."

I turned to look at my friends and coworkers. They were so beautiful and bright and sparkling, their half-masks doing nothing to disguise who they were. Their skin and smiles couldn't be hidden.

"No. Please. Y'all——"

Bea pointed at me and shooed me toward the front.

I smiled and fluffed my skirt and forced my shoulders down proudly. Swinging my hips, I led them down the hallway toward the stage, where a wide, curving staircase had been brought in to cover the orchestra pit and connect the stage to the theater floor. The seats were gone, cleared away and stacked along the wall to leave room for dancing.

I paused in the wings, as I'd been told to. At some unseen signal, the orchestra started up with a grand processional that, to be quite honest, sounded like the "Imperial March" from *Star Wars*. Head up and wearing my fangs proudly, I sashayed onto the stage and stopped at the top of the stairs. The murmuring crowd went quiet, every masked face in the room turning to watch us in hungry silence. The daimon girls fanned out behind me, and I tried to imagine what it must be like to be in the audience. In front, in shades of black and white and red, the vampire starlet promised paradise with her teeth, while behind her, a harmless, glittering rainbow of dancing girls spread like angel wings, ready to provide pleasure just for the joy of sharing themselves. It was like something out of a movie or a fairy tale, except that I felt less like a star and more like a reluctant bride, bought and paid for.

We took the stairs in time with the music. Charline brought a man to meet me at the bottom stair, a foreigner with a red-dyed beard and shoes turned up at the toes. He performed an elaborate bow, the tiny bells on his unusually colorful suit jingling. Every other man at the ball wore dress whites, but this gentleman wore mauve and plum and bright poppy red.

"La Demitasse, at last. I have traveled the entire continent to meet you, my dear."

"May I present Prince Seti, the ruler of Kyro?"

I resented the warning in Madame Sylvie's voice but was too well groomed to hiss near the man who had probably paid a king's ransom for my time. I only smiled, sweetly. "I knew I was waiting for something special," I murmured, letting him kiss my hand.

The music segued into a quadrille, and I was soon dancing, surrounded by colorful daimons matched with austere men in black, the opposite of my gawdy partner and me. The air grew hot and humid with lust, and the daimons' laughter shook the rafters. My feet hurt already in the dainty slippers, but I preferred dancing to doing what the prince expected me to do, considering the price he had likely paid for what he thought was my virginity. I would dance all night if it would keep me from the elephant.

After three songs and many polite compliments and murmured thanks, I begged to sit for a moment.

"I will bring you wine, my dear. I brought a special cask from Egypt. Have you tasted camel blud? I hear it's quite the aphrodisiac to your kind."

"I can't wait," I said, but inwardly, I cringed. Why did rich men keep trying to cram weird animals down my throat? Then again, if camel was half as good as unicorn, I would have no right to complain.

The prince disappeared, and I darted through the

crowd toward one of the niches that had been created using the velvet curtains that hung from the walls. I knew damned well they were there so the girls could discreetly provide their services without leaving the theater, but surely it was too early for one of the small enclosures to be occupied? This one still had the flaps open and drawn back invitingly.

Inside, I saw only a long quilted bench. But before I could duck in to hide, an insistent hand caught my wrist and pulled me back to the floor. I spun, barely turning my snarl into the simper that my patrons expected.

"My prince, I didn't expect you back so soon."

But it wasn't the prince, and my heart leaped into my throat. Scowling at the interloper's wicked grin, I grabbed his spotless black sleeve and dragged him into the alcove.

"What the hell are you doing here?"

"Enjoying the ball, *bébé*."

"They'll skin you alive!"

"Define *they*. Define *skin*."

Vale strolled to the bench and sat down, knees spread, arms across the back, green eyes glinting like a cat's in the light of a single lantern hanging from the tent's ceiling. A rich man's walking cane was balanced across his knees, and I wondered which tuxedo-clad client he'd stolen it from. I'd never seen him so cocky. I'd never seen him so clean. I'd definitely never seen him so devastatingly sexy. I rushed back to the velvet and untied the thick black tassels that held open the flaps. The curtains closed us in completely, and firelit darkness swallowed me whole. I tied the ropes in a double knot.

I turned to find Vale watching me, his high top hat on the bench beside him. His bare hands were buried in the plush, rubbing absentmindedly as if there was an itch he couldn't scratch, somewhere just out of reach.

"How'd you get in?" I asked, just to have something to fill the space besides my spooked breathing and his scent, that musky chai that spoke of wildness and wind blowing over a thin veil of respectability.

"The same way I always do, *bébé*. You know that."

"But why? Why risk it? What if Madame Sylvie saw you?"

"Hypotheticals don't interest me, not with you standing there, dressed like that." He curled a finger and smirked. "*Viens sur mon coeur . . . Tigre adoré.*"

My body jerked toward him like a puppet on tight strings, as if Baudelaire's words in Vale's dusky voice were a command in a language I didn't know I knew. Tiny steps in satin slippers carried me whispering across the ballroom floor, until the rounded skirt of my gown brushed his knees like a satin jellyfish.

"That's more like it."

He whipped his cane around me, holding me caged with both arms tight against my corseted waist and the polished wood at my back. His black tuxedo pants dented my dress, the distorted black-and-white designs briefly reminding me of a zebra that had lost the game and twitched under a lion's heavy paws.

"But aren't we fighting?"

"If you wish, *bébé*. Use your claws to punish me. I don't mind."

"The prince——" I started lamely.

"Forget him. He's been detained." He looked up, winked at me. "I am a bit of a prince myself, you know."

"Prince of the brigands?"

"Prince of the Brigands of Ruin. Prince of the wild moors. And my palace is a hell of a lot bigger than his."

I raised one eyebrow, suppressed a smile. "And how big is it?"

He chuckled. "Enormous, *bébé*. I'll show you one day. My palace is as big as the sky."

"Then why don't you claim it?"

He shook his head when I broke an unspoken rule of our flirting. But he recovered quickly, a golden fire dancing in his eyes. "Maybe you're right, *bébé*. Maybe I should start claiming the things I see as mine."

He jerked the cane forward and dropped it, and I fell into his open arms as it clattered to the floor. His hands were clever as he spun me, and I ended up sitting across his lap in the black-and-white cloud of my dress, his arm around my back. My mouth was still open in surprise, and before I could close it, he was kissing me, his other hand firm on my chin to hold me, just so.

Oh, God, that kiss. I'd had plenty of blood since yesterday's absinthe, but I felt suddenly as drunk and dizzy and reeling as if I had just completed a wild tarantella dance, spinning and spinning and spinning. He had kissed me before—rough as the brick in the hallway, soft as the swing of a trapeze in the breeze. But this kiss matched the cozy, heart-red velvet lair that held us, a little world outside of real life.

If Lenoir's absinthe was glitter and fairies and sunbeams, Vale's kiss was the opposite: endless star-strewn skies and the intimacy of turning your face away from eternity to steal a moment, dark and secret. His mouth tasted of spices, of cinnamon and chai and mint, of uncut cocoa and bourbon vanilla and not-quite-blood-but-close-enough.

I was careful of my teeth despite the furious passion he called forth, desperate to keep the kiss, catch the moment, intent on its path like a comet blazing a sure arc through the night.

He kissed me slowly, and I understood that he knew it, too, knew that it was precious as only stolen things could be. The prince had bought my time and, so far as he knew, my body, but Vale knew his business and would take what others didn't watch closely enough. He turned his head, his tongue dipping deep to taste me, caress me, heat me from within with the branding burn of cherry-hot iron. But he didn't taste of metal and blood to me; he only tasted of himself. And I wanted more.

The hand around my waist stroked down to explore my curves through the airy layers of tulle and satin. He groaned but couldn't reach me, even though he pulled me tighter against his body. My fingers were tangled in his cravat, pulling it untied of their own volition as I gasped into his mouth. The starch of his collar made my fingertips gritty, and I made a little growl as my talon caught in the knotted silk.

"If your hands need work, move lower down, *bébé*. We don't have enough time for the grand reveal." Holding my jaw, he kissed the corner of my mouth and moved down, slowly, softly, his lips murmuring over my throat. "Not that it's going to stop us."

"I thought—"

"Dangerous thing, thinking. Just feel."

He tipped me back over his arm, letting my head fall against the bench to expose my throat and arch my back. He pulled off his glove with his teeth and ran rough fingertips down my neck and over my collarbones, down to where the heart-shaped neckline of my corset forced my breasts up deliciously on a clever little shelf.

"Close your eyes, *bébé*."

"Isn't it my turn to participate?"

"Not yet. You perform for everyone, all the time. Let me perform for you. You'll get your chance to star, I promise."

I searched his eyes, but it was as hopeless as hunting for something lost on the moors. I was mesmerized by the hunger and an odd kindness there. Did I trust him?

I trusted him enough with my body . . . . if not yet my heart.

I closed my eyes and tipped my head back all the way, giving myself up to him for the second time. He slid me down so my ass was on the bench, my back arched over the bulge in his lap, and my head on the other side of the softly cushioned seat. I didn't know what to do with my arms, but he placed them, one by one, over my head. My legs stretched out under the poof of the skirt, and I kicked off the little slippers to rub the soles of my feet on the velvet, the closest thing I'd felt in years to walking barefoot in mown grass. My body had never felt so alive, so open, so straining and wanting. I was willing to let him have his way again—for a time.

I thought he would go for my breasts, taking advantage of the benefits of gravity and a supportive corset. I held my breath, waiting for the sweet rasp of fingertips on aching nipples. Instead, his palm cupped my jaw, his thumb tracing my eyebrows. One finger brushed over my false eyelashes like a butterfly kiss, then drew a line down my nose and over each cheekbone. As he traced my lips ever so gently, he murmured, "So beautiful. So beautiful, *bébé*."

I lifted a corner of my lip, showing a fang—half dare, half self-pity.

"Even that. Ferocious little tiger. The men of my tribe like fierce women."

He touched a finger to the fang but didn't test its sharpness. I could feel my heart beating in my ears, my breath coming fast and forcing my ribs against the corset. I squirmed, wishing for his hands in the places that called for them. All this touching and tenderness was a fine gift, but now was not the time for pleasantries. The beast inside me was done with worship and ready for action.

I sat up, sinuously arching and twisting to straddle him, my knees on either side of his hips.

He laughed and held my hips tight. "Like that, is it?"

"You said you liked fierce women."

"Did I mention I like them in my lap?"

"You talk too much."

He started to say something else, but I kissed him first, sloppy and open-mouthed and injecting every single thing I wanted into the way my tongue swirled and plunged against his. He moaned and rocked his hips, and somewhere under the poof of my skirt, I felt his response and settled more firmly down. Oh, yes. That was exactly what I wanted. Knees spread wide, I put weight in my ass and rubbed, slowly, up and down his length. For the first time in Sang, I had cause to thank Aztarte or Saint Ermenegilda or whoever made up the rules that there were no germs and no accidental pregnancies, at least not for Bludmen. My body knew exactly what it was doing, and what it was doing now was getting ready to fuck a brigand insensible.

I took what I wanted, ferociously, unapologetically,

and he loved it. His hands clenched my hips, grabbed my ass, helped me move, grinding with me in time with the orchestra's waltz. I had always liked long hair, but the curves of his skull under my hands had a sensual quality, an intimacy, that I found interesting. I ran a finger along his earrings and captured his jaw to hold him while I changed angles. He lifted me a little, and my hands fell onto his broad shoulders, onto a tuxedo jacket that hid too much of his body for my taste. I tried to pull it off, but he grabbed my hands, one on each side.

He spoke directly into my panting mouth. "Time is short, *bébé*. Use your imagination. For now."

When he loosed me, I grabbed the back bench behind his head to steady myself. He used a thumb to flick one breast over the edge of my corset, his lips tightening over the taut nipple. I went still as he sucked, his teeth lightly scraping as he lifted the other breast from the corset, too. I couldn't breathe as he toyed with one, suckled the other, licked them with wide strokes of his tongue. While his hands and mouth were busy, I reached to the front of my skirt and yanked the ribbons that held it in place. The knot came undone, and the grand skirt billowed away like a magnolia falling to the ground.

Vale whistled low against my chest, making me shiver. His hands ran down the corset and over the skimpy, lacy undershorts.

"Damn, *bébé*. I like your dark magic."

"That's not magic. That's my ass."

He gripped both cheeks, kneading for a moment before jerking me close against him, just a few layers of cloth between us.

It was entirely too much of a barrier for my taste, and

my hands went straight for his buttons. He caught my fingers, brought them to his face, and ran my fingertips over his lips.

"Kiss me, *bébé*."

I took him in another messy kiss, and he reached between us, the sound of crisp suiting and metal buttons shushed in the quiet dark. I knew he was free when he sighed, one hand moving back and forth briefly. I sat down again, savoring the feeling of his body pressing against the ruffles and right over the place he'd once licked me into ecstasy. His fingers ran up the insides of my thighs, dipping with familiar intimacy under the lace edge to stroke me.

"*Mon dieu, bébé*. So hot and wet. So ready."

"*Je le sais.*"

I sat up a little on my knees, and he obliged by pulling the bloomers as far aside as he could and guiding me back down. The press of him, right there, right against me, was maddeningly delicious, and I rubbed, just a little, enjoying the suspense and inevitability of what was to come. With his hands firm on my hips and my fingers gripping the back of the bench to either side of his face, he turned to kiss the inside of my wrist. Our eyes caught, and it was like falling, and ever so gently, I eased down, taking him inch by hot, delicious inch inside me.

I held his gaze, savoring it, reveling in the warmth in his eyes and the way his lips were parted, just a little, as if he would stop breathing if he closed his mouth. I had to kiss him, and I did, and he kissed me back, and then we were moving together with slow, hard rhythm, as steady as the gallop of his bludmare across the wildness of the moors.

He hadn't been lying; it was big. And it was wonderful.

I moved in slow circles, swirling up and down, my muscles contracting and pushing and yearning to take everything he had. He moved with me, against me, rocking me, holding me down and holding me up and running his hands up and down every inch of my body. His lips found my nipples, his tongue found my throat, his hands slipped like feathers over my bare shoulders and down to the tender insides of my elbows and wrists, down to my hands, weaving his fingers with mine and squeezing briefly before moving on.

After the night on the trapeze, I could only conclude that like any good thief, he knew my tells, knew how to read my sighs and groans and growls and twitches. His hands ran up my legs to the place where we joined under my loose bloomers, his finger finding the same bud he'd caressed with his tongue. He flicked it gently, perfectly, pinching and pressing in time with his thrusts. Mostly dressed, totally alone, still I felt the hot thrum of the crowd outside, the beat of the orchestra's drums in my bones, and the wickedly distinct possibility that at any moment, someone might lift the flap of red velvet and see exactly how cheaply the star of Paradis sold herself.

That only made it hotter.

I'd ridden his horse, and now I rode him, head thrown back and hair coming undone down my arched back. I was getting so close, could hear the little mewls and whimpers escaping me with each breath.

"*Viens, bébé. Viens.*"

As if I'd been waiting for his permission to fall to pieces, I tensed and cried out as everything inside me hit the grand crescendo, as sweet and high as a violin's string drawn out and vibrating, echoing and dancing with the stars in time with the drumbeat of my heart. He kept moving, pounding a primordial rhythm, and as my own release ebbed, I focused on him, clenching my muscles around him. I didn't even realize my teeth were scraping his throat until I felt his hand on my jaw, firm with warning. I took his mouth instead, plunging my tongue to crash against his, moving and twirling with the powerful grace of an acrobat, pulling him with me into oblivion. He followed willingly, shuddering into me, his arms wrapped tightly around my waist and his mouth open against my lips. He made the most delicious noise, this low, ragged growl that I felt deep in my belly with his last forceful thrusts.

His eyes fluttered open and met mine, and I was instantly shy, despite the fact that he was still inside me. Or maybe because of it.

"I told you you'd get your turn, *bébé*."

In response, I tightened my muscles and felt him start to go hard again. His eyes rolled back in his head, and he slumped down.

"You are going to kill me, little tiger. Or get me killed. Hurry, now. Get dressed. Before we are found."

He gently lifted me, and I blushed and lurched to my bare feet, holding the untied skirt around my hips. I felt a breeze on my bare legs, a cold dribble down my thigh. As he buttoned his pants and tried to dab off the stains with a silk handkerchief, I blushed all the harder. He offered a tasseled velvet pillow to me, and I only hesitated a moment before sopping up the mess with the velvet and tossing it, stain down, back onto the bench. Hitching up the mess of my skirts, I fumbled with what went where, how to get the skirt back on and smoothed down as if it had never been touched. In that moment, struggling in the darkness, waiting to be discovered, I felt a strange sort of shame. And then the Bludman in my heart rose up and said fuck the shame. I turned to face Vale, the cloud of skirts in one hand.

"One day, we're going to do that, and then you're going to hold me in the crook of your arm while I sleep."

His eyes went soft, his fingers curling and uncurling on his thighs as if he ached to hold me, right then. He'd already slipped his white gloves back on, and his hands looked alien, too white for having touched my body so recently. "I will do that, yes. There is nothing I want more."

"This meant something."

"It did, *bébé*."

"We're going to find Cherie."

"We are."

"But first, I have to go out there and find the prince, because that's my job."

His eyes went dark and flat. "But you're mine."

I bared my teeth at that word. "Not to control. Not to own."

"That's not what I meant, *bébé*. When will you see that it's a different sort of possession?"

"When men stop trying to claim me like wild animals pissing on their territory!"

He blanched and swallowed hard. "Perhaps you are right, then. I only wanted to cherish and protect you, but I see how that could be misconstrued. Better find a place to wash away the smell of me, then."

My jaw dropped open, and I hid my rage and shame by turning my back to him as I hastily tied my skirts tighter and arranged them to fall just so, a blooming flower again. How many times did I have to tell the jackass that I wasn't sleeping with anybody? How long before he believed me? And how dare he try to make me feel bad when I was still dizzy from our time on the bench?

"Vale, I don't—" When I turned around, he was gone. "You enormous ass," I muttered as I slipped on my shoes.

Just then, Auguste poked his head into the tent.

"There you are, *mademoiselle*. The prince is waiting."

There was no mirror to check my tumbled hair, no way to know if it was obvious why my cheeks were flushed. All I could do was nod and run a finger around my lips and sweep my bangs to the side.

Auguste held open the velvet flap, and I stepped through into a swirling chaos of sight and sound, a blizzard of sequins and feathers and eyes bright with lust and hunger. I hunted for the prince but saw only a sea of tuxedos until a slender gentleman in foreign dress stepped forward and gave a strange bow, the same one the prince had used.

"*Mademoiselle*, my master awaits you in the pachyderm."

With a gracious nod, I took his arm, noting that he smelled of pipe smoke and hot metal under an unrelenting sun. As he escorted me down the brick hall that led to the elephant, did he feel my fingers tremble? Perhaps for the first time, I missed my gloves. For what the prince of Kyro had paid, biting him would never be enough.

22

The normally bleak courtyard was lit with twinkling lanterns, and I had to shove one aside as the prince's servant led me to the pachyderm's door. He bowed again at the bottom of the stairs, and I nodded regally, my eyes drawn to the swaybacked lines of gently swinging lamps. It looked so romantic and innocent down here, the sort of place where a young couple might huddle together over steaming cups of coffee, waiting for the perfect moment for their first kiss. But no. This was Paris, and Mortmartre, and Paradis, and there was only one thing that brought couples to the world-famous copper pachyderm late at night. Well, two things. And I was pretty sure the prince wanted them both—at the same time.

I took a deep breath and put on my professional smile before I opened the door to the stairs. If there was one thing I had learned in my short time at Paradis, it was that men could be easily fooled into thinking that you utterly worshipped them, so long as your smile and your eyes focused on them as if they were the only thing in the world.

Upstairs, I swanned into the room like a queen. The prince wasn't facing the door, waiting for me expectantly, so my carefully practiced smile was utterly wasted. The room was empty. Which had to mean he was in the bedroom area, which was awfully presumptuous, even for a prince. I heard the door to the courtyard close and lock, far below me, and resigned myself to getting out of the elephant as quickly as I could and without the prince making any more headway than any other wealthy suitor had. Slipping a hand into the hidden pocket of my skirt, I made sure the sleeping powder was there. If I had to use it early, so be it. I wasn't sleeping with the prince of Kyro or anyone else.

"*Bonjour*, darling," I called, but there was no answer. "Prince Seti?"

Confused and a little off-kilter, possibly because the blood hadn't returned to my brain after my time with Vale, I walked around the screen and into the bedroom. It was empty, too.

"What the hell?"

I sat on the bed, then fell dramatically back, making the blankets and my huge skirt poof around me. Everything felt sincerely stupid. Why was I even here? It wasn't as if the prince was a local who might have a bead on my missing friend or some secret note hidden in his pockets. I was no closer to finding Cherie, and everything with Vale had just gotten infinitely more complicated, and there was this constant, whiny yearning in the back of my throat for Lenoir's absinthe and dark, measuring glare. Back in Criminy's caravan, I had wished for excitement and fame and complications, but I certainly didn't feel satisfied now that I had exactly what I'd wished for.

A low rumble began somewhere above me, and I bolted upright. Was a dirigible crashing? I stood and walked to the window in the elephant's face, which was normally covered, as everything in Paradis was, by velvet curtains. Everything outside looked totally normal, and there was nothing visible in the dark, cloudy sky. Even the moon hid from view, and I didn't blame her.

With my bare hand on the windowsill, I felt the first tremor shudder through the thick copper plating. The noise grew louder, the grind building with the pump of pistons like an old-fashioned train starting up. I grabbed the sill with both hands as the entire elephant lurched sideways with a screech of rending metal. The world outside tipped, and I stared down in time to see one of the giant legs tear free from the ground in a shower of bolts.

I screamed and fell sideways, desperate to find something solid. I managed to get both hands wrapped around the iron-scrollwork headboard, bracing my knees on the bed as the next lurch and screech of metal signaled the freedom of another leg.

"Prince Seti? Auguste? Anyone? Hello?"

The only answer was terrifying chaos as the behemoth tipped sideways, sending the unsecured furnishings and trinkets raining around my head. I ducked as a little table crashed past and clung to the bed like a monkey on a ladder. At least the bed was bolted to the floor. Above me, an engine pumped and groaned, while below me, the next giant leg pulled free from its moorings with a shudder I felt in my teeth. I couldn't imagine what sort of power it took to move something as large as a building or what the prince—or whoever was controlling the elephant—thought he was doing. But I wasn't about to be kidnapped in a giant robot. It was finally time to test the indestructibility of a Bludman's body.

I waited until the pause after the last leg broke free and leaped off the bed, dashing for the ladder set against the round interior of the elephant's stomach. I'd noticed it the first time I'd been brought here for an assignation and had assumed it led to a romantic gazebo topside, since you couldn't really see it from the ground. Considering that the elephant's head and belly were occupied and that the grinding gears were coming from overhead, I was guessing the pilot, or at least the engine, was somewhere up the ladder. Whether I was facing a man or a machine, I was ready to throw a wrench into the works.

I tripped on my skirt and went sprawling, narrowly avoiding a concussion, thanks to an ornate urn that was tumbling all over the place. Growling in frustration, I made it to my knees and untied my skirt, then whipped it off and tossed it to the ground before taking off again on my journey to the copper ladder. Ricocheting awkwardly between the bed and the wall, I managed to reach the ladder and start climbing up the rungs. The elephant was really moving now, the metal creaking and swaying as if we might fall with each heavy footfall. I pushed down a wave of nausea. Seasick and about to barf blood from riding in a runaway steamwork elephant—how ridiculous could this world get?

The hatch at the top of the ladder was loose, and it only took a few turns before I was able to lift it. Hot, oily air spanked me in the face. The steaming engine roared with such a thunderous rumble that the figure seated on a captain's chair didn't hear me or turn around. I climbed into the cockpit with utmost stealth, grateful that I'd dropped the huge skirts, even if it meant I faced my enemy wearing my lacy underpants. After slipping off my satin shoes, I tiptoed across the warm metal. Along the way, I selected a weighty-looking wrench from a bolted-down box of tools and held it aloft. Whoever the dude was, he was going down.

Just behind him, I could smell his expensive hair oil and see the etchings on the brass of his posh pilot's goggles. He'd taken off his tuxedo jacket and had his white sleeves rolled up as he pulled levers and pushed buttons and twisted dials. The elephant was moving as smoothly as could be expected, the legs working in tandem to propel us through the streets with a lolloping rhythm. The windshield showed screaming crowds scattering on the cobblestones and conveyances rattling away down side alleys on two wheels. A throng of gendarmes up ahead was readying a catapult, and I knew that whatever Sang had for defense, I wanted the elephant to stop moving before I suffered for the driver's insanity.

As soon as the pilot chuckled darkly and reached for a lever that looked too much like a joystick with a trigger, I knew it was time to act. I whipped the wrench down and cracked him across the skull. When he tried to turn around and grab the wrench from my hand, I smacked him again, harder and at the temple. It wasn't as easy to put a man out as it looked on TV.

He slumped over, his hands forcing the two large levers forward as he fell.

And the elephant fell with him.

It caught me by surprise, and I slammed forward, right into the windshield. The glass cracked beneath me and gave just a little as the entire monstrosity continued in a slow, graceful fall forward. I reached wildly around me, trying to find something solid to hold on to as, bit by bit, the glass behind my back caved outward. When the unconscious driver crashed into me, the glass finally gave, and I fell out with a gentleman kidnapper and a million-pound copper elephant right on top of me.

I wanted to pass out, but I didn't. It hurt like hell, a hundred times worse than my fall from the catwalk at Paradis. And it didn't help that I was covered in broken glass and twisted metal and the hot, heavy body of my kidnapper. Luckily, I'd fallen out of the window seconds before the entire elephant collapsed, so the cockpit had basically fallen around me, forming a protective, air-filled bubble. Still, I was completely trapped in the pitch-black dark, and no one knew I was here, except for the dead guy on top of me.

Wait.

No, he wasn't dead yet.

As the fear ebbed away, his smell replaced it, forced into my nose and mouth by his closeness. I was pinned, with no way to rid myself of his weight. I tried to shove him away, but he was limp and thick and floppy, and I only succeeded in making the meaty part of his arm fall against my mouth.

Screw it. Dude tries to kill me with a copper elephant, eating him is totally fair game.

Considering the fact that I wasn't trying to woo him or bring him any sort of comfort, I just flat-out bit the bastard's arm, sinking my fangs in like traditional vampires do and ripping a little until the blood really started to flow. The sustenance was more than welcome, considering the fear and exhaustion weighing me down. I'd never felt more like an animal, a creature with no empathy or kindness or reason. In the dark, I became nothing, just an appetite.

Only at the very last moment did I come to myself and remember that you couldn't question dead people. If there was any hope of finding out this guy's motives, he had to be alive when they found him.

Oh, shit.

And if there was any chance of me not going to jail or facing whatever grisly fate Sang used in place of jail, the driver needed to be undrained. I stopped drinking and held my hand around the wounds, willing them to stop bleeding. There wasn't much blood left, but his breathing was shallow, and his heart was still beating, so there was some hope. The machinery creaked and squealed overhead as the gigantic beast settled, but it was quiet enough to hear voices in the small space. I put my mouth right up to his ear and swallowed back my hunger.

"Why did you kidnap me?"

Nothing.

"Who do you work for?"

No answer.

"What do you want?"

At last, a low chuckle, breathy and barely more than a flutter. "Mal—" The machinery overhead groaned and resettled, cutting him off.

"Mal what?"

But his breathing had stopped. *God. Damn. It.*

I kicked a slippered foot against the metal, and a cacophony of new sounds took over. Shouting, clanking, and the hum of a great machine starting up. I eased my arm out from under the man's body and rapped on the closest metal wall. The shouting outside escalated, and I heard an answering knock but not quite near me. I knocked again, and we knocked back and forth until I could feel the metal-muffled ring of a fist against the palm of my hand, playing a Sang version of Marco Polo. I knocked frantically until someone shouted, "Quiet!"

I went silent, waiting.

The voice was muffled but slow and careful. "Shield your eyes, and back away from this wall. We have a saw. Do you understand? Knock once for yes, twice for no."

I knocked once.

"Here we go!"

I maneuvered the man's body so that his arm covered my face; I'd let the dead bastard bear the brunt of whatever damage the rescuers inflicted. The whine of a saw started up outside, and I squeezed my eyes shut as it shrieked against the metal toward my side. Hot sparks sizzled against my arm, and I tucked it in more tightly, hugging the dead body to me and shrinking as far away as I could. I was mostly indestructible but not stupid, and a saw wound would majorly mess up my act, not to mention Lenoir's painting.

Soon I felt a welcome breath of fresh air, or at least what passed for it in the cities of Sang. The metal curled back like a bit of apple peel, and a pair of heavy clippers helped widen the hole. Strong hands in thick gloves reached in to lift me gently from the ruins of the cockpit like a baby bird from a cracked egg. I didn't realize until they laid me on a stretcher and covered me with a rough woolen blanket that I wore nothing but the ruined corset top of my fancy dress and my stained and ruffled bloomers.

"There's another one in here," a man called, and I quickly added, "Don't let him get away. He's the villain who tried to kidnap me."

"He won't be running anywhere, *mademoiselle*. Nearly dead, he is."

I feigned surprise as I sat up and looked on the stretcher beside me. The face was unfamiliar. He could have been any one of thousands of seeming gentlemen who had passed through Paradis since I'd started just a few days ago. Slender, slicked-back blond hair, thin lips. Very pale, but that was mostly my fault.

"Lie down, *mademoiselle*, and we'll get you to the chirurgeon. You might have broken bones."

My heart jerked in my chest. Perhaps Charline had paid well to keep a Bludman in the bounds of Mortmartre, and perhaps Louis had brought enough security to keep us safe on our jaunt to the Tuileries, but I was willing to bet that me showing up in a hospital next to a drained body would cause legal trouble and possible hysteria among scared Pinkies or any men who'd heard of me.

I scrambled to my bare feet, holding the blanket around my body like a cloak.

"I'm fine, really."

All three of the men digging through the rubble of the gigantic elephant stopped to stare at me.

The lead one who'd helped me out was an older gentleman, a barrel-chested human gendarme with a sharp gray beard.

"You are . . . fine?"

I smiled confidently. "Totally fine. Can I return to Paradis, please?"

One of the other men was a daimon, and he leaned in to hiss, "La Demitasse."

The leader shook his head in confusion and disbelief. "If that's what you want to do, *mademoiselle*. Did you leave anything in the, eh . . . pachyderm?"

They'd opened the entire cockpit up, showing a tumble of gears, wires, cogs, levers, and gauges. I didn't see my skirt, but I had no qualms whatsoever about snatching up the kidnapper's abandoned tailcoat and exchanging it for the rough blanket.

"Would y'all mind if I borrowed this?" I asked in my most charming voice.

The gendarmes looked at one another. "Seems fair enough," the leader finally said.

"Then I'll thank you for your time, brave gendarmes." I went up on tiptoe to kiss each of them on the cheek and turned to stroll a few short blocks to Paradis, where the brightly gowned daimon girls and their tuxedoed escorts had crowded out behind a very annoyed barricade of Madame Sylvie and Mademoiselle Charline to watch the chaos. Auguste was already running toward me with a real cloak, but I wanted to keep the tailcoat for myself to see what hints it might hold about its owner.

"Please give the prince my regrets," I said to Sylvie as I sashayed past.

The crowd split to allow my passage, the girls standing sentry between the goggle-eyed gentlemen and my barely dressed form. No one spoke, but Bea's hand lingered on my arm as I passed.

As soon as I was in the building and out of sight, I cracked my back and allowed myself to limp. Damn, that hurt. I went straight upstairs and locked my door. After tossing the oil-stained tailcoat on my bed, I went over every inch of it. There was nothing unusual, just a handkerchief soiled with engine grease and a half-smoked cigarillo. No name tag, no packet of calling cards and bills like so many gentlemen carried in their breast pockets. Whoever the bastard was, he'd planned the kidnapping far enough ahead that he'd remembered to empty his pockets.

I wadded up the coat and hid it in the petticoat drawer of my armoire, undressed, and fell into bed. My head swam, half woozy with blood and half hyped up on fading adrenaline. Someone knocked on my door, and hours later, someone else scratched quietly. I ignored them both. I'd had more than enough excitement for one night.

The next morning came all too soon and, with it, the ache of bruises in places that had never been bruised before. I stretched and pointed my toes, feeling limp all over. As if they'd been listening at the door, which they probably had, Mel and Bea slipped in and approached my bed as if I might bite their heads off or faint.

"Oh, la. I can't believe it. I just can't. Are you . . ."

Bea signed *alive*, and I laughed.

"Y'all, I'm fine. Giant metal elephants run away with me all the time, and I haven't died yet."

"It's all over the papers. Shows are sold out for weeks. Everyone wishes to see you. *Mon dieu, chérie.* You're the most famous girl in Mortmartre. Ever."

I could not care less that everyone wanted to see me.

But wait. Someone more than wanted to see me—someone was expecting me. I'd promised Lenoir a full day of sitting, and the thought of that dizzy, drunken, golden time under the relaxing and dreamy effects of the Red Fairy was a mighty powerful lure. I would heal faster and not feel as much pain, and I would have a bit of respite from the wagging tongues and clutching hands of the gentlemen who would be showing up later tonight to see the girl who'd lived through a pachyderm rampage.

Bea held out a tube of blood, and I took it and thanked her. They had a rushed conversation of signs, and I barely understood that there was something Bea wanted to tell me that Mel didn't want me to know. And I did want to know, but I didn't want them to know that I was learning more sign language. And I also didn't want anything to come between me and Lenoir's studio.

I drank the blood faster than usual—not that I needed it after draining the pilot last night. When I went to my ewer and began to bathe hurriedly, Mel rushed over.

"*Mais* . . . surely you're not going out today, are you? You need to rest."

I smiled and continued trying to clean off the smudges of grease and blood. "I'm off today. And I have an appointment with Lenoir. I can't be late."

The two daimons exchanged a weighty glance.

"It can wait."

I pulled clothes out of my armoire and darted behind my screen to change. "It really can't."

"Demi, *ma chérie*. We understand. We really do. But you are already a star. A portrait by Lenoir will not make life any different. You're as high as you can go already. But you have to take care of yourself."

I stopped furiously pulling the strings of my corset to glare at her over the screen. I'd had just about enough of this line from her and from Vale. And I couldn't even tell the daimons about how my main goal with everything was simply a front to get to Cherie.

"I *am* taking care of myself. But what I need most is not a bunch of mother hens and sassy-pants roosters telling me what I need. I'm not going to Lenoir's studio because I think it's going to make me a star. I'm going because it's relaxing there. Because he's the only person who understands me, who gets what I'm going through. When he's painting me . . . I don't know. It's peaceful. Relaxing. Nothing here is ever relaxing. Here, I feel like someone owns every aspect of me, every moment of my time."

"And when he's painting you, you don't feel like that?" Mel asked carefully.

I rolled my eyes. "It's not like that. I just don't have to be what everyone else wants me to be."

Bea frantically sketched signs in the air, and Mel sighed. "She says . . . well, I don't think you should tell her that. Oh, la. As you wish, my love. Long ago, the daimons believed that—"

The door burst open with Charline in a long purple robe that grazed the ground and a fancy headdress. Behind her stood two human gendarmes and what had to be Paris's version of a reporter, a dapper daimon with a gravity-defying mustache who held a very large and unwieldy camera-type thing.

I huddled behind the screen. "Mademoiselle Charline, I must protest. I'm undressed!"

A sharp flash blinded me and filled the room with pink smoke.

"Well, that's her job, ain't it?" the reporter said, and I pulled my lips back to show my fangs.

One of the gendarmes looked as if he wanted to hide under the bed, but the other one, the older one from yesterday's scene at the toppled elephant, growled and grabbed the reporter by his arm.

"That's no way to speak to a lady," he barked at the reporter as he dragged him out of the room and slammed the door.

"Oh, *mon dieu*. We'll be on the front page of all the papers," Charline wailed, an elegant arm over her eyes, probably to hide the dollar signs that had appeared there.

"I'm Monsieur Bonchance, and this is my associate, Monsieur Legrand. We're sure you're upset and in need of recovering, *mademoiselle*, but we do need to ask you just a few questions so that we can better understand what happened yesterday," the mustachioed gendarme said, his voice gentle, as if I were a dog that might bite him. "Did you know the fellow in question?"

"I'm afraid not. I was expecting Prince Seti, but then the elephant just started walking. I climbed up into the engine room and asked him who he was and what he was doing, but all he said was 'Mal.' Do you know what that means?"

"We'll ask the questions here!" the younger gendarme barked, and I raised an eyebrow.

"I think what Monsieur Legrand means is that as the gentleman died in your presence and under curious circumstances . . ."

"The little doxy drained a human being, inches away from us! In broad daylight!" Legrand barked.

"It wasn't daylight; it was after midnight," Mel burst in

as Bea wagged a finger in the surprised policeman's face.

"*Monsieur*, I do believe that under the circumstances, it is considered self-defense, *n'est-ce pas?*" Charline lovingly dragged Mel and Bea out the door. "If she were a Pinky—I mean, a human—and she had used a hammer or a knife to dispatch her kidnapper, would that not be perfectly within the law?"

Legrand sneered. "All due respect, *madame*, but a hammer ain't teeth. Teeth's personal."

I glanced at the clock and blanched. "*Messieurs*, might I make an appointment to speak with you personally, in private, that we might share information on this incident?" I batted my lashes and slunk around the screen, almost dressed, to take Legrand's narrow, pale hand in mine. He blushed beet-red, perfuming the air with the scent of blood. When I licked my lips, I'm sure he thought it meant something other than polite hunger.

Bonchance answered for him. "That would be satisfactory, *mademoiselle*. We shall expect you tomorrow morning."

"*Merci mille fois, monsieur.*" I bowed over his hand and gave him my most charming smile.

"And I do hope you fine gentlemen will accept these tickets to tonight's show? Mademoiselle Demitasse is understandably too upset to perform, but the daimon girls will astound you."

The younger, angrier gendarme accepted the gold-trimmed tickets and cleared his throat. "We'll leave you to your business, then, *mesdames*. Good day."

Once the gendarmes were out the door, Charline turned to me, her eyes as sharp as a crow's on a busy highway. "You," she started, and I held up a hand.

"I'm off. You promised."

She sighed heavily. "Tomorrow," she said slowly, "will not prove to be your favorite day."

I buttoned up my jacket and gave her my most charming smile. "Provided an enormous copper elephant doesn't fall on me, I suspect I've experienced worse."

I didn't understand half the things she muttered in Franchian as I sashayed out the door, and I didn't care.

I was going to see Lenoir.

23

When Lenoir met me at the door to his flat, my heart stuttered prettily.

"I heard you went for quite a ride last night, my Demitasse. I didn't expect you."

"Water under the bridge, *monsieur*." I fluttered my eyes behind my fan. "But today, I am yours."

Rare and bright, his smile startled me. "And I couldn't be more pleased."

I followed him upstairs, mentally comparing his body with Vale's as the cats twined around my ankles. The two men were built differently, and Lenoir was much older, but I had no complaints. In a way, I felt a little sorry for the men of Sang. With so many petticoats and hoops and bustles, they had no way to judge a woman's true shape until they got her undressed, which didn't happen often. In Sangland, from what I understood, the Pinky women were so terrified to reveal their skin to the noses of bludrats that they rarely removed all their clothes, even for lovemaking. Sometimes I regretted being bludded, but when it came to personal freedoms and safety and how good it felt to take off thirty pounds of fabric and breathe at night, I was definitely on the right team.

Upstairs, I changed quickly and relaxed into my chair with a tranquil sigh. Although it had been gray and oppressive outside, the sun danced in prettily through the window, the motes of dust falling like magic snow upon my arms, where the tiny hairs stood up in ripples. A narrow crystal flute appeared in my hand, pink bubbles fizzing.

"This is not the usual drink," I murmured, taking a sip and then a deeper one.

"Blood and champagne, my dear. They call it the Tsarina's kiss. It's too early for absinthe." He smiled again. "For now."

I nodded, enjoying the sweet fizz tickling my nose. In moments, I'd downed the blood-tinted liquor and wiped a rogue bit of foam off my nose. I had forgotten since landing in Sang how satisfying and refreshing carbonated drinks could be. As a little girl, I had often awoken in the middle of the night so parched I thought I would die, and nothing felt as marvelous as gulping down soda straight from the bottle in the fridge. Before I could mention it, Lenoir had exchanged my flute for another, which I sipped more slowly, as the first one was already bubbling straight up to my head.

I sank deeper into the chair, slowly unfurling in the sunbeam the way a flower greeted the morning. The champagne glittered in my goblet like laughter made liquid, like the lighter, sweeter, more forgiving sister of the dark red wine laced with blood and absinthe he usually gave me for our meetings. With every sip, I told myself it was only a prelude to the bliss yet to come. I let my eyes go soft, trading focus for the fuzzy, dreamy world of Lenoir's studio. I didn't realize I was sighing until Lenoir looked around the canvas at me, his eyes the opaque dark blue of blackberries and threatening to seep in and fill me completely.

"Close your mouth."

I smirked and licked my lips, missing the bright pink gloss I would have worn in my own world.

"I'm not your plaything," I said. "For all that I'm merely an object in your still life, I still have free will. And I'll sigh if I goddamn want to."

"You're harder to paint than a horse. At least they express their annoyance through twitching tails and ears."

The champagne had to be getting to me, for the answer fell from my lips like ripe fruit from a tree. "Horses, *monsieur*, are best kept for riding."

One eyebrow shot up, and I knew my little barb had found the target. Finally, the stark, austere man showed some sign of passion outside of his paint. "I have no time for leisurely riding, *mademoiselle*. And my interests lie outside the acceptable." His words were clipped as he disappeared behind the canvas, his twitching brush belying the break in his usual coolness.

I took another sip, rolling the champagne and blood over my tongue. There was something else there, something sweet and cloying and syrupy. Not absinthe, not even a hint of wormwood and anise, and I didn't know if that was disappointing or comforting. But whatever the unknown addition was, it made my spine go loose, my arms limp, my lips numb. Might as well have been absinthe, for still it made the dust motes dance like fairies, just out of the edges of my vision. But what had he said about his interests?

"Do you know, my dear, that I have traveled?"

My mouth quirked up, and the empty glass spun lazily in my fingers, which seemed altogether too long and as if they had grown another joint. "I would assume so, *monsieur*. A man of your age and tastes would wish to experience the world."

His night-blue eyes peeked around the canvas like a child cheating at hide-and-seek. "I've been to every corner of the globe. Which has no corners, as I suspect you are aware. I've sampled the . . ." He paused daintily, and I could imagine his spade beard twitching as he chose between the word *women* and the word *blood*. "Wares of every bazaar, every bodega, every grand hotel."

"And?"

I was surprised to hear footsteps and looked up to find Lenoir staring down at me, his eyes gone the indigo of caverns cleaved in rock where things are buried forever, hidden until they crumble away to shadowy loam. He looked cold and remote in a way Criminy never had, as if growing older had ossified his heart and caused his veins to shrivel into sharp things, claws that forever grasped. He leaned over, and I found my hands hovering over my chest as if begging him not to snatch out my heart in his twisted talons.

"And I have found that everything in this world has a price." He leaned closer, close enough that I could smell the blood on his breath. "Except, perhaps, yourself. And do you know what that tells me, *mademoiselle*?"

My breath caught, and I tried to smile and utterly failed. "That you need a bigger checkbook, *monsieur*?"

Although I'd considered every smile from the suave older man a triumph, the one he gave now chilled me to the bone. "It tells me that I simply need to find the right cage and the right lock."

I took a shuddering breath and sat up, my backbone suddenly going from gaseous to solid, sublimating into rage and defiance. "There's no cage," I said distinctly, "that can hold me. I've broken out of four so far, and I'll beat my wings against the bars of the next one, too. Right until it fucking breaks."

I was so scared that my knees trembled under my skirt, but his eyes were pinned on my face, and so perhaps he didn't see. And yet something about the way his nostrils flared, like a dog scenting a mailman, told me that he knew. And he liked it.

Lenoir raised his chin, spun, and returned to his palette and canvas slowly, his boots silent on the thick carpet, as if he walked on the moon.

"The funny thing about cages, Mademoiselle Ward, is that if you build them just right"—he winked at me before disappearing behind his canvas—"the creature within need never know it's been trapped."

I heard the rasp of dry bristles on canvas and instinctively moved my arm back into place, my mouth freezing of its own volition into a smile I no longer felt. Not until the cool glass kissed my lips did I realize that he'd moved to my side and refilled my champagne flute, that the glass pressed heavily against my mouth, demanding to be consumed. But the liquid within wasn't light and bubbly and as frivolous as butterfly wings and fairy glitter. No. The moment I scented it, I knew it for what it was. Absinthe. And blood. And other things that, I knew now, had been there all along, hiding under the heavy nightmare of anise and the coppery heat of hunger. His fingers pressed the glass to my lips, urging them apart. My own hands were frozen on the chair. I had no choice but to drink.

By the second sip, I no longer cared what it was.

By the third, I'd forgotten I had wings at all.

After that, time ceased to pass. I seem to recall cool hands on my arms, pulling laces, tugging on shoes, moving me like a grand, cold doll. I remember a slight thump as my head hit the wall on the way down the stairs. I recall, like some faraway dream, Auguste's shocked gasp and his soft murmur. "*Monsieur*, is she even alive? It's too much." And then the beat of an engine, the rocking of the stairs, and the beloved, dark, infinite quiet of silk sheets sliding over my body.

When I slept, I dreamed of dark angels and deep wells of wine, floating with bones. And dancing. Always dancing.

Heavy knocking roused me, just a little. My eyes were smeary, my limbs forged of lead. I tried to move, but I was all tangled up on my bed.

"Demi? Are you here?"

I had to swallow a few times to find my tongue. "*Entrez.* Or something," I called, struggling to figure out which way was up. My head felt as if it was stuffed with wine-soaked cotton balls, heavy and wobbly.

The curtains parted, and Vale appeared like a giant bat: upside down and flapping. I laughed my ass off.

"Oh, no, *bébé*. What have you done?" The words were lazy, slow, and overloud, as if he were shouting underwater, and yet his steps were oddly fast as he crossed the soft rugs to reach me.

"Might still be a bit drunk," I answered, staring at his boots, which were wet and caked in filth. He'd come from the sewers under the city, then. "And you're getting shit on my rug."

Warm hands caught me under my knees and behind my shoulders, and my stomach flipped for a dozen reasons as he set me upright, or what I had to assume was upright, as everything suddenly ceased being upside down. He kneeled, his golden-green eyes boring into mine like corkscrew grass. I opened my mouth a little, hoping he might kiss me while I was too drunk to act surprised about it. But instead of settling his lips over mine, he simply breathed me in.

"Drunk on what?"

I licked my lips, marveling that the champagne and wine and anise and wormwood and red blood could merge to taste like candy, hours after the fact.

My voice went low, playful. Rebellious. "This is Paris. What do you think I've been drinking? *Café au lait?*"

"Absinthe. *Mon dieu, bébé.* How much?" He shook my shoulders, making my teeth rattle like the bone dice Louis had shaken in a cup in the pleasure gardens.

I wiggled out of his grasp and turned onto my hip to splay myself gracefully over the bed in a similar attitude to the pose I'd adopted for the artist. I'd sat this way for hours, my face frozen in a teasing Mona Lisa smile, waiting like Pavlov's dog for the moments when Monsieur Lenoir would set down his brush and refill my goblet with a splash of his potent cocktail. Funny, how things as normally repellent as red wine, absinthe, and blood could mix together and not curdle in the glass. But the taste was a thousand times better than any ingredient alone, and the high was the opposite of caffeine.

And it only got better, each time I had it.

"How much, Demi?"

I shrugged elegantly and nearly fell off the bed. "Just a glass."

Vale leaned close, his face more serious than I'd ever

seen it. Normally, I was the stiff, controlled diva, and he was the mischievous brigand, the clown. But now I was loose as a goose, and he was so tightly wound you could almost hear the gears grinding inside.

It struck me as funny, and I swallowed a giggle and poked his nose with my finger and said, "Boop."

Vale was so tense he was all but vibrating. "Demi. *Mon dieu*, woman. Will you never listen to me? Not even once? Absinthe is serious, *bébé*. It is poison. It is dangerous." His hands cupped my face, but again, the kiss didn't come. With his thumbs, he pulled down my eyelids, and I rolled my eyes. "Drink all the bloodwine you want. Get drunk every night, preferably in my vicinity. But I'm begging you never to take absinthe again."

I wrenched out of his grasp and rubbed my eyes. "You're totally harshing my buzz, man."

"You could go into a coma, Demi."

"Your mom's in a coma."

"You could die."

"I'd die happy." I flopped back again and rolled my head over the pillows, my attention caught by what I thought was a brass octopus offering me millions of diamonds.

Vale's hand cupped my scalp behind the sweat-plastered curls, pulling me forward and out of the little reverie inspired by the glittering chandelier. "I wouldn't," he said with a heavy gentleness. "And neither would your friend Cherie. Have you forgotten her already?"

That finally broke through the dizziness—that anger. "Of course not. Of course I haven't forgotten her. She's like my sister!"

"And are you any closer to finding her? Have you done a single thing today, asked a single question? Or have I been running around Paris, spending my hard-earned francs to buy up teeth, in the hopes that you'll see how much I care for you?"

I pushed away from him, but my arms were too weak to have any effect. He only held me tighter. But he couldn't stop me from talking. "I don't know where to begin, Vale! This life eats me up. There's not a spare moment. I'm lost and dizzy and exhausted and constantly hounded, and I'm still no closer, just rolling old men's bodies, my hands deep in their moist pockets. Just waiting every moment to be kidnapped, to be stolen away like a child in the night." Something knocked at the back of my brain, and the sudden realization would have taken me to my knees had Vale not been holding me. "Oh, shit. I should've just let the elephant take me away. I had my chance, and I totally blew it. It's what I want most, and it terrifies me. I just had to fight, didn't I?"

"You are a fighter, *bébé*. Do not blame yourself for following your instincts."

"But I do. And these teeth—are they even hers? Will they bring me any closer to finding her at all? If I stop to think about it for even a heartbeat, I nearly go mad with grief and frustration. But the absinthe quiets it. Only the absinthe and your mouth give me any peace at all, you bastard, and how dare you throw it back in my face?"

I wanted to shake my head, but I wanted his hands on my body more, so I let him hold me there and give me a significant look that made me feel even more warm and loose-limbed than I already was. I swallowed hard and sat forward, and Vale's hand slipped around to cup my jaw, his thumb stroking my cheek. "Please, Demi. Please, *bébé*. We'll look harder. But no more absinthe."

My lips parted as I leaned forward to kiss him, and he jerked back. "Why, Vale? I don't understand . . ."

"I can taste it on your lips."

"So?"

"So I want nothing to do with wormwood and blood."

I moved forward again, murmuring, "Don't be silly. Lenoir said——"

He stood smoothly, from his haunches to his feet before my eyes could track him. He'd managed to lay me gently on my pillows, but I felt the loss of his touch so keenly. "Lenoir," he breathed. "What else did he tell you, *bébé*?"

"That it was harmless. That the stories weren't true. That Bludmen weren't . . ."

"Weren't . . .?"

I sighed. "I forget the word."

"Of course you do. He wants you to forget."

"He doesn't. He wants to paint me. Wants to make me an even bigger star. Wants my portrait hung in the Louvre, surrounded by crowds." I was in his arms again before I could blink, my head cradled against his shoulder like a child.

"What he wants," Vale whispered in my ear, "is for you to give in completely, a little at a time." He placed my head back down, and I puddled limply amid the down pillows. With infinite care and a face as hard and sad as weeping stone, he drew the covers over me.

"But he's an artist——" I started.

"Oh, *bébé*. He's a man, and all men are liars."

He slipped out the window without looking back, and I giggled softly to myself.

"Liar!" I yelled to the darkness.

*   *   *

When I next heard banging on my door, I was far less drunk and much more annoyed, in part because I couldn't remember what had happened at Lenoir's or why Vale and I had quarreled. He had refused to kiss me—I knew that much. And there was something about Cherie, about me not trying hard enough to find her. As if plundering bodies and making myself a sitting duck weren't enough.

The knocking made me grind my teeth, tasting something black and twisted, licorice and soot.

"Go away!"

The knocking continued, louder and more insistent, and I took off my boot and threw it against the wood.

"Demitasse, forgive me, but the gendarmes are here for you."

I sat up, blinking back against the sun piercing my curtains. "Am I to have no peace?"

The door opened, and Charline smirked at me. "You wanted to be a star, and stars have no peace. Dress quickly. The photographers are outside the front door, waiting to snap you."

I groaned and rolled to my feet, testing whether my legs would hold me up. It was iffy. Bathing with rose water from the ewer, I couldn't help noticing my face. It was a total mess, the kohl and mascara dribbling down my cheeks in dried tear tracks and the lipstick bow smeared across my chin. God, and Vale had seen me like this last night? No wonder he hadn't kissed me. I looked like Courtney Love after a bender. I scrubbed it all off and rubbed in an expensive cream made of crushed pearls— a gift from a nameless suitor—before reapplying my makeup and touching up my hair. Even dressed to the nines, I felt itchy and off, and I vowed to take a long, hot bath after the night's show, even if it meant I had to pay Auguste to drive me to a public bath house. My time at Lenoir's yesterday had promised to be relaxing, but I felt more tightly wound than ever, as if nothing would satisfy me until I tasted the absinthe again.

Wait. Had I promised Vale I wouldn't drink it again? I didn't think I had.

He'd been right about one thing, though: I had let the giddy whirl of fame get to my head, and I wasn't trying hard enough to find Cherie. By light of day, I felt silly and lazy and guilty. And ready to get tough about finding answers.

With every hair in place and long satin gloves covering my arms, I sashayed down the stairs and out the door, blowing kisses to Mel and Bea and the rest of the girls, who watched and whispered. And no wonder—I'd nearly been killed in a giant elephant and had then disappeared for a day with the most famous and notorious artist in the world and come home too drunk to walk. Even for a cabaret girl, I lived a wild life.

Are you okay? Bea signed, and I nodded and signed, *Thank you.*

As soon as Auguste opened the front door, flashes of light and clouds of powder erupted. The photographers crowded around, their reporter partners shouting questions in Franchian and Sanglish and waggling huge feather quills in my face to get my attention. I drew the veil on my hat down over my eyes and took the hand the mustachioed gendarme offered me. But instead of gently holding my hand as if I were getting into a carriage, his leather glove clamped down around my wrist, and he all but dragged me into a waiting constabulary conveyance. The appointments were far rougher than I was accustomed to, and I clenched my hands around the wooden bench as the thing grumbled down the cobblestones, battering me against the sides behind iron bars.

"At least I'm not in manacles," I grumbled.

The younger, nastier gendarme snorted. "Against my recommendation, I might add. Please cause trouble. I beg you." He not-so-subtly stroked the sleek gun resting against his hip. It looked like a futuristic metal ray gun, but I was willing to bet it was filled with seawater that would burn my skin and possibly leave me with permanent scars. He'd probably never had a chance to use it before and was just praying to give it a whirl.

I crossed my legs and gave him a sultry smile. "You're not the first man to say that to me, Monsieur Legrand."

He scowled and stared at his clenched hands. I had an enemy for life, but it was worth it.

The conveyance stopped in front of a grand edifice, all soaring white stone and gargoyles and carvings, classic Paris in this world or my own. Inside, it was noticeably less charming, the windows mostly covered and the gaslights a sickly yellow. The floor was dark and slick and made each footstep echo, each muffled thump or shriek bounce eerily off the walls. I walked between the gendarmes, head back as if they served me instead of compelled me. I still wasn't exactly sure what they wanted, but I knew it wasn't good. My job now was to turn the tables and get what I wanted in the most dramatic and diva-esque way possible.

"Pastry, *madame*?"

I gave the older gendarme a quirked eyebrow as he

held up a pretty lavender box of *éclairs* that I had to assume were the Sang version of cop doughnuts.

"Unless they're filled with blood, *monsieur*, I must demur."

"Oh, la. I had forgotten." He stifled a laugh and shook his head, and I liked him the better for it. He would clearly be playing the role of Good Cop in today's drama. "I'm afraid we don't keep blood on hand, *mademoiselle*. I do believe you're the first Bludman we've had in the station."

I waved him off. "I understand. A few years ago, I would have gladly eaten half that box."

His jaw dropped, showing teeth that had clearly seen too many pastries. "But . . . you were once human? I have heard tales but assumed it was merely supposition."

"I was born just as human as you, *monsieur*." I batted my eyelashes, knowing that when I wanted to, I could look like an innocent seventeen-year-old. "Fortunately, on the cusp of death, my godfather was able to change me over. But I do miss the sweets."

The younger gendarme spit on the ground. "Blasphemy. The girl is clearly lying."

I fought the urge to hiss and claw his face off. "Tell me, are those *éclairs* filled with vanilla cream, chocolate *ganache*, or pudding? I always preferred the vanilla cream, myself. Especially the real kind, made with butter and Madagascar vanilla."

The older gendarme's mouth twitched. "These are chocolate *ganache*," he said, patting his belly. "My favorite."

"Let's get this over with," the younger one grumbled, and they led me through a thick metal door with a small, barred window near the top. Inside was a sturdy wooden table and three chairs. The older gendarme pulled out my chair for me, and I sat daintily, crossing my legs at the ankles. The gendarmes sat across from me, each one shuffling his papers and preparing his pen.

"Sergeants Bonchance and Legrand, questioning Mademoiselle Demi Ward, also known as La Demitasse, regarding the events of March nine," the older gendarme said loudly and clearly, glancing at the window in the door in a way that told me we had a witness.

"Please proceed," a metallic voice boomed through a rudimentary speaker.

"Mademoiselle Ward, please tell us everything that happened on the night of March nine."

And I told them, conveniently leaving out the bit about having the hottest sex of my life with a costumed brigand in a private alcove. When I got to the moment when the copper elephant ripped free of its moorings and began to charge through the streets, the younger gendarme, Legrand, raised a hand.

"*Mademoiselle*, just to clarify, could you please tell us why you were to meet the prince in this pachyderm?" The nasty quirk of his thin lips told me to tread carefully.

"I have no idea what he might have had in mind, *monsieur*. I was merely asked to pay my respects to a visiting dignitary."

"On your knees, *mademoiselle*?"

I smiled sweetly. "I'm a citizen of Almanica, *monsieur*. I kneel to no one."

"So you're saying no money changed hands? That there was no understanding?"

"Not with me. I had barely spoken twenty words to the prince beforehand. Whatever expectations he might have had are his own business. But pray tell, Monsieur

Legrand, how does this apply to my attempted kidnapping?"

"That's Sergeant Legrand," the smaller man growled.

Bonchance put a kindly hand on his arm. "Let's get back on track, lad." He gave me a sympathetic look. "Now, can you tell us how you incapacitated your kidnapper?"

Another saccharine smile. "I hit him twice in the head with a heavy wrench. I assume that self-defense isn't yet against the law?"

Bonchance shook his head no, but Legrand leaned avidly forward.

"Interesting. But how did the gentleman in question come to be exsanguinated?"

My nostrils flared, and I put up a gloved hand. Funny, how I'd never had so much power before now, the first time I'd been a minority. And I wasn't taking his shit. "Please, *monsieur*. If I might ask a question? Would you be interrogating me if you thought I had killed him with the wrench? Or a knife? Or any other weapon at hand?"

"That question is not pertinent—"

"An attorney might think it is."

Legrand went silent, and Bonchance stroked his mustache.

The older cop leaned forward, speaking out of the side of his mouth as if we shared a secret. "You must understand, *mademoiselle*, that as Bludmen are rare in Paris, this is a new conundrum for us. Technically speaking, it is against the law to drink from a human. But if it was self-defense against someone who clearly meant you harm, we must consider it carefully."

"*Messieurs*, I beg you. Please remember, during your deliberations, that I was trapped in a very small, dark room with a man who had already tried to kidnap me." I blinked, letting my eyes tear up. "And I'm also fairly certain that the crash had damaged him internally. Do you have any idea who that madman was?"

Legrand scoffed. "This is a police investigation, *mademoiselle*, not your personal gossip mill."

I sat up straighter, dropping the doe-eyed act. "I have a right to know the identity of my attacker."

"That remains to be seen."

"And I'd also like to discuss the disappearance of my dear friend Cherie, who was abducted by slavers on the road to Ruin."

"That is not part of the current investigation," Legrand snapped.

Bonchance added, "And only the city of Paris itself is in our jurisdiction, you see."

"You'll not even take a statement? Not even send out a bulletin with her information?"

Legrand looked as if he might spit again. "The whereabouts of . . . *cabaret girls* is not our top priority. Girls disappear frequently, mostly as a result of the unsavory habits of your lifestyle. If we spent our time chasing down every loose woman who fell on hard times, we wouldn't have time to investigate important things, like murders. We're the ones asking the questions, *mademoiselle*; you'd do well to remember that."

I stood, the chair clattering to the ground behind me. "I'm sorry, but are you telling me that you're satisfied to let slavers kidnap innocent travelers? And that when a madman kidnaps me in a giant machine, I'm not only prevented from knowing his name, but I'm also on trial for killing him in self-defense? Because I'd like to speak to a lawyer. Attorney. Barrister. Whatever you call it in this insane excuse for a justice system."

Bonchance held out his hands. "Now, *mademoiselle*. Let's stay civil and reasonable."

Legrand's lip twisted up. "I hate questioning women. So melodramatic."

Anger flared, my cheeks blazing hot. "So when women are kidnapped, you treat them like criminals? This is clearly a case not only of misogyny but also of racism. Were I a human man, you'd be clapping me on the back and handing me a cigar. But because I'm female, a Bludman, and, in the words you're too cowardly to speak and which aren't actually true, a whore, I don't deserve justice?"

They both stared at me, mouths open.

"*Mademoiselle*—" Bonchance began, and I almost felt sorry for him.

"Tell me, either of you. Tell me you think that because of who I am, because of what I am, I deserved it. I dare you."

"We didn't mean—"

"Tell me," I said clearly, turning to let my eyes bore through the window in the door, "that every word I just spoke isn't true, and I will cease to be, as you say, melodramatic." I sat down daintily. "And I'll wait for that lawyer now, while I compose my remarks for whichever reporters would consider my little story worthy of their time."

After a long, dangerous, and painful pause, the speaker squawked, "The *mademoiselle* is free to go."

Bonchance opened the door, and I flounced out of the room like the queen of goddamn England. Now I just had to discover who had kidnapped me and where he had planned to take me. I had to find Cherie and prove all those self-righteous good-old-boy hypocrites wrong.

24

Back at Paradis, I ignored Charline and all my curious coworkers and went straight to the tailcoat I'd stashed in my armoire. There had to be something I'd missed. Gentlemen always left a signature of their grandeur in this world.

I stretched the garment out on my bed, running my fingers along the seams and searching for a tailor's mark, a tag, a button, anything. It was well made and of the latest fashion, but tiny white stitches showed where the tailor's tag had been torn from the lining. I sniffed at the thick fabric, scenting oil and hot metal and an unsavory, magic funk. It was vaguely familiar, but I couldn't place it. An odor clinging to the cuff made me gasp—Bludman and pine and vanilla. Cherie. I put my lips to it, breathing it in.

"Did you just lick a coat?"

I spun, hands curled into claws, as Vale swung his other leg over to sit on my windowsill. "Do you ever knock?"

He grinned. "Not if I can help it."

His fingers drummed on the sill as the gauzy white curtains billowed around him, highlighting the deep gold of his skin and the brightness of his eyes. He was back in his brigand's gear, all black and shadows, and I unconsciously licked my lips, remembering what it felt like to pull him close by tuxedo lapels and devour him.

"Aren't you supposed to be mad at me?" I asked.

He shrugged. "My anger burns off easily, like clouds on a sunny day. And you're not drunk or drugged, so I'm hoping you took my warning to heart."

"You're not my boss."

The grin deepened, quirked, took on a new meaning. "Didn't say I wanted to be."

I looked down and swallowed hard, all my earlier bravado fled. "Thank you for the book."

"*De rien, bébé.* I'm glad it pleased you, even if I didn't."

"You did, but . . ." The apology was on the tip of my tongue, but something held it back.

"I didn't come here for thanks, you know."

I sat down on the edge of the bed and jumped right back up, suddenly skittish. "What do you want, then?"

He stood, took a confident but tentative step. "Just this moment or in general?"

"Your choice."

"You want to have this discussion now, *bébé*? Might be easier after a bottle of wine."

But after my outburst at the police station, I was done with being misunderstood. "Tell me the truth, Vale. Why did you offer to help me find Cherie?"

"You know why. Because I have a soft spot for lost girls. And so I would have an excuse to keep seeing you."

"What do you want from me?"

"Everything."

I blushed and turned away, twisting the tailcoat between my black fingers, aware now more than ever how other I had become. In the police station, I'd been furious at their prejudice, at their assumptions. But now, faced with the truth about someone who had no such qualms, I felt strange and unlovable and desperately alien. And so close to my goal yet so very far away.

"What did you think would happen once we'd found Cherie?" I asked.

He stepped close, so close I could feel the heat of his chest against my back. "More truth? As you like. I did not expect to find her. We've never found a girl after the slavers took her, at least not whole and undamaged. But I was willing to do anything to find her. For you. And if we did and she was beyond help, I would hold you until you were done crying and help you move on. Give you a reason to move on."

I clasped my hands against my heart. In a tiny voice that was more human than anything I'd said in years, I said one word: "Why?"

"Oh, *bébé.*" His arms wrapped around me with the same silken warmth as his sigh, and I leaned back into him. "Biggest star in Mortmartre, and do you not even know your own worth? You're an adventure. A beautiful, wild, strange, intelligent, rebellious journey of a woman. No cookfires for you, no bookkeeping or weaving or collecting of ribbons. You're the kind of woman who would leap onto the back of a strange bludmare behind a stranger, gallop for hours without complaint, and plunge into the sewers without a second thought. The kind of woman who willingly walks into a trap to save someone she loves. The women of my tribe are fierce but not as fierce as you." He planted a little kiss behind my ear. "And you make me laugh. I dearly love to laugh." His hips pressed against me, a quick brush that was more a statement than a question. "And I like to do other things, too."

"Stop, Vale. Be serious."

"And you don't think sex is serious? It's the driving force of nature, *bébé*. Everything a man does is for love or sex." He chuckled. "Power is about sex. Fame is about sex. Food keeps you alive so you can have more sex. Clothes make people want to look at you, think seriously about bedding you. Not that I generally take anything seriously. But still. You are a fool if you discount what really motivates every single person and creature in Sang." He paused, sighed in my ear. "You turned me into a poet, *bébé*. Even the best songs and books are about love."

"Which one are you talking about? Sex or love?"

He swayed against me, making my hips move. I didn't fight it; I felt liquid and dizzy. "Maybe both," he said, and he spun me around to face him, catching my face in his hands and pulling me in with delicious slowness for a deep, lapping kiss that melted my hips into his.

A knock on the door made me jump guiltily away from him, my teeth bared at the innocent rectangle of wood. My door at the caravan had been mostly left alone, and I'd grown to find all the knocking and demands of Paradis as vexing as the spam e-mails I'd received back on Earth.

"What?" I barked, and the door opened just enough to admit Blaise. I hadn't seen him in a while, and his big, dark eyes trembled with fear.

I beckoned him in, smiling. "Don't worry, *chou-chou*. I'm not annoyed with you."

He perked up and placed a sharp envelope in my hands, the paper thick and heavy with portent. I turned it over, noting that the blood-red wax seal featured crossed paintbrushes and the letter L. Forgetting that I wasn't alone, I ripped the flap with no panache and pulled a creamy folded sheet from within. The impeccable script in dark purple ink matched the flecks of flower petals embedded in the paper.

> *La Demitasse, ma chérie,*
>
> *I must request one final sitting to complete the masterpiece. It shall soon be ready for display at the Louvre, where all may gaze upon your beauty and tremble. Come to me one last time, my star. Tomorrow.*
>
> *L.*

Pride and a strange sort of hunger-lust bloomed in my chest. One more taste of that amazing, delirious draught. One more golden afternoon under Lenoir's dark and delicious gaze.

The postscript was messier than the rest of the letter, as if he'd lost just a bit of that tight control. "I shall miss our quarrels, *ma chérie*," it said. "But I shall enjoy more than words one final toast to your fame."

"You're not going," Vale said, and I spun away from his prying eyes.

"Reading over my shoulder? That's low, even for you."

He made a strangled noise, half groan, half growl. "*Bébé*, please. We both know that's a fancy invitation to fuck you on the canvas."

We stood just a few feet apart, but suddenly, a wide and uncrossable gulf opened between us. As if he could see it, too, Blaise backed away and darted out the door.

"For your information, Monsieur Hildebrand, I've only fucked one person since I arrived in Paris."

"That is the past." He pointed at the letter still in my hand. "While this is an obvious offer for something in the future."

"You don't trust me?"

"Of course, I trust you! Otherwise, I wouldn't leave you alone in this glorified whorehouse long enough to hunt teeth and secrets in Darkside. It's him I don't trust. Lenoir." He wrapped a hand around the bedpost, his knuckles white. "Do you even remember last night? You were beyond drunk, as open and easy as a flower. Anyone could have done anything to you, and you would have just lain there, laughing, smiling."

"So why didn't you?"

"Because I want you awake and looking into my eyes while I tell you with every stroke that you're mine. Not insensible and silly. Any man who wants that . . ." He set his forehead against the wooden post and sighed. "He's a coward. And a villain."

"And what makes you think I won't sit for the portrait one last time, raise a glass of champagne, and leave with a kiss on the back of my hand? He's never touched me, Vale. He's never tried."

"That's the thing about absinthe, *bébé*. When the time comes, he won't have to try at all."

I opened my mouth to say a million more things, but then I remembered that I alone knew Lenoir's secret. That he was a Bludman, like me, and that I needed that fellow feeling in a foreign place, surrounded by strangers. Something told me that if Vale ever learned anything about that, the smile would finally drop off his face forever.

One more trip to Lenoir's studio, and then it would be over.

One more sip of absinthe, and then I would be done.

Then I would be good.

Then I would be a star.

And Vale didn't need to know that.

"Maybe you're right," I said.

His eyes were wary as I walked to the fire and tossed in the note and the envelope, but as the paper caught and burned, he relaxed and finally let go of the bedpost. He came to stand by my side, sliding an arm around my waist with comfortable ease and pulling me against him.

I watched the paper curl, breathing in the smoke that rose from the cherry-red edges. I tasted violets and anise and something darker, woven into the paper along with the dried flowers. I wondered, briefly, what might have grown from the letter had I planted the paper in some dark place and watered it and kept it warm.

I was so lost in my reverie that I'd almost forgotten Vale was there, difficult as that was. Something about the smoke, about Lenoir's letter . . . I finally blinked back to reality when he said, "Changing the subject, *bébé*: You never answered. Were you licking the coat?"

In his hands, the elephant pilot's tailcoat seemed limp and harmless, and I walked over to finger the place on the collar that should have held the tailor's tag.

"He removed the tags. And the buttons are completely average. And I wasn't licking it; I was smelling the sleeve. He's been near Cherie. I think. It's hard to tell with all the clockwork grease."

"From running the pachyderm, I suppose?" He held out the arms, inspected the fabric between two fingers. "It's been there since Paradis opened. I don't think anyone knew it could move, that it was useful for anything but . . ."

I raised one eyebrow, daring him to finish it.

"I didn't even know you could go into the head," he finished with a smirk.

"Me, neither. But then again, I spend as little time in there as possible."

"I know."

We glared at each other for a few moments, just until I noticed him staring hungrily at my lips.

"And you never told me why you broke in through my window."

"What, is it not enough to crave your company?"

"Oh, it's enough." I dragged a finger up the dark stubble on his throat just to watch him swallow. "But that's not why you're here."

He laughed with his usual good humor before shaking his head and clearing his throat, uneasy as a dancing horse. "Right as always, *bébé*. Two things, both disturbing. First of all, I found another fang and put it into the hands of a glancer. All she could glean is that the Bludman in question is somewhere deep underground and miserable. So if the fang did come from Cherie, we know she is not a concubine in a cabaret or a servant in a duke's palace."

"But she's underground and miserable! And we don't even know where to start looking or if she's underground in another city . . ." I broke away from his orbit and paced the room. I'd always felt it was better to know the truth than to wonder, but now his news had killed my foolish hope.

"And here is the other thing—also bad news but a clue nevertheless."

The item he pulled from his waistcoat pocket was small and heavy and cold in my palm. I pushed the curtain aside to let sunlight fall on the oil-smudged metal of a tie tack. "Is that a skull? With wings?"

He nodded. "A raven skull with bat wings. And a top hat."

"Where did it come from?"

Vale pointed to the jacket on my bed. "From his cravat."

"How did you get it?"

Vale shrugged. "I have my ways." I stared harder. "I am a brigand, *bébé*. Had you forgotten?"

"I remember. I just haven't seen you do many . . . brigandly things."

He grinned. "That just shows you what an excellent brigand I am."

"What does it mean?"

"That your kidnapper tied a natty cravat."

At the end of my rope, I curled my fingers into Vale's shirt and hissed at him, hard, my bared teeth inches from his lips. He stumbled back with a look of such surprise that it was almost comical.

"Did you just hiss at me?"

"You deserved it. Now, stop being clever and explain to me what this is, why it's important, and why this guy wanted to kidnap me in a fucking elephant. It's . . . not subtle."

Vale held out his hand, and I dropped the button into it. He bit the edge and turned it over with one wide finger, and I noted how odd it was to see a man's bare hand; I still wasn't used to it. "It's cast of solid gold, which is unusual. The symbol is not one that I have seen before, but among my people, it's sinister. A raven's skull is used for dark magic. Bat wings signify nighttime. The top hat is a very expensive kind, extra tall, favored only by the very wealthy men who can afford it. So whoever he was, he had money and dangerous leanings."

"But you don't know who he was?"

"No. But I expect that some of the daimon girls might. It's an extraordinary man who isn't known somewhere in Mortmartre. Especially if he has the money to buy the rare things that take his fancy."

"Do we have a picture of him? A description? He was blond and completely forgettable."

He shook his head. "The gendarmes are covering it up, for some reason. I caught this little dainty before they could stuff everything in the incinerator."

"Hmm." I ran a finger over the design. It was pretty, if evil. "So lots of money is involved."

He threw back his head and laughed. "It doesn't take a lot of money to make the gendarmes dance, *bébé*. But yes, judging by the fact that they were going to burn solid gold instead of keeping it, I'm guessing many francs changed hands."

I tried to think back, but I had never really seen the kidnapper's face, thanks to his goggles and mask.

"He said something to me. Before he died." I paused, rolled the button back and forth on his palm. "Mal."

"Mal?"

"That's it."

"What does it mean?"

"I dunno. It means nothing to me. What's it mean to you?"

He rubbed a finger over the dent his tooth had made in the button. "*Mal* means bad, evil." But the way he rubbed his chin, his eyes shifting like moor grass . . .

"There's something more, isn't there?"

"Maybe. There are rumors . . ."

"Yes?"

"I've heard whispers of something called the Malediction Club. Its members are high up, very high, and sworn to absolute secrecy on pain of death."

"But what is it?"

"I don't know, not exactly. I had always assumed it was just a party of the usual powerful men sitting around with cigars, patting one another on the back. But between this pin, your kidnapping, and the way the gendarmes are sweeping it all under the rug, I suspect the Malediction Club is real and this is their crest, their sigil." He glanced up at the clock and then to the window, his fist curling around the pin. "Come on."

I followed him out my door, expecting him to drag me into the sewers or through dark alleys and into Darkside. Instead, he went right across the hall to knock on the room shared by Mel, Bea, and Blaise. After a moment, Bea answered with a halting smile.

"Demi needs your help," Vale said plainly, and Bea stepped back to let us in, her small hands blanching sky-blue against the wood.

Mel lay on the wooden double bed, curled on a bright red and green blanket and reading a book, which she quickly shut and slid under a fluffy white pillow. Both girls were in simple shifts, and I noticed something that completely floored me, something I'd never noticed before.

They had no tails.

Every daimon I'd ever known had had a long, somewhat prehensile tail. Luc and his brother at the caravan used them for balance while doing incredible dance moves, and I had also met daimons who used them for building, painting, or self-defense. But Mademoiselle Caprice and every daimon I'd ever seen at Paradis had always been dressed in layers and layers of costume, and I had taken for granted that their tails were curled up under voluminous skirts. I caught myself staring and looked away.

"You need help, *chérie*?" Mel asked, and Bea sat down beside her on the bed, their hands clasping unconsciously and merging Bea's blue with Mel's green for a beautiful teal that made me smile.

"Are you sure—?" I started, and Vale nodded.

"What do you know about the Malediction Club?" I asked.

The color drained out of Bea, leaving her a sickly grayish-white, her eyelids fluttering as if she might faint.

Mel wrapped an arm around her and drew her close, giving me a reproachful look. "Nothing," she said. "Nothing more than anyone. It's a rumor, something whispered in the dark. Wealthy men who do horrible things. But no one's ever seen it."

"Do you recognize this, then?" Vale held out the button, and Mel took it, examining it.

With sudden violence, Bea dashed it to the ground, where it skittered across the room.

"What's come over you, darling?" Mel asked. "Do you know more?"

Bea shook her head and hid behind her hair but wouldn't lift her hands to sign.

"I've seen that symbol before," Mel said slowly. "On a

cravat, here or there. Figured it was just something the Pinkies enjoyed."

"Do you remember any of the men who wore them?" Vale asked.

Mel shrugged and gave a small, defiant smile. "Oh, la. All the Pinkies look alike to me. But it is always fancy gents—I remember that much."

"What about the fellow who tried to kidnap Demi? Did you know anything about him?"

Mel shook her head. "We couldn't see him, with the pachyderm fallen and the gendarmes all around. Did they find that pin on his body? How wretched."

Bea's fingers twitched in her lap, and one hand rose, shaking, to make signs. I recognized a few of the letters as she spelled something out. After the last one, her hand fell limply back to her lap, and she slumped over, drained and defeated.

"*Charmant*? Darling, I don't think it's charming at all." Mel drew her close, stroking her hair and her back and kissing her forehead as Bea shuddered, eyes closed.

"Monsieur Charmant?" Vale asked quietly, and Bea shook with a sob.

"That's enough," Mel said, eyebrows drawn down defiantly. "I don't know what you're getting at, but she hasn't been this bad in years. I think you need to leave now."

"Bea, I'm so sorry—" I started.

"We're going." Vale took my hand and dragged me out, leaving the gold button winking on a threadbare rug.

The last thing I saw was Bea sobbing violently, silently, in Mel's arms.

25

Back in my room, Vale made straight for the window.

"Who is this Monsieur Charmant?" I asked, rushing to catch his sleeve before he could slip away.

"A dark daimon. An apothecary. He's the one who buys the tails."

"What tails?"

He paused, one leg on either side of the sill, and sat on it like a pawing stallion. "Demi, *bébé*, stop playing dumb. You saw, just now. I watched it reach your eyes. When the daimons come to work in cabarets, they must have their tails amputated. The human men won't touch them otherwise. Their magic comes from their tails; their poison, too. They go to a daimon chirurgeon to have it done and sell their tails by the pound to Monsieur Charmant."

"What the hell does anyone want with a tail?"

He shook his head in disgust. "Magical properties. They powder it for use in potions and draughts. Use the leather to make grimoires or charms or boots. Sell the meat as a delicacy."

I stared at him, jaw dropped. A fly actually, literally, seriously landed on my tongue, and I coughed and hacked and danced around until I'd spit it back out. "Are you shitting me?"

"Oh, *bébé*. You've only seen the sweet side of Mortmartre, and how sweet has it been? If this is Paradis, how do you imagine life goes in Enfer? Have you ever walked through the mouth of hell? There are daimons and humans with far darker desires than you could ever dream, and if they have the coppers, they can get whatever they need to find satisfaction."

I dragged my feet to the bed and sat down heavily. All these beautiful, seemingly carefree girls around me, and they'd all basically given up a limb to be here. From the outside, they were as pretty and bright as songbirds, but on the inside, they were crippled things, their smiles as fake as the feathers they glued to their eyelashes. I had wanted so badly to taste fame that I had ignored their suffering and simply stepped among them and sometimes on them on my way to the top. A blud tear fell on my taffeta skirt, then another and another. Vale hurried from the window to put an arm around me.

"Don't, *bébé*. We all choose our paths. This is a safer place than most."

"But Paris seems so . . . sweet and simple. So clean. You would think that when the people don't have to eat, there wouldn't be so much wretchedness."

"The humans still have to eat, and the daimons need the humans. But daimons have other needs, too. Some turn to drink and gambling and get addicted to absinthe and dark magic. Every creature walking has a fire burning inside that demands to be fed. And for many of the girls here, a few pounds of flesh and magic was a small price to pay for freedom."

"Are they paid for their tails, at least?"

"They're paid very well. And their clients pay them. And Madame Sylvie pays them. The girls who do well will eventually have enough to leave and find new lives."

"Promise?"

A genuine laugh surprised me. "*Bébé*, in just a few moments, we're going to pass by a dollmaker's shop, a dressmaker, a stationer. You'll see dancing schools and open-air painting studios and tiny daimons with swishing tails carrying books wrapped with leather belts. A few years of hard work in the cabaret can buy a lifetime of comfort for an entire family, if a girl is savvy. Outside of Mortmartre, real life gets lived in Paris, I promise you."

I sniffled and wiped my nose on the handkerchief he handed me. "In a few moments?"

"You have several hours before tonight's show. We're going to go talk to Monsieur Charmant. See if we can't learn more about that button. I want to know who tried to kidnap you. And if he has friends who have been stealing innocent girls, I want to find them." His hand curled around mine, the limp handkerchief dangling between us. "And we will end this together, you and I."

Since arriving via the sewers, I'd seen many different doors to my cabaret home. I'd hurried out the back door of Paradis. I'd been paraded out the front door with movie-star pomp. But I'd never hitched up my voluminous skirts and clambered out the window, as Vale did. Now that I knew there was a convenient ledge that led to an easily climbed drain spout appointed with handy gargoyles, I might take this route more often. In fact, it was so easy to climb into and out of my window into a dark, anonymous alley that I couldn't help wondering if the building had been designed for just that purpose.

Vale shimmied down the drain spout first, and when he looked up, I was more glad than ever for my bloomers. Just because he'd seen me *en déshabillé* in a dark room didn't mean I wanted to give him the usual cabaret girl's view from the street. As soon as I'd stepped off the last gargoyle, he offered me his arm and led me down the streets of Paris at a quick pace.

And he was right about the charming shops and studios we passed. In between the cabarets, with their gaudy signs and lights, I saw a ballet class for little girl daimons, a toy shop of handmade puppets, and an atelier filled with paint-splattered artists arrayed in a circle around a live and angry bludmare stamping against the wooden floors to which it had been tethered with bell-covered ropes. Banners and pennants were strung between the tall buildings, and bright posters fluttered against brick walls. A red daimon who reminded me of Luc from the caravan strolled by playing a violin, and I checked to see if his tail was intact, which it was. Of course. It was the women who had to give up their limbs for art and sustenance.

We passed Enfer, the darker twin of Paradis, and I gaped at the lurid mouth carved around the deep-set door. A shiver ran over me. I didn't want to see how horrible Mortmartre could be. Unless Cherie was involved. But surely, if she was in Enfer, we would know?

As if reading my mind, Vale said, "I checked. She's not down there. It's dark, but it is not that dark."

Around the corner, I saw more doppelgänger cabarets

from my art history books. Le Chat Noir and even Moulin Bleu, which was oddly small and cramped-looking. As we turned down another alley, I recognized the narrowing brick walls and increasing shadows that signaled every city's Darkside. I'd only seen two such entrances, with Criminy's red-gloved hand clamped firmly around my wrist. He had wanted me to see what horrors the cities held for our kind, and I had only entered the spiked gates of two pathetic little towns before I chose to sit out his errands to the Bludman's district of magic shops and bloodsellers.

Vale hurried under the sign, but I had to stop and look up. This arch was stone and resembled the gates of a cemetery, with black-streaked gryphons flanking the sides of a rusted iron gate. All were designed to intimidate.

"You coming, *bébé*? Or are you scared?"

I tossed my hair. "Scared? This is what I am, Vale. I'm a creature of Darkside."

He shook his head. "Not here. In Paris, things are different."

This time, I reached for his hand, and his fingers curled reassuringly through mine. The buildings were narrow and thin, the alleys crooked and riddled with shadows. Bludrats roamed, big as cats and bristling with fur the color of dried blood, sometimes a lighter mauve. They ignored us, and we ignored them. When one skittered by with a child-size hand in its mouth, I kept my eyes up from then on.

The shops we passed were typical for Darkside and yet decidedly . . . well, darker. In London and Manchester, Crim had told me, there was a malevolent area of Darkside that no one but villains visited. Deep Darkside, they called it. In most cities and smaller towns, though, Darkside was composed of compulsory ghettos and shops specifically catering to Bludmen. Here, it was like an evil version of Main Street in Disney World. The shop fronts were elegant and intricate, with wood carvings and stone gargoyles and gleaming windows, but the things behind the windows were twisted and strange. When Vale stopped before the only shop with windows blocked by black velvet curtains, a shiver ran up my spine.

"Maybe it's closed," I said hopefully. "No sign."

The look Vale gave me was grim and somewhat pitying. "He does not need one."

Instead of pushing the door open or knocking, Vale pressed his thumb to the sinister fang of the bludbunny-shaped door knocker. When he smeared a drop of blood against the peeling black paint, the red sank magically into the wood. The door swung open on silent hinges, revealing a crowded room shot through with smoky beams of light piercing the black curtains. The walls were redder than red, cracked in the corners, and lit with buzzing carnival lights around the edges.

Vale stepped in first and pulled me through. I hesitated for just a moment on the threshold, and the door slammed shut, almost smacking my hip. I spun away and nearly stumbled into the carved white fangs of a herd of screaming, carousel-horse heads arrayed on spikes. Stumbling back, claws outstretched, I bumped into a stuffed owl swinging from the ceiling by a hook. Off-balance, I sought Vale's side, sighing in relief as his hand curled around my waist.

Across the room, a counter sat unmanned, the greasy glass obscuring glittering objects within. Big jars of peculiar items sat in rows on shelves, and I noted powders, the twisted pink petals of dried bludrat ears, ivory-yellow teeth of all sizes, and one jar filled with liquid and what appeared to be sheep eyeballs. A dusty dentist's chair of metal and ripped fabric lurked in the corner under a cone light, making me shiver when I saw the rust-flecked instruments hung on the wall behind it.

"Touch nothing," Vale whispered.

"Didn't wanna," I whispered back.

A cacophony started up, somewhere in the building. Mad barking that reminded me of reading *Cujo* as a little girl, far before I was old enough to handle it. There were no doors that I could see, no curtains to other rooms, and Vale pulled me behind him and turned to face a gaping hole that had appeared in the floor, roughly hewn from the wide wooden boards. I was sure it hadn't been there only moments ago. Nails clicked on stone far below, and the barking intensified. I hadn't noticed him move, but there was suddenly a strange and evil weapon in Vale's hand, like an intricately cast version of Wolverine's claws. I plucked a parasol from an umbrella stand made of a polar bear's head and open jaw and prepared to face whatever nasty thing was growling and slobbering up the steps.

"Monsieur Charmant!" Vale barked. "We wish to parley!"

There was no answer but a sudden silence as the first dog's head came up over the stairs, its lips pulling back to growl so low and deep that it vibrated my ribs. Slow claws clicked, more growls joined it, and the thing appeared in the scant light.

"Are you shitting me?" I shouted, letting my parasol drop. "French poodles?"

"Franchian wolfhounds," Vale muttered, "Bludhounds, for short."

I stifled a giggle. Because they were totally French poodles, cut into the usual balloon-dog shape, with poofs on their heads and butts and around their ankles.

Then I looked closer and saw the fucking fangs. Like a saber-toothed tiger's, they curved down over the jaw until the things opened their mouths and howled, which was even worse.

Six of them crawled up from hell and took the floor, spreading out around us. They were nearly as tall as I was, their heads canted downward and their shoulders hunched like hyenas.

"You think those are . . . wolfhounds?"

He nodded, weaving back and forth and limbering up for a fight. "They bred some local type of dog to bludwolves, long ago. The gendarmes keep them for tracking and chasing down daimons. And they trim them like that so they won't get too much blood in their fur while feeding but will still run hot."

"How the hell do you trim one of those things?"

One feinted experimentally at Vale's leg, and he swiped at it with his claw-knife.

"Very, very carefully." He cracked his neck. "Lots of chains. Put your back against mine, *bébé*. They're behind us, too. Get ready to fight, and don't hesitate to kill."

I spun around and found three more monster dogs quietly hunting us, materializing from behind counters and trunks on the floor, silent but for their clicking toenails. I couldn't think of them as anything but bludpoodles, which made them only a fraction less terrifying.

And then I remembered, or my body remembered for me: I was a monster, too.

I hunched over and ripped off my gloves, fingers curling into claws, glad I hadn't let Blue trim my talons all the way down just to placate the clients of Paradis. An answering growl buzzed up from my belly, my teeth bared and my vision going over red. One of the bludpoodles facing me hunched down as if it was going to leap, and I pounced on its back before it could spring.

I forgot everything but the kill. My claws latched into shaved skin, piercing the hide and veering off ribs. On instinct, I slammed a foot on the ground and fell onto my back, pulling the thing over in a bear hug. With its legs pawing overhead, it whimpered and raked the air with useless toenails, and I bit deeply into its neck to drink. The thing went limp in my arms, and I'd sucked down one deep draught of blood before the next one slammed into me.

As I rolled to the floor, howling in fury, I caught a quick glance at Vale. He moved like a dancer, the giant claw-knife in one hand and a wicked dagger in the other. One bludpoodle lay near the counter, its head at an unnatural angle. Four-inch saber teeth snapped inches away from my nose, red-tinged slobber flecking my face. With an irritable grunt, I punched it in the face and felt the crunch of bone.

I counted six wolfhounds: three dead on the ground, two circling Vale, one trying to sneak up on me. But I could smell it, and I pounced before it could and sank teeth into its throat. I'd never used my teeth and talons like this, not since becoming a Bludman six years ago. I'd never been reduced to a fighting machine, a predator, a monster that lusted for the enemy's blood, no matter what species it was. I sat on the floor, my legs and fluffy skirts poofing around my legs as I dragged the dying wolf-monster into my lap to take what was rightfully mine. Hot blood spiced with fury and madness slid down my throat as I watched Vale dispatch the last hound and straighten, wiping blood off his face and rubbing it on his black trousers, where it disappeared as smoothly as the thumbprint he'd pressed to the door.

"Demi?"

I grunted, and he spun around to stare at me.

"*Mon dieu, bébé.* You look like a child with an ice cream cone."

I shrugged but didn't stop drinking. He looked half disgusted and half proud. When footsteps sounded on the stairs, I dropped the fuzzy carcass and got back into fighting stance, but Vale merely straightened and held the blood-spattered claw at his side.

"Quite a welcome, Charmant."

The daimon who rose from the floor like a devil born from hell looked as if he belonged in a barbershop quartet, but evil rolled off him in waves. He tipped a straw boater at us, mouth twitching under a spectacular mustache and skin the color of Mountain Dew.

"Oh, customers? Tut. I was just letting my pets out for a little walky." He glanced around, noting the carnage of pony-sized vampire poodles with one raised eyebrow. "They don't breed bludhounds like they used to, you know." He turned back to the hole in the floor and shouted, "Coco! Bring the broom and dustpan. Again."

After the bludhounds, I wouldn't trust anything spit

forth from that dark rectangle. A heavy clanking from deep below got louder until a copper orangutan emerged, hobbling on long arms like crutches. It clambered over to me with red eyes blinking impatiently and held out fingers that clicked open and shut in annoyance. With a last pull at the sluggish blud, I placed the drained body in its grasp, and it swung down the stairs, enveloped in the darkness. A series of meaty rips and grinding noises made me glance away.

"I should charge you for that, you know," Charmant said with a fussy and exaggerated sigh, and Vale laughed.

"For what? Destroying illegally bred bludhounds? The gendarmes would pay us in gold for that."

"Gendarmes are more easily bought than bludhounds. Why are you here, brigand? Come to buy more teeth for your collection?"

I stood and shot Vale a measuring look. He had neglected to mention he had come here to pay this devil with cash. He shrugged unapologetically.

"I'm here to inquire about a gold pin seen around town. The crest is a raven's skull with a top hat and bat wings."

Charmant rubbed filed black nails against the sharp lapels of his red-and-white-striped jacket. "Pish-posh. Sounds enigmatic."

"You know what it is, and you're going to tell us."

Charmant's mustache curled with his smile. "Am I, now?"

The clockwork orangutan clattered back upstairs and gently shoved me aside with a knuckle and an apologetic, tinny "Ooh ooh." It picked up another bludhound and carried it downstairs over one arm like a coat as the two men glared at each other. I wasn't sure how or why, but the copper ape looked downright sad.

Vale crossed his arms, the silver claw dangling over his taut bicep. "You'll tell us, yes."

Charmant finally giggled, an oddly mad sound. "Depends on what you're going to give me for the information, I suppose. A few of her fangs? A tube of your mixed bastard blood? A favor? Your firstborn? Perhaps you have a unicorn horn or a selkie skin to trade or some lovely Yssian scales?" Charmant's eyebrows waggled like dying caterpillars.

Without a word, Vale reached into his shirt and withdrew a silk scarf, testing its weight on his palm. Charmant snatched it up without touching Vale and unwrapped it like a kid at Christmas.

"Oh la la," he purred. "A bludmare's lucky horseshoe. A fine trade, indeed."

Charmant caressed the rusty U in a thoroughly unappetizing way, then tucked it lovingly into his jacket and dusted off his hands. Turning on one heel, he disappeared into the hole in the ground, tail slithering, snakelike, behind him. I was about to protest his abandonment, but Vale put a hand on my arm and shook his head. After a few moments of silence, the orangutan swung up and knuckle-walked to Vale. Its long arm extended, a folded card grasped in dexterous fingers. Vale opened it so we both could read it.

"Anatole Fermin, Artificer, Boulevard Saint-Germain."

"Do you know who that is?" I asked.

Vale shook his head, angry. "Let's go find out."

The orangutan held open the door, its mournful red eyes tracing our steps as we left, as if somewhere under the metal plates and gears, the thing had a heart and had lost all hope long ago.

"Ooh ooh," it said again, and I wasn't sure if it meant *good luck* or *good-bye*.

Tears pricked my eyes for a reason I couldn't name, and I held out a hand. The orangutan's fingers softly wrapped around mine, its eyes blinking up.

"Thank you, Coco," I said as we hurried away.

Outside, even the dim light of a cloudy afternoon felt suddenly bright. Vale pulled me aside in the doorway of an empty shop and licked the pad of his thumb to scrub at my face.

"Back off, Mom." I wriggled away.

"You're covered in wolf blud, *bébé*. We'll never make it to Saint-Germain unless I can clean you off a little." I sighed and held up my face. To my surprise, he planted a kiss on my lips before dabbing at me again and again with his thumb. "Thank heavens you were wearing burgundy today."

My eyes were drawn to a flash of golden skin through his black jacket. And beneath that, blood. Half-Abyssinian blood that smelled all kinds of wrong. I wrinkled up my nose and grabbed him.

"You bit?"

He shrugged. "That's what killed the last one. I told you, *bébé*. My blood is dangerous stuff."

"It won't turn you into a . . . like, a werewolf or anything, will it?"

He snickered and pulled my jacket over my chest, buttoning it up to my chin. I hadn't been so covered up since the carriage ride with Cherie, and it rankled. And choked. I tried to yank the stiff collar away from my throat, and Vale gently pulled my hands down.

"Do not worry about me. Worry about you." He caught my hand, his thumb caressing my palm. "If you lost your gloves, use your pockets. It'll be easier if you act like you're not the famous lone Bludman of Mortmartre."

I smiled to myself. The *second* Bludman of Mortmartre, actually. But he couldn't know about Lenoir.

We hurried out of Deep Darkside, and I didn't look back. Except at the end, because I had the strangest feeling, as if we were being followed. I didn't smell anything unusual, but after being attacked by gigantic rabid monster poodles, I wasn't going to start trusting reality.

The world brightened even more noticeably as we passed under the archway and reentered the colorful domain of the daimons. Street after street, Vale pulled me along by my elbow, silent, intent on his errand.

Finally, I couldn't stand it anymore. As we reached a quiet place on a bridge, I murmured, "How much did they cost you?"

"*Ne t'en fais pas, bébé.*"

"What does that mean?"

"Don't worry about it."

I stopped and, God help me, stamped my foot. "I know what it means, ass! How much, Vale?"

He turned to face me, gone from gruff to amused in a heartbeat, thanks to my little snit.

"A gentleman doesn't name prices."

"Well, I just . . . I mean . . . thank you."

He grinned, a spark of humor back in his eyes. "*De rien, mon chou.*"

"I'm not your cabbage. Cabbages don't drink blood," I grumbled.

"So you do know some Franchian." He eyed the slant of the sun and jerked his chin toward the other end of the bridge. "If you want to find out who this mysterious Fermin is and get back in time to perform, we must hurry."

My eyes were drawn to the water as we scurried over the river. I couldn't help jealously eyeing the carefree daimons and children laughing in large paddle boats shaped like demented pink swans or tossing crumbs at regular ducks and geese from dinghies floating in the teal-blue water. Bathers reclined on the grassy shores in straw hats and the sort of half-revealing bathing suits no one in Sangland would touch, even if they had a death wish. Sure, they were guarded by an electrified fence and a guard with a seawater gun and a bludrat net, but they still looked mostly relaxed. I'd spent one giddy night at the Tuileries and one brief and stolen night at the Louvre, but no one had ever offered to show me the beauties of Paris during the daylight, and it made me desperately sad. I hadn't been born a creature of the darkness.

Soon we were on the other side of the river. The Tower loomed over us, closer than I'd ever seen it, spindly and wrapped with wires and lights and spikes to keep the pigeons from roosting. Surrounding the elevator at its base was an unwieldy metal generator crackling with electricity like something out of Dr. Frankenstein's lab. After another block, the palpable buzz in the air subsided, and we entered a district that smelled of coal, fire, and iron. Some of the storefronts had been hollowed out and equipped with iron gates to show soot-stained daimon blacksmiths, swordsmiths, and jewelry artisans hard at work pumping bellows and hammering cherry-hot steel with a cacophonous *clank*ing that felt like horses galloping over my brain.

"Ugh. Please tell me we're not going to hang around here long."

"I do not know what we're looking for, really. This is Boulevard Saint-Germain. I haven't spent much time here, for obvious reasons." He nudged me in the side. "At least it's not the leather-tanning district, *n'est-ce pas*? Or the one where they process civet and ambergris?"

As we passed between the forges and storefronts, reading every sign, the sun slowly sank. We didn't have much time left before I was expected to be in costume and on a chandelier. When we came upon a blacksmith taking a rest on a bench outside his forge, Vale bowed slightly and said, "*Pardon*, but do you know where we might find the artificer?"

The blacksmith grunted, his thick tail twitching against the cobbles. "We're all artificers, *monsieur*. Which one in particular?"

"Anatole Fermin."

The blacksmith pointed a black-singed finger down the street, ahead of us.

"Idiot got himself crushed. They are moving his junk now." He shook his head, his curly mustache and muscles making my heart ache with thoughts of the buff but kindly strong man, Torno, back at the carnival.

"*Merci*."

We jogged down the street, and I noticed for the first time how Vale's fighting claw slid into a sort of scabbard along his thigh. A bludmare screamed up ahead, marking our destination: a shop being emptied, the goods stacked outside as daimon workers packed them into crates and hammered boards over the tops before stacking them on a pallet behind the coal-black horse. The tasteful sign over the storefront read simply, "A. Fermin, Artificer," and the air around the open doors stank with an odd and familiar mix of oil, metal, and magic.

Vale being Vale, he maneuvered around the crates, ignored the daimons' shouts of protest, and slid in through the door as if he belonged there. Me being me, I followed him.

"Can I help you, *monsieur*? *Mademoiselle*?"

The voice was cold, and the man it belonged to was even colder. His sneer made it clear that we had been instantly judged inferior, which made me automatically hate him. He even had a little Hitler mustache and a monocle.

"We seek Anatole Fermin," Vale said.

"You can check the morgue. Good day."

The man cleared his throat and looked down at his clipboard. My eyes were drawn to the pin on his cravat: a gold sigil that I now knew well. So I did what any cabaret girl would do when confronted with an uppity fellow who had something she wanted. I simpered.

"Ooh, *monsieur*." I moved up close, setting my chest practically on his clipboard and batting my eyelashes. "What a pretty pin. Trade it for a kiss?"

His lip quirked up in disgust, and he took a step back, dusting off his paperwork. "*Mademoiselle*, you're embarrassing yourself. Please vacate the premises before I call the gendarmes."

"Some fellows can't get it up," I whispered to Vale, elbowing him in the ribs and making him cough.

I couldn't help it. I hated the snotty guy with the clipboard.

And he hated me, as he was turning such a bright shade of burgundy that he was beginning to resemble a daimon. Stepping so close I could smell the cloves and tobacco on his fetid breath, he whispered, "I could have you killed ten different ways by Sunday. Get out before I change my mind."

Vale was between us in a heartbeat, his fist wound into the guy's shirt. "How dare you insult the lady? You will not live to see Sunday, talking like that."

The man jerked back and tried to straighten his shirt and jacket, failing utterly. "Consider yourself a dead man." He spit on the floor, a quivering glob.

"Not yet." Vale gave him a cocky grin. "But we'll take our leave." He all but dragged me out by my elbow.

Once we were out the door, he pulled me against the brick wall, out of sight of Ugly McClipboard and his beady little pig eyes. With an impish grin, Vale held out his hand to show me the gold pin he'd ripped from the man's paisley cravat during their scuffle.

"That's two," he said.

I heard a gasp. One of the daimons loading crates close by watched us anxiously. When he saw me returning his stare, his eyes went wide, and he hurriedly walked in the other direction, darting down an alley.

"Come on," I murmured, and Vale followed me.

The daimon was quick, but my nose was quicker, and I finally cornered him behind a sculptor's studio, hiding behind a stone statue still covered in dust, shaking with fear.

"You know something," I said.

"And we'll pay you to tell us," Vale added, holding out a shiny franc.

The face that peeked around the statue was the flaccid purple of near-death, one eye covered with a cheap silk patch and the other round and wide. Twisted scars cut across his face as if he'd been whipped with a metal-tipped lash. He gulped as he stepped into view, and I noted he had no tail. And that he was very young, barely a teenager.

"I have seen that before," he said, nodding at Vale's fist. Vale's fingers uncurled, showing a glint of gold, and the daimon flinched as if he'd been struck. Putting sticky-padded hands to the wall, he scurried straight up the building, quick as a lizard, disappearing onto the roof.

The words were whispered from the sky, silky and foreboding.

"That's the crest of the Malediction Club," he said.

Vale tossed the coin straight up. It never landed.

26

I looked up and muttered, "Why do they always run?"

Vale rubbed his chin. "They are most likely still alive *because* they always run. It does not matter; we have what we needed."

"We do?"

"We know the rumors about the Malediction Club are true. Considering Anatole Fermin was an artificer recently crushed, we must assume he is the same mad-man who tried to kidnap you while wearing one of these pins, yes? Perhaps to take you to the club?"

"I don't know. This is your crazy city. No one's ever tried to kidnap me in an elephant before."

Vale shook his head and started walking. The sun was setting, the purple clouds streaked with blood red and blazing orange. Black columns of smoke rose from the artificers' roofs, and I was glad enough to breathe the slightly fresher, cleaner air as we crossed the bridge.

We came to a major cross street, and Vale swung out his fist, hailing a rickshaw powered by half a clockwork horse and driven by a monkey of a man perched on its neck like a jockey. Handing me up into the carriage, Vale kissed my hand quickly.

"I have more questions to ask, *bébé*. Be careful tonight."

"What? Where are you going? Vale!"

He handed the man a twist of coins and rapped on the buggy, shouting, "Paradis in Mortmartre. *Vite vite!*"

With a creak and a clatter, the driver began pedaling, and the rickshaw pulled into traffic. I sat up and looked behind me, hunting for a close-cropped head and the wink of bright green eyes.

But he was gone.

Paradis welcomed me back like an angry mother hen. Charline met me at the door, tutting in Franchian under her breath and shedding ostrich feathers from her robe as she ushered me into Blue's room. The girls were in their final preparations for the night, gluing on their eyelashes and contouring their cheeks and fluffing each other's skirts. Mel ran up to grab my hands and kiss me on my cheeks as if I'd been gone a long time, and I hunted around her for a familiar blue face.

"Where's Bea?" I asked, and Mel blushed green. She shook her head, eyes tearing up, and ran out of the room. "What—?"

Blue grabbed my wrist and yanked me to the makeup counter, not gently.

"Don't poke your nose into nasty things, kid," she barked. "Might get bitten."

"I'm not poking for fun."

She held my chin and turned my face back and forth, wiping off chunks of bludhound gore that Vale had missed.

I tolerated it for a moment before leaning forward to

whisper, "Have you heard of the Malediction Club? I think they're the ones who tried to kidnap me."

Her eyes went flat as she attacked me with a kabuki brush of powder. "*Tsk*. The gendarmes will sort it." Every time I tried to open my mouth to argue, she stuck the brush into it.

I went into a coughing fit, hoping she'd used the new-fangled powder that didn't contain belladonna. When I could speak again, I put my mouth to her ear and breathed, "The gendarmes burned his body, Blue. They're covering it up."

She leaned back, gave me a look so sharp it felt like a slap. "If the gendarmes are scared, you want to pry deeper? Malediction's no sewing circle." Pinching my chin so firmly I felt sure she'd leave marks, she lined my eyes and smudged the kohl.

I shook her off. "They tried to take me. They might have my friend Cherie. And I'm not going to stop looking."

She shook her head sadly, looking a thousand years old. "Bad things happen to girls who get nosy. Make sure you're not one of 'em, eh?" She spun me around and patted me on the bustle. "Get in costume. Show starts soon."

"Is Mel coming back?"

The old blue daimon glanced at the ledger I'd seen on my first day in her domain, the one filled with crossed-out names.

"Hope so. Too many don't."

I scanned the faces around me, my heart heavy with how many names I hadn't learned. Had more gone missing in just a week? When had Jess and Edwige disappeared? Why did no one talk about it?

Madame Sylvie's husky purr rang out over the tumult

of the dressing room, welcoming the audience and urging them to clap and stomp and begin their salivating. The girls bustling around me went quiet and hurried to their places. I ran for the ladder and scurried up to my perch, content to wrap chalked hands around the smooth metal of my chandelier and grateful that since my earlier fall, Madame Sylvie had assigned Auguste to check the ropes, equipment, and catwalk before each performance.

I felt safe, so high up. No one could touch me here. This was real. This was solid. This was who I was, what I did. The fame, the gilt, the feathers, the princes, the parties—none of that was real. At the heart of my identity, I was a contortionist, a performer, a dancer in the sky. And although it made me miss Cherie more than ever, I was glad to climb onto the metal cage and get into position, stretching out my limbs and pointing my toes and waiting for the jerk of rope that would lower me into the spotlight. It was good simply to be exactly what I was.

My performance was flawless, every move sinuous and graceful. The applause thundered, the men standing to stomp their feet and whistle through fingers still sweaty from expensive gloves. I bowed, I danced, I linked arms with daimons and kicked high in the can-can that everyone thought I had invented. But as I looked around at the glitter, the glitz, the madness, the daimons' smooth skirts unmarred by waving tails, I felt a grand emptiness. The caravan may have been boring, but at least it was more real than this seductive farce.

After the last bow, I scurried backstage in the rustling crowd, breathless and weary. A gentle hand on my elbow pulled me aside. I expected Vale, but it was Auguste.

"You're wanted in the costumer's, miss," he said in his usual quiet tones.

Charline and Blue jumped on me at the door, drawing me inside and undressing me with plucking fingers before I could protest. The outfit they tossed over my head was barely half a bed sheet, draped like a toga on a nymphomaniac Greek goddess and secured with tiny gold buttons at the shoulders. They pulled the pins from my hair and lured it to tumble down my bare back in dark waves and slipped sandals on my feet.

"What the hell?"

Madame Sylvie appeared in the door to look me up and down as if I was a show dog, as if she was hunting for faults or bared teeth. "Hush. Tonight is the night."

Charline stepped to Sylvie's side. Their avid eyes made my blud run cold, their horizontal pupils unblinking and their arms crossed. Sylvie's flesh-colored powder completely creeped me out; surely that didn't fool the men? Or perhaps that was why she mostly stayed hidden in her room—who knew what her skin truly showed?

"Tonight's *what* night?" I asked.

Charline smiled too brightly. "*The* night."

Blue darted in with her brush, painting my lips with a blood-red Cupid's bow. Her own mouth was drawn down in a frown, darker blue in the wrinkles.

Madame Sylvie's eyebrows shot up in drawn-on arches. "You know what to do, *n'est-ce pas*? Where everything goes? In theory if not in practice?"

I went stock-still, frozen. They still thought I was a virgin. And they still thought I was for sale. And apparently, they had finally earned a price high enough to ensure that they got a receipt, elephant or no.

"I'm not a whore." My voice was tiny, needle-thin. But as strong as a needle, too.

"Of course not." Charline patted me as if I was a fractious lapdog. "You're a courtesan. And the highest-paid one in all of Paris. Possibly all the world one day, if you're any good at it. Impress him, and you might find yourself on the *Maybuck*."

Bile rose in my throat. When had I eaten last? Ah, yes. A vampire poodle. No wonder it tasted gamey. I swallowed it back down. "I don't want to go on an airship brothel. And I'm not sleeping with whatever rich asshole you sold me to. Period."

"That's no way—" Charline began.

"How dare you—" Madame Sylvie barked at the same time.

But Blue held up a hand. I was utterly surprised when both Sylvie's and Charline's mouths snapped shut, and Blue gave them both a benevolent and forgiving nod. "You're a girl. A beautiful, talented girl with a unique flair that draws men to you like bludbunnies to a baby carriage. What are your choices?" She counted the options off on her stubby blue fingers. "Marry well. Unlikely, as you're not landed or human. Make enough money in the cabarets to set up your life. Probable, if you don't make enemies, but they'll always want more. Stand your man up tonight, and you might wind up dead, for he's not the forgiving type." She pinned me with a gimlet eye. "You could be someone's mistress. Possible, but you'll need to be damn fine in bed and willing to put up with a nagging wife in the background. Become the greatest and most well-paid courtesan in Paris, with just an hour's worth of work." Her last finger was a thumb, scarred with years of sewing and needle pricks. She pointed it at my chest. "Or get kicked out of here and fall into the gutter as so many girls do. Take less and less money for doing more and more against the filthy bricks of back alleys. Waste away on drops of absinthe. Fade into nothing."

The thumb disappeared.

"You've got five other fingers," I hissed.

Blue held up a fist. "Only if you're a man."

"He's waiting, darling. We know you'll choose wisely," Charline said.

"Or else," Madame Sylvie added.

Charline's hands curled around my shoulders and squeezed, ushering me toward the door. My feet were leaden in gold sandals so thin I could feel the nails in the floorboards through their soles.

"If all else fails, just moan and think of the Tower," Blue called.

That struck me as odd. In my world, they told people to think about England.

"Why the Tower?"

The old blue daimon snorted. "Because if you want to die, you need only touch it."

Nothing but twisted moorings and broken concrete remained of the copper pachyderm where I'd once met my suitors. Instead, Charline pulled me down the hall and up the stairs, and a cold foreboding descended on me. So the deed was to happen in my own room? The only privacy I had in all of Paris? The place I had stolen and claimed for my own?

But when she opened the door . . . it wasn't my room anymore.

It was a bower. A beautiful, otherworldly bower. They'd brought in potted trees, draped flowering vines across the walls, and hung warmly glowing lights between them. My bed had been replaced by a monstrous boat of a four-poster thing, draped with fluttering white gauze. The windows were thrown wide open to let in the breeze, and a tiny sliver of moonlight shone upon the thick rugs and furs they'd draped everywhere, as if the magic depended on one's feet never touching the ground.

Charline sat me on the bed, my limbs wooden and numb in her claws. Madame Sylvie watched from the door, a skeletal and austere shadow. Twisting my shoulders away, Charline slipped leather straps over my arms and buckled them tightly. Something soft and ticklish brushed my bare back and the tender skin of my elbows.

I had wings.

"This is a nightmare," I whispered.

"Only for you. For him, it is heaven. Paradis."

"Paradise Lost," I mumbled.

I yelped as she grabbed a twist of skin inside my arm and pinched hard. "Enough. You've been given every-thing. Now it's time to earn your keep. He owns you now, that man. At least for tonight. If you don't wish to be tied down, beaten, and raped into silence, I would suggest you pretend that he is worthy of worship, that his every touch excites you beyond belief."

I turned slowly, eyes wide. "You would let him . . . do that to me?"

Madame Sylvie stepped close, into the warmth of the lights. I saw her color change, even through the heavy layers of paint and powder that made one forget she was a daimon at all. She shivered over with faint leopard spots, fierce and suddenly alien. "For the night, he has bought all of Paradis. You two will be the only ones in the entire cabaret." She leaned close, her breath heating me with sulfur and brimstone. "No one would hear you scream. And no one would find your body."

I flinched as if she'd slapped me, and she took a step back, letting her normal color descend and putting on that charming crocodile's grin.

"*Bonne chance*, my dove!"

She was out the door in a heartbeat, with Charline in her wake, and I hissed at the trembling door that slammed and locked behind them.

I had forgotten to ask who had bought me.

It didn't really matter.

My mysterious master kept me waiting, and I alternated between fear and fury. I paced the room, the furs tickling my feet through the sandals and the long, feathered wings trembling against the backs of my legs through the thin muslin of the shift. Pausing in front of the mirror on my vanity, I ran a hand through the flames of an army of dripping candles. Lifting my red-painted lips, I inspected my fangs.

Wait. Fangs.

My bed was gone and, with it, Cherie's fangs. Vale had bought them from Monsieur Charmant for some mysterious sum that he refused to discuss, and they had become relics, reminders of my quest, of what was at stake. I scrabbled through the compartments of my vanity and ripped the graceful vines off my armoire to dig through the drawers. The fangs were gone, as was my lucky bludbunny foot. And that was what finally tipped me over the edge.

My choices were play nice, get raped, or die?

Yeah, no.

"Demitasse, *ma chérie*?"

I knew that oily, insinuating voice.

It was the prince. Again. Of course. Apparently, twenty-four hours after your preferred virgin's kidnapping was a sufficient time to wait to claim your prize. My lips drew back, my hands curling into claws tipped with blood-red enamel.

The door opened slowly, and Prince Seti stepped inside in another vibrant folly of a sultan's costume, his perfectly trimmed beard tied in a braid and his eyes outlined in kohl, an insult to Bludmen everywhere. In his onion-head hat and ridiculous vest and striped silk pants, he was meant to look kingly, exotic. To me, he looked like a sad little man playing at being important. A collection of amulets jangled on his chest, and I saw something there that cinched it for me: a gold disk with a raven's skull, bat wings, and a top hat. I took a step back, the billowing curtains brushing my calves.

"Long have I awaited this moment," he breathed. The bells on the curly toes of his stupid harem shoes jingled as he crossed the carpets toward where I waited, one hand on the windowsill.

"Me, too," I murmured.

With trembling hands, I undid the soft leather straps, turned my back to him, and let the angel wings flutter to the ground, revealing my naked back.

"Is my beautiful angel ready to fall?"

Instead of answering, I parted the curtains and jumped out the window.

27

Or at least, he thought I did. Instead, I hooked a hand on the sill and swung over to the side, rushing along the ledge with a Bludman's speed and grace to scurry down the drain spout, the toga flapping around me in the wild night wind.

"My angel!"

Prince Seti's stupid beard poked out the window as he stared down at the empty street in confusion. Then he looked to the side and saw me clinging to the gargoyle heads like a mad squirrel, climbing away from him as fast as my claws could carry me. His face went dark, his voice changing entirely. "I will see you drained for this." His head disappeared as I landed on the cobbles and hailed the first closed conveyance that would stop.

"To Lenoir's studio," I called, wishing that I could go to wherever Vale stayed, when he wasn't climbing in my window. But I didn't know anything about his life in Paris, and I couldn't linger where the prince could find me.

The driver muttered, "An address?" and I racked my brain before spitting out the number from the painter's door. "*Oui, mademoiselle.*" He revved the engine, hurtling us into the street. I held back the curtain and looked up to my old room.

So that was the end of my time at Paradis.

I would miss Mel and Bea, especially, and Blue and Blaise and the other girls I hadn't gotten to know. I would miss the hot lights of the stage and the feel of the ladder under my feet as I ascended to the catwalk. But there were other cabarets and other cities, and I refused to believe that Blue's five scarred fingers represented every option I had. Hell, at the very least, I could always walk back to Callais, busking to pay for a quick air trip across the Channel. Criminy would take me back. He'd very likely dock my pay—which he'd basically been holding hostage, anyway. But maybe I could persuade him to use his money, his reach, and his magic to find Cherie. I just had to survive long enough.

The streets glowed with gas lamps, the traffic still lively even after midnight. It was Mortmartre, after all, and I passed open carriages that left echoing laughter and billowing feathers and glitter in their wake, the scent of lust heavy on the air. Every cabaret spewed its own brand of color and light and music, while windows lit with red bulbs beckoned lonely fellows upstairs for a treat, if they had the francs. We passed a gendarme on the corner, his arm taut as a giant bludhound strained at the end of its chain, the ridiculous poof of hair on the thing's head at odds with the silver muzzle cap tightly squeezing its mouth shut but revealing its madly twitching nose. We locked eyes, and it shivered all over and lunged for my carriage until the gendarme yanked it back.

Finally, we stopped in front of the familiar town house, and relief flooded me. The invitation had merely named the date, not the time, so technically, I was here by request, even if many hours early and half-dressed. Lenoir would understand. He always understood. And a drop of bloodwine and absinthe wouldn't go amiss, shaken as I was.

I hopped out of the carriage before the driver could help me and tossed my golden hoop earrings into his lap.

"Jewelry is not accepted currency," he said with a Franchian sniff.

"What about blood?" I smiled, showing my fangs. He drove off in a hell of a hurry.

While the cabaret districts had been lively, this was a residential area, and my knock rang loud in the shadowy night. I shivered on the doorstep. Not from the cold, because it wasn't a cold night and I was a Bludman. But because I was just a half-naked girl in a strange city, reduced to begging from a benefactor. And I hated it.

After a long while, a light went on upstairs, and the door opened to reveal Lenoir. He was fully dressed, not a hair out of place and eyes bright and amused as ever despite his stern mouth. And he seemed entirely unsurprised to see me.

"My dear *mademoiselle*. You've the date right, but your clock appears to be incorrect."

I almost apologized and then thought better of it. I was a Bludman and a star. Not a lost little girl, even if that's exactly what I'd felt like right up till he'd opened the door.

"It would appear my living arrangements have changed, *monsieur*. Do you perhaps have a guest bedroom where I could freshen up?"

His lip quirked up, just the barest bit. "Thrown out of a cabaret? Good heavens. I can't imagine what sort of shenanigans you've perpetrated."

He stood in the doorway a fraction longer than he

needed to, and I understood that he was letting me know who was in charge. That he could still slam the door, ruin my reputation, or toss me out on my bustle. But luckily, he stepped back, gave a slight bow, and held the door open.

"Of course, my dear. You know my home is open to you. But I take it this means the prince has lost his bet?"

I stepped inside, where the air was still and cold, the lamps unlit.

"What bet?"

He locked the door, turned to the stairs, and motioned for me to follow. I briefly wondered if I'd gone from the frying pan into the fire, if his price for sanctuary was as high as what I'd been expected to give to the prince. Scurrying in his wake, I was glad that this time, he led. With my back exposed, I felt vulnerable and breathless in the chill of the shadows, and I didn't wish the great painter to see the goose bumps rising over my spine.

"Surely you knew. You're on the books. Any new and interesting girl is. There are numbers for who will bed her first, whether she's a virgin, if she'll moan or cry or claw his back. Your odds were terribly high, but the prince eclipsed every other bet. A very confident man, Seti."

"He said he would have me drained."

"Then you definitely turned him down." I thought he would stop on the second level, where I had assumed the bedrooms were, but he continued to the attic. As he twisted the gaslights on and flicked the switches of a few electric lamps, he kept his back to me. "Thank you for that. I was betting rather heavily against him."

"I can't imagine you need money, *monsieur*." I glanced around at the subtle trappings of his wealth, scattered around the atelier. The marble statues and urns of hot-house flowers and little salt dishes filled with jewels, not to mention the rich paints and soft sable brushes.

"It's not about money, *ma chérie*. It's about prestige. Pride. A man's reputation is a precious thing, you see."

"How much did you win?" I asked, but he ignored me and gestured toward the changing screen with an open arm.

With the window showing cloudy darkness and the sconces burning orange, the room didn't carry its usual haze of golden sunshine, but he went about his paint preparations as if it were a normal afternoon, as if he'd been expecting me. With a shrug at the oddness of it all, I gladly changed out of the scrap of a toga and into the chocolate-plum dress. It felt deliciously heavy and cool against my skin, and I sighed as I hurled the toga into the fire already burning in the grate. Stretching until my back popped, I walked around the screen in bare feet and melted into my usual chair.

The goblet was in my hand before I'd noticed Lenoir at my side, and I sipped it gladly, anxious for a taste of dreamy oblivion, for the strange passage of time that made me feel like a butterfly caught in amber. I felt as if I couldn't exhale, as if all the anger and fear and worry were bottled up inside my chest and the drink would help it unwind like pulling a bit of yarn to unravel a sweater. As the liqueur slid down my throat and into my belly, a strange feeling overcame me. Instead of making every-thing warm and fuzzy and glittering, it seeped into me with cold tendrils like liquid ice. I licked my lips.

"Something's different."

Lenoir appeared by my side again, not in his usual

painting coat but in a high-necked white jacket that looked like something a doctor might wear. In his hand was a brass syringe, the sort I'd seen hanging on the wall at Monsieur Charmant's shop, beside the dentist's chair. This one was smaller and far cleaner, but the needle still reached past my Bludman's bravado to the human deep within and terrified me.

"I won a great prize, *mademoiselle*."

The goblet dropped from my trembling fingers, which had gone numb. I couldn't close my mouth, couldn't move my arms. As if from the bottom of a frozen pond, I saw Lenoir loom overhead as he pulled an artificer's complicated goggles down over his eyes and settled the lens attachments with one hand, his other hand tense on the syringe. My eyes were open and tearing and cold, locked onto the small gold pin attached to his high collar.

Raven skull, bat wings, top hat.

"Are you ready, *mademoiselle*, to see the Malediction Club?"

No, no, no. I couldn't shake my head, couldn't speak. When the needle pierced my neck, right over my jugular, it was like cracking through a crust of ice. I had no choice but to watch in horror as he pulled back the plunger and sucked out my blud, my soul.

28

Forever and forever we were locked there, me frozen and him killing me. He was taking more than my blud, somehow, drawing some necessary life force from me, stealing all my warmth. And I could do nothing about it, could only choke silently on the freezing potion coating my throat. Lenoir didn't speak, but he did smile for real for the first time, and it was the hangman's cruel grin, a skeleton's fangs that shone in the light.

When he was done, I was but an empty husk filled with panic and shadows. He held the syringe as if it was filled with liquid gold and carried it reverently to his canvas. With a flourish, he turned the uncovered painting toward me, letting me see his work for the first time.

Terrified, frozen, broken, drained, and dying, still I was awed by the perfection of it. It wasn't me, not quite. But it was the most beautiful painting I'd ever seen.

"I can see from your eyes that you're pleased. It's a masterpiece. But it still needs one final touch." His head swiveled around like a snake. "Your blud. Mixed properly with Charmant's draught and a few of my own inventions. I'll trap your very soul in the painting, lighting it from within. No one will be immune to its spell. It will hang in the Louvre, and they'll line up to see it. They'll weep. And no one will know that they are looking at your soul, and you are trapped within, looking back." His smile curled. "And then I'll switch it with a clever reproduction and hang the real you somewhere much, much darker."

I couldn't even cry. Couldn't even whimper.

My blud oozed out of the syringe and onto a rainbow-splattered wooden palette. He selected a brush made of dainty silver-white hair, utterly pure and sparkling with a magical glow

"Unicorn-tail hair, they said." He held it up to the light. "But I knew it for what it was. The virgin hair of a Blud Princess. Even more magical than a unicorn's pelt, for my needs. Worth every silver."

He licked his fangs as he mixed the deep red blud with his paints, adding a splash of some clear liquid, a pinch of something glittery, a sparkle of gold dust. Still I couldn't move, could do nothing but look on in horror and hope that his words weren't true. To be trapped in a painting? Even in Sang, it didn't seem possible. And yet, thinking back to the malevolence surrounding Limone's portrait at the Louvre, I finally understood why it had unsettled me so.

Her foul soul was trapped in the paint.

With tiny strokes that melted into the canvas, the brush caressed my hair, my lips, my fingertips. Each part he touched went dead, beyond numb. My heart cried out, straining against my chest, the only part of me that could protest.

"What's that, ma *chérie*? You wonder what will happen to your body? Do you feel it emptying, becoming merely a comely shell?"

He paused as if I could speak, as if he could hear me silently screaming. His smile was dark, dark as the hole in Monsieur Charmant's floor.

"We have uses for pretty flesh at the Malediction Club."

Inside, I howled and beat upon the cage of my own bones, the blud slowing in my veins. But there was nothing I could do. Nothing I could move. Nothing I could say. I couldn't even cry, couldn't even close my eyes.

"And you'll be our second Bludman. Finally, a matched set."

Lenoir's eyes flicked to his palette, and he picked up the syringe to squeeze more blud into the puddle of glistening paint. And that's why he didn't notice the strangely glimmering object that flew across the room to lodge in his side.

29

But I recognized it. The silver thing looked like Wolverine's claws. As Lenoir spun, hands curling into talons, Vale hurtled out of the darkness and punched him square in the teeth. Even from where I lounged, immobile and terrified, it seemed a foolish move, busting his knuckles into a Bludman's mouth, until I smelled something sharp.

Vale's blood.

Lenoir reflexively licked his lips as he ripped the claws from his side, painting the floor with blud. "You idiot. Do you have any idea who you're dealing with?"

Vale shook his hand out, sending splatters of his own blood everywhere. Red danced in my eyes, spots and streaks like the scattered stains left by the white-haired paintbrush Lenoir had dropped on the carpet.

"I did not know you were a Bludman, at first." Vale straightened and walked over to the crouched and wounded artist as if inspecting the painting. "Rather lucky for me, don't you agree?"

Lenoir had one arm over the three puncture wounds dribbling red through his jacket and one hand to his mouth, scrubbing at his pale lips as if he could erase the blood he'd already ingested. "Abyssinian," he wheezed.

His skin was going over pale, his nostrils wide and his eyes all black with widening pupils.

"Tell me how to save her, and I will give you a gift." Reaching into his black waistcoat, Vale pulled out a tiny glass vial that glistened metallic gold. "An antidote."

"No antidote." Lenoir hissed. "For what you are."

"But of course there is. We just keep it a secret so bloodsuckers like you will avoid us." He held up the vial, just within snatching reach of Lenoir, who made a clumsy grab for it. Vale danced back. "Talk first."

Lenoir's legs buckled, and he fell to the floor, curled around like a dying centipede, legs twitching.

Vale kneeled over him, wiggling the little bottle back and forth.

Finally, Lenoir sucked in a long breath and exhaled two whispered words. "Burn it."

He reached for the glass antidote bottle, but Vale ignored him completely and grabbed a paintbrush from Lenoir's jar of spirits. An evil stench went up when he stuck it in the fire, and it got even worse when he held the flaming brush to the painting of me. Lenoir let out an unholy wail as bright blue flames licked over the canvas and caught, the entire thing suddenly alight and crackling.

"Antidote," he hissed. "Antidote!"

But Vale was by my side, taking my cold hand, rubbing it between his own. "Still in there, *bébé*?" he asked, his pin-prick pupils telling the truth of his concern.

For all his jaunty swaggering, the boy was so scared I could smell the fear rolling off him in waves, although, strangely, I couldn't smell *him*. I took a shuddering breath and felt my fangs dig into my lips. A few seconds more, and I was able to nod my head, just a bit. My eyes blinked and reopened on a vision of myself, a work of ultimate beauty, aflame and dripping paint and belching smoke. He must have turned the easel to face me so I could watch it burn. Vale touched my face, stroked my hair, flexed each of my hands, and ran thumbs down the soles of my feet until they feebly kicked. The ice that had run in my veins ebbed, leaving me warm, as if I'd been breathing in the cold and was finally indoors again.

I sat up straight and stared down at Lenoir. Vale nodded once and turned to him with the antidote, but I finally found my words.

"Don't give it to him yet."

All eyes locked on me.

"Demi?" Vale asked gently.

"Tell us where the Malediction Club meets."

Lenoir was foaming at the mouth now, red bubbles leaking from his dry white lips. He laughed, his head spasming and his eyes going mad and glittery. "Wasn't. The deal." He wheezed a laugh. "Antidote!"

Vale sighed and kneeled. "I did promise him."

I was too tired to protest and leaned on the chair's arm, too drained to hold myself upright. Surely there would be some way to compel Lenoir, if we kept him alive. Vale unstoppered the vial carefully and used the dropper to squeeze a stream of golden liquid into Lenoir's mouth. The once-handsome painter lapped at it like a starving dog but quickly spit it back out, coughing up red foam.

"You said. There was an antidote."

Vale grinned. "Oh, there is one. That's just not it." He licked the stopper and scrunched up his face. "Oh, la. It would seem that's my aunt Merle's famous hot-pepper sauce. We consider it the antidote to poor cooking. Spicy, *n'est-ce pas?*"

Lenoir uncurled and straightened in a creepy rictus dance that resembled an exorcism. His trembling hand went for his pocket, but Vale stomped on it, grinding it into the floor.

"None of your blud magic, *monsieur.*"

After clenching his teeth and trembling for a moment as he fought to get his hand from under Vale's boot, Lenoir pinned him with his indigo eyes, the veins bloody and wet and starting to seep into the white. "Going to curse you. For lying to me."

"Think back carefully, *monsieur.* I did not lie."

Lenoir breathed out, spewing bloody froth. His eyes went lucid and crafty then, and he began speaking in Sanguine, slurry and slow. Before he could get out more than a couple of words, Vale kicked him in the throat, and he choked and fell onto his back.

"Of course, if you'll tell us how to find the Malediction Club, I have the real antidote right here."

A twist of paper appeared in Vale's fingers, but Lenoir was past caring. With the last of his energy, he pointed at the smoldering painting, then at me, then drew his trembling finger across his own throat. His hand fell on his crushed neck as his head lolled sideways on the carpet, blood spilling from mouth and eyes and bubbling from the holes in his stomach, which would have healed themselves quickly if not for Vale's half-Abyssinian blood.

"But—how will we find it now? If he's dead?" I shuddered and sobbed. "How will we find Cherie?"

With an angry growl, Vale rushed to a heavy desk in the corner, flicking on the green banker's light and shuffling through the drawers and papers, throwing everything he found onto the ground. "There must be something here, somewhere. An invitation. A bill. A card. Something."

I tried to stand, to hurry to his side, but I could barely move. As it was, I was able to pull myself up holding the back of the chair, then collapse against the windowsill and shuffle along the wall, grabbing each warm sconce like Tarzan reaching for vines. Vale had pulled all the drawers out of the desk by the time I got there, and I fell gratefully to the ground in a puddle of skirts to paw through the spilled papers.

Vale took his search to a series of deep shelves that held rolls of canvas. As he pulled them out and threw them onto the floor, I untied the leather thongs to let the fabric unfurl. I saw fruit, dogs, creepy dolls, cathedrals, haystacks, dead rabbits, piles of bones, people on trains. It was as if he'd plundered an art history book and copied every painting ever, trying out styles from van Gogh, Monet, and even Picasso. They had irregular sides, as if maybe he'd sliced them out of frames. None was signed; hell, maybe they were originals of Sang versions of the artists I revered. With Lenoir dead, there was no way to know.

As Vale moved through the shelves from left to right, the paintings got better and more nuanced. Finally, the figures began to appear, graceful daimon bodies caught in repose or ballerinas holding their legs aloft. There were nudes sprinkled in, too. The first few daimon girls had tails, but after that, the tails disappeared, and the paintings graciously neglected that part of the daimons' anatomy, perhaps to avoid the inconvenient scars that must have remained after removing so large a limb.

"Oh, *mon dieu*." Vale held an uncurled canvas in front of

him so that all I could see was the blank, khaki-colored back.

"Did you find something?" I asked, trying to stand and barely making it to my knees.

"Not something. Someone."

He turned the painting around to show me, and the breath caught in my throat.

It was Bea.

The painting had never been finished. The background was washed in red with hastily sketched-in details, and it was a more intimate portrait than I was familiar with, based on his work. His name in Sang was Lenoir, so close to Renoir. But most of his famous paintings were based on those by Toulouse Lautrec, bright and messy visions of cabarets and dancing girls and ballerinas. This one showed Bea dancing in a feathery ivory ballgown, her hair coiled up and one arm raised. The look on her face was more dreamy and relaxed than I'd ever seen her, not at all guarded and jumpy. In fact, now that I considered it, many of Lenoir's paintings shared the same unfocused gaze.

It had to be the drink.

For me, it was blood and absinthe. For the daimons, perhaps he mixed his powders into one of their fiery brews. But I understood instantly that Bea had once stood before Lenoir, just as I had, and fallen under his spell. The only difference was that her painting had never been finished, while mine now smoldered on a stand. What I didn't understand was why she'd never said more about him than her vague, general warnings. Her fear had been real, but she should have told me the truth. I glanced at my portrait; I'd totally forgotten that a fire burned across the room. It was merry and crackling, just about to reach his bottles of turps and tubes of paint lined up along the easel's edge. The painter himself lay on the floor, huddled up like a smushed bug, his hair fallen to a pile on the floor around his head and his black lips drawn back over ivory fangs set in shriveled gums.

Vale rerolled Bea's painting, stuffed it down the back of his collar, and reached down to collect me.

"Fire's working fast. Time to go, *bébé*."

I waved him away. "I know. Get his pin first. We might need it."

Vale gave me a determined nod and snatched away the damning bit of gold from the painter's jacket. I half expected Lenoir to bolt upright like Lestat and try to strangle the brigand to death, but there was nothing left in the shell of his body. When I held out my arms, Vale gently gathered me to his chest and hurried away from the growing fire. As he rushed down the stairs trailing my chocolate dress, I caught a last glimpse of the Siamese cats on the landing, curled together like parentheses, dead. Their downy white fur had fallen to the floor, their black lips twisted back over fangs, just like their master.

Instead of heading for the front door where I had always entered, Vale plunged into the darkness of a spare kitchen, nearly banging his head on hanging copper pots.

"Where are we going?"

"Into the alleys, the same way I came in. Trust a brigand, *bébé*, you don't want to be seen stepping out a rich dead man's front door."

The courtyard out back was far less fancy than the

sidewalk in front, and Vale neatly sidestepped rubbish bins that rankled of turpentine and neatsfoot oil. He navigated the back alleys like a streetwise cat, keeping us entirely away from gaslights and gendarmes and conveyances, carrying me as if I weighed nothing. I tried to speak once, but he quieted me with a quick peck on the lips and a wink.

"Brigand rule two: if you don't wish to get caught, be silent," he whispered against my ear.

I didn't recognize the route he took to Paradis, not until we entered the elephant's empty courtyard.

"Vale, I can't go in. I ran away from the prince after he'd . . ."

"Paid for you?" He gave me a dark look as he scooted sideways down a narrow alley. "I know. I watched. You were magnificent."

I drew back, which was hard, considering he was carrying me and I was still nearly numb. "You were eavesdropping?"

He shook his head. "I was coming to your room to visit, but then I saw you dressed in that . . . scrap, pacing around like a bludrat in an oven. When he arrived, I watched to make sure he didn't hurt you."

"But I went out the window and didn't see you."

"I can be rather quick when I need to be."

Placing me gently to lean against the alley's bricks, he tapped a broken edge, and to my great surprise, a knee-high door swung open on a crawlspace. I breathed in, always distrustful of small places, but all I caught was the scent of cold stone, old wood, and, oddly enough, hard liquor.

"Can you crawl?"

I flexed my arms and knees. "I think so. Blood would help."

"Crawl to the end of the tunnel, and you can have all the blood you want."

My mouth watered, and I dropped to my knees and wiggled into the hole with Vale's face pressed against my bustle.

"It's a straight shot, *bébé*. There is one turn-off that goes to the main hall of Paradis, but that hatch is probably sealed. Just keep going." I nodded, knowing he couldn't see it, and focused on forcing my sluggish limbs to move. "Best view on Sang, and I can't see a damn thing," he muttered behind me.

My muscles limbered up with movement, although my knees and skirts were suffering against the rough boards. When Vale murmured, "You should be able to stand up now," I pulled myself up the wall and leaned for a moment, catching my breath.

"You'd better not be lying about that blood."

"I never lie about going to the bar, *bébé*."

A dim light appeared up ahead, and then I realized we were in part of the tunnel Bea had taken me through that first morning at Paradis when they had neglected to feed me. I almost drooled, thinking about the supply of blood they'd brought in once I'd proven myself a star. When I found the familiar door, I unhooked the latch and peeked into the bar and the empty theater beyond. My keen Bludman's senses came in handy; there was no one there at all, but I could feel the warmth just beyond, the girls snoring in their beds upstairs. But one thing still bothered me.

"Why can't I smell you?"

Vale chuckled. "Magic, *bébé*. A brigand's secret among telling noses. Now, drink."

So I finally knew how he'd managed to sneak up on me. But considering it had just saved my life, I wasn't about to pick a fight.

Breathing deeply, I went straight to the low hum of a brand-new, still shiny blood warmer. Dozens of vials waited inside, each labeled with a fancy parchment tag showing the vintage. I couldn't have cared less about quality and grabbed the first two, popping their corks with both thumbs and guzzling them like a baby with a bottle. It was gourmet stuff, probably taken off virgin blue bloods, and it washed away the spicy funk of magic and anise from Lenoir's potion. I tossed the empty vials onto the counter and grabbed two more while Vale watched, bemused. I eyed the bowl of oranges I'd noticed on my first trip back here.

"Those aren't blood oranges, are they? I could use something sweet as a chaser."

His grin deepened. "They aren't oranges at all."

I dropped the vials and stared at him.

"Wait, what?"

He plucked an orange and held it up. When he rapped on it with his fist, the sound was hollow. He held it out to me, stem first, and I noticed a circular etching in the peel. When I pulled the stem, it revealed the orange as hollow.

"If a gentleman wishes to spend the night with a lady, he comes to the bar and buys an orange. If he offers it to a girl and she accepts it, that means she has agreed. When the deed is done, she keeps the orange and brings it back here to get paid."

"But I've never seen a girl carrying an orange . . ."

He chuckled. "Would you keep a symbol like that where anyone could see it? Or steal it? No, they mostly hide them until they cash them in in the morning. Most likely, you are still asleep when that happens."

"How much do they cost?"

His eyebrows rose significantly. "I wouldn't know. I have never paid." He jerked his chin at the pile of vials on the bar. "You have had enough?"

I stretched, cracked my neck, and gave him a wicked grin. "I could always use a little more."

"And I would be glad to take you up on that soon. But for now, I think we must wake Bea and discover what she knows. As soon as the world understands that Lenoir is dead and his studio burned, the Malediction Club might move headquarters. Because after what Lenoir said, you agree that Cherie is there, yes?"

I could only nod.

"Come on, then. There is still time, if we hurry. Something tells me this club stays wicked long after midnight."

I was curious about whether he knew a secret way up to the bedrooms, but we took the usual hallway and stairs.

"What about Charline and Sylvie?"

"They're both absinthe addicts. Hence why it's forbidden. Probably collapsed in one of their rooms next to a bottle. Sisters, you know."

Upstairs, the low-burning gaslights revealed a new sign on the door where my own name had hung just a few short hours ago. Looked like La Goulue would get her chance to rule Paradis next, and she was welcome to it. No sounds came from Mel and Bea's room, and I hesitated to knock, knowing that whatever Bea had to say, she was going to be even more upset than she had been earlier, when Mel had asked us to leave.

Before I could get up my nerve, Vale knocked gently.

There was rustling inside, and the door opened just a sliver.

"It's late," Mel said, worried eyes darting from me to Vale. "And we're not allowed to talk to her."

"We must speak with Bea," Vale said. "It is imperative."

She chewed her green lip, still streaked with red paint. "Oh, la. I think that's a bad idea."

"Is Blaise with you?"

"No. He's with Blue tonight."

Vale nodded to himself and pulled the canvas tube from his collar and unrolled it. I held out the gold pin.

"I know it is bad, Mel, and I hate to ask. But Lenoir tried to kill Demi tonight, and we killed him instead. We have only a few hours to find the Malediction Club and shut it down. Permanently."

Mel's skin shivered over to a pale and sickly light green, her eyes going wide and scared as she stared at Lenoir's painting of Bea. Finally, she took a shuddering breath and stood back to let us in. Bea was a blue smudge by a bedside lamp turned low, her arms spotted under a colorful afghan. Before she could sit up enough to withdraw her hands and sign anything, Vale held up the painting. She slumped to the side, pale blue against her white pillow, her shoulders heaving as she shook her head back and forth in useless negation.

Mel crossed the room on bare feet and curled around Bea, stroking her gently and murmuring to her in Franchian.

Vale's voice was gentler than I'd ever heard it, as if he stood over a newborn foal, something spindly and easily snapped. "Bea, we're so sorry, *chère*. We need to know about Lenoir and the Malediction Club."

She shook her head, her eyes squeezed shut. *No no no no no.*

Mel caught her hands and held them up. "Yes, love. Yes. You have to. Did they do this to you?" One green finger gestured to Bea's throat.

Bea's hands went up and clenched, and her face screwed up as if she were were caught between trying to throw up and trying to hold something in. Her teeth chattered and clacked, her eyes starting to bulge as some secret, silent battle raged in her chest.

Vale exhaled hard beside me, his pale eyes filled with grief and worry. His hands went to fists at his sides, as if he could feel Bea's pain. And then his fingers snapped open. "Wait. Let me try something."

He looked from Bea's painting to her tortured face, then thrust the canvas into the banked fire in their grate, where it caught with the same blue sparks as mine had. Bea's eyes flew open, her hands to her heart, and Mel wrapped her arms firmly around Bea's shoulders, their skin merging into teal.

The room was silent but for the painting's crackling, all of us transfixed as the dancing figure dissolved into ash. When it collapsed into the grate, Bea let out a silent but massive sigh, shook Mel off, and sat up against the headboard with a determined set to her chin and a spark to her eyes I'd never seen before. They exchanged a glance, and then Bea's hands began to fly, fast and furious, Mel's voice soft and halting at first, then hurrying to keep up and shaking with rage.

"She could not say it before now, could not communicate anything about Lenoir and the Malediction Club. There was magic in the painting to stop her, imperfect but clever. She is sorry that she was unable to tell you." Mel stroked Bea's arm fondly, tears in her eyes. "Oh, la. *Mon amour*, of course."

Bea flapped her hand at Mel, who said, "I'm sorry. I know it's important. But you're important, too, love." Mel chuckled and dashed away tears. "Bea says it happened eight years ago. She had just come to Paris, still had her voice. She had no plans to join the cabaret, was talented enough to perform on the true stage. Lenoir heard her practicing in the Tuileries one day and came back another time to sketch her and listen to her sing." Her hand landed on Bea's knee, soft as a dove. "She had a beautiful voice, then, and was going to be a star in the opera. Lenoir sent a card, invited her to sit for a painting. He wasn't famous yet, just rich and mysterious. She went, and he gave her daimon drinks and told her she was beautiful. She felt homesick and alone and enjoyed the peace she found in his atelier."

Something twisted in my gut. I knew exactly how she felt.

Bea stopped a moment, her hands fallen in her lap. As she gazed into the pitch-black night, beyond the window Mel's fingers traced her shoulders and neck and back, one going lower to rub what I suspected was the large, painful scar that had once carried a tail.

"Then, one night, he put something strange in her drink. She fell asleep. When she woke up, she was in a . . . a dungeon. Somewhere deep underground, cold, all stone. Looked as old as the catacombs, maybe older. There were skulls everywhere, and it was very dark, and she was so scared. She could hear bludrats eating something and the sounds of women crying and screaming. Soon men in strange, pointed masks and long black cloaks came. They took her down, they . . ."

Mel trailed off, let out a few hiccuping sobs. Vale's eyes met mine; we knew exactly who those men were. But Bea was intent, her signs angry and forceful.

"I'm sorry, *ma chère*, I just can't . . . it hurts me to think of that happening to you." Mel scooted closer to hug Bea, but Bea shooed her away and gestured. "Okay. Okay. I'll finish," Mel said.

"Bea feeds on comfort and joy. When she was hanging in the dungeon, she was starving. There was no comfort or joy. So when the men took her down—she could smell they were men, you see. Human men. Didn't have to see their faces or bodies to know they used the same soaps and colognes as the cabaret clientele. But they took her down and used her, and the only way to stay alive was to feed on their lust and passion for hurting her." She shook her head, her eyes pleading with us. "It was barely enough. You can't understand how awful that is, for a daimon. For a woman. It's the worst kind of torture."

I nodded numbly.

And Vale stepped closer. "How did you escape?"

Bea tapped her throat as Mel translated.

"She had singing magic, but the men kept her gagged and her tail bound. They didn't amputate for the opera. One night, she managed to work the gag loose. She sang the bludrats to her, had them fetch powders and potions from the men's laboratory. She was able to dissolve her manacles and get a few other girls down before someone came to check on them—one of the dark daimons who worked for the wealthy humans. When she started singing her magic, he took her voice." Bea's slender blue hands circled her throat, her mouth opening and closing like a fish. "He knew what she was. They fought, and he killed one of the other girls. Bea wounded him and managed to escape with one other daimon. They wandered the catacombs for days, trying to keep each other alive. Bea found enough comfort in being away from her captors and having another girl with her. But without her voice, Bea couldn't do enough to sustain the other girl, who needed lust and happiness to survive. She starved and withered before they could find sunlight."

Bea doubled over, sobbing silently, her shoulders heaving and the white of her chemise splattered with tears. But her fingers kept moving, even as they trembled.

"She had to leave the other girl's body in the darkness. The next day, she stumbled into the ladder to Paradis. Blue was the one who found her and took her in and found the books on sign language so she could talk. I went with her to have her tail removed so she could stay here. And when we found out Bea was pregnant a few months later, everyone helped out. We never knew . . ." Mel pulled Bea close. "She wouldn't tell us where she came from, who Blaise's father was, why she couldn't talk. I had always assumed she was born mute; it never mattered to me. But I understand, *ma chère*. I understand why you wouldn't tell." Because of the magic. *Because they would kill me*, Bea signed. *They would kill Blaise*.

"How would they know?" Vale asked.

Bea sat up very straight, eyes burning. Her fingers spelled one word. *Auguste*.

"Auguste is one of them?"

Her hands moved jerkily, as if she was tearing flesh into strips.

"Auguste was the daimon who tried to stop her from

escaping. A few years after she arrived here and had Blaise, he showed up to sweep the floors and tend bar. He never spoke to her. But he watched her. And he . . ."

Mel's jaw dropped, and she grasped Bea's hands. "He uses her when he wants to. In return for not telling the Malediction Club she's here. Oh, Beatrice. Oh, why didn't you say?"

The girls fell on each other, crying, one loudly and one silently.

Vale stepped closer, slipped an arm around me, and pulled my body against him as if I, too, fed on comfort. And it did help. Even with the blood I'd guzzled downstairs, I still felt wobbly, especially after hearing Bea's story. We now knew we had a unified enemy: the Malediction Club was behind Cherie's abduction on the road, my attempted kidnapping in the elephant, Lenoir's plot to steal my soul, and Bea's abuse and the theft of her voice.

"You know we will kill Auguste when we find them, yes?"

Bea gave Vale a wobbly, determined smile and signed something short and sharp.

"She says." Mel cleared her throat. "'Kill them all.'"

I couldn't be silent anymore. "We killed Lenoir and couldn't find anything in his studio that had an address or a map. And we couldn't hunt through Fermin's lab. Do you know any other members? Can we question Auguste?"

Bea snorted and shook her head no, and my hopes fell. But then she signed something

In a very quiet voice, Mel said, "She knows where they meet. She couldn't tell us, but she has always known."

"How?"

Bea tapped her throat again.

"Because she left her magic there."

"So you could lead us there?" Vale shifted, stretching his shoulders and twitching his fingers as if longing to feel his claw in his fist.

"She says . . . you don't understand. They're too powerful. The richest men in Paris. Barons and chirurgeons and gendarmes and barristers. They're everywhere. They have money and magic and weapons and servants, and they're accustomed to taking what they want. By force."

Bea's slender arms gestured to each of us in turn. Sitting there, raw and empty of tears, she reminded me of a plant that had been crushed but kept growing anyway. "The four of us against the Malediction Club? It's laughable," Mel said for her.

All I could think about was Cherie, shackled to a stone wall, deep underground, maybe dying. Broken bodies, crushed minds, empty hearts, all kept like pets by men who'd forgotten that women were people, if they'd ever known at all.

"I bet every girl in this cabaret has lost a friend or someone she loved," I murmured.

Mel nodded. "Oh, la. So many girls disappear. We never know what happens to them."

"We know now," Vale said.

"And if we hurry, before they know we know, maybe we can do something about it."

They all stopped to stare at me.

"Get up, and get dressed. Put on your thickest corset and heaviest boots. I've got an idea."

30

We went from door to door down the hall of Paradis, knocking until the sleepy-eyed daimon girls answered, clutching thin shawls and rumpled sheets around their shoulders against the spring chill. Vale and I gave each girl the same message: "We're taking down the Malediction Club tonight. They have hostages. If you've lost some-one you loved and don't wish to live in fear, bring every weapon you have, and come fight with us."

Most of them nodded, their eyes going sharp and hard. In ones and twos, the hallway filled with dancers turned assassins, standing tall in their steel-boned corsets paired with leggings and boots and skirts slit for fighting. Some were armed with knives or claws; some had only let-ter openers or hammers found lying innocently around the theater. A few had small crossbows or strange leather satchels, rigid and hinged like an old-fashioned doctor's bag, and I was curious about what they hid inside. Criminy had one like that in his wagon, tucked tidily under his desk. There was so much I still didn't know about my coworkers.

One of the newer daimon girls had shyly handed me a pile of my own clothes, given to her a few short hours ago, after the prince had left the cabaret in a petulant

storm. I thanked her and ducked into her room to trade
Lenoir's hateful heavy gown for leggings, a thick corset, a
buttoned jacket, and scuffed boots. Considering that we
were on our way to fight, I left off the bustle and skirts, as
did many of the daimons. There was no sign of the posh
star of Mortmartre in the spitfire Bludman hissing at me
in the mirror. And I liked myself better this way.

"Where's Auguste?" I whispered to Vale while we waited
for Mel and Bea to emerge from their room.

"His shift ended at midnight. After that, who knows?
Perhaps he is at the club now."

I nodded. That made sense. As many times as the
daimon had delivered me to the elephant or to Lenoir's
doorstep, I'd never seen him when I returned from my
assignations or on that delicious night when Vale had
found me on the trapeze.

"I can't believe he would do that to Bea. To anyone." I
shivered, and Vale slung an arm around my waist, ground-
ing me. I still hadn't fully recovered from Lenoir's potion.

"Other species do not share your moral code, *bébé*.
Daimons who feed on lust think monogamy is a laughable
idea, and dark daimons don't care any more for their prey
than bludrats worry over a crying infant. But if Auguste
is there and the girls find him, he will be ripped to pieces.
He has most likely been acting as a spy, tipping off his mas-
ters. And betraying a daimon to help a human is unforgivable among their kind."

I searched around my emotions like a tongue pressing
around a rotten tooth, hunting for the pocket of pain.
Nope. I felt no regret for Auguste. He'd known exactly
what he was doing, delivering me to Lenoir's studio.

Finally, the door opened, and Mel and Bea stepped out,

their hands firmly clasped and glowing turquoise. Bea's eyes were wet and tear-stained, but her dimpled little chin was set in determination. With one hand, she pointed to the stairs. We didn't need a translation to know it was time to go and fight.

Bea led us down the stairs, through the hallway, and straight to the trapdoor in the stage, the very one through which I'd entered this twisted cabaret of mixed beauty and grotesquerie just a short time ago. It seemed as if a lifetime had passed, as if I'd shed my skin and now longed to have it back as easily as my clothes. Vale pulled open the trapdoor as the girls lifted old-fashioned kerosene lamps from a shelf behind the bar and lit them with long matches. Even the bartender was with us, her human mask gone to reveal speckled skin that matched the oranges she'd once guarded. She handed me a vial of blood and held up a softly glowing lantern.

"Best drink up, pet. It's about to get dark."

I gulped the blood and flopped onto my belly, sliding my legs into the square of darkness and poking around with my boot toes to find the rungs. Ever since we'd visited Monsieur Charmant, the catacombs below Paris felt sinister, coiled like a sleeping snake and waiting to devour me after any wrong step. The underground of Paris had vomited forth the bludhounds and driven tortured daimon girls to death. What would it do to me, where we were going? But the blood settled in my belly and radiated outward, giving me new strength. And when I realized that I was finally on the right track to Cherie, I moved faster down the rungs with a fierce grin on my face.

Finally, a real enemy. Finally, something to fight.

Strong hands gripped my waist and steadied me as I stepped to the uneven ground, enveloped by darkness.

"Did you bring your pendant, *bébé*?"

I flooded red with shame. "It broke. My first day at Paradis, when Limone pushed me off the catwalk. I was fine, but it shattered." Strong fingers urged my chin up; I couldn't see his eyes, but I could feel them, probing and gentle. "I'm so sorry, Vale. I saved the pieces. I know it was special."

"I am the one who's sorry. I wanted to give you comfort, not bits of crystal."

"You did. You do. Don't we need to hurry?"

His hands didn't budge from my hips. "Stay with me in the back, *bébé*. At least until we get close."

"Why?"

"So I can do this."

He lifted me, twirling me around and pressing my back against the cold stones. I gasped, and his mouth settled over mine, catching me wide open. I had to hold myself carefully back, mindful of my fangs but filled with an animal hunger for him, for his strange taste, for the hot hardness of his knee rammed between mine and whatever instinct told animals to rut before a battle. His hands slid under my jacket and stroked the curve up and down my corset, his thumbs brushing hard over the nipples exposed by his sweeping fingers. I moaned and pressed against him, arching my back off the bricks.

As I changed the angle and pulled his face closer, I heard an answering moan that most definitely wasn't Vale. My eyes flew open. Three daimon girls stood behind him with lanterns held high, their faces on us and dreamy yet focused like birds waiting for a worm to surface from rain-wet ground. I pulled away from the kiss and snapped my knees together, forcing Vale away.

"Can I help you?" I asked.

One of the girls, a violet-skinned daimon named Lexie, shrugged unashamedly. "Little snack before the fight can only help, *non*?"

I scowled over Vale's shoulder as he held in a chuckle. I could only suppose he was more accustomed to being daimon fodder than I was.

"Please don't . . . I don't know. Don't eat me. Or whatever you call it."

"*Pfft*. We don't eat people." She gave me a significant look that made me blush. "But love and lust are free game."

I grabbed Vale's hand and stormed down the corridor, following the bobbing lights up ahead.

"Try some anger, then," I growled as we passed.

Vale allowed me to pull him along, but he stayed safely silent. Which was good, as I couldn't think of anything he could say that wouldn't annoy me. Still, he slowed down as we approached the bigger group of determined girls stomping on bits of bone as they marched down the tunnel, shedding fluttery bits of feathers in the dank water.

"Love and lust, *bébé*?" he finally asked, giving my hand a squeeze.

I ignored it and hurried faster.

"You have nothing to say?"

He stopped walking but didn't let go of my hand, and I was forced to halt or jerk my shoulder out of the socket. So I stopped, because I couldn't kill people with a bum shoulder. But I didn't turn around. I didn't want him to see my face flushed red. The three daimon girls hurried past on the other side of the water trough, giggling. One left a lamp at our feet; another carried a large ball of yarn that she'd tied to the ladder rungs, and the bright red string unfurled behind her, leaving a path.

"Let's go, Vale. We have an evil cabal to destroy."

"They'll keep five minutes. And what is the point of vanquishing evil if you are not sure you will get what you want afterward, anyway?" He wiggled my arm until I turned around, chin firmly down.

"I don't want to talk about this now. I can't. I need to fight. I need my head in the game. Lenoir almost . . . I don't know. Killed me? Paralyzed me and raped my soul? I don't know what that was. But you saved me from it, and I haven't thanked you. So thank you."

His fingers lit on my shoulders, crept on moth feet down my arms to my hands. "There. That wasn't so hard, was it, *bébé*?"

"I'm fine at gratefulness."

"But commitment is another story?"

"A completely different book. A library on a different planet."

His finger grazed my cheek, a hot brand I felt all the way down to my toes. "*Bébé*, you are talking to a nomad. I have never lived in one place longer than a couple of months." He stepped closer, tipped up my face. I could barely see him in the low light, but I could feel his breath on my lips, feel a tense tremble in his muscles. "Here is the thing about brigands: when they see something they want, they find a way to take it. Sometimes by force but most often by patience and cleverness. Following, studying, waiting for the perfect time to swoop in."

"What are you saying?"

"Swoop."

He kissed me again, softer this time. As I always did whether I wished it or not, I melted into him, opening for him. Kissing boys on Earth and in the caravan had always been exciting but taxing, as if it took work, took something out of me. But kissing Vale was a gift, filling me with strength and comfort. I guessed the daimons were right; love and lust were free game, as far as sustenance went.

"Oh la la," I muttered as he drew away.

"Then it is settled." Entwining his fingers with mine, he started back down the corridor.

I didn't move. "Nothing is settled, Vale. Nothing."

"But—"

"I mean, is that how brigands do it? One kiss, and everything's done? I feel like I know you so well, but I don't know what you want for the future. I don't know what you dream about, if you want kids, how your career as a brigand would support us, what parts of you they would cut off if they caught you stealing. Are you going to challenge your father or get in a cage match with your brother? If he didn't slice you in half, where would we live? Which continent? In a wagon? In a tent? What if I want to keep performing? I'm never going to settle down and be some grouchy old woman cooking stew I can't eat around a campfire for a dozen good-looking, green-eyed children, you know. I'm never going to be tamed."

"I would never want you tamed."

"I don't want a wagon or a house or a clockwork dog."

"Details."

"Kind of important ones. And what if we *did* have kids? They would be, let's see, a quarter Abyssinian, a quarter human, and half Bludman. What do you even call that?"

He chuckled to himself. "A dangerous little fiend, that's what."

I almost growled but started walking instead. He wouldn't let go of my hand, and enough of me wanted to let him keep holding it that I didn't fight it. At least he walked with me this time, once he'd scooped up the lantern.

With the flow of water dripping down the trough, we had to walk one in front of the other down the ledge, with my arm pulled behind me. It was strange to remember the last time we'd walked down here, me so uncertain and frightened, him steady and playing the clown, trying to keep my spirits up. Maybe I didn't have all the answers I wanted from him, but I understood that in a short period of time, he'd come to be a solid part of my life in Paris, a wall I could always count on to hold me up. And this fight we were having now, if you could even call it a fight, was more like married people bickering than new lovers having a quarrel. And he knew it, which was why he let me tug him along.

Truth was, he'd swooped in long ago, and I'd let him.

"Tell me, then," I said softly.

As I kept my eyes trained on the lanterns up ahead, he murmured in a voice low enough for my ears only. "I want to marry you. I want to run away with you. I want to have children with you but not so many that you go crazy. I don't want you to grow old by a campfire. I want to travel, see the world, pursue the sun. I don't want to lead, but I don't want to follow. I don't ever want you to stop being wild, but I wouldn't mind harnessing your ferocity. Perhaps we could start our own cabaret, treat the girls better. I don't know. I have only been thinking about this most nights while I stare at the stars and wait for your light to go out so I know you're alone when it does."

I tensed, fingers squeezing his tightly. "You've been spying on me?"

"I've been protecting you, *bébé*. I knew that one of these days, no matter how strong and smart you are, the men of Mortmartre would find a way to put an end to your teasing and claim you once and for all, against your wishes and protestations. And I wasn't going to let it happen."

"I don't know whether to be grateful or furious."

"Both, probably."

"Jesus, Vale. How are you so goddamn blasé about this? You love me, you want to marry me and start a cabaret, you've been stalking me, but it's for my own good. And we're walking into the lion's den right this moment, and you don't seem to give a shit. Do you ever take anything seriously?"

He laughed outright then. "I take everything seriously; I simply refuse to be serious about it. What is, is. What is done, is done. You don't think much like a Bludman. And whoever said I loved you, *bébé*?"

I skidded to a stop, half terrified and half furious. "But you—"

"I do, though. Quite honestly, I feel on track for the first time in my life. I actually want to do the thing that needs doing, and you're right here with me, hand in mine. The worst that can happen is I die fighting for my woman, and for a brigand, that is an enviable way to go."

"You won't die. I can always . . ." I trailed off.

"You can't. That's the irony, *non*? I'm the only one you cannot turn into a Bludman."

My heart clutched itself behind my corset, and that's

when I knew how much I cared about him. The biggest weapon in my arsenal was being a Bludman. I was hard to kill, a dangerous predator in my own right, and gifted with the ability to turn a dying human into one of my own, thereby saving his life. But since I couldn't drink Vale's half-Abyssinian blood, he was right. I couldn't turn him. I realized I was crushing his fingers and relaxed my hand, suddenly seeing him as fragile as a butterfly.

And he recognized it instantly and squeezed harder. "Don't be careful of me, *bébé*. I am still difficult to kill in my own right, and I grew up in a brigand's camp. I always have weapons up my sleeves, you know."

"But still—"

"I forbid you to worry about me. Worry about Cherie instead."

We were almost caught up to the group of girls, and they turned as one down another tunnel to the right, fanning out behind Bea. Unlike the well-defined archways that led to the other turn-offs and crypts, this entrance was like the crack in a broken tooth, and I paused before stepping over the jagged bricks and turned to face the man who loved me.

"Something else is bothering you, Vale. I can smell you again, and you smell of worry."

"Ah, yes." He chuckled, and I breathed in the strange spice as the blood hit his cheeks in a blush. "You never answered me. I basically poured out my heart to you, very unbrigandly, I might add, and you just continued walking."

I glanced through the crack in the bricks. Somewhere up ahead, the girls had stopped. They all held their lanterns aloft, and I could just barely see a set of stone steps going, oddly, downward. A bizarre melange of smells reached me: fine cologne and old Scotch, oil and metal, sex and sadness, all overlaid with the greasy sweetness of dark magic. We had reached our destination. And the daimons of Paradis were waiting for us to lead them.

I went up on tiptoe to plant a firm kiss on Vale's lips.

"I think I love you. Now, shut up and help me kill a bunch of people so we can figure out the rest."

31

As I passed through the cluster of daimon girls, I felt hands fall softly on my arms, light touches on my shoulders and back and a few on my head, as if they could draw strength from me along with sustenance. Or maybe they were offering blessings. I felt a brief moment of shame that I had spent so much time in their world, living among them, and had never really taken the time to learn about them and their ways.

"What now?" Mel whispered.

"Stick to the plan," I whispered back.

We'd figured it out while waiting in the hall, and it had spread from girl to girl like flames licking a cursed painting. Just like onstage, everyone knew her own part and was ready to play it. The daimons set down their lanterns against the wall, away from the rippling skirts that many of them had worn and carried high above the water of the catacombs. The weapons they'd held while walking disappeared into the corsets, up their sleeves, under their hats, tucked into blouses behind their backs. They twisted their heads to crack their necks and twitched their shoulders, limbering up. Those high kicks we'd been practicing were about to come in handy. The next step was a strange one, but we'd discussed it back at Paradis, and at least the first installment of the plan was familiar to them. Bea had told us exactly what would be waiting beyond the door.

Vale gave my hand a final squeeze and melted back behind the group. I took the steep steps carefully, my skin going frigid as I descended. Instead of a trapdoor with a ladder like the one at Paradis or a hole in the floor with steps like Monsieur Charmant's, this entrance was more civilized, as if the denizens within didn't care to sully their hands or boots with climbing or crawling. Even the door was elegant—dark wood, oiled and carved. I was willing to bet the hinges wouldn't dare to squeak.

Ever so slowly, I turned the knob, but the door wouldn't budge. I had no pins in my hair, and with their tails removed, the daimon girls had no magic of their own. Even with all of our stashed weapons, no one had an ax.

Beside me, Vale put a hand on my shoulder. "Let the brigand handle that, *bébé*." He fiddled with the keyhole for a moment and stepped back with a cocky grin. "Your turn."

This time, the knob turned easily. I sidled through, drawn to a break between indigo velvet curtains that hid the door from the larger room beyond. Peeking through the crack as if yet again in the wings of a grand theater, I shook my head at the perfection, the gilded beauty, the most very definite wrongness of the scene. It was like a grand church mixed with a cabaret, far below Paris. Music floated in from a three-piece band of bright-eyed daimon men who, I noticed, still wore their tails. The room beyond the band was large and open, a ballroom like one might find in a public dance hall or a rich man's mansion. The floor was light and polished, reflecting the bright chandeliers overhead and the swirling, jewel-hued skirts of the girls who danced in the arms of tuxedo-clad gentlemen. I had expected to find them in the bird masks I'd seen at the carriage fire, but what need did they have to hide here, in their secret club, where their victims would never escape the catacombs with their minds and hearts intact? There had to be at least three dozen of the bastards, although only half of them were dancing.

My heart wrenched as I inspected the girls more closely. They moved with daimon grace, dressed like dolls in revealing cabaret clothes. But their faces were blank, their eyes wide, and their mouths slack and unsmiling. They were drugged or ensorcelled, in some sort of stupor, dancing as if caught in someone else's dream. On tables and in corners, partners and more unorthodox groupings of partially clad bodies writhed in ways that drew moans only from the men.

The daimons of Paradis gathered around me, vibrating with anger and fear. I looked to my left and my right, and the girls I had come to know on sight had changed utterly. Their skins, always a riotous rainbow, were now all the same color, the ephemeral smoky gray of shadows and darkness. As we'd discussed, they split into two groups. One group shimmied and shook themselves until they were back to their bright, beautiful selves. The other group remained shadow-dark and disrobed completely.

The naked girls became chameleons, every part of their bodies and hair blending in with their surroundings as they skirted the dance floor, slinking like cougars. There were about twenty of them, and I quickly lost sight of their bodies as I tossed their clothes back through the door and into the tunnel. The remaining girls fixed each other's hair and fluffed skirts as they did backstage at Paradis. Then, as if we'd coordinated it perfectly, a grandfather clock struck two, and they sashayed past the curtains and onto the dance floor, hips swinging and smiles wide.

They'd caught the men mid-waltz, and with practiced motions, each girl found her mark and twirled the gentleman right out of his partner's grasp. The nearly invisible girls guided their sleepwalking sisters to the curtains, herding them toward us like confused cattle. Bea, Mel, Vale, and I darted out to grab them, grasping each dazed victim's arm through the curtain and carefully propelling them toward the door to the catacombs, where more girls waited to lead them back to Paradis, following that red string through the maze of tunnels.

The first girl I grabbed was pliant, her eyes dumb and her steps sluggish in slippers worn down to nothing. I didn't realize until I was pressing her hurriedly forward that it was Limone—or what was left of her. The proud acid-green of her gold-dusted skin had faded to the the color of a molded lemon. All the hate I'd felt, facing her portrait in the Louvre, was gone. She was empty, a shell, but her hair was in perfect ringlets, and her eyelashes were long and false, proving what was more important to her captors.

"I'm sorry," I muttered over her shoulder, the heat in my cheeks acknowledging that she wouldn't be here if I hadn't shown up exactly when I did to steal her spotlight.

Once I'd shoved her through the curtain as gently as I could, I ventured out farther for two more girls, tugging them behind me as if we were dancing. The daimons of Paradis were doing their job well, keeping their partners' faces turned away from the curtains. Somehow, the men missed the fierce cast of their smiles; the girls were working their seduction as an act of revenge, and it was as natural as a lioness hunting the man who had taken her cubs.

I was going back for my fourth girl when a scuffle began, and one of the men shouted, "Dammit, girl. Let go of me!"

The sound of his open hand striking her cheek didn't even stop the musicians. But the sound of her boot cracking his chin did.

"You dare to strike your master?"

In answer, she kicked him again. The room went so quiet that I heard the clatter of his tooth hitting the floor. Vale rushed past me, carrying two girls under his arms like sacks of flour. I fetched the last drooping daimon victim through the curtain as the girls stepped away from their partners and drew their weapons.

"Magician! What is the meaning of this?" a familiar voice called, and I followed the duke's gaze to a balcony up above, where an acid-yellow daimon stood in a red-and-white-striped suit, his taloned hands curled around the balustrade. Without a word, Monsieur Charmant turned and fled.

"It means your little club's over, *monsieur le duc*," the nearest girl spat. The duke grabbed her hair and yanked it, and she shoved a letter opener deep into his stomach. With that thrust, the fight was on.

The daimon girls had originally taken on the matching skin tones of the dancing partners they'd replaced. But as they whipped out their weapons and howled their war cries, they burst into vibrant, angry hues of red and black and fierce tiger stripes. Vale rushed past me and waded into the fray, the ornate silver Wolverine claw sweeping before him and striking home in the back of a double-wide tuxedo. Of course, he was here, my first interviewer, the gatekeeper. Monsieur Philippe. The blades slipped into the black fabric, right under his ribs where the kidneys nestled in fat, smooth as butter. Philippe fell to his knees hard enough to make the floorboards creak. I should have been fighting, should have taken up a weapon, but I couldn't stop watching Vale. His fragility terrified me, but the man was damned beautiful in a fight.

Vale ripped out the claw and wiped the blood spatter from his cheek before kicking Philippe over. The overfed gentleman sobbed on the floor, flailing like a turtle on its back.

"You're, what, Philippe—the curator? You choose the girls?"

"I meant no harm. I didn't know—"

"You were dancing with Limone. You knew exactly what you were doing."

Philippe covered his eyes with sweaty fists. "Please, *monsieur*. I beg you. Whatever you wish is yours."

"There's only one thing you have that I want."

"Women? Money? Riches?"

Vale snorted, his humor gone completely. "Revenge."

I turned away before I saw the final slash of the claw, but I couldn't plug my ears against Monsieur Philippe's gurgles and the wet sound of gizzards hitting the wood. Then I smelled the blood and remembered my best weapon. Vale's hand brushed over my cheek as he went to help Lexie, who was struggling with two men. His knuckles had painted me with a slash of red, and I licked it greedily from my lips.

"They owe you blood, *bébé*," he said, voice husky. "Take your due."

I nodded and turned away from what was left of Philippe. He was cooling quickly, so I scented the air for something strong that needed to be destroyed. My hands were already curled into claws before I found my prey, and I was across the dance floor, leaping over bodies and slipping in puddles of blood, aiming for his throat.

The gentleman was familiar to me, one of dozens of nameless faces from the boxes of Paradis. His fine, smooth hands were wrapped around Leola's slender neck, his thumbs boring into her windpipe as her eyes rolled back. I slashed his throat open with my claws and began drinking before he'd even let her loose. Leola shook herself and stood.

"*Merci*," she mumbled, before wading in to help the next struggling girl.

Something tugged my leggings while I drank, and I spun around, hissing. It was the prince, as I'd never seen him before. Dirty, deflated, bruised, covered in blood, and sniveling in a puddle of snot, his colorful suit stained and slashed to show pasty white skin underneath.

"Demitasse, my beloved. Help me. Heal me."

I shook him off and wiped my mouth with the back of my wrist. Licking the blood from my chin, I tossed the man in my arms halfway across the room and stared at the prince as if he were an alien. An animal. A fluffy little bunny.

It was difficult remembering how to use words and talk around my fangs. "Heal you?"

He rubbed his face on my ankle, and I kicked him away. "Your blud. Make me what you are. We will rule together. You will be my queen."

I remembered how to laugh then. Throwing my head back in a wild half-cackle, half-howl, I kneeled over him, noting the pulls in the silk of his silly jacket. A few sad worms of hair scraggled over the bald pate he'd hidden under his turban.

Putting on a kind smile, I leaned over him until my lips brushed his ear. "No one owns me," I whispered. "No one ever will."

I bit down too hard, and it was over quickly. His blood tasted of far-off spices and too much wine. And I smelled something else, something familiar. Abandoning his pulsing jugular, I put my nose to his collar, his lapel, his lips.

He smelled of Cherie.

I jerked away before he was completely dead and surveyed the scene. Most of the men were down, and the girls were working in pairs now to dispatch the rest, calling Vale and his claw over to finish off the gents who struggled. There was no sympathy in my heart for these men, not from the predator or from the girl. It was bad enough that they came to the cabarets and bought their pleasures with oranges and francs and empty promises. It was more damning that they forced the girls to give up their tails and their magic, an intrinsic part of their lives that they would never see again. Knowing that the dead-eyed girls had been brought to this underground lair of debauchery and used—the men deserved even worse than what they'd gotten.

But there was more I needed to know, and so I hunted out the one who was still the most alive and undamaged. Unsurprisingly, it was Auguste, the slippery bastard. Three girls had him cornered, but he still had his tail, and it curved over his head like a scorpion's stinger, pointing at each girl in turn as she approached.

"Save him for me," I growled.

Auguste's head snapped up, and he spit on the ground at my feet, his normally pleasant face twisted into a sneer and his once-indigo skin as yellow as Charmant's. "You should have done as you were told, bloodsucker. This is on your head."

His tail pointed at me, his hands balled in fists at his sides. My nose quivered, but my eyes didn't budge from his. I had to keep him talking. "Yeah, I'm pretty proud of that. So how much did they pay you to torture your friends?"

He leered. "They paid me in pain, not coppers. Your *petite amie* Cherie can really scream."

My talons bit into my palms, my fangs grinding for a taste of his throat. Daimons weren't satisfying, and no Bludman in her right mind would crave one's blood; it was the same way I felt about Brussels sprouts back home. But as Criminy had always told me but never encouraged me to discover for myself, the enemy's blood was always the sweetest, and you didn't notice the taste so much in the heat of battle. All I had to do was find a way past that tail.

Just before I completely lost it, Vale appeared behind Auguste, bloodstained claw in hand, and said, "I wonder how loud *you* can scream."

With one swift slice, Auguste's tail fell to the ground. Seeing his only weapon disabled, I went for his throat. The girls gasped as I ripped into the yellow flesh, and after a few rage-fueled sips, I sat back on my haunches and spit on the ground.

"Ugh. That taste is just . . . wrong."

Vale held my shoulders and helped pull me back up to standing. "Bad news, *bébé*. He was the last one."

I looked around the blood-spattered ballroom, inhaled deeply. He was right. They were all dead. I wiped the dregs of Auguste off my lips. "*Merde*."

"But where is Cherie? Can you smell her?"

I shook my head and looked to Bea.

Mel was on the verge of tears, her arm wrapped around Bea's shoulder. Bea was back to her usual blue, covered in gore and sporting a line of four Malediction Club pins on her jacket like hunting trophies. At least it was less grisly than ears or scalps on a string.

With a general's surety, Bea pointed to a nondescript corner. Since the walls of the ballroom were draped in indigo velvet curtains and tapestries to ward off the cold that seeped through the stones, I had imagined it was simply one large room. But as she crossed the boards and twitched the curtain aside, I saw another door. The last one had been ceremonial, carved, ancient, morbidly beautiful. This one looked as if it had been designed by a master artificer. It was thick, riveted metal, with heavy reinforcements and a complicated lock that I was willing to bet even Vale couldn't pick.

"Can we break it down?" Mel asked, and Bea shook her head and pointed back to the ballroom, signing something. "She says the door is new and heavier than the one she escaped from. But one of the men will have a key."

Without a word, we spread out, each girl kneeling beside a dead gentleman to rifle through his pockets. It was eerily similar to what I'd been doing every night in the copper elephant. I checked Auguste, but he carried nothing that resembled a key. Probably just a lackey, even after all this time. I did find a fang knotted into a handkerchief, which I retied and tucked into my own pocket. Chirurgeons in Sang could do amazing things, but I didn't know much about reconstructive dentistry.

Several girls came up with keys, which was good, since it took two of them to open the damn thing. In the end, it was Bea and Mel who turned the keys and swung the door open on a scene more sickening than I had imagined. It was like Frankenstein's laboratory crossed with the worst kind of animal shelter crossed with an art museum. Daimon girls were locked in cages, manacled to the walls, or strapped to beds like mental patients, the walls around them filled to the ceiling with portraits in heavy gold frames. The girls in the paintings all shared the unique, lively beauty of Lenoir's masterpieces, and the girls curled in the cages and struggling against their bonds showed signs of being drained and nearly as dead-eyed as the girls we'd freed. Mel, Bea, and all the other daimon girls cried out and hurried to help their compatriots.

But I only had eyes for Cherie.

I ran to where she lay, eyes closed, strapped to a narrow bed with thick leather bonds, shackles digging into her wrists and ankles. Beside her on an easel sat a nearly finished painting of her at her most beautiful, familiar brushes soaking in turpentine. The scent of oils now made me ill.

"Demi? Is that you?"

Her voice was weak and rough and sounded wrong—because her fangs were gone. I couldn't remember what it was like, having a mouth full of blunt teeth, and my heart ached for her.

"It's me, honey. Hold on. We're getting you out of here."

I fumbled with the thick leather straps, and Vale came to help me. The iron manacles were tougher to get undone, but Bea brought over a key, and I was soon pulling Cherie into my arms, limp as a rag doll.

"Blood? Did you bring any blood?"

"I didn't. I'm sorry. We'll get some soon."

I hugged her so tightly she squeaked and pushed away. Her long blond hair was carefully pinned into an updo, her sunken cheeks rosy with fading paint. She looked around the room, and her button nose twisted up in a very Cherie gesture. "Daimons and an Abyssinian? Am I dreaming?"

"Nope. We're here to rescue you."

"And the men? Charmant? Are they—"

I shook my head in anger. I'd forgotten about Charmant.

"The men are all dead, but Charmant escaped. Lenoir's dead, too."

Her arms wrapped around my neck, and she sobbed into my hair. "Thank Aztarte. Oh, Demi. I can't even describe . . ." She trailed off and looked up at the half-finished portraits crowded on the walls. Some were almost complete, just awaiting final touches and varnish. Others were in their early stages, rough outlines and splashes of color. "We're trapped in the paintings. Lenoir does something, and you're drained afterward. I feel like half a girl. And if he's dead . . ."

"Vale?"

"Yes, *bébé*?" He turned to look at me, and a rush of love filled my chest.

"Burn the paintings. Burn them all."

Cherie sighed softly, her eyes rolling back as she went unconscious in my arms.

32

My best friend weighed almost nothing. Her breathing was shallow, her heart beating fast, as I placed her back on the bed. When I went hunting for vials to fortify her for the catacombs, I was horrified to find the opposite of what I was looking for: Cherie's blud in tiny, ornate vials, marked for shipment to a Darkside winery. She couldn't drink them, and I couldn't find any human blood to sustain her, and all the gentlemen outside were cold. I tried to soak up puddles of blood with a handkerchief, but when I put it to her lips, she took one suck and turned away.

"Oil and magic," she muttered, dashing it to the ground. "Floor wax and poison."

The only answer was to hurry back to Paradis as quickly as possible and pour as many vintage vials down her throat as she could handle. But first, I had to see the Malediction Club ended forever.

Heading out, the daimons looked like survivors of a war. The gore-stained dancing girls of Paradis supported the half-broken, barely alive girls from the cages, hobbling past the bodies of their captors and hurrying into the catacombs. One girl was so far gone that Bea and Mel had to carry her strung between them. There was a lot of strange machinery hidden in the laboratory, and some of it looked liable to explode once we started a fire. But the paintings had to burn, and with them, the men who had brought women deep underground to use them against their will, raping their bodies and minds. It was dirty work, dragging heavy corpses into the laboratory. I found one still barely breathing, but he was gone by the time I presented him to Cherie where she sat on the narrow cot like a queen, commanding us in the proper stacking of tuxedoed lords. She managed a few token sips before drawing back with a shudder and wiping at empty spots that had once held fangs.

"Cold. And he stinks of piss."

I smothered a giggle. Cherie's prissiness and disdain were back, but I'd never heard her utter a single curse word. Perhaps they hadn't destroyed her spirit after all.

The dragged bodies left slug trails of blood from the grand, soaring ballroom to the smaller laboratory. When Vale began pulling down the paintings and piling them on top of the men, I wordlessly went to work with him, knocking them down with a broom when they were too high up. Men and art were soon piled too high to reach the top, and my shoulders ached by the time we were done.

"Is there anything else here we need?" Vale asked Cherie.

She shook her head primly. "Everything should burn."

I reached for her hands, careful of the places where her talons had broken off. "If Lenoir used the same magic on you and the girls here that he used on me, you should all go back to normal once the paintings have been destroyed."

Cherie's beautiful eyes went faraway and hard. "We will never be normal again."

Vale picked her up like a child and carried her to the door. I went to a sconce bolted to the wall and used the flame within to light one of Lenoir's expensive brushes. The oil-soaked bristles went up so quickly that I singed my fingers, and I tossed it onto the pile of paintings with a grim smile. Brush after brush, I stuck the soft hair into the fire and held them to tuxedos, to frames, to raw canvas, to the prince's curly-toed boots. The flames crackled and caught and spread until sweat soaked my chemise and I choked on oily smoke.

I had saved Cherie's painting for last, and I selected a long-handled brush to paint it with flame. The portrait was nearly complete, and the surface flared into a blaze of blue, the corners curling as it burned. I had just thrown the brush on top of the pyre and turned to run when someone burst through the door: Bea, with Mel right behind her.

"Bea, love, no! This place is going up quick. We must run." Mel tugged at Bea's arm, unintentionally tearing her shirt to reveal blue skin splattered with blood. But Bea shook her head and stumbled past me, past the pyre of paintings and into a corner of cabinets that I'd ignored, assuming it was just a collection of paints and turps or possibly horrible instruments that I certainly didn't want to see up close, much less touch.

The smoke was thick and getting thicker, and Bea's mostly silent cough was one of the saddest sounds I'd ever heard. Ignoring us, ignoring the flames, ignoring every shouted warning, she ripped open the cabinet and began knocking its contents to the ground. The first jar that broke carried the stink of Monsieur Charmant and his magic, and the brief snatches I could see through the smoke showed me the same sort of dark ingredients and talismans I had seen in the daimon's Darkside shop. Soon I couldn't see what was happening, could only hear the crashes and clanks of Bea's bizarre desperation.

"Seriously, Bea. This place is about to explode. We have to go!" I shouted. Mel tried to run around me and make a break for Bea, but I caught her around the waist and put my mouth to her ear. "She can't last much longer in this smoke, and you can't go over there. It's too dangerous."

"I have to get her!" Mel's voice was part cough, part sob, part scream as she thrashed in my arms.

"No, you don't."

The voice was husky and rich and utterly unfamiliar. Every hair on my body rose as Bea fought through the smoke and into Mel's embrace.

"I am here, my Melissande," she said, and for the first time, we heard her sob with joy.

Mel danced her around in an ecstatic hug, and I couldn't resist putting a hand on Bea's back, hoping she could feel the insane amounts of comfort and happiness I was experiencing, knowing that she had found and reclaimed her voice.

Something exploded in the corner where Bea had been tossing the cabinet, and I caught them both by their sleeves, pulling them toward the door.

Bea grinned at us. "Let's go," she said, and I knew I would never get tired of that beautiful, magical voice of hers.

In a confused jumble of hugs and coughs, we dragged

one another out the door. I slammed it behind me, twisting the submarine-like wheel to lock it. Vale waited by the curtain, Cherie's slender arms around his neck and her face held away from his skin as if he smelled like wet dog.

"Is it done?" he asked.

"Completely," Bea said, and Vale's face lit up.

Taking Mel's hand, Bea darted through the curtains and into the catacombs. The amount of joy in the last five minutes had put wings on the girl's feet, and I couldn't wait to hear her sing. But I had to get topside, first.

I rubbed my eyes with soot-stained fists and stumbled toward Vale and Cherie. Neither of them would leave without me, of course. A muffled boom made the floor shake, and I hurried past and held open the curtains.

"We'd better get out of here before the catacombs start to collapse."

Vale sucked air through his teeth. "Oh, *merde*. I did not think about that part. Can you make it back on your own feet, and fast?"

"I can do anything."

"I believe it, *bébé*. I believe it."

The daimons had left us two lamps, and I took them both and led the way up the slick stone steps. It was warmer in the catacombs, and the dry rasp of rock and bone under my boots was reassuring and familiar. I followed the red string, foot after foot, sometimes putting a raw palm against the wall to steady myself from falling into the sewage. Behind me, Vale shuffled sideways, careful not to hurt Cherie. After the third time her slipper struck the wall, she grunted.

"Oh, this is ridiculous. Carry me on your back."

I held the lamp up to her face, and she looked ten times better than she had, her eyes bright and her lips pursed in annoyance. I couldn't help smiling. "How do you feel?"

"Utterly wretched in the best possible way. And thirsty. Now, get that light out of my face and move me around so I don't break a foot on this hideous wall."

With his usual grace and good humor, Vale managed to maneuver Cherie onto his back, her ragged slippers wrapped around his waist. After that, we went faster. It was a nightmare, stumbling past piles of fallen bones and tripping over loose rocks. But I could smell Cherie behind me, hear her familiar little sighs of irritation, and the relief thrummed through me with every heartbeat. Burning her painting had killed the magic. She didn't have fangs, but she was still my Cherie.

A few moments later, the tunnel around us shook with a heavy boom, and Vale hurried to shield me under his arm. We had to close our eyes as dust rained down from the stone ceiling, but the passage held.

"There goes the Malediction Club," Vale said.

"Not if Charmant is still alive," Cherie added, and a ripple of unease chilled my spine and set my exhausted feet to a faster trot.

The way back felt longer than the trip out, and even after gorging on my opponents, I'd never been so tired. "Shouldn't we be there already?" I asked.

Vale faltered behind me, and I turned to stare at him. The left side of his face was bruised, and he was limping, and blood trickled from a gash on his neck, which was probably why Cherie was careful to lean away from him.

"I was waiting to make sure, but I'm sorry, *bébé*. I think we're lost."

"How can we be lost? We're following the yarn."

I leaned down to pick up the red string. I gave it a tug, but instead of pulling taut as it should have, it slithered down the rocks toward me. Far away, a howl echoed out of the tunnels, jolting me awake and setting my fangs on edge.

"Oh—"

"*Merde, bébé.*"

Vale spun, his back to me. Cherie's back pressed against my corset, and a rush of familiarity settled through me before I realized what Vale was doing: anticipating an attack.

"Do you think—" I started.

"Shh."

It rankled, but I shut up. Everything beyond our lantern was dark, which made the eerie howls seem as if they came from every side. I threw out my senses, trying to detect how far away the bludhounds were— because they had to be more of Charmant's demon dogs, cut loose to run free in the catacombs. The half-dead daimon girls would be such easy pickings; we had to get to them soon and do what we could to protect them.

Up ahead, something moved, just a subtle rustle and a rock loosened from a pile. I breathed in deeply, seeking past the scents of stone and sewage and age-old bones and seeping, oily metal smoke to something alive. And there it was, up ahead where the red string slithered into the darkness, a rank scent that I knew well.

Charmant.

"You two stay here," I whispered.

"No, *bébé*. Let me."

"I'm harder to kill, and if I get hurt, you're the only

one with a hope of getting us out alive. So please, shove down your bad-boy brigand thing and let me do what I do best."

"Oh, Demi. Always so dramatic." Cherie sighed. "Just—"

A scream echoed down the tunnel, along with heavy splashing and a victorious bark, and Vale's head whipped around to stare into the darkness.

"That's Mel," he said gently.

I sighed and put a hand on his cheek. "Then go help her. I've got this. Come find me, once you've saved her like a big damn hero."

I reached up on tiptoe to kiss Vale's lips, hoping I wasn't giving him one last taste of me tinged with the stink of Auguste's daimon blud. "*Je t'aime*," I murmured, so low that he might not have heard.

"*Je t'aime aussi.*" He touched his forehead to mine, kissed me again, and took off with one of the lanterns.

With him and Cherie safely away, I left my lantern on the floor and ran into the darkness like a bat out of hell heading right back in. My eyes adjusted, my fingers curled, and my mouth opened to taste the scent of my prey. I locked onto the daimon where he crouched, waiting in the shadows of a niche up ahead. With a silent snarl, I sped up and launched myself into the crypt.

Even though he had to be expecting it, he gasped as I drove him into the wall. The force dislodged some heavy stones, and skulls and bones fell around us, smashing against the floor and raining against my back. Part of the crypt collapsed behind me, the air going suddenly thick. Luckily, I'd landed against Charmant's chest, which meant his venomous tail was trapped beneath him, or at least somehow hindered from piercing me. As I plunged my teeth into the first skin I found, I felt something hot and hard punch into my back. Two gulps of sour blood in, I realized it was a knife.

33

Monsieur Charmant snickered. ·

"There's poison on the blade, you know. You'll never make it out of the catacombs, Demitasse."

His voice was slick and cruel, his laughter a mad chittering. And I was done with it. I could have told him how wrong he was, how I would never stop. How I'd died in my world, been dragged into this one, almost died again, and lived to keep going. How he couldn't kill the daimon girls, and he couldn't kill me.

Instead, I made the most eloquent argument imaginable: I ripped out his throat.

He tasted rancid, like old eggs mixed with stomach acid. Still, in case he wasn't lying, I took in as much of his nasty blood as I could, hoping it might fortify me against his venom. And then, once the predatory urge receded, I had the good sense to pull the blade from my back, hack off his tail, and take it with me. Criminy had once told me that poison often held its own antidote, and judging by the numbness creeping into my legs, I didn't have long to find out the truth. Normally, a knife strike wouldn't take down a Bludman. But Charmant's poison was insidious. And fast.

The niche was half collapsed, and the stones were too heavy to budge. I wouldn't have made it out if I hadn't been a Bludman and a contortionist to boot. As it was, I had to dislocate both shoulders to slip through a tiny crack. I fell out of the niche and crept along the tunnel, first on my feet and then on my knees. I kept waiting to see the lantern up ahead, to hear Vale's voice calling me or smell Cherie or find a piece of red yarn with a brush of my hand. At the very least, I began to hope the bludhounds would make short work of me before I died alone, one hand trailing in sewage. Instead, I felt cold stone on my cheek and saw only darkness without a single star.

Time stopped as I lay there, numb and freezing and empty, for the second time that night, listening to froth drip from my lips. The bastard hadn't been joking, then. The tail clutched in my shaking fist would be useless. I managed to move my hand, twitch a few fingers. But I couldn't hear anything but water, cold and forever running, and my eyes bulged open, blind.

But then I felt something strange: cold, smooth metal. Breathing in deeply, I could smell it, too, just a little. Copper, brass, clockwork oil. I twitched a finger, and the metal wrapped gently around my hand and squeezed it. Strange that I would die alone in the dark under a foreign city that I'd never seen in my world, dreaming of robots.

Something probed and poked along my back; my arms, as if feeling me out. Metal cradled me, turned me, held me aloft. My head swung back and forth, spineless and light, as I was carried away in the darkness.

34

I didn't wake up so much as unfreeze. The first thing I saw was Vale. The second was Cherie. And the third was a brass monkey.

No, scratch that. A copper orangutan, the one from Charmant's shop. Its soulful red eyes blinked at me, its head cocking to the side in a gesture so human, so sympathetic, that it was almost creepy. Now I understood why I'd felt metal: the orangutan had saved me.

"Thanks, Coco," I whispered through dry, cracked lips.

"Ooh ooh," it responded in a tinny voice. It patted me with one metal hand, hobbled across the floor of my old room at Paradis, and swung out of the window. It was possibly the most bizarre thing I'd ever seen, like the Lone Ranger galloping into the sunset. Maybe my killing Charmant had set the sad-eyed creature free.

"That clockwork carried you to us." Vale stepped close, gently wrapping my hand in both of his. I winced; my palm was still red with burns from the pyre of paintings. "What happened?"

I tried to sit up and failed. "Found Charmant in a niche. It collapsed on us, and I killed him, but he stabbed me with a poisoned knife. Tried to crawl away but didn't get far."

"That was smart of you, *bébé*, to bring his tail. That's why you're alive."

"That and Coco."

"Yes, love. That and Coco. It led us back to Paradis and followed us up to watch over you. Such a strange piece of machinery."

"She," I said, not knowing how I knew. "Coco's a she."

"In any case, she saved your life. And we didn't lose a single girl."

"Where are they?"

Vale grinned. "The Malediction victims are hidden. Staying with a friend in a baker's basement across the city. And don't worry; they're recovering. As soon as the paintings burned, it was like snow melting to reveal flowers. The Paradis girls are back and recovering, thanks to the adoration of their audience. The bludhounds went for Bea and Mel, but the girls weren't badly hurt."

"Quite the fighter, your man," Cherie murmured.

I reached for her as she stood there, pink tears streaking down her cheeks. She looked a hundred times better than the last time I'd seen her. She took my weak hand in both of hers, and I tried not to look at her broken talons.

"Pretty good blood, right?" I asked.

"Better than they gave us at the caravan." She grinned, showing an all-too-human smile, with her fangs gone. "And my bed here is a lot bigger, too. I could get used to Paradis."

"And Paradis would be glad to have you, *ma chèrie*. Demi has told us that you two are partners." Madame Sylvie must have been listening at the open door to pop through like that at just the right moment. She put a flesh-colored hand on Cherie's shoulder, and I would have slapped it away had I yet figured out how to move again. The smile Charline leveled at Cherie as she sashayed in beside her sister was so empty, so hungry, so obviously manipulative that I couldn't believe I had ever fallen for a single word either daimon had said.

I shook my head. "No way. We're out of here tomorrow. I expect my wages delivered in francs by morning."

Charline flew to my side, batting her feathered eyelashes and *tsk*ing. "Oh la la, my dear. You're weak. And even with Lenoir and the most wealthy gentlemen gone, you're still the brightest star in Mortmartre. Take a week off. See the city. And then we'll build a new show for you and your Cherie." She tried to touch me, and my fangs snapped the air by her fingers.

"Oh, hell, no. If Vale has to carry me on his back, we're gone."

"I beg you to reconsider. The Malediction Club is destroyed. Mortmartre has never been safer." Madame Sylvie dismissed my words with the flap of a powdery hand. "You'll make your fortune!"

"I already made one." She looked away, a little muscle by her eye twitching. "And just because we put an end to the Malediction Club doesn't mean that suddenly the audience is filled with kind-hearted gentlemen who just want a good show. There will always be predators in Mortmartre." All three of us glared at her meaningfully, and she cleared her throat. "This place is like a Venus flytrap. And I'm done."

"How much is she owed?" Vale asked.

Charline tapped a foot and studied the ceiling, and Madame Sylvie waved a hand. "Not as much as you would guess. We must deduct the costumes, the board, the laundry, the elephant she destroyed, the blood—which was a very fine vintage and not easy to procure."

"They talked about you, you know." Everyone turned in surprise to focus on Cherie. She spoke quietly, as if her throat was still bruised from what had passed in that laboratory underground. "I heard the gentlemen talk about how Charline kept the best girls, how Sylvie knew just what the club wanted and always delivered on time." Even without her fangs, she looked like a murderous doll, the way she bared her teeth at the daimon sisters. "What do you think they meant about delivering?"

Sylvie's color slipped, the human flesh rippling briefly with dark spots like thumbprints. "Bah." She turned and sashayed out the door in disgust. "You'll have your francs tonight, and you'll leave before show time, before you poison the others with your lies. I'm a businesswoman, not a nun."

Charline just shook her head. "Such promise," she said. "All lost."

"It's not lost." I smiled, showing fangs. "It's just getting the hell out of here."

I spent the rest of the day in bed, mostly sleeping. Vale and Cherie stayed with me, but a rainbow of anxious faces came and went, hands touching my forehead or pushing hair out of my eyes or just briefly stroking my arm. I heard the word *merci* so much that it chased me in my dreams.

Vale woke me at dusk, one hand gentle on my shoulder. "*Bébé*, it's time."

I was able to sit up, at least, and I found Cherie waiting on a steamer trunk by the door, where Blaise's blue face peeked curiously through the crack. When I smiled at him, he ran up with a grain sack dragging behind him and heaved it onto the bed.

"What is this?"

"From Madame Sylvie. Your wages."

I opened the bag and bit my tongue. They weren't just francs; they were mostly silvers. She must have been terrified that we would spread the truth about her or exact our own vengeance. Truth be told, it wasn't sitting well with me, just letting Sylvie and Charline go on at Paradis. If they could find another way to line their pockets, they would.

"All this is mine?"

Blaise nodded. "You're the most famous act in Mortmartre, *mademoiselle*."

"Not anymore."

Mel stepped into the room, with Bea just behind her. "So it's true, then? You're leaving tonight?"

They were both in full costume and makeup, so very different from how they had looked in their fighting clothes and natural skins, painted with blood. These daimons, they never gave up.

"I can't stay here." I hefted the bag of coins; it took two hands. "And I don't have to."

It was still so strange and wonderful to hear Bea's voice. "But where will you go?"

I opened the bag and stared at the pile of glinting metal. When I glanced up at Vale, he looked as if he was about to burst out laughing.

"What's so funny?"

"I'm waiting for your answer, *bébé*. You can do anything you want, and I can't wait to hear what it is."

I plucked a silver from the pile and flicked it at Blaise, who caught it neatly.

"I want to go back to Sangland." They all stared at me, waiting, not breathing. I let the moment go on a little long, just to see who inhaled first. It was Vale. "And start a cabaret."

"But Demi, there are no cabarets in London," Cherie said, her usual know-it-all self.

"Not yet there aren't. But just think of it—a theater in London, daimon girls who wouldn't have to sleep with the audience if they didn't want to. Performers honing their craft. We could even trade carnivalleros back and forth with Criminy's caravan, if anyone got bored." I reached for Vale's hand and squeezed it. "You up for it?"

He rubbed his stubble with his other hand. "A disgraced Brigand of Ruin in Sangland, working at a Bludman's cabaret." He threw back his head and laughed. "It would appear I finally found a way to make my father angry and yet stay far enough out of his reach that he cannot strangle me."

Mel and Bea signed quickly; they would always have their secret language. Then Bea took a big breath. "Can we come with you?"

Mel nodded. "We're good workers, and—"

"And Blaise is a good boy, willing to learn a trade—"

"And there is no greater costumer than Blue—"

I realized I could finally move, and I held up wobbling hands to sign *Yes*.

Mel squealed, and they hugged and kissed, Bea's arm around Blaise's shoulders.

"What's going on in here?"

Lexie appeared in the doorway, and then all the daimon girls were crowding in, dressed in their cabaret finest. I couldn't help recalling how hard they'd fought, how strong and faithful they had been, as they worked to free their friends. And I was just supposed to leave them here in Mortmartre, under the greedy eyes and empty hearts of a pair of evil tiger bitches like Sylvie and Charline?

Hell, no.

"Y'all want to come to Sangland and work in my new cabaret?"

Needless to say, Paradis gave out a lot of refunds that night, as there wasn't a single showgirl left. They all followed me out the front door.

35

Six months later . . .

I leaned back against the plush velvet seat of my private box, then immediately sat forward again, eyeing the shining boards of the stage. Did I see a loose nail? Surely not. Vale and I had helped fix the floors ourselves. I would've noticed any problems while polishing every inch of the stage on my hands and knees.

"Opening night's always an utter flub. Relax, pet."

I bit back a hiss. "You're not my boss anymore, Criminy."

The caravan ringmaster sighed and sipped bloodwine from a sparkling glass. He looked especially dapper in his city clothes, the top hat and well-cut tailcoat just as smart as those of any of the Pinky gentlemen surrounding us and his dark hair brushed back into a tidy queue. Tish sat beside him in the sort of tasteful but painfully colorful gown the city humans preferred, buttoned up to her throat but splashy in black with bright red poppies that matched her ruby locket. I was the only one still wearing the heavy cloak demanded by a London winter night. Their gloved hands were intertwined, and although Criminy observed the cabaret's setup with the critical eye of a ringmaster, Tish only had eyes for him.

"I was barely your boss before, Demi. Mentor, perhaps. But Aztarte knows you never listened, in the caravan or out. I suspected you would give poor Mademoiselle Caprice the slip, because it's definitely what I would have done. But it was awfully poor taste to end up kidnapped in a copper elephant."

"I did escape," I mumbled.

"And eating your kidnapper was a stroke of genius." He turned the full power of his grin on me, and I felt as if after all these years, I'd finally won his approval simply by committing my first murder. "So what's the opening act?"

Vale grinned. "Wait and see."

I was proud of him; he was possibly the first person I'd ever met who wasn't intimidated by my godfather. Well, Veruca the Abyssinian in the caravan didn't take any of Crim's shit, either, so perhaps it was an Abyssinian thing. Still, they'd hit it off, and I was more relieved than I would admit. Buying and renovating an old theater with a rogue brigand from Franchia wasn't Criminy's idea of a smart business move, but we were about to prove him wrong.

Criminy held out his pocket watch, and before he could comment on the time, the lights dimmed. An amplified organ started off at a sinister gallop, and I smiled smugly.

"What the bugger is that racket? Surely you didn't . . ." Criminy started. He sat up, gloved hands biting into the rail as he looked down at the spotlight and hissed.

"Yep. I didn't think the Maestro would say yes, but I sent the telegram, and here he is."

Below us, Casper Sterling commanded the room with his masterful playing of a song no one in Sang had ever heard before. I knew it, of course. It was the opening to

The Phantom of the Opera, and the only reason Casper wasn't being completely overrun by crazed fans and reporters was the half-mask we'd provided for him and the fact that his name wasn't listed in the playbill.

The banister squeaked under Crim's fingers. "Can I kill him?"

Tish snorted, pulled Criminy back by the tail of his coat, and shoved him playfully into his seat. "You know the rules, buster. Never kill anyone at the theater," she said.

"That only counts for the audience." Criminy tried to look innocent and utterly failed.

"Then that's the second rule: you're not allowed to kill the performers, either. Besides, he's a Bludman now, and also, you know, kind of the king of Freesia. So you should probably go down to greet him after the show and give him flowers." Tish grinned. It was so weird to think she'd ever actually considered running away with Casper. It would never have worked out; they were ten kinds of wrong for each other.

Criminy's growl made the rest of us laugh; he still couldn't forgive himself for taking Casper in when he'd appeared as a Stranger on the moors all those years ago, giving him a job and teaching him how to stay alive in Sang. It was bad enough that Casper had become a Bludman; it was even worse that he was now the prince consort of Freesia and thus untouchable without starting an international incident.

"Bloody Strangers," Crim growled.

Tish smacked his arm lightly. "You did get the girl," she reminded him. That was enough to recall him to the present, and he gave up on Casper to lean back between us and hold Tish's hand on the armrest.

"And maybe he'll introduce you to Ahnastasia if you ask nicely," I added, which had Criminy leaning forward again, avidly scanning the crowd for his favorite celebrity.

I looked out at the audience, and my heart pounded like it might burst. We had a full house, and the theater was a masterpiece. From the plush boxes like ours that rose all along the walls on three levels, down to the tiered benches for the shopkeeps and artisans, and all the way down to a special sort of elegant cage I'd built so that the Bludmen could finally enjoy a show without terrifying the humans, the design had been a work of love and madness between Vale and me. Turns out he had a good eye for design and knew a little carpentry.

Between the two of us, the girls of Paradis, the recovered victims of the Malediction Club, and a Scottish handyman named Thom whom Casper had recommended, we were able to get the half-decomposed theater up and running and still have some money left over. And just wait until the audience saw the daring costumes designed by Blue and Casper's daimon friend Reve. London had never seen anything like the show we were about to put on.

Every nerve in my body sang, and I only hoped my wide smile wouldn't ruin my careful makeup. I would never have admitted it, but throwing open the theater doors for Criminy to show him what I'd made of myself had been one of the proudest moments of my life. I'd left his caravan longing for adventure, and I'd finally found my purpose.

Casper's song built to a crescendo, and his spotlight snapped off. Vale leaned close to plant a kiss on my hair and squeeze my hand.

"Break a leg, *bébé*."

At just the right moment, I stood and let my heavy cloak fall to the ground. A spotlight fell on me, making stars dance all over the walls from the sequins and jewels on my daringly low-cut dress.

"Oh, this'll be good," Criminy murmured in approval as I stepped onto the balustrade in knee-high boots.

I slipped the small silver hook from my sleeve onto the invisible wire and struck a pose. A collective gasp went up from the audience, and I heard hundreds of voices murmuring, "Is that Demi? Is that La Demitasse herself?" With a smile on my face, I leaped into the air, hurtling toward the stage on my zip line, my skirt billowing behind me. The curtains opened as I hit the wooden boards, and the first show of the Demimonde Theater began to thunderous applause.

**Because the best
conversations happen
after dark . . .**

Announcing a
brand-new site for
romance and urban
fantasy readers
just like you!

 *Visit **XOXOAfterDark.com** for free reads,
exclusive excerpts, bonus materials, author
interviews and chats, and much, much more!*

XOXO **AFTER DARK**.COM